GOLD RUSH

by

Jennifer Comeaux

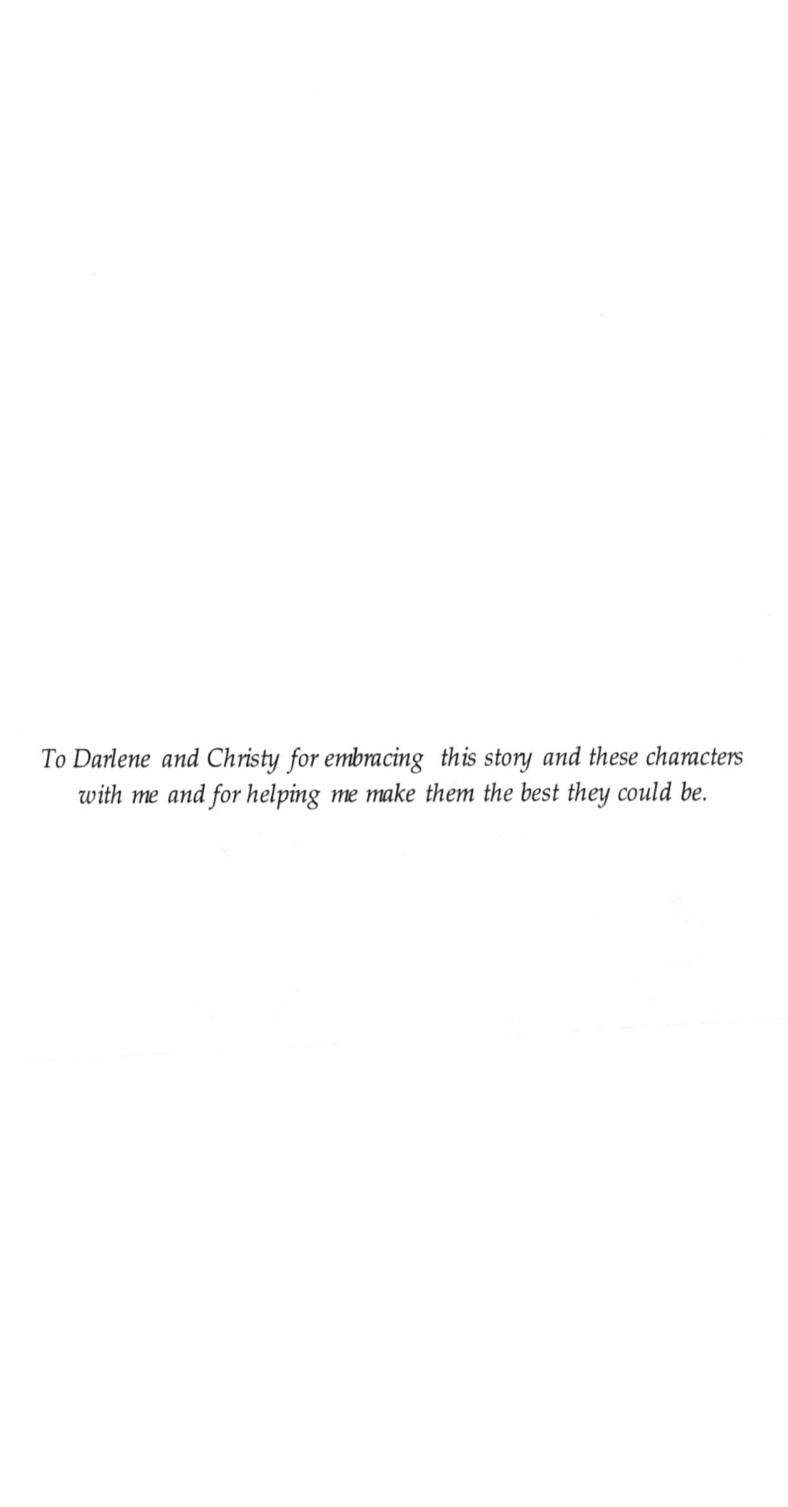

To Darlene and Christy for embracing this story and these characters with me and for helping me make them the best they could be.

Summer

CHAPTER ONE

June, 2013

DEATH WAS IMMINENT.

I couldn't breathe, my heart was slamming against my chest, and every muscle in my body burned like hellfire. Eight months away from potential Olympic glory, and I was going to die while skating the first full run-through of my new long program.

"Push, Liza!" my dad/coach Sergei called out from the corner of the rink.

My skates tried to obey his command, but my knees wobbled as I approached my final jump. I slowed to a crawl, unable to summon any more energy, and I jabbed my toe pick into the ice, not generating nearly enough upward force for three rotations. I came down cross-footed and tumbled hard onto the ice, caking my butt with snow.

My rink mates clapped and shouted encouragement as they practiced around me. I popped up, fighting against my sore body, and heaved myself into the closing spin. The music of Debussy finished well before my final turn, but I held my ending pose as if I was standing in front of the judges.

I was still alive.

Liza – one. Summer training – zero.

I moved away from center ice, giving way to one of Dad's novice pair teams since their music was next in the rotation. Setting off on an easy glide, I began circling the edge of the rink for my cooldown. Slowly I regained a normal heart rate, and my lungs no longer felt like they were going to explode.

My leisurely trip around the rink reminded me why I loved the sport so much. Nothing topped the feeling of freedom I had when I was on the ice. I could fly as fast as I wanted, the cool breeze rushing over my skin, and no one stood in my way. It was just me and a blank white canvas where anything was possible.

As I exited the ice, Dad hustled over and draped his arm across my shoulders. Looking into his deep blue eyes was like looking into my own, and he focused his on me with a smile.

"You did good. This is the hardest program you've ever done."

"I killed the opening minute. The last three not so much."

"We might need to change the jump layout in the final section. I don't like that Lutz so close to the end."

We sat on the bleachers beside the ice, and Dad gave me all the technical observations he'd made during my run-through. When he finished, we parted with a warm hug. My home training base was in New York, where I lived with my mom most of the year, and Dad was only my part-time coach when I spent summers and weekends with him on Cape Cod. Since I'd graduated from high school a year ago, though, I'd been spending more time on the Cape. I'd worked with my New York coach for years, but Dad gave me a sense of comfort only he could provide.

The loud whirr of the Zamboni replaced the sound of classical music, and all my training mates fled the ice. My friend Holly, a pair skater at the junior level, separated from her partner and gave me a double thumbs-up while climbing onto the bleachers.

"You got through it without dying," she said as she smoothed the flyaway hairs from her short brunette ponytail.

"We should totally celebrate," I said. "I'm taking the munchkins to the baseball game tonight if you want to come." My six-year-old twin siblings were entertaining company, but adult conversation would be more than welcome.

"A Cape League game with hottie college players? Of course I'm in."

"So, the eye candy is why you're coming. Not the fun of hanging out with me." I turned my head away with pretend hurt. "I see how it is."

"Fun is always had when Holliza hang out. The eye candy is just a bonus."

I laughed and tightened the laces of my sneakers. "It's time for Holliza to hit the gym. Ready to have a fantastic time busting our butts?" I bounced up from my seat, putting mind over matter – the matter being my aching muscles.

"You enjoy the pain of working out way too much."

"The more I hurt now, the less I'll hurt at the end of my program next February in Sochi."

"Go get it, girl. Eye on the prize."

I picked up my phone and pulled up the countdown clock app, set to the day of the Olympic short program. I looked at it every day after skating as a reminder of both how much and how little time remained. Dad wouldn't approve if he saw it because he was all about focusing on the moment at hand, but the prize of Olympic gold was too big to put out of my mind.

Two hundred and forty-three days to go.

❧

I YAWNED AND STRETCHED my legs on the blanket we'd spread over the outfield grass. The scoreless game between the

Yarmouth-Dennis Red Sox and the Brewster Whitecaps wasn't giving us much reason to cheer. The Cape Cod Summer League consisted of teams of college players from schools around the country, and games were played at small ballparks across the island. Since I lived and trained in South Dennis, the Red Sox were considered my home team.

Holly and I had already gone through our tradition of rating the starting lineups on a scale of one to ten. The Sox shortstop and left fielder had garnered perfect scores from both of us. Couldn't argue with dimples and tight pants.

"Double play!" my brother Alex yelled.

"He's so into it." Holly laughed. Her hands were pressed to the blanket so Alex's twin sister Quinn could paint her nails bubblegum pink. She was a surprisingly good manicurist for a six-year-old.

"He's been obsessed with baseball ever since my dad took him to Fenway last month. He knows all the rules," I said.

"I know all the rules of skating," Quinn said.

"You could probably be a better judge than some of the ones we have now." I ruffled her springy blond curls.

The small crowd cheered as the Red Sox center fielder caught a deep fly ball, and Alex scrambled over to me on his knees.

"Can I have a Slush Puppie?"

I stuck out my tongue. "That's like drinking pure sugar."

"Mom said we could have one treat."

My stepmom Emily hadn't said any particular snacks were off-limits, so I pushed myself up and grabbed my wallet.

"What flavor do you want?" I asked.

He tapped his chin. "Orange. No, cherry. No–"

I held out my hand. "Come with me so you can decide on the way. Quinn, you want one?"

She only shook her head as she intently stroked the polish onto Holly's thumb.

Alex went back and forth three more times before

deciding on orange as we joined the short line at the concession stand. Since it was still early summer, the Cape hadn't been bombarded yet with the usual tourists and summer residents. When we got closer to the Fourth of July, the crowd at the high school ballpark would be twice the size it was tonight.

"Can I have a hamburger, too?" Alex asked.

I shook my head with a little laugh. "We just had dinner."

I couldn't blame him for asking, though. The smoky aroma of the burgers grilling made me wish Em hadn't cooked a nutritious baked chicken dinner.

As we inched forward in the line, a loud, hearty laugh caught my ear. I looked up and saw it had come from a guy working at the concession stand. He was sliding two of those awesome-smelling burgers toward two kids at the counter.

I watched him chat with the kids and noticed how easy and genuine his smile was. It reached all the way up to his eyes. He wore a navy Red Sox cap, and his light brown hair peeked out from under his hat and curled around the edge.

His eyes shifted in my direction as if he sensed me staring at him, and his smile took on a flirty gleam. My face grew warm, and I quickly looked away. There was nothing I knew less about than flirting with boys. Correction – doing *anything* with boys.

I fiddled with the end of my long, dark braid and kept my head down as I listened to Counter Boy help the couple in front of us. Even his deep voice relayed his cheerfulness.

Our turn came to step up to the front, so I put my hand on Alex's shoulder. My eyes met Counter Boy's, and my cheeks flushed with more heat that I couldn't blame on the smoking grill.

"Hey." His gaze dipped slightly and then returned to mine. "What can I get you, Liza?"

My order stuck in my throat, and I stood gaping at him. He'd mispronounced my name, but how did he know it? Did he recognize me from skating?

"Your necklace." He pointed to it, obviously seeing my confusion.

My hand went to the gold name pendant Mom had given me for Christmas. It wasn't large or blinged out, so the guy was very observant. *Should I correct his pronunciation?* I usually just let it slide with strangers, but for some reason I wanted him to have it right.

"It's umm… it's *Leeza*," I said.

"Oh, my bad." He still wore a huge grin. "I can sympathize. My name's Braden, and people always call me Brandon. I mean, do you see two n's in there?"

He was so smiley, so *alive*. Energy radiated off the guy like warm sunlight. I felt my own mouth curve upward in response.

"So, what can I get you? Popcorn? Peanuts?" He motioned behind him with his thumb. "Have you tried our donut burgers? They're insane."

I was still so thrown off balance that it took me a second to remember why the heck Alex and I had gone there.

"We need one orange Slush Puppie."

Alex tugged on the bottom of my T-shirt and shook his head.

"You changed your mind again?"

He made me lean down so he could whisper, "I want blue raspberry."

I turned back to Braden. "Sorry, one blue raspberry Slush Puppie."

"I can never decide either," he said as he filled a small cup with the frozen syrupy mixture. He set the drink and a straw in front of Alex. "There you go, little man."

Alex didn't waste any time slurping away, and I handed over two dollar bills to Braden. A jumble of colorful woven bracelets and a green rubber wristband bearing the word *Faith* circled his tanned wrist.

"Nothing for you?" he asked. "We have all kinds of ice cream, penny candies... our famous Cape Cod chips if you're more of a salty over sweet person like I am."

A normal girl would buy something else to stall and flirt, but my instinct to flee whenever any guy gave me attention had already kicked in.

Alex pulled on my hand. "We're missing the game."

Saved by the kid.

I tossed a parting "Thanks" at Braden and let Alex quickly lead me away from the stand, but I found myself glancing backward. Braden's eyes followed us with great interest. I swung my head forward and scampered to the blanket with Alex running ahead of me.

Quinn peered at Alex's drink, and I didn't even have a chance to get settled before she asked, "Can I get one, too?"

"I just asked you and you said no."

"I didn't want it then."

"That was five minutes ago!"

She launched herself at me and threw her arms around my neck. "*Pleeaasse.*"

"I can't go back to the concession stand when I was just there."

Holly blew on her nails. "Is someone monitoring how many trips you make?"

"No, it's just..." I untangled myself from Quinn, and she flopped down next to Alex. "There was this guy working there who was all chatty."

Holly's eyebrows perked up. "Was he cute? What did he say?"

I wasn't answering her first question because I didn't want her to know how cute he was. He would've scored eleven on our rating scale.

"Nothing. He just gave me this vibe."

"The vibe that he was interested in you?"

I watched the first baseman tag out the runner, taking my

time in replying, "Maybe."

She hit my arm. "Then get yourself down there and chat him up."

"Yeah, that would go *so* well." The mere idea of it made me feel close to losing my dinner.

"Talk to him about the game. If he's chatty, he'll make it easy for you. This could be your chance to go on a date!"

"I've been on a date."

"You can't count taking your gay friend to the prom."

"He was still technically in the closet."

Holly gave me one of her *come on* looks. "That closet had a glass door."

I laughed. "Look, I know you think I'm a freak because I haven't been on a real date, but I went to an all-girls school and I spend the rest of my time in an ice rink – not exactly a mecca of straight guys."

"And you shoot down any who try to talk to you."

She was absolutely right, but I wasn't up for discussing my social deficiencies.

"I could've totally misread this guy's chattiness," I said, hoping she'd drop the subject. "He seemed talkative with everyone."

"There's only one way to find out." She lifted Quinn's arm. "Take your little sister to get a slushie."

I thought about telling Holly to take Quinn herself, but I couldn't trust that she wouldn't set me up somehow. I sat still for a minute before finally getting to my feet. "This is going to look so obvious."

"You can't help that kids whine for things."

"I don't whine," Quinn said.

I took her hand and held it tighter than necessary as we walked past the metal bleachers. I felt absurdly anxious about talking to Braden again.

He didn't see us until we made it to the head of the line, and his eyes widened a bit with surprise. I got a better look at them, and the color of hot cocoa immediately came to mind. His ever-present smile beamed at me.

"Hello again." His forehead wrinkled, and he pointed to Quinn. "Do you have a brother?"

"Alex. He's my twin."

"Aha. I thought my eyes were playing tricks on me. Let me guess – you saw how delicious that Slush Puppie looked and you want one, too."

She nodded enthusiastically.

"Blue raspberry like your brother?"

"Yes, please."

He grabbed a cup and set it under the machine. "Sure I can't get you one, Liza? Not that I mind if you have to come back again."

There was something in the way his eyes held mine when he spoke to me that made me feel like I was the only person in the ballpark. That plus his smiley energy was setting off wild flutters in my stomach.

"No… no thanks," I sputtered.

"You look really familiar. Do you go to UMass by any chance?"

He'd probably seen me on TV or in the local papers. I'd been getting a lot of press and had done a few ads as the media geared up for Sochi. What was the most humble way to say I was a two-time world champion figure skater?

"She's the best skater in the world," Quinn announced. "She's gonna win the Olympics."

That takes care of that problem.

"Yes, that's it!" He snapped his fingers. "Wow, I should get your autograph or something."

Was he serious or was he flirting? This was why I couldn't talk to guys. I had to scramble to think of a funny reply.

I laughed nervously and spread my hands open. "I left all my signed photos at home."

He chuckled and glanced under the counter as he gave Quinn her drink. "I'm sure I can find some paper around here."

Oh, God, what if he asks me to write my phone number? The irrational panic I'd felt before in this situation tensed my whole body.

I placed the money on the counter and nudged Quinn toward the field. "I don't want to hold up the line. I'll probably be back again!"

But I had no intention of returning.

I thought I heard Braden call out something, but I didn't look back that time. Holly practically jumped off the blanket when she saw me.

"How did it go? Did you talk to him?"

"He was *cuute*," Quinn said between slurps. She now had a blue tongue.

"Was he chatty again? Did you get his name?"

"Jeez, chill for a second." I sat and folded my legs under me. "I feel like I'm on the witness stand."

"Hey, would you like to buy some raffle tickets?"

I looked up, and one of the reserve players and an intern girl stood beside our blanket. The team had a split-the-pot raffle every game as a fundraiser.

"Not today, thanks." Holly shooed them away and returned to scrutinizing me. "Back to the boy."

I checked my phone and waited a few moments to answer her just to mess with her. "His name is Braden, and I think he goes to UMass."

"Okay, good start. He's in college, age appropriate. What else?"

"I didn't get anything else."

She sighed with frustration. "Did he seem interested?"

"He wanted her autograph," Quinn said.

I could always count on the town crier to fill in all the details.

"So, he knows who you are. Wait, he's not a skating fan, is he? He might be playing for the wrong team."

"I didn't get that feeling from him," I said.

"Then tell me you gave him an autograph and included your number."

I played with my phone again and wiped a speck of dirt from the purple case. "He couldn't find any paper so I left."

"You didn't give him a chance to find paper before you high-tailed it out of there. Am I right?"

I avoided her penetrating gaze. "We were holding up the line and–"

"Girl, what am I going to do with you?"

"I know, I know." I covered my face with my hand. "The whole thing just freaked me out and made me so nervous."

"You can't be afraid to put yourself out there. You have *so* much to offer. You just need to have the same confidence with guys that you do when you skate."

She made it sound like such a simple task, but it wasn't. Skating was like breathing for me. I'd worked so hard on it for so long that confidence came naturally. But because I'd spent so much time in my skating bubble and not doing normal teenager things, I was behind in the dating world. And the longer I waited to dive into it, the more terrified I was to expose myself.

"Getting out there and going on that first date will make it so much easier. Even if the guy turns out to be a total dud, you'll have the experience." Holly paused and tapped my arm. "You know I'm just harassing you because I think you're fabulous, and I don't want you to miss out on something good because you're scared."

I gave her a little smile. "You're right that I need to be pushed. But I can't go back to that concession stand tonight without looking completely nutso."

She laughed. "Fair enough. We'll work on your flirting game so you'll be prepared next time. Whenever and wherever it happens."

CHAPTER TWO

On the table before me sat fabric samples in every possible shade of blue. My mom had brought a suitcase full of them to the costume designer's shop in Boston, where my stepmom Em and I had met her after morning practice. My short program costume was almost complete, but we hadn't finalized the color or design of my long program dress yet.

"I love this color." Mom picked up a bright blue swatch and held it against the front of my black bodysuit. "It matches your eyes perfectly."

"I was picturing something lighter." Em fingered two of the more muted shades. "Since the program is so soft and balletic."

She coached alongside my dad, so she'd watched the program come to life the past few weeks. My choreographer Josh had also consulted with her on a couple of sections.

"The dress has to make a strong impression. It can't be too light," Mom said.

"What do you think, Liza?" Em asked.

I groaned to myself. Mom and Em got along fine for the most part, but they were very different people who tended to have differing opinions. When they didn't agree, I always got stuck in the middle, and it ticked off Mom whenever I sided with Em. Which happened more often than not.

I picked up a slate blue sample and draped it around my middle. My long program music was "Prelude to the Afternoon of a Faun," and a softer color would indeed make more sense.

"How about this one?"

Mom pressed her deep red lips together as she studied me. "It doesn't look exciting enough."

"I don't know about that," my designer Louann piped up. "It's a unique shade, and it still makes her eyes stand out."

Good thing I was accustomed to being in the spotlight because the three of them couldn't stare me down any harder.

"I like it a lot," Em said. "We should keep it clean, too. Not too many stones. Lots of sparkle wouldn't fit the program."

Cue Mom's rebuttal in three, two–

"With this color she needs more sparkle, not less."

"But my music isn't flashy," I said. "I'm not skating to *Moulin Rouge* or *Burlesque*."

"I'll start off with some subtle stones and we can see how it looks," Louann said, ever the peacemaker. She'd been stuck in the middle as many times as I'd been.

Em and Louann went over to another table to look at the preliminary design sketch, and Mom continued to admire the swatch she was holding.

"I wore a dress this color when your father and I won Junior Worlds. Also when we landed our first triple jumps. It was my good luck color."

I knew she was hinting that it could be my Olympic good luck color, but I'd been compared enough to my parents over the years without dressing like them, too. They'd been pair skaters for Russia and had been touted as future Olympians. Until I'd unexpectedly come along.

"Maybe I can use it for my show program dress." I attempted to compromise. "Josh and I are going to work on a new exhibition later this summer."

"That would be nice. It really does look stunning on you."

She wrapped it around me and turned us to face the long mirror. We were the same petite size and could easily pass for sisters. Mom kept in great shape teaching ballet at my New York rink. We had the same porcelain complexion, and I hoped my skin would be as pure and smooth as hers when I was in my late thirties. There were no signs of gray in Mom's dark bob either.

"I made a few adjustments to the neckline," Louann said as she showed me the sketch. "I think it makes it more romantic, more special."

I traced my finger over the vee design. "It does, and I love the placement of the stones."

"This cut is deeper than we discussed." Mom leaned over my shoulder to squint at the paper. "It's too revealing."

"It's not that deep," Em said. "Louann knows what's suitable and what's not."

Here we go again.

Mom folded her arms. "I just want to make sure she's portraying the right image."

"The dress is perfectly classy. She's going to look amazing in it," Em said.

"Once you see it on her, I guarantee you'll love it," Louann said.

Mom didn't look convinced, but I wasn't going to give her time to put up more resistance. At our last visit to Louann's she'd gone on a five-minute tirade about modesty and the use of illusion fabric.

"Em, we should go so we're not stuck in traffic," I said.

"Are you coming home this weekend?" Mom asked.

"Umm... probably not. Holly and I might go to the beach."

We'd only vaguely talked about it, but I liked being in a house full of action as opposed to the quiet of just Mom and me. In addition to the twins, one of Dad and Em's pair students also lived with us. Courtney was only a few years older than me, and she was like a member of the family.

"Elena, why don't you stay with us tonight?" Em suggested. "You can drive back to New York tomorrow."

"I appreciate the offer, but I have to teach a class tonight." Mom caressed my hair. "I miss having my favorite ballerina there."

I smiled a little. I did feel guilty leaving Mom alone all summer. She had her boyfriend George, but he lived in Manhattan and couldn't always get away to White Plains to see her. He was raising two teenage daughters of his own.

"I'll come visit after the Fourth," I said.

She gave me a long hug as we left the shop, and she waved as I climbed into Em's SUV. Whenever I felt bad about leaving her, I reminded myself that if I had a normal life I'd be away at college most of the year. I just knew how hard it was for her to have an empty nest since I'd been her main focus for so long.

The heat of the city was stifling compared to the pleasant air on the Cape, and we had to blast the A/C until we reached the outskirts of Boston. Em's phone rang through the car stereo, and she pressed the hands-free button on the steering wheel to answer the call.

"Hi, Mom," Alex's tiny voice came through the speakers.

"Hi, sweetie. How was camp today?"

"We went swimming, and I put my face in the water."

"Good job, buddy," she said while I chimed in, "That's awesome." Alex had taken a long time to warm up to the idea of swimming, while I was convinced Quinn had been born a mermaid.

"I asked Dad if we can go to the baseball game tonight, and he said to ask you when you'll be home."

"We're on our way now, so we can definitely go."

"Yeah!" Alex cried. "I'll tell Dad."

Baseball game? The image of Braden smiling at me appeared in my head, and jumping beans appeared in my stomach. A week had passed since I'd met him, but I still had a crystal clear memory of his face. His extremely handsome face.

Once the stereo returned to music, I said, "I might go with you guys. Court's working tonight, so I'd be bumming around the house by myself."

Em's bright blue eyes swung over to me. "I think I know the real reason you want to go."

What? Holly wouldn't have said anything to Em. Oh, but Quinn would have.

"All those hot guys on the field?" Em said. "I used to go to the games for that same reason when I was your age."

I laughed with relief. "Yeah, you got me."

It was bad enough I had Holly hounding me about Braden. I didn't want Em to get in on the crusade. Unlike my parents, who'd kept a firm seal on my skating bubble, she'd actually be excited by the prospect of me socializing with the opposite sex.

If I decided to talk to Braden, I could make a trip to the concession stand to see him. If I decided I didn't want to open that door, I could stay out of sight and enjoy a nice summer evening at the ballpark with my family. Option two sounded like the safe and logical choice, but something about option one excited me a little. It would also save me from the wrath of Holly.

❦

I TAPPED MY FINGERNAIL on the phone screen and scanned my surroundings. I was looking for an Instagram-worthy shot of the game, but nothing interesting was jumping out at me. My vantage point was from the outfield, where we'd set up three portable chairs and a blanket.

Quinn was stretched out on the blanket, drawing pictures with markers, while Alex sat on Dad's lap as he taught him how to keep score. I smiled at how apple-pie American they looked in their matching red and blue Sox caps and T-shirts. I snapped a quick photo of them and sent it out into the digital universe with the caption – *The family being precious #GoSox*. All the skating fans who voted Dad as "Hottest Coach" on the message boards every year would appreciate the picture.

I posted a lot on social media to stay connected with my fans, even though the haters and creeps made it difficult sometimes. With Russian parents and the last name Petrov, some people thought I shouldn't be the face of American figure skating, and they constantly let me know it in their online comments. Forget the fact that I'd only lived in Russia one year of my life, and I'd been Team USA since I'd first put on skates.

Em returned with popcorn for the kids, and Quinn sat up from her art studio to dig into the bag. I was so curious to know if Braden had taken Em's order. The game was only in the second inning, so I had plenty of time to do a scouting mission on the concession stand. I hadn't figured out yet what I'd say to Braden if I made it all the way there. Would he even care that I hadn't gone back last time? He probably met a hundred girls per game.

I clicked on the ereader app on my phone and opened the young adult romance I'd been reading. The sweet story of first love might give me inspiration for how to interact better with guys. It could also get my creative juices flowing for the short story I'd been writing. I'd found that experiencing romance through my characters was a good outlet for a perpetually single girl.

"Hey, Liza."

I looked up directly into the smiling face of Braden. He was holding the raffle bucket, and a Sox player stood beside him. I was so unprepared to see him that I couldn't even get a "hello" to come out of my mouth.

"Would you like to buy a raffle ticket?" he asked.

I felt weird having him talk down to me while I sat, so I sprang to my feet. "Hi. Umm… yeah, I'll take a couple."

"Cool. How many?"

I bent to get my wallet and pulled out a five dollar bill. "As many as this will get me?"

The player tore a strip of tickets from the big roll and gave them to Braden before moving on to solicit Em and Dad, who were watching Braden and me with rapt attention. Braden set the bucket down and slowly separated my part of the tickets. Now that there wasn't a counter between us, I could see his full physique better. The top of my head only reached his chin, so he had to be more than half a foot taller than me. He had a slender build, but he wasn't scrawny. The short sleeves of his polo showed nicely-defined biceps.

"I remember you," Quinn said.

Braden laughed. "I remember you, too."

Quinn might also remember Holly and me discussing Braden's date potential. I quickly stepped between them so Quinn couldn't see him.

"I thought you worked concessions," I said.

"I'm an intern, so I go wherever they tell me. I like doing the raffle better because I get to see more people."

His eyes held steady on mine in the I'm-only-looking-at-you way they'd done at the concession stand. How was I supposed to come up with witty conversation when my heart was pitter-pattering so loudly I couldn't even think?

"Were you going to visit me at the concession stand? I'm still waiting for my autograph." He cocked his head with a sly grin.

"Oh… yeah. I'm sorry. I wasn't sure if you were really serious."

"I definitely was. I've never met anyone as talented as

you. I watched a video of you at the world championships, and you were incredible."

"You Googled me?"

"What kind of twenty-first century guy would I be if I didn't?"

I had to break away from his gaze because I felt redness taking over my face. *If only I could be incredible and confident right now.*

Braden's companion had left and was chatting with another family, so Dad and Em had returned to staring at me. Em with a smile, Dad not so much. I turned and my eyes fell on Quinn's art supplies, giving me an idea. I reached for a sheet of green paper and a black marker.

"Can I borrow these?"

She nodded and kept drawing, so I took the paper and wrote *To Braden* and scrawled my signature in large letters across it.

"Here you go." I handed it to him. "I don't give many autographs on construction paper, so this is very special."

Look at me being flirty.

"Perfect spelling on my name," he said.

"One n, not two." I smiled, and he grinned wider.

"This is awesome. I'll frame it and put it next to my Tom Brady signed football, which was bought off eBay and not personalized so it's not nearly as special as this."

I'd used up my few clever lines, so I was at a loss for a comeback. I shifted from one foot to the other before I finally pointed to my ticket stubs. "Should I take those?"

"Yep, these are yours." He gave me the small red tickets. "And I need you to fill out the back of our copies." He hesitated but kept his eyes on mine. "With your name and phone number."

The thumping of my pulse grew louder, and I blabbered in a nervous rush, "Don't they just announce the ticket number of the winner?"

It was Braden's turn to blush. "You're gonna make me work for this."

"No, I'm… I'm not trying to be coy. I'm just not used to…" I had no clue how to say what I was trying to say without sounding totally lame. "It's just that… my life is a lot different from most people."

He nodded. "I get that. I'm sure you have to be very careful."

If he only knew how careful and closed off I'd been. This was the longest conversation I'd ever had with a guy who'd shown any kind of interest in me.

"How about I give you the 4-1-1 on me?" He put his hand on his chest. "I'm from Fall River. I have two older sisters, a younger brother, and a black lab named Big Papi. I'm currently a sophomore at UMass, majoring in business." He paused for a beat. "I enjoy watching sports, running, and bingeing Netflix. And most importantly, I do not have a criminal record."

I laughed. "That's a lot of good information."

"I also promise I'm not asking for your number because you're famous. I wanted it the moment you stepped up to my counter."

I didn't know it was a real thing, but I actually felt my heart skip a beat. I dipped my head for a second and then looked up at him. "I bet you say that to all the girls you wait on."

"Only the ones with cute little blond kids who order blue raspberry Slush Puppies."

Oh my God. You.Are.So.Adorable.

There was no way I could turn him down after all that, and I didn't want to. For once, I didn't want to crawl deeper into my bubble and hide. I wanted him to keep giving me this fluttery feeling that excited me and terrified me all at the same time.

I uncapped the marker and smiled. "Wanna hand me

those tickets?"

His face lit up beyond its usual sunniness. "I'll let you put it in my phone."

He placed it in my palm, and I typed around the long crack in the screen. "My last name is Patrick, by the way," he said. "It's only fair that you can Google me, too."

"I think I'm still at a big disadvantage. My whole life story can be found on the internet."

"I watched a few of your videos but didn't read anything. I wanted to wait and let you tell me all about your life."

"You were that confident I'd give you my number?" I said as I handed him his phone.

He looked surprised, like he wasn't expecting me to challenge him, but he smiled brightly. "Confidence is the key to making things happen. I'm guessing you know that as a world champion, though."

"My dad preaches it to me all the time."

The Sox player holding the ticket roll found his way back to us and slapped Braden on the shoulder. "Hey, we need to hit the other side of the field."

Braden picked up the bucket of stubs. "I'd better get back to work, but I'll definitely be in touch." His eyes locked on mine, and I had no doubt I'd hear from him. As he took a few steps, he held up the autograph. "I'll keep this safely by my side until I get home."

"Have fun. I'll be over here Googling." I waved my phone.

He laughed as he walked backward, finally spinning forward just before he reached the bleachers. As I processed everything that had just happened, my heart rate accelerated as if I was in the middle of a workout.

I gave my number to a boy.

He's going to call me.

I might be going on my first date.

I dropped onto my chair as excitement and anxiety

muddled together in my chest. *Take a breath. You have time to prepare. You're not going out tonight.*

"How do you know him?" Em asked.

Her question brought me out of my daze, and I slowly exhaled. "He was working the concession stand last week when the kids and I were here."

"He seemed really nice." She lowered her voice. "And he was very cute."

"Did he ask you out?" Dad asked. His tone was the complete opposite of Em's. So was his expression.

"He asked for my number."

"Liza's got a boyfriend," Quinn sang.

"Having my number doesn't make him my boyfriend."

"So, what's his story?" Dad asked.

"I don't know, I just met him. I haven't even had a chance to internet stalk him yet."

"Give me his name." Dad pulled out his phone. "I'll look him up."

Em swatted his arm. "Let her have some space, love."

The worry crease between Dad's eyebrows deepened. "I just didn't know you were interested in dating right now."

"Dating implies a series of outings. I haven't even been on one yet."

"One can lead to many, and you have a lot on your schedule coming up."

"She deserves to have some fun," Em said. "You and I dated when I was skating."

"I was your coach so I understood what you were going through and how important your time was."

I planted my hand against my forehead. "You guys are jumping so far ahead. Can you not make such a huge deal out of this? He might not even ask me out after we talk again."

"I'm pretty sure he will. There was a definite spark between you." Em smiled. "I felt it all the way over here."

Dad appeared to have his own opinion to share on

possible sparks, but Alex interrupted, "What number is the shortstop again?"

He pulled Dad's attention back to their scorebook, and I put mine on the opposite side of the field. Braden was tearing tickets, but he was clearly looking in my direction as he did so. My heart began to beat quicker again, and I looked down at my phone.

What am I getting myself into?

CHAPTER THREE

"Hold that moment there," Josh said, and I froze with my arms open and one leg in attitude position behind me. Staring straight at me was my reflection in the wall-to-wall mirror of the rink's ballet studio.

Josh paused my long program music on his phone and gently tipped my chin upward. "Make sure to keep your head up. This is the moment you set the tone for the whole program."

We'd spent the last hour reworking the opening of the program off the ice, focusing on the smallest details. Every look, every bend of my fingers had a purpose and a home within the music.

"I love that I'll be skating directly toward the judges as I'm doing this," I said, finally breaking the pose. "It's like I'm telling them, 'Here I am, ready to lay my heart and soul on the ice. Please be kind.'"

Josh laughed. "They'll be more than kind when they see how brilliant you are with this music."

"I don't think I'm quite to the brilliant stage yet. More like the still-trying-not-to-die stage."

"It'll come. You're owning every movement more each day."

"Can I tell you again how in love I am with this program? It's damn hard, but all the elements flow together so perfectly. I feel powerful but also like I'm floating, if that makes sense."

"That was my goal when I first pictured you with the piece."

"Then a gold star for you." I held up my hand for a high five, and Josh obliged. At twenty-six he was one of the youngest choreographers in the business, but he had an incredible ear for music and an innate understanding of body movement. Some of the bigwigs of the U.S. Figure Skating Federation had questioned why I wasn't using a "big name" choreographer for the Olympic season, and Dad had helped me argue my case. Besides being extremely talented, Josh was one of Dad's students and a friend that I trusted with the most important program of my life.

"Productive session?" Courtney asked as she poked her head into the room.

"Very." I slipped on my warm-up jacket. "Your boyfriend is a genius."

"Well, that's old news." She smiled and went over to Josh. "I have to run a few errands. Meet at your place before work?"

"Sounds good."

She stood on the tips of her toes and gave him a kiss. "Love you."

"Love you, too." He pressed their lips together once more.

Court was small and blonde, while Josh was tall with hair as dark as mine. That contrast gave them a striking look as partners on the ice. Off the ice they worked nights at the same local restaurant – Court behind the bar and Josh on the piano – and they relished every minute they spent together. They'd had a rocky start as a couple, but I'd never doubted they were perfect for each other.

Court scooted out of the studio, and I took a healthy swig of water. "Relationship goals," I said.

Josh grabbed his skate bag. "Goals for you and Braden?" he asked with a knowing smile.

"Does Court tell you everything?"

"Pretty much."

I stashed my water bottle in my bag and fished out my phone. The notification light was blinking, causing my jitters to activate. I kept my phone on silent at the rink, so I could've received a call or a text or an email or–

Just check it, already!

I tapped the screen to life and saw a missed call from an unknown number. I also had a voicemail.

"Did he call?" Josh asked.

I bit my lip. "I think so."

"I'll give you some privacy." He headed for the door. "Bring him by the restaurant so Court and I can inspect him. I mean, meet him."

"Ha ha."

The heavy door clicked shut, and I dialed my voicemail while pacing along the shiny laminate floor.

"Hey, Liza, this is Braden." I couldn't help but smile at the enthusiasm in his voice. "I'm guessing you're on the ice right now, working on continuing your world domination. Or you might be screening your calls if you Googled me and found some of my high school pictures. I admit I made some unfortunate hairstyle choices, and I assure you that I'll never go near a bottle of peroxide again."

I giggled and leaned against the ballet barre. I had indeed found photos of Braden and his high school baseball teammates, all sporting bleached blond crew cuts. He'd still looked super cute.

"Anyway, I was calling first to say how glad I was that I saw you again yesterday, and second, to ask if you'd like to hang out this weekend. There's a big barbecue on the beach Saturday night. It's part of the Summer Celebration? If you're free, gimme a call and we can make a plan."

He went silent, and I wasn't sure if the call had dropped, but then he said, "Talk to you soon, Liza."

I slid down so my butt hit the floor. Saturday night was only two days away. My *first date ever* was only two days away.

If I said yes.

I could easily not call him back (I'd have to avoid all Y-D Red Sox games, but I could manage that). Then I could continue my easy romance-free existence and just live vicariously through my fictional characters. No anxiety, no racing hearts, no complications.

But also no more of the warm, gooey feeling I got just hearing Braden say my name. It was *such* a good feeling.

There's no harm in going on one date, right?

As Holly had said, getting the experience was the important thing. If I ever wanted to feel comfortable around guys, I needed to actually hang out with one.

I had to find Holly so she could cheerlead me before I called Braden back. I got to my feet and went out to the rink, and I spotted her inside the snack bar.

"I need you." I pulled her away from the group of pair skaters at the table.

She saw the phone in my hand and squealed. "He called?"

I led her into the much quieter lobby before I answered, "He left a message asking me to the barbecue on Saturday."

Her squeals were suddenly accompanied by bouncing, and her loose topknot appeared on the verge of collapsing. "I'm so excited for you! The barbecue is perfect for a first date. It'll be casual and relaxed, and there'll be lots of people around to keep it entertaining."

"Should I meet him there so I can leave if it goes badly?"

"It won't go badly. From what you've told me, he seems like a fun guy. You need to have the full date experience, so he should drive you."

"My dad is gonna go into scary Russian mode when he sees Braden."

"It's a rite of passage we all have to go through." She slung her arm around me. "You haven't lived until you've been mortified by your parents in front of a guy."

I gripped my phone with two hands and rested my chin on its edge. "I should call him before I lose my nerve."

"Do you want me to stay for moral support?"

"No, you watching me will make me even more nervous. I'll go outside."

I stepped out into the sunshine and sat on the steps, shedding my jacket in the process. I suddenly felt like I couldn't breathe.

He's just a person. Talk to him as if he's one of your friends.

I quickly dialed his number and hoped he'd answer because God only knew how awkwardly I'd ramble if I had to leave a message.

"Hey, Liza." He sounded out of breath, and there was a loud noise in the background that sounded like gushing water.

"Hey, is this a bad time?"

"No, just give me a sec."

I heard him say to someone, "I'll be right back," and after a minute the noise quieted.

"Sorry about that. My day job is noisy sometimes."

"You have another job besides the internship?"

"The internship isn't paid, so I'm working for a painting company, too. We're power washing a deck today."

I'd never had one job, much less two at a time. I'd been so lucky that my mom took care of all my skating expenses, and I only had to work on being the best skater I could be.

"We can talk later if you're busy," I said. "I don't want you to get in trouble."

"No, it's okay. The guy I'm working with is cool. He knows I was waiting for a very important call."

I felt his smile over the line, and the gooeyness returned. We started speaking at the same time, and we both laughed.

"Go ahead," he said.

"I umm… I was just going to say that the barbecue sounds great. I'd love to go."

"Yeah?" His excitement came through clearly. "I was hoping you didn't have plans already."

"I have plans with a friend earlier in the day, but Saturday night is all yours."

I cringed. *Was that too much? I should've rehearsed this.*

"It starts at five-thirty, so I'll pick you up around six?"

"That sounds good. I'll text you my address."

"Awesome. I'm really looking forward to it."

I exhaled a little. "Me, too."

A pause followed, and we started talking over each other again. And again we laughed.

"Ladies always first," he said.

"I was saying I'll let you go since you're working."

"Yeah, I should get to it. Thanks for calling me back so soon. You just made the rest of my day a lot better."

So much gooeyness. *So much.*

"I'm glad I could help."

"See you Saturday, Liza."

I locked the phone and set it on the step. Holding my hands in front of me, I noticed they were trembling. Perform alone on the ice with millions of people watching? No problem. Chat with a guy for five minutes? Shaky mess. I really had to do something about my nerves before Saturday night.

❧✠☙

"WHO WANTS ICE CREAM?" Dad asked.

"Me!" Quinn and Alex shouted in perfect unison.

I waited for Dad to dish out their post-dinner dessert before I stepped up to the kitchen counter with my bowl. "I'll take a little."

He dropped two scoops of chocolate into the bowl, and I said, "That's more than a little."

"It's coconut milk with one gram of sugar. Two scoops won't hurt you."

Dad and Em were always watching out to make sure I ate enough and didn't go overboard in counting calories. As an Olympic gold medalist, Em knew the right diet for a skater at my level, and luckily for me she was also a fabulous cook who made healthy meals that were tasty.

The twins took their ice cream outside to the back deck, leaving me alone with Dad and Em. I'd needed all afternoon and evening to work up the nerve to tell Dad about my date. He would have a million questions for sure.

He took a few steps toward the sliding door to the deck, so I knew I had to get it over with already. I quickly blurted, "So, that guy Braden asked me out. We're going to the beach barbecue Saturday."

Dad froze with his spoon in his mouth, while Em shut the dishwasher with a smile. "That'll be so much fun."

"Did you find out more about him?" Dad asked as soon as he swallowed.

"He's my age and he goes to school in Boston. From what I've seen online he seems to have a nice family."

"How could you tell that?"

"I don't know … they looked normal enough."

"Give me his last name so I can look for myself."

I tipped my head back and groaned. "*Dad.* Can't you trust my judgment?"

"You don't know enough about him to make a sufficient judgment."

"That's why I'm going out with him. To get to know

him."

Dad put his ice cream on the granite island and rubbed his hand slowly over his chin. "He should come over here first so we can meet him and talk to him."

I shook my head violently. "No way. That would be *so* awkward."

"Is he picking you up Saturday?" Em asked. "We can meet him then."

"He is. And I don't want him to be interrogated."

Dad crossed his arms. "I don't like the idea of you riding with a guy you barely know."

"He's not going to kidnap me."

"He could do a lot of things you're not expecting like drive you somewhere isolated or put something in your drink or... or..." Dad's wheels of doom were spinning so fast that he couldn't keep up with his own thoughts.

"She's a smart girl with good common sense," Em said. "You have to trust her to take care of herself."

"She's never been out with a guy before. She doesn't know anything about what they're thinking, what they might do–"

"Thanks for having so much confidence in me, Dad."

"You know I do." He must've heard the hurt in my voice because he softened his. "But this is an all-new experience for you. I have a right to be concerned."

"I appreciate the concern, but I'm not doing anything that a million other girls haven't done. Can you try to be cool about it and not act like this is some world-changing event?"

I hurried out of the kitchen and looked for my phone in the living room, but then I remembered I'd left it in the library. I found it on one of the cushions of the black leather sofa. Before dinner I'd sent Braden my address and asked how his day had gone. My mood immediately lifted when I saw I had a text message.

I sat cross-legged on the sofa and held my ice cream in

one hand and the phone in the other, using my thumb to open Braden's text.

Braden: **Got it! Power washing was uneventful, which I learned last week is a very good thing. How was skating?**

I set the bowl aside and started typing.

Me: **Also uneventful. Also a good thing.** ☺

Braden: **How many hours a day do you practice?**

Me: **Four hours on ice and a couple hours of off-ice workouts/ballet/Pilates depending on the day.**

Braden: **That's hardcore. You must be exhausted every night.**

Me: **Some days are worse than others. Usually have to keep it pretty low-key on weeknights.**

Braden: **So no wild partying tonight? ;)**

I laughed out loud in the empty room. There was sadly no wild partying *ever* in my life.

Me: **LOL no. How about you? Hot date with Netflix? ;)**

Braden: **You know me so well already.** ☺

Me: **Which show are you currently bingeing?**

Braden: **Friday Night Lights**

Me: **OMG that's one of my favorite shows ever. What season are you on?**

Braden: **Only the first, but it's awesome so far.**

Me: **I watch the reruns all the time. Season 1 was amazing.**

Braden: **You're welcome to come over any time and binge with me. Perfect low-key activity. ;)**

Hanging out with a guy at his place? I could already feel the aftershocks from Dad's head exploding.

I wasn't sure how to respond since we hadn't even been on our date yet, but I knew I had to play it cool.

Me: **Sounds fun.** ☺

Texting was so much less nerve-wracking than talking face to face. Could we have our date via the phone?

He didn't respond right away as he'd been doing, so I

scooped a big spoonful of the now soupy ice cream into my mouth. Should I try to find a way to wrap up the conversation so he didn't feel obligated to continue?

My phone dinged, taking care of the question.

Braden: **Any chance I'll see you at the game tomorrow night?**

Me: **I'd love to be there, but I have an interview.**

Braden: **An interview?**

Me: **One of the networks is coming to do an at-home fluff piece on me. A lot of them are shooting footage now to air during the Olympics.**

Braden: **Is there going to be paparazzi following us on Saturday?**

Me: **LOL no I'm not THAT famous.**

Braden: **From what I saw in your videos, you should be.**

Me: **How many have you watched?**

Braden: **Just two or three… or ten. ☺**

A few goosebumps popped up as I pictured him watching my performances. I put so much of myself into every one, and I'd had some glorious moments but also some not-so-pretty ones.

Me: **You've probably seen some of my epic falls then.**

Braden: **You don't fall much. You're crazy good.**

More goosebumps.

Me: ☺

Braden: **You make it look easy but I know from experience it's not.**

Me: **Not much of a skater?**

Braden: **I played hockey when I was a kid but I was sorta terrible.**

Me: **You should give skating another shot. It's such an amazing feeling to fly around the ice.**

Braden: **Is that what keeps you going during all those hours of training?**

Me: **Definitely. The gold medals are good inspiration**

too. ;)

Another long pause came, and I switched to reading my ebook until my phone lit up again.

Braden: **One of my roommates needs a ride, so I have to run out. You gonna stay out of trouble over there?**

Me: **Haha I'll do my best.**

Braden: **Hope you have another uneventful day of skating tomorrow.** ☺

Me: **Thanks! Hope you have a good day too!**

I stretched out on the couch and realized my face mirrored all the smiley emojis in our messages. Scrolling through our conversation, I reread all of it and then did it again. If I could channel the ease I felt while texting Braden when I saw him on Saturday night, I'd be set. That is, if Dad didn't threaten his life first.

CHAPTER FOUR

"How should I do my hair? Keep it down and natural?" I combed my fingers through my long, straight locks.

"Hmm... it might be windy on the beach, so a braid would probably be more comfortable," Court said.

"Can you do it for me? I feel so spastic right now."

I flopped down on my bed, and Court sat beside me with my hairbrush. She was helping me get ready, and Holly was texting me every ten minutes from work for outfit updates. Court and I had put together five different outfits before choosing the sleeveless turquoise romper and gold sandals I was wearing. The sandals had slinky straps that tied around my ankles, which Court had deemed "sexy." That had unleashed a boatload of thoughts about what Braden would think when he saw me and all the possibilities that could occur before the night was over.

"Do you think he might try to kiss me?" I asked.

"If you both have a great time and the moment feels right it could happen."

"I wish I felt more prepared. I'm not used to doing anything without practicing it a thousand times first. A few years ago my gay friend Jordan offered to let me kiss him to practice. I should've taken him up on it."

"You'll be fine. Don't stress about it. If it happens, just relax and melt into it."

I let out a laugh. "Melt into it?"

"That's the best way I know how to describe it." She looped a hair band around the end of my braid. "Don't overthink it. He'll likely know what he's doing, so follow his lead."

"I just don't want it to be obvious that I have zero experience."

"It's okay that you're new to all this. You're not the first nineteen-year-old to have never been kissed. You have nothing to feel weird about."

I reached out and touched the matted fur of my teddy bear that sat against the pillows. I'd had Peter since I was three, and I had the sudden urge to hold on tight to him.

"You know, I didn't tell my mom about Braden. I couldn't deal with her freaking out on top of my freaking out."

"She's pretty anti-dating, isn't she?"

"There's a reason she sent me to an all-girls school."

The doorbell chimed, and I jumped up. "He's here already?" I looked at the clock on the nightstand. "He's fifteen minutes early."

"It's okay. You're ready." Court set her hands on my shoulders, bringing my eyes to hers. "Breathe with me. Slowly in and out."

We took a long inhale and exhale together, and she wrapped me in a hug. "Relax. Have fun. And remember – you are beautiful and amazing and Braden's probably as nervous as you are."

I squeezed her tightly and grabbed my purse and sweater. "I'd better get down there before Dad has a chance to grill him."

Court followed me down the stairs, and Braden looked

over at me as soon as I hit the creaky final step. He was dressed in a dark red polo and khaki shorts. It was the first time I'd seen him without a baseball cap, and his light brown hair was thick and slightly wavy.

His eyes swept over me, and his whole face glowed with a smile. "Hey, Liza."

There were four of us in the room, but Braden's attention was only on me. Now I had tingles on top of jitters.

"Hey," I said.

"Sorry I'm so early. I was telling your dad that traffic wasn't as bad as my phone said it was. I was going to wait outside, but I figured it would be better to come in than sit in my car like a creeper."

I laughed, and Court came forward to shake Braden's hand. "Hi, I'm Courtney."

"Another sister?"

"We act like it, but no."

"Court's one of my dad's students and she lives with us," I said.

"Where are you living this summer, Braden?" Dad asked. He'd been in a firm stance with his arms folded over his chest since I'd come downstairs.

"I'm rooming with a couple other interns at a house in Dennis."

The door from the garage opened, and Em and the twins spilled into the kitchen. Quinn and Alex were jabbering loudly, but they stopped abruptly when they saw Braden. Alex took his usual spot behind Quinn when new people were around.

"You again," Quinn said.

Braden laughed, the big hearty laugh that had first made me notice him.

"I know Alex, but I never got your name," he said.

"Aquinnah Rose Petrov."

"You can call her Quinn," Em said. "Hi, I'm Emily, Liza's

stepmom. It's great to meet you, Braden."

The doorbell rang, and Court said, "That must be Josh."

Someone put a tent over this circus.

She welcomed him inside and made the introductions, and I wanted to get out of there before anyone else showed up to witness the wonder of me going on a date.

"Ready to go?" I asked Braden.

"Let's do it." He waved at the crowd in the living room. "It was nice meeting all of you."

Dad stalked behind us out to the front porch, and I gave him a what-are-you-doing look.

"Braden, you won't be drinking tonight?" he said as a questioning command.

My face burned surefire bright pink. There was the mortification Holly had mentioned.

"No. No, Sir."

Dad nodded stiffly, his arms still folded. "Be careful because other people will be." He turned to me. "Call if you'll be late."

My whole body felt red with embarrassment. "Okay, Dad."

I rushed off the porch and hoped Braden was still with me and not looking for an escape route. I headed for his older model black Jeep along the curb, and he caught up to me as I reached the door.

"I'm so sorry about that," I said as Braden opened the door for me.

"Oh, it's cool. I've seen worse." He came around to the driver's seat. "My dad's a cop, and he used to scare the hell outta my sisters' boyfriends."

"Your dad's a cop?"

"A detective in Fall River. I should've told your dad that to give myself some cred."

I laughed and buckled my seat belt. As Braden put on his, I noticed he was wearing the *Faith* wristband and colorful bracelets again. He'd had them on both times I'd seen him at the ballpark.

"Let me plug in the directions to the beach." He typed on his phone. "Unless you know how to get there?"

"Just go back out to the main road and take a left."

"I came to the Cape a few times when I was a kid, but we never stayed around here."

"I've been spending summers here since I was nine, so it's like a second home for me," I said.

"Where's home the rest of the year?"

"New York. Right outside New York City."

"Uh oh." He braked softly at the stop sign. "If you tell me you're a Yankee fan, I'm turning the car around."

"If I was a Yankee fan, would I be going out with a guy who named his dog after a Red Sox player?"

He laughed. "That's great."

I laughed with him, and my shoulders relaxed a little. Braden gave off such warm energy that he was already making me feel at ease.

"Take a right at the next light," I said.

He curved the wheel with one hand and tapped his leg with the other in time to the alt rock on the radio. "Since you're here with me, I'm guessing your internet search didn't turn up anything too damaging."

"Is there something out there worse than the bleached hair?"

"Ahh, you did see that. You're lucky you play an individual sport. That's what happens when team peer pressure goes terribly wrong."

Telling him I thought he looked cute in the photo would be a definite flirty move, but not one I had the nerve to make yet. *Just keep the conversation going.*

"I saw you're on social media, but you don't post much," I said.

"I'm mostly there to follow my friends and get sports

news. I've never gotten the whole concept of telling the world every mundane detail of your life."

I kept quiet because I was guilty of sharing what some might consider mundane details. That morning I'd Tweeted about bathing my ghostly self in sunscreen before I went to the beach with Holly.

"Did I just put my foot in my mouth?" He cringed. "You post a lot, don't you?"

"Kinda."

"Well, you're a special case because you're well-known. Your fans probably eat that stuff up."

"I don't Tweet every time I leave the house like some people do."

"You mean you didn't let the world know you were going out with the coolest guy you've ever met?"

I glanced at him with a smile. "Maybe you'll earn a Tweet later. Depending on how the night goes."

"What do I have to do to earn an Instagram pic?"

"Ooh, that's huge. You'll have to really wow me."

He grinned. "Challenge accepted."

I pointed him to the final turn, and soon we were walking up to the crowded beach. A DJ was set up just off the sand, playing "Gangnam Style," and a group of kids was jumping around doing the dance craze. Past the DJ was a large tented area with rows of tables and chairs plus booths dishing out food and drinks.

Braden pulled out his wallet as we reached the entrance table, and I quickly opened my purse.

"I can pay for my ticket," I said.

"I've got it."

"I don't mind."

"I asked you out." He smiled. "I'm gonna pay."

The lady behind the table passed us a couple of tickets, and we joined the food line. I peeked around the person in front of me to see the options so I could decide on the least messy one. Braden handed me a paper plate, and I accepted a chicken sandwich from the server but bypassed the potato chips. We moved down the line to the next booth, and Braden pointed at the sign.

"Have you ever had Captain Parker's clam chowder? It's the best."

"I'm allergic to seafood. Shellfish."

"Oh, then we'll definitely keep that far away from you."

"You can have some. I won't break out in hives from sitting across the table from it."

"Nah, I can get it any time."

He turned toward the bar, and I wondered if he was skipping the chowder because he had thoughts of kissing me later and didn't want to risk sending me into anaphylactic shock. It was sweet foresight, and it also made my nerves prickle up again.

Braden grabbed a can of soda from the bar, and I picked up a bottle of water and scanned the tables for seats.

"There's two," he said and led the way to a table close to the DJ.

We sat across from each other next to a middle-aged couple, and I took a small bite of my sandwich, trying not to get crumbs on my face. Braden took a huge bite of his burger and a swig of his soda.

"So, tell me something about Liza Petrov that's not in any videos or news articles."

I patted my mouth with a paper napkin, leaving a trace of pink lip gloss. "You're starting with the tough questions."

"I don't mess around."

I sipped my water. The first thing that came to mind was the fact that I'd never been on a date before, but I sure wasn't confessing that little tidbit right now.

"I umm… I like to write."

"Yeah? Like fiction?"

I nodded. "I've always loved to read, and I started

writing when I was in junior high."

"What kind of stories do you write?"

"Usually short stories. I haven't tackled a novel yet."

"Jeez, what are you waiting for? It's not like you have anything else keeping you busy," he said with a teasing smile.

I laughed. "I know. I'm hoping to get to it one day."

"This could be your next career. You could be as well-known for your books as you are for your skating."

"That would be amazing," I said and made another tiny dent in my sandwich. Silence set in, and I remembered Court's tip for keeping up the conversation – ask questions.

"How about you? What do you want to do with your business degree?"

He finished chewing a potato chip before answering, "Dream job is general manager of the Red Sox. Before that, I just want to work for any sports team, any job I can get."

"That explains the volunteer internship."

"Serving burgers isn't part of my career plan, but I get to do other stuff with the team, so it's good experience."

"Did you ever think about being a policeman like your dad?"

"Noooo, never." He shook his head. "That life isn't for me."

He'd answered so quickly and definitively that I could tell he had strong feelings on the subject. I'd never personally known any policemen, so my ideas about them all came from TV and movies.

"Was it tough being a cop's kid? I picture him being very strict."

"Nothing ever got past him. He can smell a lie a mile away." He put his hand over his heart. "Not that I ever lied or got in any kind of trouble."

"Of course not. I can't see you being mischievous at all." I smiled behind my water bottle.

He studied me with a little glint in his eyes. "I bet you

were an absolute angel as a kid."

"What if I told you I was a complete terror?"

"Not a chance."

"I'm that transparent?"

"I inherited some of my dad's detective skills."

He was still staring at me, and I felt like he could see deeper inside me than I was ready to reveal. I lowered my head and sighed loudly. "I have to admit you're right, *but*... I did get in a fight once when I was eleven. Put some nasty scratches on a girl's face."

"What did she do?"

"She was talking trash about Emily back when she was competing."

"I like that. Defending the family." He smiled and chewed slowly on a chip. "Your parents have been divorced a long time then."

The convoluted story of my childhood would take too long to explain, so I kept it simple. "They were never married."

He nodded. "Gotcha."

We spent a few quiet minutes finishing our food and watching the kids dance with the encouragement of the DJ. He was playing every line dance and party song I'd ever heard, some way older than the kids and even older than me.

"My little brother would be at the front of the pack if he was here," Braden said. "He thinks he's Justin Bieber."

"How old is he?"

"Nine. He was a surprise baby."

"I think I saw him in one of your pictures."

"If you saw a miniature version of me with darker hair, that was Tanner."

"Alright, who's ready to do the Cupid Shuffle?" the DJ boomed.

"This should be good," Braden said.

The DJ stood at the front of the group, demonstrating the

dance, but the kids in the back were totally off with their steps.

"They're not doing it right," I said.

"You should get out there and show them."

I laughed. "I don't think so."

"Why not?" He hopped up and took my hand. "Come on, I want you to teach me, too."

The warmth of his hand around mine spread through me like lightning, flushing me all over. The sweet, gooey feeling he'd been giving me since we met had now been multiplied by a thousand. Make that a million.

"I don't know..." I said. No one over the age of ten was dancing. Also, the longer I stalled, the longer Braden would have to hold my hand.

"World champ skater afraid to dance in front of some kids?" He gave me a challenging grin.

My competitive fire never let me back down from a challenge, so he'd said just the right thing to spur me on.

"Not at all. I just don't want to steal the spotlight."

"We can dance in the back."

He tugged lightly on my hand, and I followed him to a space behind the last row of kids. They were spinning around completely off the beat.

"I'm ready when you are." He let go of my hand and clapped his together, and I flexed my fingers, already missing the quick buzz he'd given me.

I slung my purse across my body, and I waited for the chorus of the song to make my first move. With a little bounce in my knees, I took four steps to the right and then four to the left. After doing four little kicks, I walked in a circle and found Braden watching me with a huge smile.

I started the pattern over again, and he mimicked my movements until we were totally in sync. We laughed together as we put more swagger into every step, making our turns more elaborate each time. Braden was being goofy with his moves, but I could tell he did have some rhythm within him.

A few adults joined us and fell in line with our lead, and they kept dancing as the song ended and the next one began. My body felt looser, and I silently thanked Braden for making me dance out some of my jitters.

"Look at us, inspiring people to dance," he said.

"They'll have to keep it going without me. I refuse to do the Macarena."

"I'm with you."

We went back to our table, and Braden tossed our empty plates into the trash. "Want to take a walk down the beach?" he asked.

"Sure."

I shrugged on my sweater while Braden grabbed a couple of bottles of water for us. We snaked through the crowd of people watching the cornhole tournament and found a clear path heading west along the edge of the sand. A light breeze rustled the marsh grass that lined the walkway.

"Did I read you all wrong?" he asked. "You been hanging out in the clubs doing the Cupid Shuffle?"

I laughed. "No, your detective skills didn't fail you. I learned it for Spirit Week my senior year."

"So you went to regular high school? I know a lot of elite athletes are homeschooled."

"I went half a day so I got to have part of the high school experience. The weirdest thing was senior year when everyone was applying to college and going through all that excitement and I wasn't doing any of it."

"You have plenty of way cooler stuff going on, though."

"Yeah." I toyed with the hem of my sweater. "It's just a lot different from college life. Or how I picture college life."

"I can give you the lowdown on what college is like. Ask me anything."

I looked up into his smiling face. "Do you live in the dorms?"

"The UMass campus in Boston doesn't have dorms, so I

live in an apartment with a few friends."

"Are there lots of parties? I'm picturing a frat house situation."

"Oh, yeah, it's out of control every weekend."

My eyes widened, and Braden laughed. "Not really. One of my roommates is a neat freak germophobe, so he would flip out if our place was trashed."

"You're ruining my clichéd ideas."

"There are parties. They're just at the neighbors' house."

"Okay, that makes me feel better." I smiled.

"What other clichés can I satisfy for you?"

"Hmm... do you stay up all night studying? Play Frisbee on the quad? Eat cold pizza for breakfast?"

He threw his head back with laughter. "Yes, no, and sometimes."

We'd reached the outskirts of the party, so we drifted over to a bench facing the water. Nantucket Sound lapped gently at the sand, kicking up small frothy waves.

The bench wasn't wide, so Braden and I were practically shoulder to shoulder. Mixed in with the salty sea breeze I could smell his cologne – slightly musky and very masculine. It reminded me that despite the comfortable banter we'd found, I was still swimming in uncharted waters. Being this close to Braden made my stomach bob like the buoy I spied out on the horizon.

"Beach or mountains?" he asked. "Where would you rather live?"

"Beach," I said with no hesitation.

"City or country?"

"City."

"Winter or summer?"

"Winter." I peered at him. "Is this the rapid-fire portion of the evening?"

"Yes, it is. Dogs or cats?"

"Dogs. I should get to ask questions, too."

"Fire away."

"Umm… books or movies?"

"Movies. Theater or DVD?"

"Theater."

I paused to think of my next question, and Braden snapped his fingers. "Rapid fire. You have to be quick."

"I'm thinking!" I sputtered for an idea and finally spit out, "Chocolate or vanilla?"

"There's only one acceptable answer to that question, and it's not vanilla."

We continued to go back and forth until we were both stumped for questions, and then we switched to asking about our favorite things – colors, foods, games, holidays – the list went on. I learned Braden was a Halloween-loving, Trivial Pursuit fan with a secret obsession with cooking shows, and he got me to confess my guilty pleasure of watching *Saved by the Bell* reruns over and over.

The sky had dimmed to a deep orange dusk, and some of the partygoers gathered around small fire pits on the sand. The kids had abandoned the dance floor and were now poking marshmallows with skewers to roast them over the fire. The flames matched the colors between the sky's wispy clouds.

"The sunset is so pretty," I said.

"You're itching to take a photo and Instagram it, aren't you?"

"No, I'm not." I gave him a sidelong glance. "Okay, maybe I am."

He laughed. "Go ahead. I won't judge."

I took out my phone, and Braden said, "I have to ask – have I earned my way into a picture yet?"

I chewed my lip. "I don't think I should post a photo of you because it'll get all kinds of comments and questions from my followers. Some things I like to keep to myself."

"I get that. I'm sure you have a lot of fans who try to get all up in your business."

"We can still take a picture. If you don't mind it not being shared."

"Well, you have to share it with me. I promise I'll keep it safely off the internet." He held up his hand in swear mode.

"Of course." I aimed the phone upward. "Let me get the sky first before the sun goes down."

I snapped the colorful landscape and posted it with the caption *Perfect Night*. My followers would have no idea that I was talking about more than just the scenery.

"Can you take ours?" I asked. "I suck at selfies because of my short arms."

He took the phone in his right hand and casually slipped his left arm behind me on the back of the bench. I gulped as he leaned his head in close to mine for the photo.

"Ready?" he asked.

I took a calming breath and relaxed into a smile. Braden clicked twice and showed me the results. Seeing evidence of myself having such an amazing time made me smile even bigger than I had in the pictures.

"We're so much prettier than the sunset," Braden said.

I laughed. "I'll text it to you later."

His gaze shifted to the beach, and he pointed his nose in the air. "How good do those marshmallows smell? Should we go for the dessert portion of the evening?"

I usually stayed away from sugar-laden candy, but I didn't want to be a stick-in-the-mud. We grabbed a couple of skewers and found a spot at one of the fire pits alongside a family of four. Braden let his marshmallow almost burn, and I had to give him a hard time.

"It's practically black!"

"That's the way I like it." He blew on it and popped it into his mouth. "Mmmm."

We both had sticky fingers after we finished, and it was Braden's turn to tease me as I fished an antibacterial wipe from my purse.

"My germophobe roommate would love you," he said.

"I was going to share with you, but since you choose to mock me..."

"I'd be very grateful if you'd share."

I smiled and gave it to him, and he glanced at his watch as he wiped his hands. "They're probably shutting down the party soon, but we could stay and hang out on the beach. If you want," he added hastily.

"Yeah. I'd like that."

We started walking back toward our bench, and Braden's fingers brushed mine tentatively before curling around them, making me all aflutter again. His hand was so strong and warm, and I loved the way mine felt gently sheltered inside it.

We sat on the bench, and our clasped hands rested in the narrow space between us. I knew I had to text Dad to tell him I was going to be late, but it pained me to break this physical contact with Braden.

"I should let my dad know we're staying past the barbecue."

"Definitely. I don't want to lose any points with him."

I reluctantly pulled my hand away to get my phone, and I saw I had a string of texts from Holly asking how the date was going. I typed a swift reply.

Going great! Talk soon!

After shooting a text to Dad, I put the phone away and realized Braden had stretched his arm across the back of the bench as he'd done earlier. I settled back and breathed in his cologne. How could a simple scent give me so many butterflies?

As I took a stealthy glance over at him I noticed his bracelets again. "Can I ask you something? Is there special meaning behind those?" I pointed to them.

His face lost some of its light, and he bobbed his head slowly. "They're for my friend Scott who died a few years ago."

"Oh, I'm so sorry."

He didn't say anything for a minute, and I didn't know if I should try to change the subject. I was mentally fumbling for words when he started talking again.

"We got the wristbands at youth group, and some of us on the baseball team started wearing them freshman year. By the time we were juniors Scott had our whole team wearing them. He was also the one who got the idea of bleaching our hair. Everyone always followed his lead."

My curiosity got the best of me, and before I realized I was speaking I asked, "What happened to him?"

Braden's eyes dimmed further, and I couldn't believe I'd just spat that out. There were far more sensitive things I could've said.

"I'm sorry. I shouldn't have asked–"

"It's okay. It's a natural question." He looked down at the wristband. "He committed suicide our junior year."

"Oh my God," I breathed quietly.

"He was top of our class, in every club, on every sports team. He was under so much pressure to be the best at everything. I knew he was stressed, but I never thought... I just didn't see it coming at all."

A tiny lump formed in my throat as I heard the sadness in his voice. I felt terrible for asking about the bracelets. *Nice job making him dredge up painful memories.*

"You don't have to talk about it if you don't want to," I said.

"Sorry, I didn't mean to get all dark on you."

"No, you don't have to apologize. It's obviously something that's impacted you a lot."

"I think about him every day when I look at these." He lifted his wrist.

"What do the colorful ones symbolize?"

"Some kids at school made them for Scott's memorial, and everyone traded them with their friends. They're a reminder that you always have someone to count on."

I gazed at the mixture of yellow, blue, and green running through the black thread. "That's a really nice idea."

He was quiet, and I searched for what to say. The mood had turned so serious, but learning something so important about Braden made me feel closer to him. I wanted to share something important about my past, too. Something that had flipped my life upside down and made me question everything I'd thought was true.

"I know how hard it is to lose someone so suddenly and tragically," I said. "It seems so unreal, like a bad dream that you're convinced is going to end."

He turned to face me. "You've gone through it, too?"

I gave him a little nod. "My adoptive parents were killed in a car accident when I was seven."

He gaped at me, having been stunned into silence. Once the shock wore off, confusion spread across his face. "You were adopted?"

"My mom and dad skated together for Russia until my mom got pregnant with me when she was seventeen. My grandfather didn't approve of her relationship with my dad, so he made her give me up. Her American cousins adopted me, and I thought they were my real parents until after they died."

Braden's eyebrows arched higher. "Wow."

"After the accident my mom took me to Russia to live with her, and I still thought she was just my cousin. We ran into my dad one day in a total fluke meeting, and he took one look at me and knew I was his. Then everything came out, and my mom and I moved back here so I could be closer to my dad."

His mouth hung open a few extra moments before he could speak. "That's one of the most unbelievable stories I've ever heard."

"It was a lot to process as a kid."

"I can't imagine losing one of my parents, much less both of them."

The memory of my friend's mom telling me my parents weren't coming home was one I pushed far, far away whenever it appeared. That night and the entire year that followed had felt like never-ending days of tears and confusion.

"Skating was my lifeline," I said. "If I hadn't had that..."

Braden's hand cupped my shoulder, giving it a gentle squeeze. I hadn't been angling for affection with my story, but I couldn't deny how much I enjoyed his touch. It was sweet and genuine – an extension of the expression he wore as he intently listened to me.

"Had you even met your mom before you moved to Russia?" he asked.

"She visited sometimes, but we weren't close or anything. It was pretty awkward for a while, especially after I found out the truth. I was really mad at her for lying to me and keeping me away from my dad."

"Do you guys have a good relationship now?"

"Oh, yeah. She's very overprotective, but I think it's because she's never really gotten over having to give me up for adoption."

He shook his head. "I'm surprised they haven't made a movie of your life yet."

"We've actually been asked, and my mom and dad said no way. They don't like to talk about their past to the media, but it's all out there. It's the topic reporters love to bring up the most." I tipped my head up toward him. "See all the stuff you missed just watching my competition videos?"

He smiled. "This is some heavy territory we've covered for a first date."

"It is." I paused, sensing we needed a quiet moment. "Thank you for telling me about Scott. I'd love to hear more about him sometime. If you're okay talking about him."

"Yeah, for sure. I have so many great Scotty stories." The brightness returned to his face. "I'd love to hear about your adoptive parents, too. And not in a nosy reporter kind of way."

I smiled. "Definitely."

Our eyes met, and he held mine with soft intensity. There was a palpable connection between us now, the result of sharing such personal aspects of our lives. Talking to him about my past had felt so comfortable – more comfortable than I would've expected with someone I'd just met.

We sat quietly for a few minutes, watching a group of young teenagers start their own party on the beach. Braden's hand rested on my shoulder, and the slow stroke of his fingertips heated my skin through my sweater. The swirly feeling in my stomach felt even better than what I'd experienced holding hands, and that had felt ridiculously good.

Braden broke the silence by asking me about the time I'd spent in Russia, and the next hour flew by as I described life in Moscow and he told me more about life at UMass. I could've stayed on the bench and talked to him all night, but Dad would have an army of state troopers searching for me.

As Braden drove me home, I lost any feeling of comfort I'd gained, and my palms began to glisten with sweat. I felt more anxious than I had when we'd first started the evening. The "end of the date" moment was near, and all I could think about was a possible kiss and Courtney's advice of melting into it. I had a terrible fear that I was going to do the exact opposite and be as stiff as a new pair of skates.

We pulled up in front of my house, and I rubbed my hands on my sweater. Braden shut off the engine, and I longed to know his next move. Was he going to say goodnight there or was he going to walk me to the door?

He stepped out of the Jeep, answering my question. I climbed out, and he took my hand as we walked up to the porch, lit only by the dim gaslight lamps on either side of the front door. My pulse was seriously racing. I hadn't been that nervous since I'd skated at the Olympics three years ago.

Braden faced me, and I looked up into his soft brown eyes. I could barely catch my breath because my heart was beating so fast. *I'm going to have a heart attack and die before I even have the chance to kiss a boy.*

"I thought your dad might be out here with a breathalyzer," he said. "My dad actually did that with one of my sisters' boyfriends."

"Oh, no." I laughed, but I secretly hoped that Dad might pop through the front door and save me from this nerve-wracking moment.

"I'm really glad we got to hang out tonight," Braden said.

"Me too. I had a great time."

He squeezed my hand and shifted his weight, and I sensed he was anxious, too, but probably nowhere near my level of freak-out. My face and neck were growing hotter by the second, and I prayed Braden couldn't see how red they were in the low light.

"I'd love to see you again," he said, stepping closer.

I nodded. "Definitely."

He smiled and inched further forward, and I felt myself tightening with nerves. It was the same sensation I got sometimes before a critical jump in my programs, and it often meant I ended up sprawled on the ice. What if Braden kissed me and I made it just as much of a disaster?

His head bent toward mine, his mouth so very close. The panic within me took over, and I quickly turned my face, making his lips land on my cheek instead of their real target. His kiss lingered an extra moment, probably out of surprise, and I tried to figure out how to gracefully get out of the awkwardness.

I decided a hug would save me from eye contact, so I looped my arms around his shoulders. "Thank you again for such a fun night."

He hugged my waist but didn't pull me any closer. "It was my pleasure."

We broke apart, and I fumbled in my purse for my keys. When I got them into the lock, I gave Braden a quick look and smile. "Goodnight."

He echoed me, and I heard him going down the steps as I opened the door. The foyer was dark, but light shone in the living room. I took a breath to compose myself because I expected Dad to be there, ready to cross-examine me.

Surprisingly, only Em sat on the sofa, working on her tablet. Her dark blond hair was pulled up into a knot, and she was wearing her glasses. The TV was on but barely audible.

"I can't believe Dad's not in here pacing," I said.

"I suggested he go take his shower to relax." She laughed and set the tablet in her lap. "Come tell me all about your night. I'm assuming you had a good time since you stayed late."

I dropped onto the sofa beside her and fiddled with the strap of my purse. "I did. He was really, really great."

"Then how come I can tell something's bothering you?"

I twisted the strap around my finger. "The night was perfect until… Braden tried to kiss me just now and I panicked and made him kiss my cheek instead."

Em's smile turned sympathetic. "If you had a great time and he really likes you, it won't matter. Did he mention going on another date?"

"Yeah, but that was before I dodged him. He might think I'm some frigid ice princess now."

"He's not thinking that. You have a right to not kiss him if you weren't ready."

I leaned back and rested my head against the couch. I hated that three hours of amazingness were being overshadowed by five seconds of weirdness. Maybe I was making too big a deal out of it. But I thought I'd felt a change in Braden's body language after the kiss-miss.

"Is dating always this stressful?" I asked. "It might be better if he ends up not calling me again. I probably shouldn't be adding more stress to my life."

"The question you have to ask yourself is whether the good feelings you experienced tonight outweigh the angst. And for the record, I think you might be stressing for nothing." She patted my knee.

Em's advice was usually on point, and she definitely had more wisdom on this subject than I did. I thought back to everything that had happened before the front porch, and I couldn't even put into words how many good feelings I'd had that night. Was that my answer?

CHAPTER FIVE

A CLAP OF THUNDER EXPLODED OVER the rink, overpowering the classical music playing on the stereo. As if my Monday blues weren't bad enough, the stormy weather was making my mood even darker. I zoomed around a novice pair practicing their spins and sought comfort in the feel of my blades flying over the ice.

Forget about last weekend. Skating is what's important.

But I couldn't stop thinking about Braden and how I hadn't heard from him since he'd stepped off my front porch. I'd texted him our selfie Sunday morning, and I'd gotten no response. Nothing. The longer I didn't hear from him, the madder I became. Was he really blowing me off because I hadn't let him kiss me?

Speeding into an area of clear space, I slammed my toe pick into the ice and took off for the triple flip jump, but my angry stab had been too violent. I was so off-center in the air that I knew I couldn't do anything to save the landing. My hip hit the ice right on a big bruise I had from Friday's practice, and I clenched my teeth as pain radiated deep into my thigh. I slapped the ice and pushed myself to my feet.

It wasn't until I took a few strokes that I noticed the blood on my index finger. I cut across the ice and went to my bag on the bleachers for a bandage. My phone taunted me from the side pocket, and I couldn't help but check it for a text.

Still nothing.

Holly leaned over my shoulder. "The jerk hasn't replied yet?"

"How could he have been so nice and then…" I threw the phone into my bag.

"It's his loss. You should still feel great about going out with him. You got your first date out of the way, and now you're ready for any guy that comes along."

"I'm done with dating for now." I held my stomach. "My nerves can't take it."

"Don't let one bad experience take you out of the game."

"But it wasn't a bad experience. It was so much fun, and I really thought we'd clicked. Am I so naïve about guys that it was all in my head?"

"I'm sure you didn't imagine it. Boys are stupid, and they do a lot of things that don't make sense."

"Liza, your music is up next," Dad called from the corner of the rink.

I secured the bandage around my finger and hopped back onto the ice, taking long strokes around the rink to warm up for my run-through. As soon as Court and Josh finished theirs, I clapped for them and got into my starting pose to wait for my short program music to begin.

Another round of thunder boomed just as the peaceful cello notes of "Benedictus" started playing. The lights flickered twice, but I stayed in my zone, moving confidently through the opening choreography. I may have been a naïve girl when it came to dating, but I was a pro at skating, and this run-through was exactly what I needed to get out of my funk. Mom and I had seen 2Cellos in concert in April, and as soon as I heard them play this piece, I wanted to skate to it. The beautiful music had a calming effect on me – perfect for the chaotic Olympic season.

I did a few crossovers, and I arched my back until it was parallel with the ice. While in the deep Ina Bauer I sailed across the center of the rink. On the first high note of the music I rose up and pushed off from the ice for my first jump, making two and a half big turns in the air. I came down with a smooth landing and held my strong posture, head up and arms open.

The other skaters scattered as I leapt into my flying sit spin, and I silently counted the revolutions to make sure I'd earn maximum points when it came time to be judged. Loose strands of hair flew across my eyes and mouth and then settled around my face as I stood upright. I took a couple of steps and quickly knocked out another required spin, loosening more of my bun. With just a few pushes of my blades I worked my way to the opposite end of the rink, but the sight of Braden beside the bleachers made me stutter-step around the corner.

What is he doing here?

I couldn't let myself dwell on that question because I had to do the triple flip next, the jump I'd fallen on earlier. If I fell again, Dad would accuse me of being distracted by my visitor. Plus, I didn't want to mess up with Braden watching me.

Extra adrenaline pumped through me as I set up for the takeoff. Instead of an angry stab into the ice, my toe pick made an excited one, but it was still more powerful than what I needed. My body was leaning in the air again, but I felt more in control than I had before. I shifted my position slightly as I spun, and I landed just slightly tilted. I dug hard into the ice and kept myself upright and on one foot.

Exhale.

I took a peek at Braden, and he stood perfectly still, his eyes glued on me. A trail of goosebumps covered my spine, and I quickly looked down at the ice. Being overcome by

Braden-butterflies wasn't going to help my focus. *Think about the footwork. Give this footwork everything you have.*

Curving my blades deep into the ice, I hit the complex steps right on the highs and lows of the music. The pattern stretched from one end of the rink to the other, and I burst from the final step with a shot of energy. I had one jumping pass left, and it happened to be the most difficult element in the program.

I flexed my knees and picked up more speed before sailing backward into the combination, the triple Lutz-triple toe loop. Springing into the air, I pulled my arms in tight to my chest and spun three times. The moment my right blade reconnected with the ice, I picked in again and went up for three more. As I came down cleanly and spread my arms, I broke into a huge smile.

I completed my layback spin at a dizzying pace, and as I hit my ending pose applause broke out around me. My training mates and I always supported each other after our run-throughs, but that time there was a set of hands clapping louder than all the others.

Dad noticed Braden for what looked like the first time, and he made no move to welcome him to the rink. I grabbed my water bottle from the boards and took a long drink while I glided slowly to cool down. As I neared the edge of the bleachers, Braden smiled and waved, and I made a circle motion to let him know I had to do a few laps.

Holly skated up beside me. "He answers texts in person?"

"I guess so."

She glanced back at Braden. "He's even hotter than his pictures."

I snuck a quick look, too. He wore a navy rain jacket and jeans, and his hair was slightly damp. He ran his fingers through it as if to dry it, making it more messy-adorable.

"Don't remind me. Now I'm getting nervous again." I patted my unkempt bun and looked down. Sweat beaded my chest and trickled under the neckline of my black leotard. "I'm such a mess. This isn't how I planned for him to see me if we met up again."

"You look fine. Guys love that no-makeup, natural thing you've got going on right now."

"I'm naturally sweating like a pig."

I snatched a tissue from the boards during my next lap and blotted my face and neck. After circling the ice a couple more times, I stepped through the door but hesitated before I started toward Braden. I felt so exposed in my fitted leotard and pants, which showed every curve, or lack thereof, on my petite body. My jacket was in the locker room, so I had nothing to cover myself. I was just going to have to suck it up and own my current appearance.

"Hey," I said as we met halfway across the rubber-matted floor.

The once-over and ensuing smile he gave me proved my lack of assets didn't seem to bother him.

"I can't think of anything to say except, 'Wow.'"

My face warmed. Was he commenting on how I looked?

"Video doesn't do you justice," he said. "I mean, you were great on there, but seeing you skate live... wow."

I laughed to myself at my misunderstanding. Of course he'd been talking about my skating.

"Thanks. I'm still getting comfortable with the program, so it wasn't at full speed."

"That wasn't full speed? You looked like you were flying to me."

"Come back in a few weeks and you'll see the difference."

You should probably make sure there's a second date before you extend a long-term invitation.

"Sorry for just showing up today. My idiot roommate spilled beer on my phone and it's still drying out. I didn't want you to think I'd disappeared."

A broken phone. Of course. Why had I jumped to the

worst conclusion?

"That sucks. I hope it isn't dead."

"I know, I have a ton of pictures and stuff on there. Not to mention numbers I really didn't want to lose." His eyes held steady on mine. "Can I get yours again in case it doesn't come back to life?"

"Sure." I reached into my bag and found a pen but no paper. "Do you have anything to write on?"

He shoved his hands in his pockets and came up empty. Pushing up one sleeve of his jacket, he smiled and held out his arm. "It'll be safe from the rain here."

I lifted my eyebrows and wrapped my fingers tentatively around his wrist. His forearm muscle tightened as I pressed the pen to his skin. I took my time making each digit clear and also enjoying the electric energy from Braden's nearness.

"Are you off from work today?" I asked as I finished the last number.

"My house-painting gig got rained out."

"Right." I tapped the pen to my head. "That was a stupid question."

"We do indoor jobs, too, so not stupid at all." He pulled down his sleeve. "I'm actually glad it's raining so I could come by. I wanted to ask if you have plans for the Fourth."

Besides the same-ole, same-ole tradition of going to the parade with my family and then watching Dad barbecue?

"Nothing set in stone."

"Have you ever been to the concert and fireworks in Boston?"

"Just once. The first summer I spent here."

"Would you like to go this year?" His eyes opened a little wider with hope. "Fair warning – we have to get there super early to get a spot, so it's an all-day thing. If you don't want to be stuck with me for sixteen hours... and I can't imagine any reason why you wouldn't... speak now or forever hold your peace."

He flashed a big grin, and I laughed. An all-day outing sounded intimidating, but Braden had made the hours of our first date fly by so quickly. I didn't have any reason to say no.

"I'm game," I said.

I didn't think it was possible, but his smile grew bigger.

"Excellent. I'll let you know the details as soon as I have a functioning phone."

"Thanks for coming all the way over here. Especially in this weather."

"I had to get in touch before you wrote me off as a jerk."

"I hadn't totally written you off, but my friend Holly did call you a jerk."

He laughed. "She sounds like a great friend."

"She's the best. That's her in the red shirt." I pointed to the ice and saw Dad staring at us from the boards. "I'd better get back out there, too. I have another run-through to do."

"Yeah, go do your thing. Sorry again for barging in on your practice."

"It's no problem. It was a nice break."

He matched my smile and slid closer, and I buzzed with anticipation. Was he coming in for a hug? Another kiss on the cheek?

Suddenly he looked over my shoulder and stiffened. He touched my arm for a millisecond and said, "I'll talk to you soon."

I watched him go through the double doors to the lobby and then turned to find the reason for Braden's quick exit. Dad.

"Did you invite him here?" he asked.

"No, he came because he couldn't call me. His roommate–" I stopped as I realized mentioning beer in relation to Braden wouldn't be a good idea. "His phone died, and he wanted to ask me out for Thursday. To the Pops concert in Boston."

"I don't want you going to Boston that day."

"Why not?"

He gave me an incredulous look. "You have to ask me that after what happened at the marathon?"

"Security will be a million times tighter because of the marathon. It'll be safer than ever."

"It's too many people. Security can't cover everyone."

I copied his serious stare with one of my own. "You just don't want me going out with Braden again."

"That's true, but if you insist on going, he's welcome to come to the parade with us. There's plenty to do around here."

"I really want to go to Boston and support the city after everything that's happened this year."

He didn't seem to share my sentimental feelings as his stare became icier. I folded my arms in response and stood my ground. I could play the stubborn game, too. I'd learned from the master, who happened to be standing in front of me.

He finally let out a loud breath through his nose. "I suppose nothing I say will change your mind."

"Dad, you have to let me do my own thing. If I was in college, you wouldn't know what I was doing every day."

"But you're not in college, and one of the benefits of living with me is you get my expert guidance." He put his arm around my shoulders. "Almost forty years of wisdom and experience that I can share with you."

"You know where I could use your expert guidance? On the first section of my footwork."

I pulled away and led him onto the ice to end the Boston and Braden conversation. If it kept going, Dad would just find more reasons why I shouldn't dare to do something outside my ordinary routine.

The topic of the Fourth didn't come up again until I was leaving the rink with Court and Holly, and they had a much different reaction than Dad's, talking over each other as they went into outfit-planning mode.

"You should wear a cute little tank or T-shirt," Holly said.

"With your cutoff jean shorts."

"And your hair up in a ponytail with a Red Sox cap. He will *love* that," Court said.

My phone rang, and I transferred my umbrella to my left hand to see the caller. When I read the number, my thumb hovered anxiously over the Answer button.

"It's my mom. I have to finally tell her about Braden because I know she'll ask about the holiday."

"Have fun with that." Holly waved, and Court crossed her fingers.

I answered the call as I climbed into my SUV, the way-too-extravagant Lexus that Mom had bought me for my eighteenth birthday. I only got in a "Hi, Mom" before she made me call her back on the hands-free feature of the car. When she was satisfied I had both hands on the wheel she asked me about skating, and I gave her a brief rundown on my training that day, leaving out my unexpected visitor.

"How was your weekend?" she asked. "Did you do anything fun?"

"Holly and I hung out Saturday morning. And then Saturday night..." I slowed as I neared a wooded curve, but my words came out quickly. "I had a date."

"You had a date? With who? Why am I just hearing about this?" Her indignant shrill came through the speaker loud and clear.

"His name is Braden, and I met him at one of the baseball games. He's doing a summer internship with the team."

"You went out with a stranger? And your father was okay with this?"

I gripped the wheel tighter. "I'm not a kid. He couldn't forbid me from going."

Mom just couldn't accept that I was an adult. She still saw me as an innocent child who needed to be protected from the world. Since she'd missed out on parenting me until I was eight years old, I often thought that she held onto me so tightly because she didn't want me to grow up.

"Tell me about the date," she said.

Giving her details would only provide information for her to pick apart, so I had to keep it vague. "It was a lot of fun. We're going out again this week."

I wasn't mentioning Boston just yet. Mom was already riled up enough about the mere existence of Braden.

"He must've made quite an impression on you."

"He's a really nice guy."

"Did your father at least look into his background? You have to remember that you are a public figure, and you can't trust just anyone. Look at all the crazy messages you get online."

"Braden isn't a crazed fan. He didn't even recognize me at first."

She turned quiet, and I figured she was reloading with ammunition. I tugged on my seatbelt, which felt more constricting than usual.

"Why do you want to get involved with boys now anyway?" she asked. "This is the worst time for all that."

"I don't know. Maybe I was tired of being scared to try something new."

"You have the rest of your life to try new things. You know how important everything you do this year is."

"Going on a few dates won't get me off track for the Olympics."

"What if a few dates turns into a relationship? You've opened the door now for a world that I don't think you're ready for."

I shook my head. She wouldn't say it, but I knew her real fear and another reason why she'd kept me so sheltered. She didn't want me to get involved with anyone because she didn't want her history to repeat with me. Her Olympic dream had ended when she'd gotten pregnant, and though she'd never made me feel like I was a mistake, I knew that having to give up her career still haunted her.

"Liza, you are so young," she continued. "You have so many years to date. Relationships take time and energy, and skating needs to be your focus right now. Unless your goals have changed?"

"Of course not."

"Then you should tell Braden you can't see him anymore. He'll understand you have other priorities."

So that was it. She made it seem so black and white. It didn't matter what I wanted or what I was feeling. She was convinced that she knew what was best for me.

I lied and told Mom the call was breaking up so I could finish the drive home in silence. I didn't even turn on the radio. Only the windshield wipers whooshing back and forth provided background for my thoughts.

As much as I didn't want to admit Mom could be right, I couldn't ignore the impact Braden had had on me after just one week. I'd gone from anxious to giddy to angry and now confused. If I let things continue to grow between us, I was in for a lot more emotional turmoil, and I'd learned from years of competing that I needed a clear head to do well.

When I reached the house, I went straight to my room and curled up in the plush chair next to the window. I loved the coziness of my room on a rainy day. The strings of tiny white lights over my bed gave off a twinkly glow that lit up the teal walls and the black and white décor.

I stared at my laptop on the desk, knowing I needed to write a new post for the Team USA blog, but I reached for my journal instead. I'd started a new short story about a girl and a guy who meet on the ferry to Martha's Vineyard. They'd just gotten off the boat and had gone in opposite directions, but fate would have them connect again on the island that day. Getting lost in the story would let me forget about real-life drama.

My characters were about to run into each other at the

Gay Head Cliffs when my phone chimed with a text. I stared at it a second before picking it up from the arm of the chair.

Braden: **My phone has risen from the dead!**

Seeing his name gave me the little flutter that had become so familiar lately. Mom's worried voice crept into my head, reminding me that this feeling was not necessarily a good thing. I shook it off and set aside my journal.

Me: **Amen!**

Braden: **As pissed as I was at my roommate, I'm glad it gave me the chance to see you skate.**

Aww. I put my thumbs on the keyboard to reply, but another message came through.

Braden: **I can't stop thinking about it.**

There was no smiley or winky face. The lack of any emoji made his message feel all the more serious, and I had no idea how to respond to him.

I started and erased reply after reply until I decided to go with a lighthearted one.

Me: **I hope the judges are as impressed.** ☺

Braden: **They're blind if they're not. I don't know anything about skating, but I know I saw something special today.**

Me: **The music touched me so much the first time I heard it that I knew I had to skate to it.**

Braden: **I felt how much you love it.**

I rested my head against the chair and gazed at his last text. The fact that he was moved by my skating, the most important thing in my life, made me smile so big inside. I sent him a matching emoji, and Mom's warnings grew louder. Every time I talked to Braden I became more invested. Too invested?

We texted a few minutes about the Fourth and how early we had to leave for Boston, and I realized our date had the potential to end my dilemma. Braden may not be so enamored with me anymore after sixteen straight hours with me. Ditto for how I felt about him.

I knew that I should hope for a terrible day together to make things easier, but my heart had other ideas. It was imagining the two of us sharing a day of fun and laughter and then huddling together to watch the fireworks. Braden would lean into me, his eyes on my lips, and I wouldn't freeze up. I'd meet him halfway and melt right into him.

I sighed and looked at the story in my lap. If only I could write the scenes of my life to give myself the ideal happy ending, where skating and romance would blissfully exist together.

CHAPTER SIX

Eleven hours.

Braden and I had been together eleven hours, and he hadn't done anything that annoyed me, disgusted me, or turned me off in any way. In fact, he'd succeeded in making me like him *more*. Judging from his constant smile and all the flirty touching he'd been doing, I didn't think I'd tarnished his opinion of me either.

The sun still burned hot in the early evening sky, but I sat protected under the pop-up canopy Braden had brought (one of many things for which he'd earned lots of points). We'd been camped out on a blanket since mid-morning, surrounded by thousands of people on the grassy Esplanade. All of us faced the huge stage, named the Hatch Shell because of its shape. To our left, numerous boats dotted the Charles River, waiting for the fireworks display after the concert.

I reached into our sack of snacks and pulled out a bag of almonds. Braden had packed chips and candy, but he'd also included some healthy options for me – another thing that had earned him high marks. As I opened a new bottle of water, he returned from the portable restrooms, cleaning his hands with one of the many antibacterial wipes I'd contributed to our campsite. He looked so patriotic in his blue *Boston Strong* T-shirt and red shorts. The shining star of his outfit was the tall Uncle Sam hat he wore. Any guy who wasn't afraid to don a big, silly hat on a date deserved all the points.

I loosened my ponytail and took off my own cap, the Red Sox hat that had made Braden's eyes light up (as Court had predicted). With night falling soon, I wouldn't need a ponytail to stay cool much longer. I used my fingers to fluff up my hair as much as my picket-straight locks would fluff.

"The bathroom lines are officially out of control," Braden said. "We should probably cut off all liquids."

I capped my bottle. "Duly noted."

He sat beside me and looked at his watch. "One more hour of entertaining ourselves. Shall I school you some more in Gin Rummy or do you want to whip me again in Hacky Sack?"

"As much as I'd love to show off my Hacky Sack skills, exercise will make us hot and thirsty. Not good for our no-liquids situation."

"Good point. Mental stimulation it is, then."

His phone trilled on the blanket, and he gave it a curious stare. "Why is my mom FaceTiming me?"

He picked up the phone, and with a tap on the screen his mom appeared. She looked a little different from her pictures online. Her hair was longer, down to her shoulders, and she'd lightened it to a dirty blond color. She had Braden's smile and his expressive brown eyes. They brightened with joy as soon as she saw him on the call.

"Happy Fourth!" she bellowed.

"Happy Fourth," he echoed at a lower decibel.

"I didn't want to bother you on your date, but your grandma didn't believe me when I told her you were out with Liza Petrov."

I giggled and Braden said, "You called to get proof?"

Another woman stuck her head into the video, and her round face and olive complexion matched Braden's mom's. She had short, permed gray hair and wore thick, red-framed glasses.

"We just want to say hello to her, B," she said.

B. Cute nickname for a cute guy.

He laughed. "You guys are nuts."

"Just ask her to get on the call. What's the big deal?" his mom said.

"She's not here for you to gawk at."

"I don't mind," I said.

"I don't want you to feel like you're on display."

"I feel like that a lot, but this isn't one of those times." I smiled.

He smiled back and scooted closer to me until we pressed together from our shoulders down to our thighs. The right side of my body immediately needed all my blood and oxygen. We'd had the flirty touching all day, but this was the closest we'd been.

I love you, Braden's grandma.

"This is my mom Tracey and my grandma Joann." He angled the screen slightly and pointed to me. "Here she is. Now do you believe me?"

"It's wonderful to meet you, Liza," Grandma Joann said. "I'm a huge fan. I've been watching you since you were a little girl."

"Really? That's awesome."

"I hope my son is being the gentleman I taught him to be." Braden's mom eyed him with a stern glance.

"Of course I am," he said.

"I want to hear what Liza thinks."

"He's been the perfect gentleman," I said.

Braden turned his head to smile at me, and we were so close his breath wisped across my lips. He could so easily kiss me. If we didn't have an audience. And if I didn't have another panic attack.

A dog barked on the call, and Mrs. Patrick looked down at her feet. "You want to say hello, Papi?"

She squeezed the big black Lab into the video frame, and he woofed more excitedly.

"Hey, buddy, I miss you," Braden said.

Papi whimpered and lifted his paw as if he could reach out and touch Braden.

"He looks so sweet," I said. "I wish I could pet him."

"B, you'll have to bring Liza by for a visit. Papi would love that. Wouldn't you, boy?" Mrs. Patrick nuzzled his nose.

"Your grandma would love it, too." Grandma Joann winked.

Braden and I both laughed, and his mom said, "You kids have fun the rest of the night. Be careful driving home."

We all waved goodbye, including Papi with an assist from Mrs. Patrick.

"They're a little crazy," Braden said.

"They seem like a lot of fun."

"When we first got Papi, my mom complained about him all the time. Now he's like her fifth child."

"I always wanted a dog, but my mom's allergic and Em doesn't like them."

"What kind would you get if you could have one?"

"A Cavachon. Holly has one, and he's so cute and cuddly."

"Papi's a great cuddler. He lays next to me and puts his paw right here." He placed his hand on my shoulder, and I suddenly grew very jealous of his dog. Cuddling with Braden had become a top item on my short-term bucket list.

"Does he sleep with you when you're home? Holly's dog has a little bed, but he's always in hers."

"He used to, but now he goes straight to my brother's room. I'm not gonna lie – the rejection hurts." He patted his chest.

"Well, you left him behind when you went to college. He's probably got some serious abandonment issues now," I teased.

"I had a long talk with him before I left, and he licked my face so I thought we were cool."

I laughed. "Sounds like you need to have another heart-to-heart."

"Maybe you should be there with me to help smooth things over."

"You think I have some dog whispering powers?"

"I think if he looks into your eyes he won't stand a chance."

His gaze lingered on me, and my heart went haywire again, skipping multiple beats that time.

"Hey, guys." Our lawn neighbor stuck his head under the canopy. "It's time to take the tents down."

"Oh, yeah, I forgot." Braden slowly rose to his feet. "They have to come down before the concert starts."

He held out his hands to help me stand, and we stood smiling at each other an extra moment before starting to disassemble the canopy. When we settled back on the blanket we sat across from each other, and I grabbed our notepad for keeping score. As Braden shuffled the deck of cards, I snapped a photo of the sea of people, most wearing some combination of red, white, and blue.

"Any good Team USA member is expected to post a patriotic pic today," I said.

"Did your parents ever want you to skate for Russia like they did?"

"They know I'm USA all the way. My grandfather was a different story, though. My mom and I lived with him in Russia, and he was all about me representing them. He died a few months after I moved there, but he used to mention it every time we talked about skating. Well, every time *he* talked. I didn't do much speaking since I was a little terrified of him."

Braden's eyes darkened. "Did he do something?"

I quickly shook my head. "No, he was good to us. He was just very serious, very stern. I'm pretty sure he was involved in some shady stuff. Like Russian-mafia-level shady."

"Seriously?"

"He ran this huge empire in Moscow. My mom's never told me any of the details, but I've heard my dad and Em talk about it."

Braden paused while dealing the cards. "Is your dad in the mob, too? When I picked you up this morning, he looked like he wanted to give me some cement shoes."

I burst into laughter. "He's really a big teddy bear. He's just being an overprotective papa bear right now."

"So I won't be finding any horse heads in my bed? Although I guess that's Italian mafia. What would the Russians do to me?"

"Hmm… maybe smother you with a fur coat? Drown you in vodka?"

"I'll Google it later to see what I'm getting into," he said with a crooked grin.

I laughed. "I promise you have nothing to worry about."

"I'm not worried." He leaned forward, his eyes glinting in the evening sunlight. "A little mob action won't scare me away from you."

He finished dealing the cards, but he had me so swoony that he easily smoked me in our first game. I focused hard on my next hand, and using the tricks he'd taught me I finally beat him. I liked that he hadn't let me win earlier when he'd defeated me repeatedly for two hours straight. Competitiveness was a quality I admired… and also found extremely hot.

Shortly after my victory the stage came alive with the Boston Pops, and all of us in the crowd welcomed them with raucous cheers. We stood for the "Star-Spangled Banner," and I placed my hand over my heart. According to the countdown clock on my phone, I could be in that exact pose on a podium in Sochi in two hundred and thirty-one days. I stared at the Stars and Stripes on the big screen and fell into my favorite daydream – the anthem playing, the flag rising, the gold medal around my neck...

"You okay?" Braden asked.

I didn't realize the music had ended and my eyes were still glazed over. "Yeah, I was just... I was thinking about the Olympics. It's silly."

"It's not silly." He took my hand. "It's your whole life."

It *was* my whole life, and I was still unsure whether there was room for the handsome, charming boy standing beside me. All I knew was every hour that passed made the idea of following Mom's advice and saying goodbye to Braden harder to swallow.

He held onto my hand, and we returned to the blanket to listen to the orchestra and its guest vocalists. When pop singer Howie Day took the stage and began to sing his hit "Collide," couples all over the Esplanade got to their feet to slow dance. Braden stirred beside me and extended his free hand.

"May I have this dance? You won't have to show me the steps this time."

I smiled and he helped me up so we stood face to face. He slipped his hands around my waist, and I didn't know if I should rest mine casually on his chest or go for a full-on hug around his neck. I settled for the middle ground and grasped his shoulders, which were mighty nice and solid to hold onto.

We started to sway to the music, and I felt especially petite in his arms. It was a wonderful feeling, being surrounded by his warmth. He bent his head so his cheek brushed my hair, and I closed my eyes, taking in the sounds and sensations of the moment. Some people around us sang along to the love song, but Braden and I were both quiet. We rocked gently from side to side, our bodies drifting closer together, reacting to the natural pull between us.

I didn't open my eyes until I heard applause. I lifted my chin and met Braden's gaze, and I saw the look in his eyes that he'd had on my porch right before I'd dodged him. My heart was beating insanely fast, but desire had taken over my fear. He wanted to kiss me, and I didn't want to stop him.

Then *he* dodged *me*.

He backed away and rejoined our hands. Had he let the moment pass because he thought I would turn away again? If I had to wait until the end of the night for him to kiss me, I was afraid I'd psych myself out again.

After Howie Day's second song came intermission, and we went back to laughing and being silly as we played Heads Up on Braden's phone. There could be no intense moments while acting out animal noises. When the concert resumed, we belted out "Yankee Doodle" and "God Bless America" during the sing-along, the latter making all of us emotional as thousands of voices came together in perfect harmony with passionate, patriotic fervor. While I blinked back tears, Braden's voice cracked on the final high note, and he hurried to clear his throat.

"I heard that," I teased him through my sniffles.

He dabbed at the corners of his eyes. "It's a little dusty out here."

Cheers for America and for Boston spread through the crowd as we listened to the final songs before the fireworks. With the first explosion of colorful light, shouts of wonder and squeals of glee rang out in the night. I arched my neck back to watch the show, all the while very aware of Braden's presence. I sensed him looking at me a couple of times, but when I turned to him his eyes shot up to the sky. *Lord, if he's waiting for me to make the next move, we'll be doing nothing but holding hands all summer.*

The last pop of color faded into the night, and the mass scramble for the exits began. Braden carried the canopy and our bag of games, while I hauled the blanket and leftover snacks. We moved along with the river of people down Arlington Street toward the T station, where the train would take us to Braden's Jeep parked in the suburbs.

My phone buzzed in my pocket, so I shifted the blanket and the bag to see who'd texted me.

Dad: **Just checking that you're on your way home.**

I'd told him the fireworks ended at ten. Where did he think I was going? I had practice in the morning, so it wasn't like I could party till all hours.

Me: **Walking to the T now.**

The toe of my sneaker hit concrete just as I hit Send, and I stumbled forward and landed hard on my knees. All the items in my hands dropped to the sidewalk with me. The scratchy pavement hurt way worse than the smooth ice on which I was used to falling.

"Shit, are you okay?" Braden stooped next to me. Everyone else hurried around me as if I was a nuisance blocking their path.

"I think so."

I gathered my belongings and Braden assisted me up. We both looked down at my knees, and the first thing I saw was blood trickling down my left shin.

"That cut looks deep." He steered me toward a lamp post. "Let's go under the light."

He bent in front of me and carefully touched my left knee. I filled with tingles from his hands on my skin, but the awful burning below my kneecap cut into my enjoyment.

"I think you need stitches."

"Is it really that bad?" I squinted in the dim street light.

"You must've fallen on a rock or something. I had a gash like this when I fell off my bike once, and I had to get stitches."

I leaned my head back against the post. My parents were going to flip out and then dish out an endless stream of *I told you so's*. Stitches on my knee meant no skating until the wound healed. I'd seen it happen to other kids at the rink.

Braden found a wipe in our snack bag and cleaned both my knees of the blood. Luckily, my right one was just scraped.

"I can't believe I tripped on the freaking curb. It's ironic that I was answering my dad's text when he's always warning me about texting and walking."

"I should've carried the blanket. You would've been able to see better without so much in your arms."

"You had your hands full. It's my fault for not watching where I was going."

"Do you want to go to an ER here in the city or wait until we get to the Cape?"

"The Cape might be less busy," I said.

It wasn't.

We arrived at the hospital in Hyannis a little after midnight, and almost every chair in the waiting room was occupied. Too many Fourth of July hijinks gone awry? Braden snagged two seats in the far corner while I talked to the nurse at the desk. I was pleased that I actually had my insurance card in my ID holder. *Yay me for being a responsible adult.*

I filled out the paperwork and then made the phone call I'd dreaded the entire drive from Boston. I called Em's cell because having her relay the news to Dad would be much less painful than telling him myself.

"Hey, sweetie." She sounded groggy, which was understandable since she had to be at the rink early in the morning.

"I just wanted to let you know we had to make a stop so I'm going to be a little late. I fell and cut my knee, so I'm getting stitches at the hospital."

"Are you still in Boston?"

In the background I heard Dad asking, "What happened?"

"We're at the Cape hospital. There's a line of people ahead of me, so I could be awhile."

Em explained the situation to Dad, and he made her give

him the phone.

"I'm coming over there," he said.

"Dad, I'm okay. You don't need to."

"I'm coming."

He hung up before I could protest again. I sighed as I turned to Braden. "That went about how I expected."

"He's being a protective papa bear?"

"Something like that."

"Have you ever gotten stitches before?"

"I've had plenty of other injuries, but stitches only once when I was eight. Em was showing me how to do a Charlotte – it's like a vertical split on the ice – and I fell on my chin. You can still see the scar here." I tilted my head to show him. "The Charlotte is one of my signature moves now, but I think my mom still cringes every time I do it."

He ran his thumb along the scar. "That had to hurt like hell."

I had no concept of pain at the moment. I shivered from his simple touch and also the air conditioner blowing on us, its brisk breeze on my bare shoulders. A tank top had been ideal for the ninety-degree day but not for a frigid hospital.

"You must be freezing." Braden put his arm around me and slowly rubbed mine, erasing all chill bumps.

Yeah, I definitely wasn't feeling any pain.

We watched the constant activity around the desk, noting the patients' visible symptoms and making our own diagnoses. Braden had me laughing with some of his outlandish guesses.

"This is officially the longest date I've ever been on," he said. "And the best, even with the ER visit."

His words gave me more warmth, and they also gave me the opening I'd been looking for all day. I wanted him to understand that he was way ahead of me on the social-life curve.

"It's the longest and the best for me too, but... I have a

confession to make. It's only the second date I've ever been on."

His hand stilled on my arm. "When we went to the barbecue, that was your first date with anyone?"

I nodded with a sheepish smile.

"How am I the first guy to ask you out? I mean, look at you." His voice lowered. "You're gorgeous."

I'd been complimented many times in my life on my appearance by my family, my fans, TV skating commentators – "She looks beautiful in that dress." But none of those compliments had made my insides turn to mush like they were right now.

"I umm… I wasn't really open to dating before."

He studied me thoughtfully as his fingertips resumed caressing my shoulder. "What made you say yes to me?"

Maybe it was the late hour or Braden's strong arm wrapped around me, but I wasn't afraid to be completely real with him. I looked up at him without hesitation.

"The way you make me feel."

We couldn't tear our eyes from each other, and the charge in the air between us intensified. It didn't matter that we were sitting in a hospital. It didn't matter where we were or what was around us. It was all white noise.

"Liza!"

Except for Dad's voice.

I straightened up, and Braden moved his arm to the back of my chair. Dad rushed toward us and bent in front of me. His brow knitted with concern.

"How did you fall?"

"I tripped on a curb."

"Thank God you didn't break anything. This will keep you off the ice a couple of weeks, though."

"That long?"

"The cut is in such a bad spot. You can't put any strain on it or the stitches could open up."

Hearing Dad's prognosis brought me down from my cloud of swoon and reminded me of the consequences of my injury. My first competition of the season was six weeks away, and I'd been banking on having maximum ice time to prepare. It was just a small club competition on the Cape, but I wanted to have a strong debut of my Olympic programs. No watered-down technical content like a lot of skaters did at summer events.

"Braden, you can head home," Dad said as he stood.

"I'd like to stay, sir."

Dad crossed his arms and gave Braden his best intimidating glare, but he didn't budge. There were only two chairs in our little corner of the room, so I pointed across the way.

"There's an empty seat over there."

Dad didn't even look. He moved next to my chair and stood along the wall like a bodyguard. None of us spoke until the nurse called my name and Braden said, "I'll be here" as Dad and I headed to the back.

While I lay on the exam table, waiting for my knee to go numb from the anesthesia, I stared at the stark white ceiling and thought about where things were going with Braden. There was nothing like a big needle in the leg to deflate my romantic hopes and dreams. As much as I wanted to pursue the possibilities between us, I had to stop and look at the situation from the athlete side of my brain. I was lying in a hospital. That was not where I needed to be at any time during the Olympic season.

Why did I have to meet this amazing guy *now*?

Dad hovered nearby, still not speaking, and I suspected he was mulling over the "teaching moment" he wanted to share.

"I feel like you're holding in a lecture."

"You didn't do anything to earn a lecture. It was an accident." He paused. "But–"

"I knew there was a 'but.'"

"I don't like getting calls at midnight that you're in the emergency room, and you wouldn't be here if you hadn't been out with Braden."

"It's not his fault I tripped."

"I'm not saying it's his fault. I'm saying once you start doing new things like dating, there's a bigger risk of new problems occurring. Like tonight."

A nurse came in to clean my wound, and Dad stepped closer to the table to watch. He had a valid point about my date. I would've normally been home, safely asleep in bed for practice in the morning. No chance in that scenario of setting back my training a few weeks.

Warm water dribbled over my knee as the nurse irrigated the gash. Since I was lying flat, I couldn't see how much Boston sidewalk was being washed out of the cut, but Dad's grimace told me the amount.

I turned my head on the table. "Have you talked to Mom about Braden?"

"We talked last night. She said she told you her opinion."

"I know what she wants me to do and what I *should* do, but... I really like him, Dad. I know I've only been out with him twice, but we have a real connection."

He smoothed his hand over my hair. "You could tell him you'd love to go out again after the Olympics. March isn't that far away."

"It's almost a year away. That's a lifetime for a nineteen-year-old guy who probably has girls crawling all over him at college."

"If you have a special connection he'll put you ahead of any other girl."

"You didn't wait. When you and Em fell in love, you dated secretly even though you were her coach and you could get in trouble."

"And I did get in trouble, and it almost cost me my

career."

"So you regret doing it?"

He hesitated and rubbed the back of his neck. "I have a different perspective now that I have kids, and some of the decisions I made when I was younger aren't what I want for you." He gazed at me with worry in his eyes. "Your mom and I just want to protect you and to do everything we can to help you realize the dream that you've worked so hard for. You have the chance to do something incredible this year."

They *had* given me everything I'd ever needed and had supported me every single grueling step of the way to becoming a champion. They'd always steered me in the right direction even if I'd had to miss out on some other interesting paths. I wouldn't be one of the favorites for Olympic gold if I hadn't let them guide me.

It just sucked that following their advice meant the end of something awesome that had just started.

The doctor sewed up my knee with eight stitches and told me to have them taken out in ten days. As expected, no skating until after they were removed, and he suggested even a few more days of rest after that. Dad said we'd consult with the U.S. Skating Federation's medical staff.

I hobbled out to the waiting room, and Braden was right where we'd left him, as promised. He jumped up when he saw me.

"How's your knee?"

"It's still numb, so it feels okay right now." My heart was another matter. It was going to need its own set of stitches soon.

Dad led the way to the parking lot, and he stopped at the second row of cars. "We're over here."

So this is it. I had to say goodnight to Braden in front of my dad. There would be no kiss, even though I was more than ready now. There would never be a kiss, which I'd have to tell him later. I couldn't explain everything in the parking lot.

"Thank you for today," I said. "It was the best Fourth of July I've ever had."

"I promise next time we won't have to visit any hospitals."

My stomach sank, knowing there wouldn't be a next time. Maybe we could go on one more date? My logical self shook her finger at me. Seeing him again would just pull me in deeper.

We stood there awkwardly for a few moments as Dad lingered within earshot. Braden finally stepped forward and wrapped me in a hug. I held on tight, trying to sear into memory how his body felt against mine.

"I can't wait to see you again," he said in my ear.

Dagger meet chest.

I walked to the car with Dad and spent the drive home reminding myself that I was making the smart choice. The safe choice. It's what I'd always done. But I'd never felt so sad doing it.

CHAPTER SEVEN

I STARED DOWN AT MY WRITING journal and scratched through yet another crappy sentence. Quality words for my story were not coming easily. I rested my head against the back of the leather sofa and closed my eyes to the sunlight streaming into the library. I hadn't slept well with my sore knee keeping me awake.

Tiny footsteps on the hardwood alerted me to an approaching twin. I opened one eye and found Quinn holding my teddy bear Peter.

"When I get a boo-boo my bear helps me feel better, so I brought you yours."

I took the stuffed bear into my arms. "You're so sweet."

"Do you want more water?" She peeked into my cup on the end table.

"I'm good. Thank you for being such a great nurse."

I was babysitting Quinn and Alex while Dad and Em were at the rink, but they'd been taking care of *me* all morning.

"Where's Alex?" I asked.

"He's doing a puzzle."

"I'll make your lunch in a little while. How does PB&J

sound?"

"With the crusts cut off?"

"Of course."

My phone rang, and a nervous jolt zapped through me at the thought of Braden on the line. I exhaled when I saw Holly's picture.

"Hey," I answered as Quinn skipped out of the room.

"You're missing so much fun here. Your dad is being Mr. Cranky Pants since he didn't get enough sleep."

"I'm sorry. I told him he didn't have to go the hospital."

She let out a dry laugh. "Like there was any way he wouldn't."

"I'm just glad he's not here hovering. I'll have enough of that with my mom the next few days."

"You're still going to New York?"

"I promised her I'd visit. And it gets me away from certain temptations."

During my sleepless night I'd replayed my entire day with Braden, not wanting to forget any of the details. Even the smallest ones, like how he would chew on his bottom lip when he was concentrating in Gin Rummy.

"Have you talked to him yet?" Holly asked.

"He texted me earlier, and I told him I'd call him later. I'm trying to figure out how to say, 'I can't go out with you again because apparently having a social life is too dangerous for a delicate ice princess such as myself.'"

"There is nothing ice-princessy about you. I see your workouts every day." She took an audible slurp from her water bottle. "Why can't you just go out with him on weekends? It wouldn't interfere with skating."

"Everything I do, even on weekends, impacts skating. Plus, after summer he'll be in Boston and I'll be here or in New York. It would take a lot of energy to keep up a long-distance thing if we even got to that point."

"Sounds like you're trying to convince yourself you're

doing the right thing."

I sounded like my parents, which was disturbing but necessary. I'd let myself step outside the box for a moment – one glorious moment – but I needed to get back inside and let Braden be just a memory. A sweet, beautiful memory.

"It's the only way I can keep from thinking about how much fun I had yesterday."

"You should let yourself have more fun."

I kneaded my forehead with my thumb and forefinger. "You don't understand the pressure and expectations I have on me."

"Why? Because I'm eighteen and still skating in juniors?"
Where did that come from?

"Hol, you know I don't think less of you because you're in juniors. I've never said anything like that."

"I know. It's just one of those days. I guess I'm cranky today, too."

"What's going on?"

"Let's just say we didn't need the Zamboni this morning because my butt did its job."

I cringed, knowing all too well how frustrating a bad practice could be. "Do you want to come over tonight and have a Holliza pity-party sleepover?"

"I can't. I'm going out with Luke."

Her on-again, off-again boyfriend was an ice dancer at our rink. I couldn't keep track of how many times she'd flipped the switch.

"Where are you guys going?"

"Just go-carting." She paused as voices grew louder in the background. "Ugh, next session's about to start. Let me know how it goes with Braden."

I promised to do so, and we said our goodbyes. I rested my head against the sofa again and found myself staring straight at Em's Olympic gold medal, encased in a shadow box on the wall.

When she'd won the medal in Torino with her partner Chris, she'd asked if I wanted to try it on, but I'd said no. Even then when I was only eleven years old I knew. I knew what I wanted more than anything, and I didn't want to wear the gold medal until I could call it mine.

Standing atop the Olympic podium was the number one thing I'd dreamt about since I'd put on skates, and I couldn't let anything interfere with my dream. I was the perfect age and at the perfect stage in my career to be the Olympic champion. If I didn't take advantage of the moment, it could pass me by and I might never get it back.

I picked up my phone and pulled up Braden's number. I needed to call him while I still had my resolve. He answered on the third ring, his voice thick with sleep.

"Did I wake you up?" I asked.

"I guess I dozed off watching TV. All that late-night hospital partying."

I smiled a little. He always put a lighthearted spin on things. It was one of his qualities that made talking to him so fun.

"How are you feeling?" he asked.

"Okay. The twins are taking good care of me."

"I'd be happy to come over and help. You could start Season Two of *Friday Night Lights* with me."

Why did something as ordinary as cuddling together and watching TV have to sound so amazing?

"I'd really like that, but..." The words got lost in my throat, and I looked up at the shiny gold medal on the wall. *Just say it.*

"I can't see you anymore."

He was silent, and I had to laugh at the irony of me dumping someone after going on a total of two dates in my life.

"Is it because of your dad? Is he mad you got hurt?"

"He's not happy, but it's my decision. I need to focus on

skating."

"I don't want to get in the way of your skating. I know how important it is to you. But I want to keep seeing you. Any time, any way I can."

I want that, too, I silently replied as my conflicting emotions continued to battle each other.

"I know I should've thought about this before I agreed to go out with you, but I couldn't even think past the first date because I was so nervous about it," I said.

"I'm glad you didn't think about it. I've had the best time hanging out with you."

"Me, too."

"Then let's find a way to keep it going."

I massaged my forehead again as if I could push out all thoughts except those related to skating. *Fifteen years of training. You have to do everything you can to see it through.*

"I wish... I wish we could keep this going, but I have this other priority in my life right now and so many people expecting things from me. I don't want to start something with you and not be able to give it one hundred percent. I can't add your expectations on top of everyone else's."

He stayed quiet for what felt like ten minutes. I was about to check if he was still with me when he said, "What if I don't have any? What if we were just friends?"

I lifted my head. "Just friends?"

"We can hang out whenever you have time. No pressure, no expectations."

It was my turn to be silent. His idea sounded reasonable, but I had no experience with transitioning from potential romance to a platonic relationship. Was that easily done?

"What about the fact that we both want to be more than friends?" I asked.

"I'm sure it'll be hard for you to resist my charms, but I'm confident in your determination."

I laughed. "I'm serious."

"This is how I look at it – if my choices are being buddies or not speaking to you at all, I'm going with option A for sure."

I smiled and fiddled with the gauze around my knee. "I really hated the idea of not talking to you anymore. It's been so much fun getting to know you."

"And you haven't met Papi yet. That has to happen."

"Will it be weird if I go to your house since your family thinks we're dating?"

"I'll tell them what's up so there's no misunderstanding."

"Your grandma might be upset."

"When I explain that I'm helping your career, she'll be all over it."

He had such good, logical answers. It would be silly to turn down an offer of friendship from someone who made me smile and laugh so much. His positive energy could provide many benefits for a stressed out athlete.

"Speaking of my career, I have to warn you that I get a little crazy once the competition season starts. It's kind of an intense time." *A little crazy* was an understatement, but I didn't want to scare him away.

"Even more reason for you to have another friendly shoulder to lean on."

Leaning on him made me think of dancing with him at the concert and holding onto his strong shoulders. Could I hang out with him while having these more-than-friendly thoughts and feelings? I might make myself crazier. Staying in touch with him meant the possibility of something more between us in the future, though… when I wouldn't have so many restrictions in my life. That opportunity outweighed any hesitation I had.

"I feel like we should be shaking hands right about now," I said.

"Do we need to put this in writing?"

"What would it say? Thou shalt not flirt with me?" I

joked.

He didn't respond at first, but then he said, "What happens if we break the rules?"

"I don't break rules."

"Maybe I do."

A line of goosebumps formed on the back of my neck, and a fresh set of doubts about our agreement arose, but I ignored them. "Then I'll have to sic the Russian mob on you."

He laughed, and I joined him, mostly from relief to be past the awkward part of the conversation.

"So, can I visit today as a friend?" he asked. "I promise to abide by the terms of our agreement."

As much as I wanted to see him again immediately, I wasn't ready to have my emotions tested. "Today's not a great day. I have to pack and do some stuff before I leave for New York."

"You're not leaving for good?"

"No, just going for a visit. I'll be back next weekend."

Alex shuffled into the library and climbed onto the arm of the sofa. "Is it lunchtime yet?"

"I'll make it in a sec."

"Twin duty?" Braden asked.

"Yep. I guess I'll... talk to you later?" The weirdness had returned.

"Check in any time. My friends bug me at all hours. Not that you'd be bugging me because I want to hear from you. I like hearing from all my friends. You know what I mean."

I laughed. "I do. And I will. Check in. You do the same."

"HOW MUCH CELERY DO we need?" Mom asked.

I slid her tablet across the breakfast bar and read the recipe for her latest culinary venture, quinoa-stuffed bell peppers.

"It says half a cup."

Mom wasn't as superb in the kitchen as Em, but she'd come a long way since we'd lived in Russia. In Moscow we had Olga, the cook and housekeeper who helped raise Mom after her mother died when she was young. Mom had asked Olga to move to New York with us, but she hadn't wanted to leave Russia. I couldn't blame her because I knew how hard it was to be so far from home.

As Mom diced the celery with great precision, the sound of Celine Dion accompanied her chopping. She kept soft rock radio playing constantly on our house's built-in stereo. It was like living in a dentist's office.

"You should put your leg up," she said. "It must hurt after being in one position for four hours in the car. I would've driven to the Cape to get you if you'd told me you were coming a day early."

I propped my leg up on two of the barstools. "I like having my car when I'm here."

"You need to rest while you're here."

"The doctor didn't say I couldn't walk."

"The least amount of strain you put on your knee, the faster it will heal."

Of course Mom would know better than the doctor. It was useless to argue with her.

She tossed the celery into the saucepan and wiped her hands on a dishtowel. "You haven't told me how your conversation with Braden went. Did you tell him you can't see him anymore?"

I dipped my head and scrolled through the recipe. "It was fine. We're just going to be friends."

"What does that mean?"

"Exactly what it sounds like."

"I thought this would be the end of it. That you wouldn't be in contact with him at all."

I looked up in disbelief. "Now I can't have friends

either?"

"You have Holly and Courtney and other kids at the rink."

"So, I'm only allowed to hang out with other skaters."

"That's not what I'm saying, but they understand your life and what you're going through. They're much better companions for you. Remember those girls at school who wanted you to go out on weeknights and stay up late talking on the computer? They didn't understand your schedule at all."

And that was exactly why I'd never felt like I fit in during high school. I was always the girl with too many rules. It took too much effort to be my friend.

"This boy has no clue what you're facing this year," Mom rolled on. "And if he's interested in you, he's not going to stop pursuing you, no matter what he says about being friends. You'll be right back at the starting line."

I would've laughed if I hadn't been so annoyed. Mom had spent many years perfecting her English, but sometimes she butchered popular sayings.

"Braden means what he says. He knows skating is my life, and he respects that."

"Well, that's very nice, but he's still a boy and you are a beautiful girl. He may have good intentions, but can he stick to them?"

I flashed back to my talk with Braden. *What happens if we break the rules?* He hadn't sounded like he was joking when he'd said that, and a part of me felt a little thrill over the possibility of danger ahead.

Mom's phone rang on the granite island, and the caller ID made her face relax from its worry mode. She punched the speaker button and said, "Hi, darling."

"Hey, George," I shouted.

"Hey, I thought you weren't coming home until tomorrow?"

"I decided to surprise Mom."

"She must be over the moon. She's been wanting to take care of you since your accident. How's the leg?"

"Feeling much better."

"Well, I won't interrupt your girl time. Give me a call when you can, honey."

"I will later tonight," Mom said.

After we said goodbye, I stared at Mom as she stirred the onion and celery. "Why don't you just marry him already? It's been eight years."

She threw a glance over her shoulder at me. "We've talked about this. George and I agreed to wait until it makes sense for me to move to Manhattan. He can't leave because he doesn't want to take his daughters out of their school."

"You can move right now. I'm not in school anymore, so there's nothing tying you down here."

"Your rink is still here, and I teach ballet there."

"You could teach anywhere, and I could train full time with Dad."

She stopped stirring to face me full on. "What are you saying? You'd leave Kathy after all these years? She's been your coach since you were a child."

"I've been spending more time with Dad lately anyway, and we have a good thing going. Kathy's gotten so negative and argumentative. I need constructive criticism, not her picking apart my programs just because she doesn't like that Dad and Josh have better ideas."

"I know you haven't been getting along as well, but you've never mentioned ending your relationship."

"I didn't want to cause a big commotion, but it's getting worse every time I see her."

"Then I'll talk to her. You're right that now isn't the time to upset things. How would it look if you fired one of your coaches right before the Olympics?"

It would look questionable for sure, but I was so tired of

worrying about what the powers-that-be would think. Some things were worth fighting for, like when I'd insisted on hiring Josh as my choreographer.

"I'll give it more time, but if it continues the way it's been, I really don't want to skate with Kathy anymore," I said.

"I'm not going to get married so you'll have an excuse to leave her," Mom said as she whacked her knife at the tomatoes.

"That's not why I brought up marrying George. I just don't want you to feel like you have to stay here for me. You've waited so long to be together full time. You deserve to have the life you both want."

She calmed her frantic chopping and peeked up at me with a little smile. "We've had our routine for eight years and we've made it work. Another year won't hurt us. With the Olympics coming up, I don't have time to plan a wedding anyway."

"You could do something simple that doesn't require a lot of planning."

"I would like a proper wedding. Something that celebrates our relationship."

"You're not going to wear a big poofy, white dress, are you?"

"White, yes. Poofy, no."

I clapped my hands together as a vision came to me. "What if you have the ceremony on a boat with the Manhattan skyline behind you? That would be so romantic."

"It sounds very dramatic."

"Which makes it perfect for you!"

She tossed the dishtowel at me, and I used her tablet as a shield. We continued our hypothetical wedding planning over dinner, which thankfully kept Mom from bringing up Braden again. Since she wouldn't let me help her clean up after we ate, I went up to my room to unpack.

The first thing I pulled out of my bag was my teddy bear.

It didn't matter where I traveled – New York, France, Japan – Peter always came with me. My adoptive dad, Peter's namesake, had given him to me, and I hadn't been able to store him away with the other mementos from my childhood. Carrying him with me on all my journeys made me feel like my parents were still with me. Sometimes I talked to him as if I was talking to them, something I'd never told anyone.

I plucked a piece of lint from Peter's sandy brown fur and set him against the pink and purple pillows on the bed. My New York room featured much brighter colors and felt much younger than my Cape Cod room. It was also twice the size because it was two bedrooms converted into one. Mom had been accustomed to living in an extravagant apartment in Moscow, so she'd chosen the biggest house on the market when we'd moved to White Plains. Whenever other moms from the rink would come over, I saw the curiosity in their eyes, clearly wondering how my mom the ballet teacher could afford our lifestyle. I had no idea how much she'd inherited from my grandfather (and I doubted she'd tell me if I asked), but she never looked twice at a price tag, so my guess was more than a lot.

The fluffy pillows on my bed looked so inviting, so I halted my unpacking and collapsed into their coziness. My knee did feel stiff from the long drive. Not that I would admit that to Mom.

I shifted onto my side, and the framed photo on the nightstand caught my eye. It was the last picture taken of me with my adoptive parents. We were skating on the Rockefeller Center rink, the three of us holding hands. I wanted to go faster, but my dad wasn't very coordinated. He'd almost taken us down a few times, which had led to the huge laughs captured in the photo.

Looking at the abundance of happiness in the picture, it was hard to believe it would come to a crashing end just a week later. My parents had gone out to run errands on a

Saturday afternoon, and they'd never returned. I was at a friend's house playing beauty salon, and her mom delivered the news that no one should have to give a seven-year-old. I kept begging her to take me to my mom and dad even though it was too late. I couldn't understand how they could be gone, and I still didn't know the details of how the accident had happened.

The muscles in my throat tightened, and I turned away from the photo. That feeling of paralyzing disbelief and horror was why I tried not to think about that day. Eleven years hadn't been enough time for the memory to fade. I didn't know if it ever would.

My phone buzzed next to me, and I took a couple of breaths before I reached for it. I filled with immediate light when I saw the text notification.

Braden: **Hey, friend. Just checking in** ☺

We hadn't spoken since our "agreement," and I'd been waiting for him to reach out first to make sure he was still game.

Me: **It's good to hear from you** ☺

Braden: **Do you have time to talk?**

Me: **Yep. The one benefit of being a cripple.**

Braden: **I'm gonna call.**

No more than five seconds passed before my phone lit up with a FaceTime request. *He wants to video chat?* I hopped off the bed on my good leg and did a quick check in the mirror over my dresser. Teeth clean... hair decent. No makeup, but he'd seen me with a naked face before. Diving back onto the bed, I grabbed the phone and was greeted by Braden wearing glasses. The studious look gave him a new, sexy vibe.

Curse him.

"I didn't know you were FaceTiming me," I said.

"Audio only is so impersonal."

I scooted back into the pillows to get comfortable again. "I almost didn't recognize you."

"I'm having some contact issues. I wouldn't be able to see your face without the glasses, and I can't have that." He grinned.

"Are you flirting with me?"

His mouth dropped open. "How dare you accuse me of breaking our agreement already? I'm simply trying to overcome my visual handicap so I can see my friend clearly."

I laughed. "Okay, I'll let this one pass."

"So, where am I seeing you right now? The Cape or New York?"

"I'm at my mom's. I miss Quinn's motor mouth already."

"How are you going to entertain yourself there?"

"Hopefully by getting a lot of writing done."

He cocked his head to the side. "When do I get to read one of these stories?"

My face grew hot just thinking about him reading my romantic tales, complete with kissy-kissy scenes. "Umm... I don't think they're really your speed. They're all pretty girly."

"I grew up with two sisters. I've seen my share of girly stuff."

No way was I committing to giving him even a peek, so I just said, "I'll think about it" and thought of a quick subject change. "So, what are you doing with your night off from work?"

"I'm currently trying to stay out of a group text argument between my roommates – my school roommates – over who gets what bedroom in our new apartment."

"Uh oh. How many of you are there? Do you each get your own room?"

"There's four of us – me, Phil, Sam, and Ross. We all get our own rooms, but they've decided to nitpick the differences between each one, like how two of them have five more inches of space. We signed the lease today, and my phone has been blowing up since I got back."

"Which one of your roommates is the germophobe?"

"That's Phil. He already has his hazmat suit ready to clean the place before we move in. Sam is the newbie this year, and Ross is our Rain Man. The dude never goes to class, but he aces his tests because he memorizes the textbooks."

"This sounds like a reality show waiting to happen."

"You'll have to come up and meet everyone sometime. We'll give you the college experience. I'll even throw in some clichéd activities." His teasing smile filled my phone screen.

"That would be so fun. Something totally different between all my competitions this fall."

"Are you competing anywhere nearby? I need to witness the skating event experience you've talked about."

"My first event is actually at my Cape rink next month if all goes well with my knee. I'm probably doing just the short program, though."

"I hope I don't have a game that day."

"I think it's the sixteenth. It's the third weekend."

"Aww damn." His head fell back against the wall behind him.

"You have to work?"

"No, the season will be over, but I have a family thing. My dad and my brother and I go on this fishing trip every year. My dad's work schedule is so tight that I can't ask him to change it."

My shoulders deflated, sinking me further into the pillows. I'd already gotten excited at the prospect of Braden seeing me do my thing for real, not just at practice.

"That's okay. It's a small club competition, so you wouldn't get the full event experience. Maybe you can come to nationals in January. It's in Boston this year."

"At the Garden? Hell yeah I'll be there."

"The Olympic team gets picked then, so it's a circus. There's media and sponsors everywhere and so many things happening besides the skating. I'm glad I've gone through the selection craziness once before so I know what to expect."

Braden was still smiling, but he was quiet as he studied me behind his tortoise shell frames.

"You know, it probably makes more sense that we're just friends," he said. "You're so far out of my league."

I leaned toward the phone. Surely I hadn't heard him correctly.

"*I'm* out of *your* league? Have you forgotten that I've only been on two dates ever?"

"Yeah, but you're a freaking superstar. My own grandma didn't believe I was on a date with you."

I burst into laughter but muffled it as a knock sounded on my door and Mom simultaneously stuck her head inside. I shoved the phone to my ear.

"Are you talking to someone? I came to ask if you want to watch a movie."

"Just umm... just Holly. I'll be down in a bit."

"Okay. I'll give George a call while I wait."

As she shut the door I brought the phone down so I could see Braden again. He wore a cute little smirk.

"Holly, huh?"

"I'm giving her some time to digest the idea of me having a guy friend."

"She just needs to meet me to see that I'm completely harmless."

I did the studying then, and I had one overriding thought – *Are you harmless?* The butterflies flapping in my stomach were a sign of someone still vulnerable to emotional trauma. But was that really Braden's fault? He couldn't help that he was so thoughtful and funny and attractive. Who could I blame for his awesomeness? His parents?

Curse them, too.

CHAPTER EIGHT

AS MUCH AS I LOVED BEING in the ice rink, cold hands and runny nose and all, I lived for beach days. The warmth of the sunshine, the tickle of the sand between my toes, the soothing rhythm of the rolling waves – all these things equaled my personal paradise.

This particular Saturday afternoon was a perfect eighty degrees with a light breeze coming off the ocean. Add in the fact that Braden would be arriving any minute, and it had the potential to be the best beach day ever.

"Liza, check this out," Court said.

I lifted my head from my journal to find Josh holding an upside down Court over his head with one arm. They were always playing around, trying out new lifts off the ice.

"That's pretty cool," I said and grabbed my phone to snap a photo, posting it online as – *Sneak preview from my faves.*

Josh lowered his arm, and Court lost her balance, letting out a yelp as she and Josh became a Cirque du Soleil act gone wrong.

"We haven't figured out the exit yet," Josh said while setting Court's feet onto the sand.

I laughed. "Clearly."

I checked the time on my phone and glanced toward the crowded parking lot. Braden had said he and his roommates would come by after they cleaned their house for the next tenant. It was his last day on the Cape, and I'd only seen him three times over the past month, two of those being brief chats at Sox games. Between his two jobs and my training, we hadn't had much time to hang out, but we'd made up for it via text and FaceTime. I'd gotten as comfortable texting him random thoughts as I was with Holly.

Comfort did not equal loss of attraction, however, as I was quickly reminded.

Braden was walking across the sand, clad in baby blue board shorts, and he'd left his shirt behind somewhere. The car, the house… who cared? The golden tan I'd admired on his arms extended to his chest and his abs. Not quite a six pack, but tight enough to make a girl want to put her hands on them. This girl in particular.

I sat up on my towel and adjusted my sunglasses. They were going to be my lifesaver, ensuring I didn't get caught checking out my friend all afternoon.

"I made it," he said as he spread his towel next to mine. "It was dicey if I'd find my way out of the piles of garbage."

"You should've borrowed Phil's hazmat suit."

"I thought about calling him in for his expertise, but he would've been scarred for life by our kitchen."

He stretched out and reclined back on his elbows. I couldn't tell with his dark shades if he was using my stealth admiring technique, but I got goosebumps from the sensation that his eyes were slowly taking me in. My lack of any tanning ability was on full display in my pink bikini as were my obvious A-cups. I waffled between wanting to know what Braden was thinking and not wanting any part of his thoughts.

"Are your roommates coming?" I asked, hoping to distract him from everything below my neck.

"No, they crashed after we finished." He motioned to the two empty towels on my other side. "Where are Courtney and Josh?"

I hadn't even noticed they'd wandered off. I looked out at the water and found Josh knee-deep in the ocean with Court up in the air again.

"They're making up lifts." I pointed to them. "Hopeless dorks, but I love them anyway."

"Are they competing next weekend, too?"

"Yeah, all my dad's students are."

"I'm so bummed I can't be there. Total friend fail."

"You can't bail on your dad and Tanner. That would be total son and brother fail."

"My dad *would* be pissed. I just hate that I'm not going to be there to cheer you on. You've been so stressed about not being ready."

His genuine concern made me smile inside. "I need to get out of my perfectionist head and realize that I don't have to be at the top of my game right now. This competition is only the first step in a very long season."

"But it kills you when you're anything less than perfect."

"You've figured that out about me?"

"I've seen it before." He shifted his sunglass-covered gaze to the water. "Scotty was just like that. So Type A, so driven. He never gave himself a break."

I noticed the downward change in his voice, and I fidgeted with the end of my braid. "You said his parents were hard on him, too."

"They were brutal. Nothing was ever good enough. He couldn't just bring home an A. He had to get the highest grade in the class."

"Did they really think all that pressure would help him succeed? My parents expect a lot from me, but it's only because *I've* set high goals for myself. And my dad always stays positive as my coach. He tries to make sure I take away something good from every experience, even the bad ones."

"You're really lucky to have that support."

I nodded ever so slightly. "I'm sorry Scott didn't."

Braden sat up and rested his forearms on his knees. "I just wish I'd known how much it had gotten to him. If I could've helped him..." His fingers touched his wristband in what seemed like an unconscious movement.

"You can't blame yourself. I know I wasn't there, but I've seen the kind of friend you are. I doubt you let him down in any way."

He tilted his head to look at me, but before he could say anything Court and Josh returned with chatter and laughter.

"Hey, Braden," Court said while Josh reached across me to shake his hand.

"Good to see you guys again," Braden said, his delivery not up to his cheerful standard. Scott was obviously still on his mind.

"How about a game of volleyball?" Court said. "Girls versus guys."

"Shorties against giants?" I asked. "Are you looking to lose?"

"Good point. Okay, I'll take this hottie then." She hooked her arm through Josh's.

Jeez, this feels like a double date all of a sudden.

"Guess I'm stuck with this shorty." Braden grinned at me, now back to his normal self.

"I can't spike to save my soul, but I can dig with the best of them."

"So, you like getting dirty?"

His lips fought to hold back a smile, and I tried to do the same. I'd let some other comments pass, but I had to call him out on this one.

"Haven't I warned you about flirting?"

"You keep twisting my words. I'm totally innocent."

I just laughed and shook my head. We claimed one side

of the volleyball net, and all flirting (or alleged flirting) ceased as we got into competitive mode. Court and Josh made a strong team, but with Braden's vertical leap and my quick feet, we beat them by five points. We exchanged a final sandy high-five and collapsed onto our towels.

While we'd played an idea had come to me for a beach party scene, so I grabbed my journal to jot down the images I wanted to remember. Watching shirtless Braden pound the volleyball had turned out to be very inspirational.

"Working on a new story?" he asked.

"Just some rough ideas."

"There has to be one in there you can let me read."

I bit my lip and tightened my grip on the book. Court and Holly were the only ones who'd read my writing. Getting a guy's opinion could be interesting, though…

"You can ask me for anything in return," he said.

I lifted my eyebrows. *Can I touch your abs?* My eyes threatened to wander south, but I remembered I wasn't wearing sunglasses anymore.

Girl, get your head on straight.

I stared down at the pages and mentally scrolled through my story collection. I'd finished one a few weeks ago that contained only one kiss, so it might be a good candidate for sharing. I couldn't handle Braden reading any of the longer make-out scenes I'd written. Talk about Awkward City.

"I can't think of anything I want right now, but I'll definitely collect later," I said.

"Yes." He pumped his fist.

"Don't get too excited. Remember, you have to do *anything* I ask."

"And I will." He put his hand over his heart. "I'm a man of my word."

I flipped through the journal until I found the story titled "Always You." A pang of anxiousness squeezed my chest as I handed the book to Braden.

"You're only allowed to read this one story. Absolutely no peeking at any other pages. Court, you'll keep an eye on him?"

She saluted. "I got your back."

"Where are you going?" Braden asked.

"I can't watch people read my stuff. Ask Court."

"She always leaves the room."

"I'll be in the water. Take your time. Actually, finish it quickly and forget what you read."

He laughed. "I'm going to savor every word."

I scurried toward the ocean and splashed into the water. My toes sank into the dense sand, slowing my pace. When the waves lapped at my thighs, I dove in and began to swim. The water cooled my sun-drenched skin, and the workout helped relieve the tension of waiting for Braden's thoughts.

Refreshed from the swim, I made my way back to shallow water and unraveled my wet braid, using the rubber band to sweep my hair up into a sloppy bun. A glance at the beach showed Braden head down, concentrating on my journal. I turned around to face the horizon and, more importantly, to put my back to my reader. Every time a wave neared me, I bent my knees to meet it, watching it wash over my ugly new scar.

After a few minutes I heard splashing behind me, and I wrung my hands together. Braden came up beside me, and I waited for him to speak first.

"I needed to get in the water to cool off," he said. "You didn't tell me you write smut."

"What? There was one kiss!"

He laughed. "I'm just messing with you. Not about cooling off, though. That kiss was hot."

And so was I. A full-body blush burned my skin from head to toe. Did he know that he'd been my inspiration when I'd written the kiss? That I'd imagined his eyes, his lips, his hands on me?

"And I'm not flirting," he said. "I'm being completely serious."

He'd shed his sunglasses, too, so there was no hiding his feelings. His warm brown eyes shined with sincerity.

"You… you really thought it was good?"

"The chemistry between Michelle and Griffin was crazy. How do you make it so believable?"

My blushing wouldn't let up, so I continued to stop the waves to avoid looking at Braden.

"I don't know. I guess they seem like real people to me, and I just write what they're feeling."

"I wanted more. Ending on that kiss was just cruel."

I took a quick peek up at him. "I'll have to think about a sequel."

"I get first dibs on reading it."

I smiled and bent my knees again, and Braden asked, "Is this a skater exercise you're doing?"

"Oh. No." I laughed. "It's something my dad – my adoptive dad – and I used to do at the beach. I always find myself doing it still."

"Was he like your real dad at all?"

"Not really. I mean, he was caring and supportive like him but personality-wise very different. He was a total jokester, and he had all these nicknames for me like LiLi and Lizaberry."

"Lizaberry? I love that."

"He was so funny. My mom was, too. They used to crack each other up."

"Do you have any pictures of them on your phone?"

"I do. I snapped a bunch from an old album."

We headed back to the beach, but Court and Josh were cuddled close together being all touchy feely, and I didn't want to hang around that scene with Braden. I snatched my phone, and he and I went for a walk along the edge of the water.

"Darn, I have to get home in a few minutes," I said as I saw the time. "We're having a little party tonight for my dad and Em's tenth anniversary."

"Pictures first," he said.

"I know." I mimicked his hand over heart gesture. "I'm a woman of my word."

I thumbed through the gallery and showed him a photo of my parents and five-year-old me. "This was my first gold medal."

"It's bigger than you." He laughed. "Your mom and dad look very proud."

"They weren't into sports, but they learned everything about skating because I loved it so much."

I shared with him a few other photos, and he decided his favorite was from Halloween 1999 when we'd dressed up as a fruit bowl – my dad as an apple, my mom a banana, and me a bundle of purple grapes. I reluctantly ended my show and tell, knowing I wouldn't get to spend time with Braden again for a while.

"Before you go, I want to give you something," he said.

His shorts didn't have any pockets for gifts, so I was momentarily confused until he slipped one of his woven bracelets off his wrist. *Ohh.*

"Since we don't see each other much, I want you to have a reminder that I'm here whenever you need me. Even next weekend. I might not be there, but you can call or text if you're stressing and need to talk. You can always reach me."

I ran my fingers over the black and royal blue thread. "Thank you. I know how special these are to you, so I'm honored to have one."

A hug seemed like the natural show of thanks, but I hesitated at the idea of our half naked bodies pressed together. *We should be able to act normal, though, right?* I had to stop analyzing every movement.

Before I could analyze any longer, I looped my arms

around Braden's neck. He hugged my waist, drawing us together, the sand on his skin rough against my stomach. He smelled like sunscreen and the ocean, and his hands felt like fire on the small of my back.

It was the greatest hug in the history of hugs.

"I'm glad we finally got to hang out," Braden said as we slowly split apart. "My offer still stands any time you want to come up to Boston."

"I definitely want to do that."

We returned to our campsite, and I broke up Court and Josh's snuggle session, reminding them of our evening plans. After a round of goodbyes (but unfortunately no more touching), Braden stayed to nap on the beach while the rest of us headed to the parking lot.

"Did Braden give you that?" Court eyed my wrist.

"Yeah, it's a friendship bracelet."

"Right. Because you're *friends*." She used air quotes.

"That's what we are."

Josh popped the trunk of his car. "Court and I were, too, until we stopped pretending we weren't madly in love with each other."

"Whoa, don't be bringing love into this," I said. "I may still have some minor feelings for Braden, but I have them totally under control." *Says the girl who almost melted into the sand over a hug.*

Court slung her arm around me. "I hate to tell you this, but the heart cannot be controlled."

I frowned and threw my tote into the car. "I'm not loving you as my older and wiser mentor right now."

I HAD NEVER SEEN so many people packed into Tony Kent Arena.

There wasn't one centimeter of free space on the

bleachers, and the standing room audience was three deep. The Cranberry Open, our rink's annual summer competition, usually drew a good crowd, but this was ridiculous.

And I was the main event.

I didn't consider myself cocky for thinking that because it was a fact. The other girls competing weren't international level skaters. Further evidence that this was a special year was the Boston news crew that had shown up, which was unheard of for this competition. Everyone wanted the first look at my new short program. The one I'd deemed Olympic-worthy.

Breathe. Nice and easy.

I counted the final seconds of my warm-up and glided slowly around the rink, looking to Dad behind the boards for his customary smile and nod of assurance. He delivered and called out, "Calm and steady." Meanwhile, Kathy stood beside him with a concerned frown, not what I needed to see at the moment.

I took a long inhale and exhale and smoothed the front of my white dress. I was wearing an old costume of Holly's because I wasn't ready to reveal my real dress yet. That had to be saved for Skate America, my first international competition of the season.

The announcer bellowed my name, and overwhelming applause echoed off the high, curved ceiling. I opened my arms and smiled to acknowledge the reception and then came to a stop at center ice. Within the silence I quieted my thoughts and waited for the music to become my guide.

As the peaceful strains of "Benedictus" began, I came to life with soft arms and delicate steps. When the music grew louder, the power of my strokes rose with it. I sailed across the ice in a long Ina Bauer and went up for my first jump, the easy double Axel. I turned loosely in the air and came out of the jump on a shaky edge, grinding my blade into the ice to hold the landing.

Not so easy. Don't take anything for granted.

Loud cheers broke out, but I put my focus on the music. I let it guide my limbs through the sit spin and then the combination spin. My heart was beating fast, but the calming cello notes ran through me, keeping me steady.

I needed that steadiness for my next jump, the triple flip. Working up speed with the rise and fall of my knees, I zoomed into a series of turns and then stabbed into the ice with my right toe pick. The force shot me into the air, where I pulled in my arms and spun three times. I came down on my right blade, and I let out a breath as I maintained the landing perfectly.

The tempo of the music picked up slightly, and it led me into my footwork sequence, another required element. I twisted and turned my body and my blades in all directions, hoping the technical panel would award me level four when they pressed their computer screens.

I finished my final twirl one step before the boards and quickly took off for the opposite end of the rink. My favorite combination and my money element, the triple Lutz-triple toe combination was in my sights. All the top competitors did this combination first on fresh legs, but I'd planned it late in the program to earn the ten percent bonus. I knew I could pull it off, and it would give me an advantage over everyone else.

I turned my back to the boards and glided in reverse on my left skate. Reaching behind me, I picked into the ice and immediately curled myself into a tight coil, rotating three times. As I opened up for the landing, my blade carved into the ice, but it didn't feel right. The impact felt uneven, sending me off balance. I fought against the lean, still needing to complete the second part of the combination.

With all the strength I could muster, I jabbed the ice again with my toe pick and went up for three more rotations. I had very little air under me, and I came down quickly, scratching the ice with both my blades. Every muscle in my core went to work to hold me upright. The landing wasn't pretty, but I stayed on my feet.

I raced into my closing spin, and the American flag hanging from the rafters became a blur as I spun crazy fast in my layback. The crowd's cheers drowned out the quiet final notes, and I whirled to a stop facing the judges.

Not perfect, but not terrible for August.

I bowed to the judges and reeled around to see the audience. Quinn and Alex were front and center, and they jumped up onto their seats, hands clapping furiously. Em grabbed Alex's arm as he almost tipped over, and I made sure he was safe before I blew kisses to them. I also gave a big smile to my grandparents, who were visiting from Moscow. They came every other summer for a few weeks, and the only other times I got to see them were when I had competitions in Russia.

After I took my bows, I headed toward Dad and Kathy behind the boards to wait for my score. A stuffed animal came flying onto the ice, startling me, and I bent to pick it up. People didn't usually throw many gifts at these small events.

The stuffie was a chocolate brown puppy with big, floppy ears. My first thought was, *Is Braden here?* I looked up into the crowd but didn't see him in the sea of faces. Then I spotted four hands waving wildly, and I recognized their owners right away – Braden's mom and grandma.

I waved back and cradled the dog in my arms as I skated to the ice door. Dad gave me my blade guards, and I clicked them into place.

"Great fight on the toe," he said.

I took a sip from my water bottle. "The ice was a little rough down there."

"I still don't like the combo last," Kathy said. "You have no options if you miss it."

I slapped the cap on my bottle. She didn't like it because she hadn't come up with the strategy, which happened to be a good one.

"I'm not going to miss it," I said, and I felt confident saying it. I landed that element ninety-nine percent of the time.

"You almost missed it just now," she shot back.

I lowered my head so no one could see the annoyance on my face, and I noticed the stuffie had a paper tag hooked to his collar. I flipped it over and found written in black marker – *I love to cuddle.*

I broke into a huge smile and wrapped the puppy in my arms, pressing my nose to his velvety fur. Since I couldn't hug Braden at the moment, this was the next best thing.

The announcer began to read my score, and I put my attention on the crackling sound system. The number was lower than I expected with just a couple of shaky landings, but I'd have to study the protocols (the breakdown of all my elements and levels) to see where I'd lost points.

Mom came over as soon as the score was read, beating out all the little girls seeking selfies and autographs.

"It was a great start," she said as she embraced me.

"The score was kinda low. I might've missed a few levels."

"Liza, can you sign my skate?" one of the girls asked.

"Of course."

I had my water bottle and the stuffed animal in my hands, so Mom offered to take them, but I didn't want to part with the puppy. I gave her the bottle and tucked the stuffie under my arm.

A line of kids followed the first one, and when I'd fulfilled every request, I looked up to see Braden's mom and grandma waiting patiently.

"Hi, Liza!" Mrs. Patrick exclaimed and swallowed me in a hug. "It's so good to finally meet you in person." A cloud of jasmine perfume engulfed me as she rocked me back and forth.

"Thank you so much for coming. Braden didn't tell me you'd be here."

"He wanted it to be a surprise. He gave me very specific instructions that I shouldn't let you see us before you skated."

She finally released me, and Grandma Joann came in for her own hug. Braden had told me they were a very affectionate family – *I've seen my mom hug a waitress before.*

"He's so sweet," I said.

"I think he's pretty terrific," Mrs. Patrick said. "And yes, I'm biased, but it doesn't make it untrue."

"*You* were terrific out there today," Grandma Joann said. "I couldn't tell you'd lost any practice time."

"Thanks. I really love the program, so it makes it easier to focus and nail the elements."

"Your music was just beautiful. I'm downloading it as soon as I get home," Mrs. Patrick said.

"When is Braden going to bring you home for a visit?" Grandma Joann asked. "A couple of my neighbors would love to meet you."

I laughed to myself. Braden had warned me that his grandma was planning to parade me down her block.

"We've talked about it, but we've both been so busy."

Mrs. Patrick gasped and clutched my arm. "I know the perfect time. Braden's birthday party next month. It'll be at my house."

"Oh, you're having a party? I've been trying to come up with gift ideas ever since he mentioned his birthday is in September."

"If you need any help, let me know. I'm sure he'll tell you all about the party later. It's a barbecue we do every year for family and all his friends."

"I'll definitely put it on my calendar."

"Sorry to interrupt." Dad touched my back. "The news crew asked for a quick interview."

"Oh, sure. Dad, this is Braden's mom and grandmother."

He gave them a longer look and shook their hands. "It was nice of you to come."

Dad hadn't been thrilled about Braden and me staying in touch, but he'd been more accepting once he saw how little time we were spending together. He didn't know we talked every day. Multiple times a day.

I received more hugs as I exchanged goodbyes with the two women, and I made a promise to see them again soon. Dad ushered me toward the cameraman, and I answered the standard questions about how I felt about my performance and if I was thinking about the Olympics yet (duh, I'd been thinking about it all my life).

After I finished the interview, Dad and Kathy had the protocols ready for me to examine with them. As expected, I'd been docked accordingly for the sketchy landings. I checked the levels on my spins and footwork and saw I'd received fours across the board, the highest level possible. If my technique had been on point, then what was the issue? I read down the page to the program component scores, which were similar to the old school "artistic mark," and I found the problem. I usually received around nine out of ten points in every category, but the numbers before me were not in that range.

"What's up with the PCS?" I wondered aloud.

"I bet it's the program," Kathy said. "I've said all along the music doesn't have enough impact."

"Two judges came to the rink in June to critique both my programs, and they had no problem with either of them," I said.

"We'll talk to the panel to get their feedback," Dad said.

I didn't like the worried look in his eyes, but I wasn't going to panic yet. I let him seek out the judges with Kathy while I finally got a few moments with my family. My grandmother held my face in her hands and showered me with kisses. "So much beauty when you skate!" she said in her thick accent. My grandfather wasn't as demonstrative with his emotions, but the twinkle in his clear green eyes let me know he was just as proud.

Since I hadn't had a chance to change out of my costume yet, I headed to the locker room, still holding onto my stuffed dog. Quinn had told me I had to name him, so I'd declared him to be Hershey since he was the color of the chocolate bar.

As I took a pair of jeans from my duffel bag, I also grabbed my flashing phone and was greeted with a text from Braden.

How'd you do? I'm dying over here!

I smiled and started typing.

Me: **Skated pretty well. Score not great but Dad is investigating.**

I clicked on the camera and held Hershey next to my cheek, one paw in the air. It was the first stuffed animal selfie I'd ever taken. I sent it to Braden and followed with a message.

Me: **Hershey says hello. I've been cuddling him for the past thirty minutes so he's quite content.**

I didn't receive a response, so I did a quick change and went out to the rink to find Dad and Kathy. They stood near the ballet studio, Kathy with her arms folded and Dad pushing his hand through his light brown hair. A sinking feeling settled onto my chest.

"What did they say?" I asked.

"They don't–" Dad started.

"They don't like the program," Kathy interrupted, seeming all too eager to share the news. "I told you from the beginning it was too slow, too one-note. I knew I was right."

I didn't have time to be pissed about her gloating because the sinking sensation had dropped into my stomach, filling me with alarm. "How could they not like it? The judges who saw it two months ago said it was great and assured us everyone else would think so, too."

"They said it came across different in a competition setting with a full audience," Dad explained in a much gentler tone than Kathy's. "They think you need a piece with a bigger change in tempo, one that builds more to the end."

"Didn't I say the music was all wrong? It's not exciting enough," Kathy said.

Oh my God, we get it! How many times do you have to remind us? I pressed my lips together because I couldn't have an outburst. Not with people still milling around from the event.

Dad didn't even look at her, instead keeping his eyes on me. "We can run it by the federation at camp next week, but I'll start going through my music tonight for some other options."

I'd thought the annual U.S. Skating Federation camp would be a breeze this year. They always critiqued our programs, but since I'd gotten good feedback already I assumed I was good to go.

Now I had a huge, major, colossal, problem.

"If we have to change it, we'll find something you love just as much." Dad squeezed my shoulder. "We have time to work on this."

"Not much. Skate America will be here before you know it," Kathy said.

I had to get out of there before I totally went off on her. Also because I felt like I might cry at the thought of four months of work going in the trash. Along with my beautiful program that I'd imagined skating on Olympic ice.

"I need to go process all this," I said. "I'll see you at home, Dad."

I blew out of the rink and drove home with the windows down, letting the cool night air whip at my face. Changing a program wasn't an unusual occurrence. I'd had to do it my last year in juniors. But I'd found out earlier in the summer, and the stakes weren't as high then. I didn't have the whole country expecting me to bring glory back to U.S. ladies' skating.

A text message notification beeped on my car stereo, and when I saw it was from Braden, I clicked to listen to it.

"I knew you would do great," the robot-voice lady read. "And I'm glad your dad is on the case. Those shady judges better be ready for his Russian intimidation skills."

I let out a laugh, which completely surprised me since I'd been so far from laughing just a minute ago. I shouldn't have been surprised, though. Braden had the power to lighten my mood in an instant. I angled my hand on the steering wheel, and the glow from the streetlights shone on my friendship bracelet.

Another text came through, and I happily accepted it. "Hershey? Very cute. I can tell he loves his new owner already."

Even though the robot read the message, I could hear Braden's deep voice saying the words. I needed to hear it for real, and I knew I had to call him the minute I got home.

The house was dark when I got there, and I dumped my bags in my room and took Hershey and my tablet onto the back patio. I wanted to see more of Braden than a tiny face on my phone screen. I turned on the overhead light and dialed his number, and he answered right away.

"Greetings from the wilderness." He grinned. His hair was damp, and he was wearing his glasses again. The backdrop behind him was a wall of dark wood paneling.

"Caught any fish yet?"

"We had my trout for dinner," he said, puffing out his chest.

"You cooked?"

"I cleaned 'em, Dad cooked, and Tanner threw fish guts at me. Typical Patrick men fishing trip."

"I think your mom and grandma had fun on their outing today. They did a great job surprising me."

"I thought for sure my grandma would go all fangirl and chase you down before you skated."

I laughed. "I haven't thanked you for Hershey yet. A cuddle buddy is exactly what I need right now."

His smile faded. "What's wrong?"

Tanner jumped into the video frame behind Braden and peered at the camera. "You talking to your girlfriend?"

Braden shoved him out of the picture. "Get out of here." He turned to me. "I never told him you're my girlfriend."

Just hearing the word come out of Braden's mouth in relation to me had me feeling warm and fuzzy. Maybe one day he would be happy to call me that all the time.

"Don't worry, I'm used to kids saying whatever comes into their heads," I said. "Quinn and Alex have interesting imaginations, too."

"Back to what you were saying before, did something bad happen? You mentioned your score wasn't great."

"Yeah," I said slowly and tucked my legs under me on the patio swing. "Turns out the judges aren't fans of my short program, so I probably have to scrap it and start all over."

"Oh, man. Isn't it pretty late in the game to do that?"

"I have two months until my next event, but I have to find new music, get the right cuts, design a costume, and learn the new choreography so it's second nature. All while listening to Kathy say, 'I told you so' every chance she gets."

He cringed. "I'm sorry. That really sucks."

"I just hate being rushed and not feeling prepared. I need to be able to do my programs without thinking, and I can't do that if I haven't done hundreds of run-throughs. There's not going to be enough time for that before Skate America."

"What did your dad say about all this?"

"He was very reassuring and is already planning ahead, thinking about new music."

His eyes lit up. "Maybe I can help with that, too. I'm not a classical music buff, but I have a whole movie soundtrack playlist. There's gotta be some skateable music on there."

I toyed with one of Hershey's floppy ears. "According to the judges, I need something that's more exciting."

"I thought the program you have now was awesome

when I saw you practicing. It got me plenty excited."

We both realized how that sounded at the same time because Braden's face turned red, and I couldn't help but giggle.

"Excited in a sport appreciation way," he said, also now laughing. "Get your mind out of the gutter."

"I didn't say anything!"

"You act all innocent, but don't forget I've read your writing."

"You didn't even read the stories with–" I stopped, recognizing I was about to out myself and my hot and heavy scenes.

"With what? You do write smut, don't you?" He leaned toward the camera with a wicked grin.

"No, I don't." My laughter didn't make me sound very convincing.

"I'm not going to believe you unless you show me the evidence."

"I'm not showing you anything ever again."

"You shouldn't be ashamed of the smut." He tried to look serious. "Embrace your inner freak, Liza."

"You're so annoying," I said, but I was totally smiling.

How did he do it? How did he make me forget all my worries and feel so giddy? I knew the answer but hadn't wanted to admit it. *These feelings I have for him? Not so minor.*

CHAPTER NINE

DARK CLOUDS COOLED THE LATE SUMMER afternoon in Boston, making the walk to my car more pleasant than it had been when Holly and I had arrived at Louann's. Holly had picked up her long program costume, while I'd approved the design of my new short program dress. Louann had forty-three days until the costume needed to be on a plane with me to Skate America in Detroit.

"I really like the color you went with over the silver," Holly said as we crossed Boylston Street. "Fuchsia makes a statement."

"Cross your fingers it'll be ready in time to make a statement."

I opened the door to my SUV and hopped up behind the wheel. When I started the engine, the sound of Yanni's "Nostalgia" filled the car. I'd been listening to the song nonstop since it had become my new program music. I'd only been practicing with it for two days, so I needed to mentally run through the choreography to make up for the months of preparation I didn't have on the ice. Braden had tried to talk me into using music from *Star Wars*, sending me daily videos of droids rocking out to "Cantina Band." I'd never seriously considered it, but it had provided me much amusement.

Speaking of Braden, I needed to plug his address into my GPS. Since I was in Boston, it was the perfect chance to stop by his apartment. He and his roommates had just moved in and were starting classes next week. When I'd told him I would be in the city, he'd been super excited for me to visit. My stomach was swirling with anticipation and the nervousness I felt whenever I saw Braden in person. Which hadn't been since our beach day.

"Are any of Braden's roommates hot?" Holly fluffed her wavy hair in the visor mirror.

"What happened to Luke?"

She shrugged. "We're on a break."

"Again? It might be time to make the break permanent."

"I like hanging out with him. He just doesn't set my world on fire, you know?"

Oh, I knew. The guy we were about to visit had burst my world into flames. I wasn't writing smut just yet, but my kissing scenes were becoming steamier by the day. I had so many repressed thoughts and emotions about Braden that I needed to let them out somehow. My characters were enjoying all the benefits.

The GPS took us to the south side of the city, and the streets began to look dingier, the houses more unkempt the closer we got to Braden's address. I took a couple of second glances at the directions on my phone.

"This neighborhood is sketch," Holly said. "Is this where he lives?"

"Well, he can't really afford a brownstone on Beacon Hill."

"There must be some middle ground."

I slowed as we neared his block. "He said it's safe around his house."

She peered out the window and tapped her purse. "I've

got my mace if we need it."

Braden's house came into view, and I parked on the curb in front of the two-story home. He and his roommates occupied the first floor while another group of students had the upper level. The white siding could use a fresh coat of paint, but the yard was well-maintained. A row of neatly-trimmed azalea bushes sat under the two big front windows.

I straightened my T-shirt over my skinny jeans and brushed my hair over one shoulder as Holly and I climbed the steps to the front door. I pressed the doorbell and heard a guy yell, "I got it" from within.

The door flew open, and I recognized Ross from online photos. He had to be at least six feet tall with close-cropped red hair and freckles for days.

"The famous Liza is here!" he said with a huge smile.

I could see straight through the living room into the kitchen, where Braden was standing. He wasn't alone. There was a girl draped all over his back.

"Hey!" he said as soon as we locked eyes.

Holly pushed me into the house from behind, but I remained mute. The girl on Braden's back cried, "Let me have it, B!" and swiped at something in his hand. He wrangled himself loose from her clutches and said, "Not a chance" before jogging over to me.

"Hey," he repeated and wrapped me in a hug. The warmth of his body and the strength of his embrace chased away the sudden jealousy that had overcome me. Seeing his face on video chats was wonderful, but touching him, smelling him, feeling his breath against my hair was *everything*.

I looked over his shoulder and caught Piggyback Girl watching us intently while gnawing on her bottom lip. My nirvana disappeared, and my stomach turned again.

I stepped back and said, "You remember Holly." They'd met at a Sox game.

"Yeah, how's it going?" Braden gave her a quick hug.

"This is Ross." He pointed to the redhead. "And Sam."

Whoa, whoa, whoa. Sam is a girl? One of his roommates is a girl?

"Hi, it's great to finally meet you." She extended her hand.

While I shook it I sized her up. Her pixie cut was dark blond with a pink streak on one side, and she had one of those perky little button noses. She wasn't much taller than me and was equally fit, but she had more assets in all the desired places. She pretty much had my dream body, and I had a view of almost all of it in her tiny athletic shorts and tank top.

"Nice to meet you," I finally uttered, still getting over my surprise. I'd seen a girl named Samantha in some of Braden's pictures, but I'd never thought she was Sam the roommate.

"Maybe you can convince Braden to give me the last Rice Krispies treat. That *my* mom made." She reached for his hand, but he snatched it away. "He'll be nicer to you than he is to me."

"Don't drag our guests into this," he said. "Besides, your mom made them for *me*. She knows they're my favorite."

"I hate you." Sam punched Braden's arm, but I didn't see animosity there. Her eyes lingered on him, and I imagined it was exactly how I looked when he and I teased each other.

Ross turned to Holly and me. "Ladies, if you're confused, this is indeed college and not first grade."

"Let me give you guys a tour of the house," Braden said.

"Can I get something to drink?" Holly asked. "I had a protein bar and I'm dying of thirst."

"Sure, I'll hook you up." Ross nodded to the kitchen. Sam trailed behind them, still watching Braden and me.

"So, this is the living room, obviously," he said. "Notice Phil's strategically-placed coasters so we don't dare mess up the furniture."

"Is he here?"

"You just missed him. He wanted to meet you, but he had

a job interview."

I glanced around me at the common area. A long, black sofa sat on one side of the room, surrounded by two end tables and two oversized bean bag chairs. They all faced a large TV with two auxiliary speakers. The plain white walls looked freshly painted.

We went into the hallway, and Braden unwrapped his Rice Krispies treat, splitting it into two pieces. "Want half?"

"Shouldn't you share it with Sam?"

He shook his head as he chewed. "She was being a brat earlier."

I looked down and toed the wood laminate with my ballet flat. "You umm... you never mentioned that Sam was a girl."

"I didn't?" He swallowed before continuing, "We've been friends since we were kids. She's like my little sister."

Did you know your little sister has the hots for you?

"This is the first bathroom." He nudged the door open.

Everything from the tile to the ceiling was stark white like it had been drenched in bleach. The only splash of color was the green wastebasket next to the pedestal sink.

"Sam and I share this one," Braden said.

My eyes widened. So, she probably saw him in a towel or other states of undress on a regular basis. How fabulous.

I'd known her for five minutes and I hated her.

"Here's my room." Braden opened the next door.

He'd apparently lost the argument over the bigger rooms or maybe I was just spoiled from my palatial bedroom at Mom's. The double bed and a small desk took up most of the space. Above the desk were three rows of bookshelves, and above the bed was a panoramic shot of Fenway Park.

"It's cozy," I said.

"I took the smallest room since I'm not in here much. I mostly study at the library."

I scanned the shelves crammed with books and knickknacks, and I smiled as I spotted a familiar item.

"You framed it." I picked up the picture frame with my construction paper autograph inside.

"Hell yeah. I couldn't chance it getting messed up. A future Olympic champion signed that."

I aimed my smile at him and then put the frame back in its place. A bobblehead of Big Papi (the Sox player, not the dog) sat beside my autograph, and I poked it to make it dance.

"I thought about getting you one of these for your birthday, but I figured you'd have one."

"You don't have to get me anything. You already gave me your incredibly valuable signature."

"I love giving presents. Don't ruin my fun."

"Okay." He laughed and held up his hands.

He led me back into the hall and pointed out the others' bedrooms. Sam's had posters of European cities all over the walls.

"She's hoping to study abroad for a semester," Braden said.

Could I ship her off to live with my grandparents in Russia? Tomorrow, perhaps?

We backtracked to the living room, and Holly, Sam, and Ross were gathered in the small kitchen, all sipping from big plastic cups. Braden went over to Sam and offered her the remaining half of his treat.

"So you won't call me a meanie the rest of the year," he said.

"I'll still call you a meanie, but thanks." She shot him a toothy grin.

"I'm so jealous of you guys, living on your own, no parents to nag you," Holly said.

"We have Phil," Sam and Braden both said at the same time and laughed.

They even think alike. Cute.

"Holly, you should come up with Liza when she does her

college experience weekend with us," Braden said. "It's going to be epic."

"When is this epic weekend happening?" Ross asked.

I hadn't mentioned this to Braden, but as awesome as the idea sounded, I wasn't actually sure I could get away for a whole weekend. Could I chance doing something so out of the ordinary, especially since I busted my knee the last time I was adventurous? I also couldn't imagine telling my parents I was staying with three college kids. They'd think of all the worst-case scenarios that could happen during two days.

"I don't know yet. More stuff keeps getting added to my schedule." I fiddled with my bracelet, and Sam stared at it. I'd noticed she wore a couple just like it on her wrist.

"You're still coming to the barbecue," Braden stated more than asked.

"Definitely. I wouldn't miss it."

"Mama Pat makes the best homemade birthday cake," Sam said.

"Mama Pat?" I asked.

"All the kids who grew up on our street call my mom that," Braden said.

I felt like I needed a textbook to learn their full history. They could have their own college course – Advanced Studies in Sam and Braden. Spending the weekend there would be the best opportunity to closely observe their relationship. If I got up the nerve to make it happen.

Holly had to get home to her nagging mom, so we only got to spend a few more minutes chatting. Braden walked us out, and I'd barely shut the car door when Holly said, "She's totally in love with him."

"Oh my God, you saw it, too?"

"She looked like she was going to die when he hugged you and when he took you to his room."

I punched in the directions to the Cape and buckled my seat belt. "They've been friends their whole lives. She's probably been pining for him since they were in preschool. That's how it always is in books. She's the girl-next-door heroine, he's the swoony hero who takes forever to realize his feelings for her, and I'm the outsider distracting him who everyone hates."

"Okay, you need to stop reading so many romance novels." Holly laughed. "What makes you think he's going to fall for her after all this time?"

"Because they live together now. They're going to be closer than they've ever been. You don't think she'll make a play for him?"

"I know I would if I were her."

I gave her a sidelong glare as I pulled into traffic. "You were supposed to disagree with me to make me feel better."

"Sorry, I thought you were looking for validation." She reached over and touched my arm. "But even if she goes after him, it doesn't mean he'll be into it. I think he's still into *you*."

"I don't know. I'm wondering now if he flirts with and teases all his female friends."

"Some guys *are* like that."

"Again, not making me feel better."

"I didn't say Braden is definitely one of those guys. And I'm telling you..." She propped her foot up on the dashboard. "I don't think he wants to be in your friend zone."

I leaned back against the headrest. "It doesn't matter because that's all I can offer him right now. I just have to hope that he's still available when I finally have time to take him out of the friend zone."

Holly was quiet, but her lips were pinched together in her deep-in-thought face. "You know, being friends can have a broad meaning. Not everything has to be black and white. There are things you can do to make sure he knows you're still interested."

"Such as?" I asked cautiously.

"When you come back for your weekend visit, I'm giving

you one task, one typical college activity to complete."

"What's that?"

"You need to get tipsy and make out with that boy."

WITH A GIFT BAG in each hand, I strode up the sidewalk to the Patrick house and paused at the foot of the front steps. The two-story colonial exuded a homey feeling with its colorful garden and big American flag flying beside the door. The house had been in Braden's family for three generations, but I couldn't tell its age from the outside.

The sound of voices and laughter drifted from the backyard, and I hoped someone would hear the doorbell. I shifted from one foot to the other as I thought about meeting so many people at once. I was probably the only guest who wasn't a regular at this event.

The door opened and so did Braden's arms the moment he saw me. I held onto him as tightly as I could with the gifts in my hands. Our hugs got longer every time we saw each other, and they gave me so much life.

"Happy Birthday," I said. "Now you're a mature nineteen-year-old like me."

"Are you saying I was immature before?"

"No comment."

He looked down at the bags. "You brought me two gifts?"

"One is for Papi."

"Oh, you won't need to bribe him to like you. As soon as he smells you, he'll be all over you."

I put my nose to my braid. "Do I smell like bacon or something?"

He laughed. "No, he can sniff out a new person a mile away, and new people are his favorite."

"Well, the birthday boy gets his present first." I handed

over the bigger green bag.

"Let's go in the living room."

We moved out of the entryway and into the room immediately to our left. It was decorated in warm colors – browns and reds and yellows – and there were photos everywhere. One wall featured rows of graduation pictures from what looked like kindergarten through college. Braden's sisters' rows stretched a bit past his and Tanner's.

Braden dug into the gift bag, and he pulled out the gray hoodie I'd found online. The front was emblazoned with a football and *Dillon Panthers*, the team on *Friday Night Lights*.

"Aw yeah." He grinned and held it up to his chest. "I'm a Panther now."

I patted myself on the back for making the right choice. I'd contemplated getting him a Red Sox autographed team ball, but even though I could afford it, I thought it might be too much. I didn't want Braden to feel weird about accepting such an expensive gift.

"Liza!" Mrs. Patrick came in, arms spread wide. "Did you just get here? Come outside and join the party."

I stepped into her hug and then followed her through the kitchen to the backyard. I set one foot on the deck, and loud barking erupted. Papi came racing over from the grass to greet me, panting and sniffing my sandals and the hem of my sundress.

"Hey, boy." I crouched and put my hand atop his head. "I've wanted to meet you for so long."

I rubbed his neck, and he raised his nose to look at me. "I brought you a little something. I heard you like to chew on socks."

I laid the sock monkey chew toy on the wood deck, and Papi inspected it with his nose before taking it between his teeth.

"Tell her thank you." Braden lifted one of the dog's paws.

I laughed and shook it, and Braden said, "Let me

introduce you to the human members of the family."

I stood up to find everyone looking at me even while they carried on their conversations. I was actually glad to see Sam sitting on the rail of the deck because at least she was a familiar face. There were so many people that they spilled off the wide deck onto the grass.

"This is my dad," Braden said as we approached the man handling the grill.

"Great to have you here, Liza." Mr. Patrick set down his beer to shake my hand. He had a firm grip and piercing eyes that were perfect for interrogating criminals.

"Thank you for inviting me."

"Hi, I'm Dustin." Another hand came toward me, this one from Braden's oldest sister. With dark hair and fair skin, she'd clearly gotten more of their dad's genes.

"Wow, you're even tinier in person," she said.

"Really, D?" Braden said.

I laughed. "It's okay. At least she's not a creepy old guy telling me he wants to put me in his pocket."

"That happened?" Dustin grimaced.

"More than once."

"I bet fans say a lot of crazy things to you, especially online."

"You should check out her Instagram comments," Braden said. "Some people shouldn't be allowed on the internet."

"So, this is Liza!" a girl's voice said behind me, and I only got a glimpse of her before she corralled me into a hug. "I'm Tarah, B's favorite sister."

"It's true," Dustin said. "They're the same person, just the opposite sex."

Tarah had the same friendly smile as Braden, the one that lit up everything around them. *Is it weird that I already want to be BFFs with her?*

"I miss my partner-in-crime." Tarah squeezed her arm around Braden.

"You're at Providence College now?" I asked.

"Yep, getting my master's in education."

"The youth of America will be in good hands," Braden said with a proud pat on her shoulder. "Oh, and the sick and injured will be in good hands with you." He poked Dustin, the soon-to-be nurse.

"Thanks for that afterthought of a compliment. I appreciate it." She ruffled his hair and left us for the spread of food.

"We need to get you a drink," Tarah said to me. "I'm guessing you don't drink beer… too many calories. Diet soda? Water?"

"Bottle of water sounds good."

She made a beeline for the ice chest while the last of Braden's siblings ran toward the back door. Braden scooped Tanner up with one arm as if he weighed nothing, though he looked tall for his age.

"You sorta met this kid already," Braden said.

I laughed. "I remember."

"Braden said he'd kill me if I called you his girlfriend again," Tanner said.

"I did not threaten his life." Braden held up a swear hand.

"You'd better not hurt my baby," Mrs. Patrick said as she moved past us carrying a huge bowl of potato salad.

Tanner jumped onto the deck and took off to the house, Papi hot on his heels. Tarah returned with my water, and she and Braden ushered me around the yard, introducing me to aunts, uncles, cousins, neighbors… there was even a priest. "Father Randy's been a friend of the family forever," Braden said. After thirty minutes of new face after new face, my head was spinning with names. I sighed with relief when Braden suggested we grab some food.

Ross and Phil had arrived while I'd been making the rounds, and I finally got to talk to them while we filled our plates. Phil gave me a sanitary wave instead of a handshake, which didn't offend me at all. I'd shaken enough hands that afternoon to win the next presidential election.

Grandma Joann insisted I sit next to her, so I pulled up a chair at the big patio table and Braden squeezed in beside me. Our elbows kept knocking while we ate our burgers, but I wasn't complaining. Any chance I got to make even insignificant physical contact with him set off sparklers inside me.

It took me a long time to finish my burger because Braden's grandma asked me every single skating wonderment she'd ever had. From "How do you spin so fast without getting dizzy?" to "Why do some girls wear their tights over their skates?" She tackled it all. Papi fought her for my attention, so I fed him scraps from my plate while we talked. When I got up to get a fresh bottle of water, I was still laughing at some of the things I'd been asked.

"Hey, you got away from Grandma Joann," Sam said across the cooler. "She'll have you here until next week if you're not careful."

"I think we just covered sixty years of questions."

"Can I ask one more?"

I froze while opening my bottle. Was she going to ask something about Braden and me?

"Are you coming to visit us soon because I could use another girl in the house for a few days. Someone who won't give me side-eye for watching *Twilight*."

I relaxed and laughed. "Umm... I'm still not sure yet. But I watch *Twilight* every time it comes on, so I'm totally on board."

"Thank you! It's like six straight hours of SportsCenter is acceptable to the guys, but they mock all my movie choices."

Okay, maybe she's not so bad. If she wants me to visit, she can't be too territorial about Braden.

"I don't know if I could ever live with three guys," I said.

"Thankfully, Phil keeps them from being slobs, so it's just

the abundance of testosterone I have to put up with. And the smells. Why do they reek of sweat after a five-minute walk?"

"I know, some of the guys at the rink are on the ice for two seconds and I have to hold my breath around them."

"I would have it so much worse if Phil wasn't there, so I probably shouldn't complain. I've seen our upstairs neighbors' place." She made a gagging face.

I took a sip of water and slowly turned the cap. "How is it sharing a bathroom with Braden?"

I *had* to ask. I couldn't help it.

"It's not bad. His sisters trained him well since they had to share here. He does take forever in the shower, though. The other day I was going to be late for class, so I just barged in and did my makeup while he was still in there."

Here comes the Green Monster again. Now all I could think of was Braden asking Sam to hand him a towel and her admiring his wet body as he emerged from the shower.

"Speaking of the bathroom, I'm gonna go find one," I said.

"It's right past the stairs."

I spent a few extra minutes in there, freshening my lip gloss and tucking flyaway hairs into my braid. When I came out, I stopped in the quiet kitchen to check out all the photos on the refrigerator. There were a few where I couldn't tell if it was Tanner or young Braden because they looked so much alike.

The pictures of Braden with a mouthful of braces had me chuckling as did the ones of him with glasses too big for his little face. Many of his childhood photos had Scott in them – he and Braden making goofy faces with their arms slung around each other. My eyes roamed to the top of the fridge and landed on a school dance picture, and my laughter ceased. Braden looked adorable in a navy suit and red tie, but his hands were around the waist of none other than Sam.

Mrs. Patrick opened the sliding door and set an empty

platter on the counter. "Some of those pictures are so old, but I can't bring myself to take them down."

"I love that you still have them all up here." I paused and pointed to the dance picture. "When was this one taken? Sam's hair is a lot lighter." *Did that sound casual enough?*

She squinted at the photo. "That was her junior prom. She and her boyfriend broke up right before it, so Braden went with her."

That didn't surprise me at all. Of course he would step up and help a friend in need. As long as he didn't help fill her carnal needs.

"This one is my favorite." She lifted a Boston Bruins magnet and showed me a shot of Braden jumping into Scott's arms. They were wearing pinstriped baseball uniforms.

"They won the youth league championship that year. Scotty pitched and B played shortstop. Happiest bunch of kids I've ever seen."

"Braden and Scott were like brothers, weren't they?"

"Oh, yeah." She placed the photo back in its place and ran her finger over it. "He told you what happened."

I gave a solemn nod.

"When Scotty died..." She shook her head as if she still couldn't believe it had happened. "Braden was so hard on himself. He felt like he hadn't been there for him, like he'd failed him. I told him there was nothing he could've done to stop it. For reasons we'll probably never understand, God thought it was Scotty's time. We have no control over that."

I gazed at the photo of the two of them having the time of their young lives. "I think he still feels somewhat responsible. I told him he shouldn't, but..."

"I'll tell you, I was really worried after it happened that he was going to push people away... that he wouldn't trust that he could be a good friend to anyone, but he's actually done the opposite. He was always loyal and protective of his friends, but I see how he's even more protective now. He doesn't want to let down anyone close to him."

As if Braden knew we were talking about him, he popped into the kitchen with Papi at his side. The dog shot over to me, and I scratched behind his ears, eliciting a whimper of content.

"Grandma said she's ready for cake," Braden said.

"Then I guess we're having cake," Mrs. Patrick said. "Can you carry it outside? I'll get the candles."

He hauled the large square cake onto the patio, and I started to take Papi out behind him, but Mrs. Patrick called out to me.

"There was one more thing I wanted to say before." She set her warm brown eyes on mine. "I'm so happy that you and Braden stayed friends and that you're one of those close people in his life now. I think you're really good for each other." She rubbed my arm, and I smiled.

"I'm happy he wanted to stay friends with me, too, although sometimes I'm not sure why he did. I think he's given me a lot more than I've given him. He's always listening to my worries and troubles."

"He likes to feel needed like that. You've given him a lot more than you think."

She gave me another pat and turned to the counter, and I left her counting out nineteen candles. As I watched Braden blow out the inferno on the chocolate cake, I thought about my conversation with his mom. Did Braden want to stay in touch because he was worried I would break under the Olympic pressure? Were his feelings for me now more concern than any kind of lingering romantic interest?

Tarah interrupted my thoughts with her delivery of a slice of cake, and I ate around the buttercream frosting as we chatted about her childhood attempt at skating lessons. "I had no interest in following instruction. I just wanted to wear the sparkly dresses." I told her how I only wanted to wear pink dresses when I was a kid, and I refused to skate when my mom bought me a blue costume.

The crowd in the backyard began to slowly thin out, and soon there were only a handful of us under the amber sky. Sam and Dustin were helping Mrs. Patrick clean up the buffet table, so I stood up to give them a hand.

"You're not leaving yet?" Braden asked.

"No, I was just going to help your mom."

"She's got it under control. I want to show you something."

He motioned me toward the grassy part of the yard, and he took me around the corner of the house. A cluster of trees hid the yard from the street, and in the center of the cluster was a large treehouse made of dark, knotted wood.

"You know how the rink was your favorite place growing up? Well, this was mine," Braden said.

"It's so cool. I've never been inside one."

"Then this is your lucky day." He wrapped one hand around the ladder. "Normally, I'd say ladies first, but since you're wearing a dress that wouldn't be very gentlemanly of me."

His eyes flashed down to my legs, and my cheeks flushed. Maybe Holly was right and he was still interested in me.

Don't get too excited. What straight guy wouldn't be tempted to peek up a girl's skirt given the opportunity?

When I reached the top of the ladder, I crouched as I entered the open doorway. Two porthole-like openings served as windows on either side of the house, but the shade from the trees didn't allow in much light. I heard a click, and the place lit up from the lantern in Braden's hand.

"Wow," I said as I sat on my knees. "This is one pimped-out treehouse."

A sleeping bag provided cushion under my legs, and multiple pillows rested against the back wall. On another wall hung a whiteboard with a drawing of some kind of map. Below the board sat two portable speakers, a portable fan, and one of those lights that spins colors on the ceiling.

"Tanner's done some redecorating since he inherited it," Braden said.

"Is it his personal disco now?" I laughed and picked up the light.

"He's still short enough where he could practice his dance moves in here. Us not so much," Braden said as he further hunched his shoulders. "Check this out."

He pushed up on the ceiling, and an entire panel opened, revealing peeks at the orange sunset between the trees.

"A skylight?" I looked up in wonder.

"My dad and grandpa went all out when they built this."

"I can see why it was your favorite place."

He bent down and sat against the pillows. "The house was always so crowded with D and T and their friends, so this was my hideaway. Ross and Scotty and I used to sleep out here all the time."

"I bet you cooked up a lot of mischief out here, too."

"I told you I was the perfect child," he said with wide innocent eyes.

"Uh-huh."

"There *was* this one time..."

I hid my smile. "Just *one* time."

"I had this baby tooth that wasn't falling out. It was sorta loose but not really, and my mom said she was going to get the dentist to pull it. Well, I hated our dentist. He was this mean, scary old man. So, I got the genius idea to ask Scotty to pull it for me."

I cringed. "Oh, God."

"He got my dad's pliers and we came up here, and I never knew what 'seeing stars' meant until that day. It hurt so damn bad, and there was so much blood that I thought he'd ripped all the teeth out of my mouth."

I covered my eyes like it was happening in front of me.

"He managed to cut my lip with the pliers, which caused

most of the blood. I was freaking out, he was freaking out. My mom brought me to the ER and then whooped me good that night." He laughed. "We used to joke that Scotty would grow up to be a dentist."

His laughter trailed off, and I felt his sadness in my heart. I moved over to his side and sat against the adjacent pillow.

"It's nice to have a place where you feel close to him that you can always come back to," I said.

A scuffling noise came from the ladder, and Tanner's head appeared in the doorway. "What are you doing in my treehouse?"

"I was the original tenant," Braden said. "I have lifetime visitation rights."

"You said no girls were allowed."

I lifted my eyebrows and looked at Braden.

"I made the rules, so I can change the rules," he said.

"You better not be kissing in here," Tanner said. "I'm gonna have to fumigate it."

My face flushed again, and Braden started toward his brother. "You better run unless you wanna feel pain."

He scrambled down the ladder but not before making loud kissing noises. Braden's face looked a little pink, too.

"Am I the first girl in here?" I asked.

"I think D and T used to sneak up here. D and her boyfriends for sure. And Sam weaseled her way in a couple of times. But you're the first girl invited."

He smiled, and I glowed with the feeling of being special to him. It was only one of the many good things he gave me, more and more each day. I was so grateful for his friendship that I couldn't chance making things messy, no matter what Holly had said about blurred lines.

Autumn

CHAPTER TEN

"OKAY, LIZA, GIVE ME A LOOK of determination. As if you're about to take the ice," the photographer said.

I relaxed the aching smile muscles in my face and set my jaw. Wearing a deep red skating dress, I posed in a strong stance in front of the camera, making myself look as fierce as possible. I'd been asked to present the gamut of emotions during my plethora of photoshoots that day. It was all part of the Team USA Media Summit, where select Olympic hopefuls were invited to do interviews and photoshoots so the press would have material leading up to Sochi.

"I think we have everything we need," the photographer said. "Thanks for being so patient."

I returned his thanks and shook his hand, and then I went immediately to my agent Kristin for the bottle of water she had for me. I'd been hydrating like mad all day. The altitude in Park City, Utah had me feeling grateful that I only had to do media there and not compete.

"Just one more interview," Kristin said. "But it'll be a long one."

I groaned. Long meant the reporter was going to dig back

to my childhood. I was already emotionally spent from an entire day of talking to journalists and making sure I looked like the perfect face of U.S. Figure Skating.

"I'll just be a few minutes," I said. "I need to make a quick call after I change."

Mom had left multiple messages while I'd been running between sessions, so I figured I'd better call her back. Who knew how long I'd be trapped with the next reporter.

"Hey, Mom, what's up?" I asked as I slipped on my sneakers.

"I know you're busy. I just wanted to confirm that you're still coming home this week. I thought we could have dinner with George and his daughters this weekend."

"Yeah, I'm skating with Kathy Thursday and Friday, which I'm *so* looking forward to." I made my voice as dry as the air in Park City.

"Just keep trying to make the best of it."

I'd been doing exactly that, but the best I could do still wasn't a good situation. I hadn't been able to convince my parents to let me cut ties with Kathy. They kept giving me the same speech about not making waves.

After I hung up I threw on my light jacket and sent Holly a quick good luck text punctuated with numerous exclamation points and heart emojis. She and her partner Danny were competing in Europe, so with the time difference, her wake-up call would be in a few hours. I wanted my text to greet her when she started the day.

Kristin was waiting for me, and she walked me over to a small room on the other side of the sprawling Waldorf Astoria Hotel. A middle-aged woman named Alice welcomed me with a wide smile, and she wasted no time getting started. She put her tape recorder on the table beside us and placed a notepad in her lap.

The conversation began with questions about my new short program, the hot topic out of my camp the past few weeks, and then Alice worked backward along my career timeline, touching on all the significant milestones. When she got to my world junior title, tension crept into my neck. This was always the part where reporters made the comparison to my parents, also world junior champs, and then segued into asking about my adoptive parents. How deep they delved into those years varied. From the depth of Alice's questions so far, I braced myself for more than a passing inquiry.

I was right.

She first asked how I met my dad, so I described the confusing time when I didn't know if I was staying in Russia with Mom or moving back to the States to be near Dad. I wrapped it up with the happy ending of how they'd worked out their differences for my sake and how I'd been able to have close relationships with both of them.

"Even though your parents were world-class skaters, you didn't know that when you first began skating because you didn't know them at that point," Alice said.

"Well, I knew my mom, but I didn't know she was my mom." As many times as I'd said it, it still sounded like a tabloid headline.

"Did she encourage you to start skating?"

"No, I saw it on TV and wanted to try it, so my parents – my adoptive parents – took me to the rink one Sunday, and I just loved it. I didn't want to leave."

"The sport is in your blood." Alice smiled.

"That's what my dad always says."

"Do you think your parents knew when they brought you to the rink that day that it was your destiny?"

I wanted so badly to roll my eyes, but I made them stay steady on Alice's face. "I think it was just a fun family outing. They knew who my real parents were, but they never pushed me to take lessons. That was all me."

She jotted some notes and stared down at her pad for a long minute. "You were only seven years old, a week shy of your eighth birthday, when your parents' accident happened."

All my muscles tensed even though I'd known the topic was coming. It was my body's way of keeping me from crumbling. Did she really have to bring up the birthday part of it? It was an extra personal stab of hurt on top of all the other pain surrounding that time.

"Can you tell me what you remember about that day?" Alice asked.

Why? Why do people need to know this? It wasn't the first time I'd been asked to recount those events, but it was still excruciating to do every time. Unfortunately, since I'd been forced to tell the story before, I couldn't cop out and claim I didn't remember anything.

I took a long drink of water and shifted in my seat, maintaining a strong grip on the bottle. "My umm... my parents were out running errands, and I was playing at a friend's house. The doorbell rang, and a few minutes later her mom said she had to talk to me. I saw a police car through the window, and I... I felt sick to my stomach without her even saying anything yet. She sat me down and... and that's when she told me."

I couldn't repeat the words she'd said even though they were seared into my brain. I'd never spoken that part of the story out loud, and I never would.

"Did she tell you how the accident happened?"

I shook my head. "Later I found out there was a man driving the other car."

"Do you know anything about him?"

"I just know he went to prison."

She tilted her head in a sympathetic way. "I'm glad to hear there was justice. No child should have to experience what you did."

I lowered my chin and swallowed hard. I didn't know what to say, and even if I did I wouldn't be able to get it past the huge lump in my throat.

Alice let me have a couple of moments to collect myself, and then she moved on to questions about the year I spent living and training in Russia, also an unpleasant time for me to recall. When she finally turned off her recorder, I was ready to bolt from the room.

"Thank you for taking the time to talk with me," she said. "You have a remarkable story that I think will really touch our readers and have them rooting for you."

As we said our goodbyes I couldn't shake Alice's last statement. Something about it seemed so wrong. Multiple things, in fact. First, there was the tragedy of my childhood being used to sell newspapers and second, the possibility of people cheering for me because I'd lost my parents. I wanted people to root for me because of my skating and how I conducted myself as a role model for kids. Not out of sympathy or some fascination with the heartache I'd experienced.

I was still tense when I got to the room I was sharing with Court. She wasn't around, and I remembered she and Josh had gone to explore Park City after their last photoshoot. I went straight for my teddy bear, and I curled up with him on my bed. There had been days after I moved to Russia when I wouldn't let go of him for even a minute. Because I hadn't wanted to let go of *them*.

"I haven't talked to you in a while," I said, resting my cheek on his matted fur. "I hope you know it's not because I don't think about you. I've never stopped missing you."

I closed my eyes to bring up their images, and I saw my mom with her wild mane of dark curls and my dad with his reddish-brown beard. I hated that my memories grew hazier every day, and I had to rely on photos to sharpen them. I could clearly remember their voices, though, and how my dad would call out one of his twenty nicknames for me when he woke me up in the morning. "Lollapaliza!"

The blanket under me vibrated, so I peeked over at my

phone. It showed an incoming video call from Braden. I normally would jump all over it, but I didn't trust my current emotional state. If I told him about the interview I might start crying, and I'd rather he not see that.

When the buzzing stopped I shot him a text.

Me: **Can we do audio only?**

Braden: **Uh-oh. Are you wearing a top secret Olympic outfit? Do you have on the Opening Ceremony uniform!?!**

My lips twitched into a smile.

Me: **No secret outfit. I'm just having an emotional night. Not presentable for video.**

The phone rang a minute later, and I put it to my ear.

"Hey, you okay?" Braden asked. "Did one of the reporters get to you?"

I rolled onto my back and stared up at the recessed lighting. "She asked the question that I hate answering. The one that I dread hearing every time I sit down for one of these in-depth interviews. I know people think the story is compelling or whatever, but they don't understand how hard it still is for me to talk about it."

"Your parents' accident," he said softly.

"She wanted to know what I remember about that day." I pressed Peter tighter to my chest. "I try to look at it like I'm watching a movie of someone else's life when I have to talk about it, but going into detail brings up all these feelings..." My throat burned again, and I couldn't continue.

"I'm so sorry you had to sit through that."

I took a deep breath, and Braden stayed silent too, letting me have a minute to regain my composure.

"You know I've never been told how the accident happened or who the guy was that hit them?" I said.

"Is that something you want to know?"

"I've tried searching online, but the local paper's archives don't go back that far. I've always wondered why it happened and who was responsible, but when I asked my mom she said all I needed to know was that the man was in jail. I don't know if he was drunk or ran a red light or what. She wouldn't answer any of my questions."

"You have a right to know. They were your parents."

"My mom still thinks I'm a little kid who can't handle the truth."

He was quiet for a few moments. "I wonder if... maybe my dad could get the information. He might be able to reach out to the police department there or ask one of his lawyer friends."

I sat up but held onto Peter. "You think he could do that?"

"I can ask him."

For a second I questioned whether I should go there... if knowing the details of the accident would put pictures in my head that would worsen my already grim memories of that day. I couldn't deny my curiosity, though, and the feeling that I was owed an explanation for the event that had forever changed my life.

"Thank you," I said. "I didn't think I'd ever get the chance to find out what happened."

"He'll be glad to help if he can."

I smiled to myself. *Like father, like son.*

"He might ask why your mom hasn't shared the details with you, but he'll understand that you're an adult and it's your choice to make," Braden said.

"My mom would not be happy if she knew I was looking into this."

"It's your life. You have to do what feels right to you."

My life. Most of the time I felt like it wasn't really mine. It was controlled by everyone but me – my parents, the federation, the judges. None of the important decisions were in my hands, and I didn't know how to take charge of them.

"I wish it was that easy," I said.

"It can be. You've already started taking the first steps.

You went out with me when your parents didn't approve. Aren't you happy you did that?" The smile in his voice was unmistakable.

"Very happy." I grinned on my end just as much.

"Which leads us to the perfect next step – you coming to Boston this weekend. Tell me that you don't need an escape right now."

"You have no idea how much. But–"

"No buts."

I chewed on my lip. Every time he brought up the idea, I thought about how much fun it would be, but then I came back to the problem of my overbearing parents.

"I'm going to my mom's Wednesday night since my dad is in the Czech Republic with Holly and Danny. She'll go into cardiac arrest if I tell her I'm leaving Friday to stay with you for the weekend."

"What if you train on the Cape instead so she doesn't have to know? Is there an excuse you can come up with for being there even though your dad's not around?"

I hummed quietly and brainstormed potential lies. "Maybe I could say that Josh and I have to work on my show program, which is actually true. We just weren't going to do it until the end of next week."

"There you go. Totally plausible excuse."

"Except my mom and I are supposed to have dinner with George and his daughters."

"Would you rather go to a quiet, ordinary dinner or have a fun, amazing, spectacular weekend?"

Court opened the door, and I gave her a smile. "That's not a biased description at all."

"You know I'm right," he said.

I couldn't argue, and this was also one of the few upcoming weekends I didn't have any skating-related obligations. Dad being out of town was another plus. Em would probably express concern and have some questions, but she wouldn't give me a hard time.

Now is the time to start taking control of your life.

If I acted responsibly and made sure not to trip over any curbs, I should be fine. Here was a decision where I could take charge, and I knew exactly what I wanted.

"Hmm... what to do... what to do? I think..." I left Braden hanging on purpose just for suspense. "I will set this plan in motion right away."

"Sweet! I'll start getting everything ready for your arrival."

"Rolling out the red carpet?"

"Only the best for you."

I fell back onto the bed as I became a body made of Jell-O. I really had to toughen up if I was going to survive forty-eight hours of nothing but Braden.

"Court just came in, so I need to get with her on my alibi," I said.

"Yes, you work on that and I'll work on our itinerary. Can you hear how excited I am for this? If we were on FaceTime you'd see me bouncing in my chair."

I laughed. "I'm picturing it now and loving it."

As soon as I ended the call, Court sat across from me on her bed, a curious look in her eyes. "Alright, girlie, what am I giving you an alibi for?"

"Do you think Josh can work on my exhibition Thursday or Friday?" I asked as I popped upright, having regained muscle control.

"I thought you were going to New York after this."

"There's been a change of plans. I'm going to Boston this weekend."

"Ohh, your big college weekend. I thought you said you'd never be able to pull that off."

"Well, the stars might be aligning. I just need a reason to give my mom for training on the Cape Thursday and Friday without my dad there. That's where Josh comes in."

"Sneaky, sneaky." She smiled. "I'm sure he can make time. Do you have music picked out?"

"That's my project for the plane ride home."

"What are you going to do about Em? You know she's going to tell your dad."

"There's no way I can lie to her. I *think* I can pull off lying to my mom over the phone. Hopefully, since Dad will be traveling home most of the weekend, he won't be able to bug me with calls and texts every five minutes. My mom and Em don't talk, so there's no chance of being busted there."

"So, your mom will think you're on the Cape the whole time. What a tangled web we weave." She shook her finger at me.

I hopped off the bed and paced over to my suitcase. "I've never snuck out or done anything like this, so I think I'm entitled to one free pass."

"I'm just teasing you. I'm all for you having a fun getaway."

"I'm really excited, but… I'm also kinda nervous. What do I know about college parties? I didn't even go to any high school parties where there was alcohol or hooking up."

"I've been to a couple. You'll be fine as long as you remember a few key things. One – don't accept drinks from people you don't know. Two – don't take more than one shot. You don't have the size or the experience to handle it. And three – don't play any drinking games where you know you'll lose badly."

I nodded and ticked them off again on my fingers. "Stranger danger as far as drinks are concerned, one shot max, and stay away from beer pong. Got it."

"Braden's a good guy. I trust he'll look out for you and won't let you get too crazy."

That didn't sound like a typical nineteen-year-old's plan for a party, but I had to accept that I couldn't one hundred percent pretend to be in college. Letting loose still came with rules in my world. Rules that included not putting my lips anywhere near Braden's. Even if I got a tiny bit drunk.

CHAPTER ELEVEN

FRIDAY AFTERNOON AT THE RINK WAS always a fun time with everyone pumped for the weekend and ready to show off their moves in our weekly "Free-For-All Friday." Dad and Em had started the tradition of having their students take the ice two at a time to skate to whatever random song Em put on the stereo. The object was to be free and creative, and the only rule was no jumps allowed.

Court and I stood at center ice waiting for Em to surprise us, and I hoped the music would be fast because I was about to explode with excitement and anxiousness. I needed to let out some of that energy before I got on the road to Boston or I might find myself driving ninety miles an hour.

"Here we go, girls," Em said.

A driving beat came through the speakers, and I threw my hands in the air. "Club Can't Handle Me" was exactly the type of song I wanted.

"The rink can't handle me," I said to Court as I took off backward.

She laughed. "Don't run me over."

I sped into back crossovers and felt the bass vibrating

through the ice and into my knees with every stroke. Court and I lapped each other, and we each broke out into frantic footwork to match the lyrics. We high-fived as we crossed paths in the middle of the ice, but neither of us lost momentum. I danced my way across the rink, itching to jump because nothing made me feel more powerful than hitting a big triple. Since I was already breaking rules today, I decided I'd better keep my skates on the ground.

I was a sweaty mess after the workout, so I jumped in the locker room shower. With a quick hair and makeup session afterward, I was ready to go on my adventure. I slung my flowered tote over my shoulder and rolled my other bag behind me into the lobby. Em and the twins were standing near the doors with one of the ice dance coaches. Quinn and Alex never ceased to look adorable in their navy school uniforms.

"Hitting the road?" Em asked.

"You're leaving already?" Quinn hugged my waist. "You just got here."

Aww hell. Now I have sister guilt on top of liar guilt.

I caressed her curly blond ponytail. "I'll be back Sunday."

"I'm gonna walk Liza out," Em said. "Why don't you two go pack up your books in the snack bar?"

I kissed the twins goodbye, and Em hooked her arm around me as we stepped out into the parking lot. I'd been spared Dad's worries so far since neither Em nor I had told him my plans. She said she'd wait to share that information after the competition in Europe finished. We'd all huddled around Em's laptop earlier to watch Holly and Danny skate, and their silver medal had me celebrating for my friend and also thankful that Dad would be in a great mood.

"I hope you have an awesome time in Boston, but don't feel like you have to cram a lifetime of fun into this one weekend," Em said. "You'll have plenty more opportunities to live it up in the future. Remember to keep it all in perspective."

I nodded. "I will. Thanks for being so cool about everything and for talking to Dad for me."

"I'll try to keep him from bothering you too much." She smiled and gave me a long hug.

Armed with my latest piece of advice, I set off down Route Six and pulled up my new show program music on my phone. As I'd searched my playlists for song possibilities on the trip home from Utah, I'd come across "Beneath Your Beautiful" and realized how well it described my life. Part of the lyrics even closely matched something Braden had said to me – *You're so far out of my league.* I still didn't think it was true, but the rest of the verse about saying no to boys and building walls around myself was spot on.

Within ninety minutes I arrived at Braden's house, and I found a parking spot across the street. I grinned as the front door opened while I was only halfway up the sidewalk.

"Are you staying for a week?" Braden surveyed my luggage as he jogged out to meet me. "I'd be more than fine with that."

"Since you haven't given me our itinerary, I brought a semester's worth of outfits."

He reached for both bags. "I got these."

"I didn't know there was bellhop service here."

"Only for our most special guests," he said, giving me a tight sidearm hug.

The TV was loud enough to hear from the front stoop, and I caught the crack of a bat followed by Ross yelling, "It's about time!"

"We got a hit?" Braden stopped to look at the big screen. A Red Sox player stood on first base, and the scorebox indicated the team was down two runs to the Tampa Bay Rays in the playoff game.

"Looks like I got here at the right time," I said, perching on the arm of the couch.

Big Papi stepped up to the plate and promptly hit a towering fly ball that made Ross and me both leap to our feet. Two of the outfielders converged to catch it, but the ball bounced untouched behind them.

"Yeah!" Braden and Ross exclaimed while I jumped up and down.

"You're our good luck charm." Ross pointed to me. "Don't go anywhere."

I grinned and settled onto the sofa. I liked feeling that I belonged there already.

A bases-clearing double soon brought in the two tying runs, and we exchanged high-fives all around. When the inning finally came to a close, Braden picked up my luggage.

"I'll put these in my room," he said. "You can sleep there, and I'll take the sofa."

"You'd better inspect the sheets first," Ross whispered loudly to me.

"I washed the sheets," Braden said.

"You shouldn't have to give up your bed. I can sleep on the couch," I said.

"No way. Special guests get their own room."

He disappeared into the hallway, and Ross offered me his bag of Cape Cod potato chips. "Want some?"

"Oh, no thanks."

"You probably don't eat junk food, huh?"

"Not much."

"You'll be appalled when you go in the kitchen then. We've started calling Sam 'Little Debbie' because of her huge stash."

I laughed. "She doesn't look like she eats a lot of snack cakes."

"That's because she runs almost every day."

Was it a coincidence that a certain roommate of hers also had that routine?

"Does she run with Braden?"

"Who, Sam?" Braden asked as he returned. "Yeah, she does the harbor route on campus with me."

I nodded slowly. "Cool."

He flopped onto one of the bean bag chairs. "So, I wasn't supposed to work tonight, but my sub fell through. I have to help with the stats at the volleyball match, so it'll just be a couple of hours. You can come watch or if you'd rather hang here that's cool. I'm really sorry I can't get out of it."

"That's okay. I think the match will be fun. I can get the college sports experience."

"Come on, ump!" Ross yelled at the TV.

"Welcome to the playoff baseball experience." Braden laughed. "I'll be done working before nine, so I'll have plenty of time to introduce you to a typical Friday night around here."

I smiled. "I can't wait."

The three of us cheered on the Sox as they built a big lead – big enough that Braden and I weren't nervous leaving before the end of the game. Ross gave me hell about taking the good luck with me, but Braden said as long as I left behind something I was wearing I wouldn't jinx the team. I didn't question the sanity of their superstition because I'd seen plenty of weird stuff in skating. I took off my cardigan and draped it over the sofa.

Braden drove us the short distance to the UMass campus, and we went straight to the gym in the athletic building. "I'll take you around the rest of campus tomorrow," he promised.

I parked myself in one of the dark blue seats while Braden went courtside to find his boss, an associate director in the athletic department. A sparse crowd dotted the stands, so it wouldn't exactly be the hyped-up atmosphere I associated with college sports. I'd just have to clap and cheer extra loud for the Beacons.

My phone trilled in my purse, and I knew who the caller was before I even saw Dad's name.

"I'm fine, I'm safe, I'm at a wholesome volleyball match," I answered.

"It's only six o'clock there, so it's too early for partying. The question is where will you be a few hours from now?" he asked. "Don't try to sneak into any clubs. You can't risk getting into trouble."

"Dad, I'm not stupid."

"I know, but it's easy to get talked into doing something when you're in a group and there's peer pressure."

I pinched the bridge of my nose. "I feel like I'm back in ninth grade health class."

"I'm just reminding you to please be careful. You need to–"

The PA announcer began speaking, making it impossible to hear anything over the phone. The timing couldn't be better.

"Dad, I can't hear you, and the match is about to start. I promise I'll be careful. Love you."

The girls took their places on either side of the net, and I cupped my hands around my mouth and shouted, "Go Beacons!" My phone buzzed in my lap, and I wasn't surprised to see a text from Dad.

I know you want to feel like a normal kid, but you have to be cautious. Please take care of yourself this weekend. Skate America is only two weeks away.

I shook my head. What did he think I was going to do? Drink myself into a two-week coma?

Me: **I'll be fine. This is the perfect time for a little break. I'll be fired up and ready to go for Skate America.**

I put the phone away and clapped my hands. As the action heated up, I tried to pay full attention to the match, but I couldn't stop staring at Braden across the court. He looked like he'd stepped out of a college brochure in his dark blue UMass polo and khaki pants. He kept biting his lip in concentration as he worked on his laptop, and watching all his little mannerisms was more riveting than watching the ball being spiked. I got such a rush seeing him in the flesh rather than on my phone screen.

UMass won the match in three hard-fought sets, and I played on my phone while Braden wrapped up his duties. I snapped a picture of the blue bleachers along the opposite wall which featured "Beacons" painted in white. It would be a cute photo for Instagram, but Mom stalked all my social media accounts so I couldn't share anything I experienced that weekend. I finally knew what it felt like to be a sneaky teenager.

When we got back to the house, Sam and Phil were there with Ross and another guy. He was introduced to me as Jason, one of the upstairs neighbors. They were all diving into pizza boxes on the bar between the living room and the kitchen.

"I got one with half veggies for you," Sam said. "Makes it seem healthier."

"Thanks." I smiled and waited for the grabby hands to clear out before I took a slice. It surely wasn't as healthy as Em's wheat crust and low-fat cheese pizza, but one piece wouldn't hurt me.

"Did you see the Sox scored four more runs after you left?" Ross asked. "Either you or your sweater has to be here tomorrow afternoon for Game Two."

I laughed. "I'll make sure that happens."

"So, we bowling tonight or what?" Phil asked.

"I haven't bowled in forever," I said.

"You're on Braden's team then," Ross said.

"Dude, that's harsh," Braden said.

"Hey, I've lost three Fridays in a row. I'm not washing your car or doing your laundry again."

"That's fine. I'm more than happy to have the Olympic athlete on my team." Braden laid his arm across my shoulders, and I had trouble swallowing my bite of pizza. The electricity from his body made all my basic functions misfire.

I looked up at him. "You remember that I'm an Olympic

athlete because of my feet, not my hands?"

"Doesn't matter. You have the intangibles of a winner." He bent his head close to my ear. "And Ross sucks, so we got this."

The heat from his breath gave me shivers deep inside. If he kept this up, I wouldn't be able to hold a bowling ball much less throw one.

"Rain Man, what was Braden's score last time?" Jason asked.

"One eighty-two," Ross said.

Jason volunteered to be our third member, so the trash talk began between the two teams and continued until we reached the twenty-four-hour bowling alley. The rock music combined with the crashing of the pins made it a lot louder than the volleyball match had been. We piled onto our adjacent lanes and donned the garish red and blue loaner shoes, paired with complimentary Boston Bowl socks.

After we all picked out our balls, Phil scrubbed his with a wet wipe and dug deep into the finger holes. His shaggy blond hair flopped over his forehead as he focused hard on cleaning every centimeter. Ross stood next to him, watching the meticulous process and shaking his head.

"You should just get your own ball," he said.

Phil held up the wipe. "These are cheaper."

Sam punched my name into the electronic scoreboard first, saying I should start the game since I was the guest player. I rubbed my hands on my jeans and grabbed my pink ball, feeling all eyes on me. Braden started a "Let's go, Liza" chant and clap, and Jason joined him. I took a deep breath and strode toward the lane, and I flung the ball as hard as I could. It clunked onto the shiny wood and veered to the left, sliding into the gutter long before it reached the pins.

"Nice hook shot," Ross yelled.

I spun around with my hands on my head. "I told you this was going to be bad."

"You're just rusty. It'll come back to you," Braden said.

But my next ball ended up in the left gutter again, giving me a big fat zero for my first frame.

"Maybe you should stand in our lane and throw it," Ross said with a wide grin.

"Or do a triple Axel first," Phil said.

I stuck my tongue out at them, but I loved that they were ribbing me. It meant they'd accepted me into their group.

My rustiness unfortunately didn't wear off, and with Braden and Jason having off nights, we found ourselves losing more ground with each frame. I blamed some of my ineptitude on being distracted by the activity at our table. Every time I got up, Sam took my seat next to Braden, and she was always touching him and digging into his fries. I didn't see her doing that with any of the other guys.

Phil appeared to be watching them, too, so I went over to where he stood behind the table, nursing a giant cup of soda. Braden got up to take his turn, and I clapped and cheered, "I'm feeling a strike here!"

"Having fun?" Phil asked. He wasn't a tall guy, so I didn't have to crane my neck to talk to him like I did with Ross.

I nodded. "Despite how much I stink at this game."

"I'm glad you finally got to visit because Braden hasn't shut up about it since we moved in." He wore a straight face but it eased into a little smile.

"He gets very excited about things," I said.

"So I've learned the past year."

Braden rolled his ball, and I took a moment to admire the view. He'd changed into a T-shirt and faded jeans, and when he raised his arms in triumph his shirt rode up, giving me a reminder of the abs I'd seen at the beach. I'd failed big time by not taking any photos that day.

"So close," he said as one pin stood alone.

I applauded and started a "Spare!" chant with Jason.

Braden's next ball narrowly missed the lone pin, and he staggered in defeat back to his seat. Of course Sam had to pat him on the back even though they weren't teammates.

Phil's eyes had returned to them, too, but I couldn't read what he was thinking. I sensed he might be able to give me some insight into their house dynamics, though.

"Do you ever feel lost with inside jokes or anything since you didn't grow up with these guys?" I asked.

"Not really. Sam's the only one who talks a lot about old times."

"Like when they were kids?"

"Yeah, sometimes she brings up stuff Braden doesn't even remember. We should start calling *her* Rain Man." His gaze locked in on her as he chewed on his straw.

"You're up, Phillip," Ross said.

He left to take his turn, and I pretended to check my phone while still observing Braden and Sam. Did Sam talk about the past because she wanted to remind Braden of their history? Was it part of a plan to make him fall for her? He didn't seem bothered by her being all up in his personal space, but he was probably used to it after so many years of friendship.

So, how do I go about getting used to it?

STANDING IN BRADEN'S BEDROOM in my pajamas was a very dangerous situation. Not because anything was going to happen between us, but because the daydreams flooding my mind were sure to keep me up all night. It was already well past midnight and way past my usual bedtime.

I'd carefully selected a purple baby doll shirt and gray yoga pants for my pajamas for this trip, leaving my usual tank top and short-shorts at home. I pulled Peter out of my tote to reach my hand lotion, and I jumped at the knock on the half-open door.

"Hey," Braden said, pushing it open.

I couldn't get Peter back into the bag fast enough, and I saw Braden's eyes go to him.

"You brought a friend?" He smiled.

I lowered my head and finished repacking the bear. "You weren't supposed to see that."

"Hey, no judgment here."

He appeared genuinely unfazed. He also appeared genuinely drool-worthy in his choice of sleepwear – a well-worn T-shirt and long basketball shorts.

"I umm… I bring him with me whenever I travel," I said.

"He must have a lot of sentimental value."

"My adoptive dad gave him to me. I don't sleep with him. He's just… nearby."

"You don't have to explain. I'm familiar with keeping something sentimental close by." He lifted his wrist.

We shared smiles of understanding, Braden's eyes lingering on mine, and something else hung in the air between us in the tiny room. A late-night, intimate energy that suddenly had my heart beating faster.

Braden broke the spell first, taking a step backward. "I promise as soon as my dad's off this crazy case he's working, I'll ask him about looking into your parents' accident."

"Oh, sure. I don't want you to bother him if he's busy."

"My mom said he might have a better schedule next week," he said as he went to the closet. "I just need to grab a blanket and I'll be out of your way."

"Take your time. It's your room."

He reached up to the top shelf and tugged, and a pile of shirts came tumbling down. Braden snatched the blanket and shoved the door on the avalanche all in one quick motion.

"So, what did you think of your first day at college? Met expectations? Exceeded expectations?"

"I had a blast. I'm glad I got to experience bowling night

even though I let the team down badly."

"Jason and I didn't exactly pull our own weight either."

"I can help wash one of the cars tomorrow."

"No way. We're not wasting your precious time here with that. Jason and I can handle it later. I'm taking you around campus, and then there's a party upstairs tomorrow night. By that time you'll be fully indoctrinated into the college world and ready for the craziness." He grinned.

We said goodnight, and I turned off the light and climbed into bed with my phone. With my nose to the pillow, I breathed in the fresh scent. It smelled just like Braden's clothes. *Can I take this home as a souvenir?*

I had two texts from Dad that had arrived while I'd been in the shower. He asked about my whereabouts, so I typed a reply.

Safely tucked in. Have a good trip home. Love you!

I figured Holly was probably also up for breakfast across the ocean, so I sent her a text.

OMG I AM IN BRADEN'S BED.

I scrolled through Instagram while I waited for a response, and a minute later the phone buzzed.

Holly: **WHAT??!! I told you to make out with him not jump his bones!**

Me: **He's not in the bed with me! He's sleeping on the couch.**

Holly: **Oh LOL that makes more sense.**

Me: **I'd better get to sleep. Big day tomorrow for this faux college student. Congrats again, Silver Girl!!!!**

Holly: **Thanks!**

Holly: **GO FOR IT WITH BRADEN.**

I laughed and pressed my cheek to the awesome-smelling pillow. The only place I planned to go for anything was in my dreams.

CHAPTER TWELVE

THE THIN BLINDS ON BRADEN'S BEDROOM window didn't block out much sunlight, so I slowly opened my eyes to adjust to the brightness. The first thing I noticed as I came out of my sleepy state was my frozen nose. The comforter was also now up to my neck. Someone apparently liked to set the AC on fifty degrees.

My stomach growled, not accustomed to having breakfast this late. I peeled back the covers inch by inch and hugged my arms against my body. Why hadn't I packed a sweatshirt I could throw over my pajamas?

Two of Braden's hoodies sat in a pile on his desk chair, and I yearned for their warmth. I didn't think he'd mind, so I slipped the gray UMass one over my head and pushed up the too-long sleeves to free my hands.

The living room and kitchen were empty, and Braden's blanket was in a bundle on the couch. I started opening cabinets, hoping to find something suitable for breakfast. I was so hungry I'd settle for sugary cereal or a toaster pastry. Not passing out topped nutrition at this point.

The front door opened, and a laughing Braden and Sam

came in, both wearing running clothes and each with a different look in their eyes when they saw me. Sam's dropped with disappointment while Braden's widened and swept over me.

"Morning," he said.

"Good morning. I hope it's okay I borrowed your sweatshirt. I was really cold when I woke up."

"Ross likes to freeze us out," Sam said.

"You can use anything of mine you need," Braden said with a smile now in his eyes.

"Do you have any cereal?"

"I thought you'd want cold pizza to get the authentic experience," he teased.

I twisted my face. "That's one experience I don't need."

"I can actually offer you much better than cereal or cold pizza." He moved into the kitchen and took out a skillet. "I'm going to make you one of my California omelets."

"They're delicious," Sam said. "He makes them for me all the time."

"I'm gonna take a quick shower first so I don't sweat all over the eggs," Braden said.

Sam and I stood alone for a few uneasy seconds before she went over to the couch and the remote control.

"*New Moon* was on a few days ago," she said. "I should've recorded it so we could watch it."

I sat on the opposite end of the sofa and covered my legs with Braden's blanket. "That one's actually my least favorite *Twilight* movie."

She paused while flipping channels and narrowed her eyes at me. "You're Team Edward, aren't you?"

"I'm guessing you're Team Jacob?"

"He was so obviously the best choice."

"But he and Bella were meant to be just friends."

Her face tightened, and I realized the possible real-life parallels with what I'd said. I needed to proceed cautiously...

"Bella and Jacob had a lifelong bond," she said. "She just never gave him a chance because she got blinded by Edward's sparkliness." She gave me a pointed look.

What the hell? Is she saying I'm the vampire?

This is insane. We're not in a love triangle. Last time I checked we were all just friends.

I couldn't deny the urge to defend my side, though.

"I think… I think Bella and Edward had a real emotional connection… even though they just met."

"I think it was more obsession than a real connection," she said.

Now I had even more questions. Was she just talking about the movie or was she implying that Braden was obsessed with me? And if he was, what did that mean exactly?

Phil shuffled into the living room, mumbling some sort of morning greeting, and I was so happy to see another person that I wanted to hug him. My new goal for the rest of my stay was to not be alone with Sam anytime, anywhere. I just couldn't figure her out. Sometimes she was nice to me, and other times I got the impression that she didn't want me within a mile of her (or Braden).

❧

I STEPPED IN FRONT of the mirror on Braden's closet door and assessed my look. Court and I had put it together a few nights ago after consulting the internet for "college party outfit." The loose maroon sweater, super skinny jeans, and black heeled booties were stylish yet casual enough for a house party (or so all the teen magazines had said).

I snapped a selfie in the mirror and texted it to Court.

Ready to party! I feel much more like a college student after today. Tell you about it tomorrow!

I pulled up my photos and thumbed through the many I'd taken that day on campus. Braden had started the tour at the bookstore in the Campus Center, where I'd gone a little crazy buying school apparel and paraphernalia. How could I pass up a Beacons travel mug or a sticky note cube? We'd eaten lunch in the Center's upstairs food court, and I'd soaked in the atmosphere of students studying over their meals or working on group projects together. It made me think about the possibility of college and my future beyond skating, which I hadn't ever done at length. I'd only been able to look ahead as far as February to the event that would dictate said future.

My picture scrolling landed me on a photo of the harbor, and I smiled as I remembered our windy walk along the water. The campus sat in a beautiful spot on the ocean with views of the Boston skyline in the distance. Braden had shown me all the buildings where he had classes, and then we'd stretched out on a sunny patch of grass and talked until it was almost time for the Sox's first pitch. I'd wanted to get back to the house to bring my luck to the team, and I'd succeeded! With the Sox now up two games to none in the series, the party mood had started early around the house.

The footsteps creaking the ceiling above me were getting louder by the minute, so I figured it was about time to join them. I slipped my phone into my small crossbody purse and went into the living room. Sam and Braden were watching something on Sam's phone and snacking on tortilla chips. Both wore jeans and Sam had on sky-high wedges, so I felt good about my outfit choice.

"Sounds like there are a ton of people upstairs already," I said.

"Ready to hit it?" Braden asked.

"Let's go!" I said, pumping myself up for the scene I was about to enter.

I've skated at the Olympics. I can handle a wild party.

The three of us went around to the side of the house and the stairs that led to the second floor. I could feel the music vibrating in the wooden steps. When Braden opened the door, a blast of noise assaulted us, and I took a step backward. *Whoa, that is A LOT of people.*

We squeezed into the steamy living room, sliding between bodies, and Braden slapped hands with a couple of guys we passed. They gave both Sam and me less-than-subtle once-overs, and my feeling of being college-ready evaporated. I was back to feeling young and inexperienced and totally out of place.

"Hey, man, you ready to play?" A big guy who looked like he could be a linebacker smacked Braden on the shoulder. "Britt and Jason are talking shit about us. We gotta avenge last week." He just then noticed Sam and me. "If you don't mind me stealing him, ladies."

"This is Mike, my beer pong partner," Braden said. "You know Sam, and this is Liza. She's my special guest, so if she wants to play, she and I are gonna team up tonight."

As much as I wanted to be Braden's partner and maybe feel more comfortable there, I had to heed Court's advice because I knew my limitations. I needed to ease into the drinking thing.

"I'll skip this cliché activity. There might be another game I'm more suited for."

"You sure?" he asked.

"Yeah, go ahead."

"You have to come be my good luck charm."

Sam took my elbow. "I'll show her where to get a drink first."

She steered me away from him before I had a chance to blink. The traffic jam ahead of us slowed our trip, but Sam didn't say anything until we reached the kitchen.

"You want beer or the hard stuff?" She pointed between the keg and the cluster of liquor bottles on the kitchen counter. "I suggest the hard stuff."

I'd tried kvass in Russia, which was similar to beer, and I hadn't cared for it. The hard stuff was a little intimidating, but

I definitely needed something to take the edge off.

"Your suggestion sounds good."

She poured a cup of cranberry juice over ice and added vodka. She didn't measure anything so I didn't know how strong the cocktail was going to be. I took my first sip and coughed as the burn hit my chest. A couple of girls leaning against the counter looked over at me, and I saw the recognition pop onto their faces.

"You're that ice skater," one of the two blondes said with a slight slur in her delivery.

"Liza Petrov," the other girl said.

Sam finished mixing her own drink and took off. She probably wanted no part of this celebrity sighting.

"That's me," I said to the girls.

"You're like a little Russian doll." The drunker one petted my long hair. "I need a picture with you." She pulled out her phone and mashed herself against my side.

All I needed was for Mom to see me tagged in a party photo. Surrounded by alcohol.

"I can't take any pictures," I said. "I'm not supposed to be–"

"Oh, gimme a break," the more sober girl said. "You should be grateful she even asked. It's not like you're that important."

"That's not... I just can't be tagged–"

"Whatever." The girls dismissed me and left me to be gawked at by the other people in the kitchen.

This is off to a fantastic start.

I took a big gulp of my drink and fought my way through the crowd, following the sound of cheers I assumed were beer pong-related. I bumped into a couple groping each other and mumbled, "Sorry" as they gave me dirty looks.

The guy in front of me spun around and knocked his cup against mine, making my drink slosh up against the rim. I yelped as a few drops splattered on my sweater.

"I'm so sorry," he said.

"It's okay." I swiped at my sweater and started to move past him.

"Hang on a sec." He touched my arm. "I haven't seen you around before. You go to UMass?"

"No, I'm visiting a friend."

He held out his hand. "I'm Billy."

I tentatively shook it. "Liza."

He leaned toward me, still gripping my hand, and I got a strong whiff of beer, both from his cup and his breath. "Are you from Boston?"

"No, New York."

"You don't look like a New Yorker." His hooded eyes took a slow journey over my body, and my old instinct to flee from guys kicked in. I ripped my hand away, but he just moved closer.

"Why don't we go talk in my room where it's quieter?" he said.

Seriously? Do people really hook up like this?

"My friend is waiting for me."

I barreled through him and the dancing bodies around him, and I took a long inhale when I finally reached the dining area. It was the only brightly lit spot in the house with a lighted ceiling fan whirring over the table.

"There you are," Braden said. He was at one end of the table, lining up cups, and he had a drink in his hand that he was enjoying already.

"What did Sam get you?" He peered into my cup.

"Vodka and cranberry juice."

"Good choice. She tends to be heavy-handed on the vodka, so don't drink too fast."

A tall brunette slipped between Braden and Mike and put her arms around them. "Okay, your cheerleader is here. The game can begin."

"Hey, Tessa," Braden said. "This is my friend Liza."

I received another once-over, this one not as impressed. "Hey," she said before quickly turning back to Braden. "Gavin's having a midterm study sesh at his house tomorrow night. You have to come."

She had a firm grip on his bicep and stood no more than an inch from his face. She was even more handsy than Sam.

"I might stop by," Braden said, casually putting space between them. "I have a paper to finish."

"Prepare to be embarrassed again," Jason declared as he and the girl I assumed was Britt took their places at the opposite end of the table.

I retreated to a pocket of space among the other spectators, but Tessa stood right beside the table, chanting some cheer about Braden and Mike and balls. The game started, and every time she let out a flirty laugh or flipped her long hair over her shoulder, I took a swig. I needed a refill after three tosses of the ping pong ball.

"Where you going?" Braden asked.

I showed him my empty cup.

"You finished that already?"

"I'm okay. Sam must've been light-handed this time."

I started walking to the kitchen, and I felt myself leaning to one side. My feet wouldn't go in a straight line. I hadn't realized how woozy I was when I was standing still. *Guess I should've listened to Braden about drinking slowly.*

As I filled my cup with more juice than vodka, I noticed a girl staring at me like she was trying to put a name to my face. I didn't want a repeat of earlier, so I high-tailed it out of there, swaying slightly with each step on the laminate floor. Braden and Mike were losing badly, which delighted me because I had visions of Tessa laying congratulatory kisses on them (and me hurling the contents of my stomach everywhere).

I took smaller sips as I used the wall behind me for support, and I cheered inside when Jason scored the winning shot with a big bounce off the table. Braden and Mike emptied two more cups of beer, and Mike demanded they play two out of three to determine the winner. While Jason reset the table, Braden worked his way over.

"You doing okay?" he asked, his face a little flushed.

I held up my cup. "I slowed down the pace."

"That's good. I want you to be able to remember tonight," he said with a crooked grin. "I can forfeit this if you wanna do something else." He nodded to the table.

I really just wanted to talk to him or check out the music or do anything else, but if I asked him to quit, I'd be the wet blanket who ended the game. I wouldn't have any chance of blending in as a chill partygoer.

"As an Olympic athlete, I can never support quitting." I turned him toward the table. "Go finish this."

Tessa resumed her inane cheers, and I tried to tune her out by people watching. Everyone kept giving me long looks as they passed, and I supposed it was because I was the new girl. Just in case they recognized me, I brushed my hair around my face. Phil saw me and waved, and I perked up at finally seeing someone familiar, but he went in the opposite direction. I slouched back against the wall and became further acquainted with my cocktail. At least the music had been turned down so I could entertain myself by eavesdropping on the conversations around me. Braden did his best to include me in the game atmosphere, high-fiving me after a good shot or just making eye contact between tosses, but I still felt as if I was a square attempting to fit into this big circle.

Jason and Brittany earned another win, this time with a high arching shot, and I prayed they wouldn't decide to play three out of five. Braden and Mike drank up for the final time, and Tessa felt the need to give them sympathy hugs or whatever. She took her time releasing Braden, and she fisted his shirt while saying something in his ear. The fire in my chest grew hotter but not from the vodka.

You don't have any claim on him, I reminded myself. *You've known all along he has a life here that you're not a part of.*

He finished emptying his cup, and he turned away from Tessa and came over to me. All the beer had made him even more smiley than usual. He looked so damn cute that he made me smile too, despite my current mood. Some people became happy when they drank, but apparently I hadn't been blessed with that trait.

"Sorry I didn't bring you much luck," I said. "Guess I'm only valuable to the Sox."

"Did you see the couple of wicked shots I nailed? Those were all because of you."

"You don't have to do that."

"Do what?"

"Try to make me feel like I belong here."

He studied me a minute and then put his hands on my waist. I held my breath, not sure exactly what was happening. He pulled me away from the wall and into a hug, and I exhaled with disappointment as I put my arms around him.

"You do belong here," he mumbled into my hair.

He stroked my back, and I knew he was being extra affectionate because he was a little drunk, but I didn't care. I buried my face against his hard chest and closed my eyes. *THIS is where I belong.*

Someone backed into us, crashing our embrace, and I reluctantly had to let go. Jason called out Braden's name and said, "Britt and I can take on you and Liza next."

"Beer pong isn't really for me," I said.

"We need to get you into the action," Braden said. "Britt, what's a good game for a newbie drinker?"

"Hmm… what about Never Have I Ever?"

"Yes! That's perfect. Are you familiar with it?" he asked me.

I nodded, and he grabbed my hand. "I promised cliché, so I'm gonna deliver cliché."

He led me through the living room as he recruited

numerous players, including Ross and Sam. We all gathered near the couch, and Ross cleared out the two people sitting there, declaring it the official game zone.

"We have to do a pregame shot," he said.

He and Braden went to the kitchen, and they came back with a stack of cups and a bottle of tequila. When we all had our shots in hand, Ross said, "Bottoms up," and everyone drank. I recoiled from the smell of the liquor and even more from the bitter taste as I forced it down. *Okay, I did my one allotted shot. Another life experience down.*

I'd seen the game played on TV and had read about it in books, so I knew the premise and the rules. Since I hadn't done a lot of things in my sheltered life, I felt confident I wouldn't be getting plastered during this.

"Gotta play with a full cup," Sam said as she poured more vodka into mine. *No harm,* I thought, since I wouldn't be drinking much of it.

"Liza, you start us off," Braden said.

Everyone stared at me, and I scrambled to think of what to say. Did they normally do silly, fun stuff or did they do racy, probing stuff? I didn't want to sound lame, but no way was I going to throw out something salacious right off the bat.

"Never have I ever..." And then the perfect opener came to me. "Gone to college."

Braden laughed, and the others followed. "Nice," he said and tipped back his cup. "Take us all down in one shot."

I relaxed my grip on my cup and let out a breath. First test passed.

Sam surveyed the group while tapping her chin. "Never have I ever..." She gave me a sidelong glance. "Gone to the Olympics."

"Payback!" Ross said from his seat above us on the back of the couch.

"That's fair." I nodded and took a drink. The warmth from my vodka-filled gulp seeped into my veins.

Ross cleared his throat loudly. "Never have I ever thought about someone else during sex."

A collective groan came from the group. I immediately looked at Braden, and he didn't lift his cup. Sam, on the other hand, knocked back a long swig from hers. I could only guess who her fantasy guy had been since her eyes went everywhere but on Braden. I wanted to drink even though I didn't have to.

"Ross, you know you've done that," Brittany said. "You'd better drink."

"I am always focused only on my lady," he said.

Brittany let out a dry laugh. "Okay, my turn. Never have I ever had the hots for a teacher."

Mr. Lanotte. Or "Mr. La-Hottie" as my fellow sophomores and I used to call him. The image of my young English teacher burst into my mind – dimples, wire-rimmed glasses, button-downs with the sleeves always rolled up. I smiled to myself as I sipped my drink.

Braden and Ross both drank and then pointed to each other. "Miss Foster!" they said in tandem.

"I wanna play," Tessa said, squeezing onto the coffee table between two guys whose names I didn't know.

"B, you're up," Ross said.

"Never have I ever..." He paused and set his eyes on me. "Kissed a guy."

My face flamed, and I looked down at my cup. Sam, Brittany, and Tessa cried out with indignation. "Cheap shot at the girls," Brittany said.

When I didn't drink, I felt everyone staring at me. "Wait, are you gay?" Tessa asked.

"No, I'm not gay," I said quietly.

"But you've never kissed a guy?" Brittany gaped at me.

I peeked up at Braden, shooting laser darts at him. Why had he zeroed in on me? I'd told him I hadn't dated anyone before him, but I never told him I hadn't kissed anyone.

One of the coffee table guys raised his hand. "I volunteer

to be the first!"

"No, pick me," another voice said.

"We should play Spin the Bottle," the other guy sitting on the table said.

The heat from my face spread and scorched my neck and my scalp. I was the freak again, the girl who belonged more at a high school sleepover than a college party.

"B, didn't you take Liza on a few dates? How did you not kiss the girl?" Ross asked.

Oh, God, the humiliation is just getting worse.

Braden was slack-jawed as he avoided looking at me. "We're just," he stuttered. "We're just friends."

The overheating of my face combined with the warmth of the room had me smothering, and the wooziness I'd been experiencing hit me with a sudden harder punch. I couldn't sit there any longer being scrutinized.

"I need some air." I stood up and wobbled around the coffee table.

"I'll go with you." Braden jumped up and knocked over his chair, tripping on the legs while trying to follow me.

"I'm fine alone," I said.

When I stepped outside, I heard the light tap of raindrops on the roof. The overhang only covered the top step, so I huddled there with my knees to my chest. The fresh air cleared some of my shakiness, but it was colder than I'd expected. I wrapped my arms around my shins and rested my chin on my knees.

A few quiet, peaceful minutes passed before the door opened, and a couple of people streamed out and stumbled past me into the rain. I wished I could go downstairs and lay down, but Braden had locked the apartment when we left.

Another person emerged from the house, but he plopped down beside me instead of leaving. It was the guy who'd suggested we play Spin the Bottle.

"A few of us duked it out, and I won the honor of being

your first kiss." He hooked his scrawny arm around me. "So, how 'bout we do this already?"

"What?" I shot to my feet, and all the blood rushed from my head. I quickly grabbed the stair railing.

"You okay?"

I turned and saw Braden in the doorway. He glared at Annoying Guy.

"Dude, what the hell?"

"I'm trying to help out since you dropped the ball with her."

"Get out of here. Now." Braden stood over him, tight and angry. I'd never seen him so intense.

The guy got to his feet, and Braden had about six inches on him. He hesitated for a moment but then headed for the door. "You gonna take care of business now?" he snorted as he went inside.

I put my hand to my forehead and lowered myself slowly onto the step. *No more sudden movements.*

"You alright?" Braden asked as he sat beside me, almost missing the step with his butt.

"Just a little dizzy." I put my head down, hoping to regain blood flow. "I guess I should thank you for not telling everyone I was the one who dropped the ball on our first date, but I'm kinda pissed at you for starting the whole conversation."

"I'm sorry. I didn't know it would get blown up like that."

"Why did you look at me when you said, 'Never have I ever kissed a guy?' How did you know I haven't?"

"I didn't know for sure. I was... I was curious."

"You could've asked me when we were alone instead of humiliating me in front of everyone."

"I'm so sorry. I didn't mean to do that."

"Now I have random guys trying to kiss me." I shuddered as I remembered Annoying Guy leering at me.

"I won't let that happen."

I gingerly lifted my head to look at him. "What are you going to do? Be my bodyguard the rest of the night?"

He pushed up the sleeve of his polo and flexed his bicep. "I can take 'em all."

I had to laugh a little at his seriousness and the idea of me needing a bodyguard.

"I'm not joking. None of those idiots are getting near you. You deserve so much better than that." He still sounded serious, but his voice had grown softer. "You deserve to have the most amazing first kiss from someone who really knows you and who appreciates you... and all the wonderful things about you."

My heart slammed against my ribcage. Only one dim lightbulb burned above us, but Braden was close enough for me to see the intensity in his brown eyes. I let my gaze wander to his lips, and I heard Holly screaming, "Go for it!" All I had to do was lean into him and it would happen. The moment I'd been dreaming about, writing about for months would happen.

The door burst open, and a girl came out yelling into her phone. I rubbed my arms and took slow breaths to match my decelerating pulse. *It's an omen. You're not supposed to cross that line.*

"Let's go back inside," Braden said. "We can just hang out. No more games."

"And no more drinks for me," I said. "Or I won't be able to make it down the stairs."

I wasn't wild about the prospect of people staring at me with wonder/disbelief/curiosity again, but I had to find a way to ignore them and just have fun with Braden. And if I was lucky, maybe I'd get to see him go into bodyguard mode again. Because that had been seriously hot.

The game had ended while we'd been gone, and Jason and Brittany were now dancing atop the coffee table. The music had been turned up, and almost the whole living room had become a dance floor. Brittany saw me and hopped down, choking me with a hug.

"I'm sorry we made you feel bad," she said. "You keep holding out for that first kiss until it's the perfect guy, and it'll be *so good.*"

I looked at Braden over her shoulder, and I physically ached at how close that so-good moment had just been. I could tell myself over and over it wasn't the right time, but I couldn't control the longing in my heart.

"Come dance with us." Brittany took my hand and spun us around.

Braden joined us, and as we all let loose to the hip hop music, I finally got the happy effect of being buzzed. Phil taught me some basic pop and lock moves, while I showed off my ability to do a full split in a standing position. We danced until we could barely stand, and I was sweating when Braden, Phil, and I trekked downstairs. Sam had checked out a while ago, and Ross was cozied up with a girl next to the keg.

I collapsed on Braden's bed and pulled out my phone, which I hadn't looked at in hours. Two missed calls and three texts from Court made me sit up with alarm.

Get on Instagram!

Someone tagged you in a pic

It's a stealth photo

Crap!

I found the picture which showed me watching Braden play beer pong. The caption read – *Look who's partying with us tonight. #IcePrincess*

My fingers flew over the screen, removing the tag and making sure there was no other evidence of me in Boston. Mom not only monitored what I posted on social media. She also searched for all tags and mentions of my name. She'd been known to surf the internet during her bouts of insomnia, so the fact that it was three in the morning didn't mean I was safe. My only comfort was I didn't have any texts from her, so I may have destroyed the evidence in time.

I laid back on the bed and hugged the pillow to my body. What a day, what a weekend it had been. Even if Mom had busted me, it would've been worth it. Sure, I'd had some low moments, but the highs... strolling through the inspiring campus, dancing and laughing so hard I couldn't breathe, seeing how Braden had looked at me on the stairs. I wouldn't be able to explain it to anyone, but I felt like I'd really gone through something the past two days.

I felt like I'd *lived*.

CHAPTER THIRTEEN

IN MY SUBURBAN DETROIT HOTEL ROOM I paced between the window and the closet, continuously refreshing the Skate America results on my phone. Court and Josh were skating their short program downtown at Joe Louis Arena, but I had to stay at the hotel to get ready for my own short that afternoon. I tapped once more on the link and pumped my fist when I saw they'd received a personal best score. They were in a strong position to win a medal tomorrow.

I stopped in front of the mirror and did a quick check of my hair and makeup. I'd spent over an hour on my meticulous process. It included applying multiple shades of eyeliner and shadow to make my eyes bright and visible to the people sitting in the top row. Before I glammed up, I'd had a small meal and had taken a thirty-minute nap, another part of my pregame routine. Keeping a standard schedule helped me feel focused and prepared for the competition.

Unfortunately, it didn't help me feel less anxious.

The ladies' field at the event was packed with tough competitors from around the world, so I needed to be in midseason form even though Skate America was only the first event of the Grand Prix series. My two biggest competitors were Katia Safina, a seventeen-year-old jumping wizard from Russia, and Yuki Yamashiro, the Japanese champion known for her graceful style. I'd beaten both of them at worlds in March, but this was a new season, and they'd been practicing their short programs for months while I'd only had mine for six weeks.

A text message from Braden popped up, and I clicked to read it while grabbing my puffer vest from the closet. It was about time for me to head to the skater shuttle bus.

Braden: **Wishing you one last GOOD LUCK though you don't need it. You're going to slay so hard.**

I smiled and zipped my vest.

Me: **Thanks! Leaving now for the arena. Nervous, excited, terrified. All the normal pre-skate feels.**

Braden: **Just be your awesome self and no one can touch you.**

Me: ☺

Me: **Gotta run. Talk to you later!**

I rolled my bag with my costume and skates down to the lobby, where I wasn't surprised to see Mom waiting for me. She attended every one of my competitions and always met up with me before I got on the bus. She looked her usual chic self in a rose-colored silk blouse and dark wool pants.

She gave me a tight hug, and I took comfort in the familiarity of her embrace. Despite her smothering, I couldn't imagine not having her at my events. Early in my career, she'd driven me a little nuts constantly comparing her skating career to mine, but she'd learned that I just wanted to focus on the present. And unlike some overbearing skating moms, she left the coaching to Dad and never critiqued my performances; she just provided a sounding board and unconditional support.

"You look so beautiful, so sophisticated." She fingered the end of my sleek ponytail. "Remember when you used to need me to do your hair and makeup?"

"Mom, please don't get sentimental on me right now. I have enough emotions already."

"Sorry, I'll save the memories for another time." She embraced me again. "Have fun and skate great. I love you."

I gave her an extra-long squeeze. "Love you, too."

She went toward the elevators and I headed for the door, but a small group of Japanese fans stopped me for pictures. I tried to hide my nervousness behind a big smile as they snapped numerous photos. They enthusiastically wished me luck, and I thanked them and took hold of my bag again.

"Can I have another autograph?" a voice behind me asked.

I spun and then froze at the sight of Braden standing in front of me. He had on a navy Red Sox hoodie and jeans, and his presence in the lobby of a skating event was so out of context that I thought I might be hallucinating.

"How..." I sputtered.

"We drove all night." He grinned and swallowed me in a hug. "I had to come cheer you on."

While Mom's embrace had given me a moment of calmness, Braden's got my heart pumping harder, and it had already been working overtime from anxiety. I was definitely not hallucinating.

"When I looked at the map and it said twelve hours to Detroit, I knew I had to do it." He stepped back and stared at me. "Wow, you look so different."

I was still so shocked to see him that I couldn't formulate a response.

"Not bad different," he quickly said with a smile. "I'm just not used to seeing you with so much makeup. You look like a superstar."

I finally found my voice. "I can't believe you're here."

"I can't believe I finally get to see you compete. This is the best road trip idea I've ever had."

My mind hadn't caught up to the conversation and was

still processing what he'd said two minutes ago. "Did you say 'we' drove all night?"

"Sam and Phil came with me. Phil was all about driving his new car up here."

Sam tagged along? Shocking.

"Are you guys staying here?" I asked.

"Yeah, we were able to snag a room. We can all hang out tonight and watch the game."

My worlds were colliding, and my head was spinning. I had a routine, a schedule I followed at events. Anything outside that routine had to be carefully considered because nothing could interfere with my competition readiness.

"I'll have to see," I said. "I need to get on the bus before it leaves. I'll text you later."

I had to run away from him before he might hug me again. His touch did things to my body that made it shaky and unstable – two problems I could not have right now.

During the ride downtown, I put in my earbuds and blasted my competition playlist – a mix of pop, rock, and a few inspirational ballads. I gazed out the window at the freeway, but all I could see was Braden's smiling face. He was going to be in the audience watching me. Not hundreds of miles away, sitting in front of his laptop, but right there in the building where I could feel his eyes on me.

Must.Not.Think.About.That.

I'd been excited about him coming to nationals in Boston in January, but I had time to mentally prepare for it. I had zero time to prepare for this. Never in a million years did I think he'd pop up in Detroit.

The bus pulled up to the arena, and I kept my music playing as I entered the building. Two TV cameramen jumped in front of me and held their cameras on me for my entire walk to the locker room. When I came out to stretch and do my office walkthrough, the lenses found me again. I could sense them zooming in extra tight as Dad hugged me and then stepped aside to let me warm up.

I followed my standard routine, using the backstage corridor as my warm-up area, and I walked through my choreography with "Nostalgia" piped into my earbuds. My competitors went through similar paces around me, but I focused only on my own movements. Each stretch awakened my muscles and prepared me for the two and a half minutes I had to be on the ice.

As the time ticked closer to my on-ice warm-up, I put on my fuchsia costume and my skates and paced in the hallway to stay loose (and also because my twitchy limbs wouldn't stop moving). Dad and Kathy stood nearby, but they remained quiet. They knew this was my "getting into the zone" time, and I used it to give myself an internal rah-rah session.

You are the world champion.

You've won Skate America three times.

You are a fierce jumping machine.

No one can touch you.

Thinking of Braden's last text made me think of his presence out there in the audience. Where was he sitting? Had my mom seen him? Did he have any idea how much I wanted to wow him?

You can't think like that. Do not try to wow anyone. Just skate how you do in practice every day.

The cameraman inched closer to me, so I knew it was time to walk to the ice. The five other girls in my warm-up group marched ahead of me, and I took two deep breaths before stepping into the arena.

The bright lights played off the shiny stones on our costumes, creating a sea of popping sparkles, like flashbulbs firing. I tucked my name pendant inside my halter neckline and locked my eyes on the clean sheet of ice. The crowd hummed with anticipation for our group, the top six skaters in the event, but I didn't let myself look up at the faces. I had to shut out all of it.

"Would the following competitors please take the ice – from Japan–"

I tuned out the announcer and took off my blade guards, handing them to Dad. A roar accompanied my name, and I shot off across the ice. Speeding around the other skaters, I took long strides, slowly breathing in the cool air that rushed over my face. After the quick stroking session, I started my first jump setup. We only had six minutes to warm up, so I had to maximize the time. Since I was skating last in the group and had the longest wait, I needed to go full-out and practice all my jumps and spins.

A jumping lane opened up between Katia and Yuki, so I sped toward it and launched myself into the air, completing three tight rotations on the triple Lutz and then three more on the triple toe. Another loud cheer went up and an even louder "Go Liza!" from a familiar deep voice. It sounded so close to the corner behind me.

Do not look over there. Next jump now!

I pumped my legs harder and quickly moved through the traffic to complete my triple flip. Same with the double Axel. I took a breather to get a sip of water at the boards, and Dad demonstrated a slight break in form he'd seen on my flip takeoff. I listened intently while I used a tissue on my runny nose.

I spent the rest of the six minutes on my spins and doing a brief cooldown. Dad gave me my guards and my Team USA jacket, and I led the pack backstage that time. I found a quiet spot near the medical room and listened to my "waiting" playlist, which contained mostly classical and calming music.

Closing my eyes, I tried to lose myself in the soothing violin concerto, but I couldn't shake my jumpiness. My knees bounced up and down as I sat on the metal folding chair. I just wanted to get on the ice and get this performance out of the way. The first statement of the Grand Prix season was such an important one, and I had to make it with a program I hadn't quite mastered yet.

Thirty minutes later I finally stood a few feet from the ice, moments away from my turn in the spotlight. Katia had just finished her program, and as soon as she exited through the ice door I entered the field of play, the place I'd dominated the past two seasons. As I circled the rink, loosening my legs again, the announcer read Katia's score. When I heard "seventy," my shoulders tensed. Anything in that range was world-podium level.

I glided toward the corner of the rink, and I thought I saw a Red Sox hoodie in the blur of people. I swung my gaze away and skidded to a stop in front of Dad and Kathy at the boards. Dad covered my hands with his, and I put my tunnel vision on his face.

"Take your time. Breathe through each step," he said. "Just another run-through."

I bobbed my head and let out a breath. *Just another run-through.*

He patted my hands, and I skated away as the announcer introduced me, "Representing the United States... please welcome Liza Petrov."

I raised my arms and smiled to acknowledge the cheers and the high-pitched screams of my younger fans. As they quieted down another "Go, Liza!" cut through the silence. It was the same voice I'd heard earlier.

No one important is watching, I lied to myself. *It's just you and a bunch of nameless faces.*

I settled into my opening pose, hands clasped behind my back, but squeezing my fingers together couldn't stop their trembling. The music filled the arena, and after the initial piano notes I began to move. The first section of "Nostalgia" was slow, so I took soft strokes into my opening element, the combination spin. I counted the necessary revolutions in my head as I curved my body into a horizontal donut shape. Once I stood upright I took a few steps and went right into the sit spin, turning in time with the new age piano beat.

With two of the three required spins done, I measured my breathing to prepare for the jumps. Flying across the ice, I hit the double Axel right on the final note of the slow section. The tempo of the music quickened, and I matched my strokes to it as I began the footwork into the triple flip. Picking into the ice, I went up and spun three times, and I came down on my right blade for a clean landing. The only jumping pass I had left was the triple Lutz-triple toe combination.

The music heightened in intensity, and I skated faster than I ever had, leaving a hurricane-force breeze in my wake. Zooming to the other end of the rink, I turned my back to the boards and sailed in reverse on my left skate. I felt like I could fly up into the rafters I had so much energy. I stabbed my toe pick into the ice and went to pull in my arms for the Lutz, but I had no control of my lower body. My legs didn't come together like they should, and I stayed wide open in the air, coming down on both feet with no rotations completed. Everyone in the crowd gasped, sucking the air out of the building.

I'd popped the combination.

I'd popped the most critical element in the program.

It was worth ten points, and I'd earned zero.

I kept moving, gliding into the step sequence, but I was numb. My muscle memory took over as I completed the end-to-end footwork and the last element, the layback spin. When I finished the spin on the final beat of the song, the audience gave me warm and sympathetic applause, and my die-hard young fans still shrieked with excitement. They didn't know the ramifications of what I'd just done. Or *not* done.

With a weak smile on my face, I bowed to each side of the arena. A few stuffed animals and flower bouquets landed on the ice, and the little sweeper girls swarmed around me to pick them up. I headed for Dad and Kathy, my smile now gone. They both looked as grim as I expected, but Dad gave me a hug and said, "It's just the first competition."

I slipped on my guards and my jacket, and we moved onto the bench in the kiss and cry to wait for my score. I could see the commentary burning Kathy's tongue, but with a camera on us, she wasn't going to make her feelings known just yet.

Dad put his arm around me and rubbed my shoulder, and I stared down at my water bottle. I couldn't bring myself to look at the replay of my aborted jump on the monitor in front of us.

"I was just so amped up," I mumbled. "It got away from me somehow."

The announcer came over the PA system, and I dug my nails into the carpeted bench. How low was the number going to be?

"The short program score... sixty-one point two six. She is currently in sixth place."

A murmur went through the crowd, and I lowered my head and wished I could rewind time just a few minutes. I could do that combination cleanly ninety-nine out of a hundred times. Not just cleanly but better than anyone else in the world. What the hell had gone wrong in that moment?

Dad and Kathy flanked me as we walked backstage, but I had to leave them to face the media in the mixed zone. I wouldn't be invited to the press conference because it was for the top three in the standings only. When was the last time I hadn't been in that position at an event? I couldn't even remember.

I had no good explanation to give the reporters for my huge mistake, but I told each one of them I would come out fighting tomorrow in the free skate. They all reminded me that I'd have to be perfect to have any chance of winning. As if I didn't know that already.

Before I made it to the locker room to change out of my costume, Kathy corralled me away from the bustle backstage for the talk I'd been anticipating. With the cameras gone, I steeled myself for her thoughts on my performance.

"I knew when you picked this new song that it was too fast," she said. "You rushed through the whole second half of the program. All your timing was off."

She hadn't expressed any concern about the music over the past six weeks that I'd been practicing with it, and *now* she was going to bitch about it and pretend she knew better?

"You said the song for my original program was too slow, and now this one is too fast? What will make you happy?" I snapped.

She crossed her arms and used the height of her five-inch heels to tower over me with authority. "What will make me happy is my student respecting my opinion."

"Your opinion has been to fight my dad on every idea and every decision he makes."

"I was right about having the combination late in the program, wasn't I? You had no chance to make up any of the points you lost on it."

"I think you're happy I messed up so you can say, 'I told you so.'"

"You think I wanted that to happen? For my world champion to be buried in the standings and thoroughly embarrass me?"

Tears of anger and frustration pooled in my eyes, and I was *not* going to cry in the middle of the hallway. "I have to get changed," I said.

I avoided looking at anyone in the locker room while I discreetly blotted my eyes. As I shoved my costume into my bag, I stifled the scream I wanted to let out. I could not take Kathy and her attitude any more. When was Dad going to see that she only cared about her image and how my skating benefited her?

My phone buzzed with a text, and I pulled it from the bag's side pocket.

Braden: **Are you okay?**

I didn't need to ponder that question.

Me: **Not really**

I slipped the phone back into its pocket and took off for the shuttle, again avoiding eye contact. Dad fell in line behind me and followed me to the back of the bus. He had the protocol sheets in his hand.

"You got level four on everything and the PCS were right where they should be." He folded the pink papers. "So, what happened on the combo? You never pop jumps."

"I don't know," I said tersely. "I just felt like I had to go faster. I had to get it done to prove that I'm ready for this season."

"You are ready for this season. Your practices have been great. Your warm-up was great. It's not like you to let the pressure get to you."

"It wasn't the pressure. It was almost like I was too excited or something." The possibility that my excitement had been subconsciously due to Braden's presence was something I wouldn't be sharing with Dad.

"You might've been excited today, but tomorrow I know you'll be angry, and you'll use that anger in the most positive way. No one is more dangerous on the ice than you when you're mad."

"I'm not just mad about the combo. Dad, I don't want Kathy at the boards tomorrow."

He sighed. "Liza, you can't–"

"She doesn't care about me. All she cares about is getting an Olympic gold medal on her resume. Ever since I won my first world title, she's made everything more and more about herself. She wants to be quoted in every article about me. She wants to be in all the news videos of my training. She hates that I rely more on you and your opinion, and she acts like she's the all-knowing queen of coaches. I can't take it anymore."

"I understand everything you're saying, but if we fire her now, especially after a big mistake like you made today, it's going to start all kinds of rumors," he said. "If you want to cut back your lessons with her to a couple of days a month, you can do that."

"That's not good enough. I'm telling you that I don't want to take any lessons from her and I don't want her at my competitions. She cannot come to Paris," I said, thinking ahead to my next Grand Prix event in four weeks.

"The arrangements have already been made."

"They can be cancelled. Dad, this is *my* career, *my* dream. Why shouldn't I be able to do what I know is best for me?"

"I'm just trying to protect you from the potential backlash. She's been coaching you for so long that everyone is going to have questions about why you're letting her go."

"I'll just tell them I'm tired of traveling between two cities and I want to have a steady training schedule this year, the most important year of my life. People make up BS excuses to give the media all the time. That's what my publicist is for."

He looked at me a long time, and I thought I might finally have gotten through to him.

"Sweetheart, you have to trust me that I'm making the right call here," he said.

I didn't respond to him. I plugged my ears with music and closed my eyes for the remainder of the ride to the hotel. Storming into the lobby, the first people I saw were Braden, Sam, and Phil at a table in the elevated section. Behind me I was sure Dad saw them, too. I was embarrassed that they'd all seen me flop after Braden had probably hyped me as the greatest skater of all time, but I couldn't ignore them since they were staring right at me.

I went over to them, and Braden shot up to give me a hug. I made it the quickest one we'd ever shared.

"Thanks for coming all this way," I said. "Sorry I didn't give you guys much to cheer about."

"You were amazing," Braden said.

"You didn't fall," Sam offered.

"Falling would've been better than popping," I said. "At least if I'd tried the jump I would've gotten a few points."

Braden put his hand on my back. "It was still a great performance even with the one mistake."

"It was a ten-point mistake."

"But you can come back from that. I remember you telling me how people have made up big deficits to win."

"It's possible, but I have no room for error now."

They were all silent, and the uncomfortableness draped further over us. This was why having my worlds collide wasn't a good idea. My family and my friends in the skating world understood the ups and downs of the sport. People on the outside did not.

"Why don't you come get dinner with us and then watch the game? It'll help take your mind off everything," Braden said.

"I need my mind to be on skating, and the game doesn't start until after eight. I have to get to bed early to be ready for practice in the morning."

Phil and Sam exchanged glances at my pissy tone, and Braden said, "Can we talk alone for a sec?"

We moved over to the corner of the lobby, and I watched Dad observing us from afar as he talked on his phone. Braden shoved his hands in his jeans pockets and shuffled his Converse.

"I feel like you're upset with me for coming here," he said.

"I'm not upset. I'm just... I don't like surprises at competitions, and you popped up out of nowhere right before I had to compete."

"I'm sorry. I didn't think it would be a bad thing. I just wanted you to know you had extra support here for you."

"I know you meant well. It's just that things here are

really intense, and I need to have my head in the right place at all times."

"I thought having friends around would help you be less stressed."

Out of the corner of my eye I spotted Mom heading for us, and my stress level jumped up another twenty notches. *Just when I thought this day couldn't get any worse.*

"Hello," she said. "You must be Braden."

He stuck out his hand. "Hi, it's great to meet you."

She shook it while giving him a full appraisal with her dark eyes. "Liza didn't tell me you would be here."

"She didn't know. I surprised her earlier."

"Oh." Mom slowly nodded. "Well, that was nice of you to travel so far."

"Do you want to walk with me upstairs?" I asked her in hopes of ending this latest episode of my worlds colliding.

"Yes, let's do that. It was nice to meet you, Braden."

"Same here." He touched my arm. "Call me later if you have time. We'll be hanging out here all night."

"Okay," I said and hustled Mom toward the elevator.

"He's a very dedicated friend to make that long of a trip for you," Mom said, the suspicion in her eyes obvious.

"He would do it for any of his friends." I punched the elevator button. "That's just the kind of guy he is."

"Did you see him before you left for the arena?"

"Yeah, right after I talked to you."

She looked back at the lobby before stepping into the elevator, and then she put her scrutinizing glare on me. "Is he the reason you weren't yourself on the ice?"

My defenses shot up, and I stared at the floor numbers to avoid facing Mom's penetrating look. I might question myself about whether Braden affected my performance, but no one else was allowed to go there.

"It had nothing to do with him. That was all me rushing too much."

The elevator dinged for my floor, and I started through the door. Mom pushed the button to hold it open.

"Do you want any company for dinner?" she asked.

She knew my post-skate ritual of eating in my room, where fans and officials couldn't take notes on my mood or the food on my plate. I'd once read an entire play-by-play of my meal on a skating message board.

"No, thanks. I think I'll watch a movie. Something funny and light."

"Okay. I guess I'll see you in the morning then. Love you."

I retreated to my room, which I happily found empty. I loved rooming with Court, but sometimes I needed solitude. I just wanted to decompress and relax not only my body but my brain.

I kicked off my sneakers and carried the room service menu and my tablet to the bed. I went to click on the Netflix app, but my finger hovered near Twitter. Dad reminded me again and again not to read social media during competitions, but I had a hard time resisting the temptation. The messages of support were always a great boost. It was just the nasty internet trolls who posed a potential hazard.

Clicking on Twitter, I decided to scroll through my feed first to see if there were any interesting posts by people I followed. I came upon one from Sam.

In Detroit watching figure skating. There's something I never thought I'd say.

And I'd never thought I'd see her in Detroit watching me skate, so I supposed we were on the same page. Summoning my courage, I peeked through my fingers and clicked on my Twitter notifications tab, which contained all Tweets directed at me. The first few were positive, so I kept reading.

LOVE your new short! You're gonna hit that combo tomorrow!

Shake off today. You're still the bestest of the best.

So proud of your fight out there today!

Sixth place is perfect for a spoiled bitch like you.

I flipped the tablet over and pressed it face down on the bed. Despite the number of insults I'd received over the years, I still got a sick feeling in my stomach every time I read a new one. What possessed people to spew so much hate? And to a person they'd never even met?

A soft knock sounded on the door, and I checked the peephole first. Em stood alone in the hallway, still in her dress and heels from coaching Court and Josh at the pairs event. I let her in, and she hugged me before saying anything.

"I came to see if I could talk you into dinner downstairs. I know you want to stay away from prying eyes, but Quinn and Alex would love to have you there."

"Using the twins to guilt trip me?" I smiled a little.

"Their adorable faces have a lot of power," she said.

"I don't like disappointing them, but I wouldn't be great company, and I already turned down my mom."

"She can join us, too."

"Thanks, but I have to pass. I might be tempted to get into it again with Dad about Kathy, and that wouldn't be good dinner conversation."

"Can we talk a minute about that?"

Em had been my ally on many issues, so I hoped she was going to tell me she'd try to change Dad's mind. I sat on the edge of my bed, and she sat on Court's, smoothing her red dress.

"It might seem like your dad is being overly cautious with your career, but it's only because of the issues we had when he was coaching me. Both of my Olympic seasons had so much drama, and he doesn't want you to go through that. He's so afraid of making the wrong move and letting you down."

"He wouldn't be letting me down. I'll take full responsibility for firing Kathy. It's my decision."

"It is, but he just wants to be sure you're making the right one."

My head hurt from going in circles. I pulled my ponytail loose and slipped the rubber band around my wrist. "What happened in the past when he was coaching you is totally different from my situation. He needs to understand that."

"Maybe you can try talking to him again when we get home and emotions aren't so high."

"Maybe." I was tired of talking about it with no action, and what I wanted more than anything at the moment was to be alone again.

I stood and walked toward the door. "I need to take a shower before I order food."

Em got the message and followed me to the door. After she left I spent a long time in the hot shower, letting the steam and the warmth of the water unwind the knots all over my body. Eating dinner and escaping reality with the romantic comedy *13 Going on 30* further eased my tension. Its sweet fluffiness was the perfect mood lightener for me.

I checked the time on my phone and remembered the first pitch of the Sox game was in a few minutes. I pictured Braden, Sam, and Phil in their room, laughing and joking as they geared up for the big playoff contest. I'd had so much fun watching the game with Braden and Ross at their apartment. Why shouldn't I be able to hang out with Braden now?

It only took two seconds for my voice of reason to answer. If I went to his room, I'd get sucked in and wouldn't want to leave after just an hour. I saw him so infrequently that any time with him was like an oasis in the desert. I'd end up staying for the whole three-hour game, and I'd be dragging when my alarm went off in the morning for practice.

Hanging out might not be an option, but calling him to apologize was something I needed to do. I dialed his number, and he picked up after the first ring.

"Hey, I was just about to text you," he said. The sound of the TV plus Sam and Phil talking loudly filled up the background.

"You were?"

"Yeah, just wanted to see how you're doing." The voices quieted as it sounded like a door closed.

"I'm sorry I was so short with you earlier. I was mad at myself and my dad and I took it out on you."

"You don't have to apologize. I should've given you a heads up that I was coming."

"It was totally acceptable for you to want to surprise me. You didn't do anything wrong."

"Maybe so, but you have a lot on your mind, and I should've thought about that. I might be a huge sports fan, but I've never been on the inside like this. I didn't really have a grasp of how the smallest thing can affect your mindset."

Oh, honey, you are so NOT a small thing to me.

"I told you I get a little crazy during competition season. I just didn't think you'd see it so soon."

"You're not crazy. You have incredible drive, and you're trying to achieve the ultimate greatness. Anyone in your position is going to be wound up sometimes."

I pushed the room service tray aside so I could stretch my legs over the blanket. "I really do appreciate you being here. You gave up your whole weekend to schlep to Detroit."

"Yeah, I'm missing so much. Bowling and beer pong will be there next weekend."

I laughed. "If the Sox win tonight and make the World Series, you'll be missing a big celebration at home."

"We're all set for our own party here. Sam and Phil raided the gas station for snacks." He paused. "Any chance you can join us?"

Knowing he was so close, possibly just down the hall, made it *so* hard to say no. I looked down at my pajamas. It wouldn't take but a few minutes to make myself presentable.

And once I got to Braden's room it would take me three hours to realize what a mistake I'd made.

"I wish I could, but I should stay hunkered down here. Court will be back soon, so I'll have a buddy to watch the first few innings with before lights out."

"Is there somewhere I can see you tomorrow after your practice?" he asked. "See, I'm scheduling in advance this time. No surprises."

I smiled. "I have to eat breakfast when I come back, so I'll text you after I'm done."

"Cool. I'll see you then."

CHAPTER FOURTEEN

I POKED THE LAST PIECE OF melon on my plate and reached for my phone as I chewed. The late-morning breakfast crowd in the hotel restaurant was thin, so there weren't any gawkers Tweeting about the big blueberry muffin I'd eaten. While I brought the phone screen to life, Mom stared at me across the table.

"I hope you're not reading social media," she said.

Too late for that.

"I'm texting Braden so we can meet up in a few minutes."

Mom combed her fingers through her short bob. "I have to give him credit. He's stuck around a lot longer than I thought he would."

"Gee, thanks. I didn't realize I was such terrible friend material."

"That's not what I meant. Anyone would be lucky to have you as a friend. I just meant that as a college boy I thought his attention would wander since there's no chance of you sleeping with him."

"Oh my God, Mom." I covered my face. "Not every college guy is a manwhore."

"It's very common behavior."

"How do you know?" I had to laugh. "From watching reruns of *Beverly Hills, 90210?*"

"You don't know any more than I do. You've never seen what goes on at his apartment."

A rebuttal edged onto my tongue, and I clamped my lips shut. I had firsthand knowledge of the goings-on at Braden's apartment, and none of the guys had brought home girls when I was there. The only girl around was pesky Sam.

I typed a message to Braden and received an immediate reply to come up to his room. I wiped my mouth with the linen napkin and pushed back my chair.

"I'll see you before I get on the bus?" I asked even though I knew Mom would be in her usual spot.

"Of course, sweetheart. Try to get some rest."

I only got two steps out of the restaurant and into the lobby before a cluster of fans rushed me for pictures. As I smiled for the last one, Quinn and Alex ran over and the fangirls turned their attention to getting photos with Em. Seven years later, her Olympic gold still brought her admiration as well as opportunities and endorsements. With her earnings and her connections, she'd been able to set up a scholarship fund for skaters in financial need, and it had grown bigger every year. Seeing how her life had benefited from the gold medal gave me an idea of what I might experience if I won. Both Em and my agent Kristin had told me there would be no limit to my opportunities.

"Liza, did you see the game?" Alex asked.

"I only saw the first three innings, but I heard we won!"

"Dad's gonna get us tickets to the World Series!"

"That's awesome. I went the last time they made it, and it was so much fun."

My phone dinged with a text.

Braden: **You still coming up?**

Me: **Yep got delayed in the lobby.**

"Okay, munchkins, give me hugs for luck." I spread my arms wide.

They squeezed me until I couldn't breathe, and I raced to the elevator before anyone else could stop me. I only had to knock once on Braden's door for him to open it.

"How late did you guys stay up celebrating?" I asked. The desk was loaded with soft drinks and bags of chips and candy, but they were all neatly arranged, surely thanks to Phil.

"Sam crashed first from the sugar high around two," Braden said.

She sat stretched out on one of the beds, and she looked up from her phone. "I never should've eaten that whole bag of jelly beans."

Phil was laying on his stomach on the same bed, watching SportsCenter. "I tried to stop you, and I got called a party pooper. Now who's wishing she'd been a pooper, too?" He tickled her ankle.

She let out a yelp/laugh and jerked her leg away, and Phil chuckled. "What was that?"

"You didn't know that's her weak spot?" Braden said. "If you ever need information out of her, always go for the ankle."

I didn't like thinking about Braden's knowledge of Sam's body or him touching any part of her. Especially not now when I needed to keep my mind clear of disturbances. Maybe it had been a mistake to go up there.

"Interesting," Phil said and slowly tiptoed his fingers across the blanket to Sam's other leg.

"Don't you dare." She pulled both knees up to her chest.

"How was practice?" Braden asked me.

I refocused on him. "Good. I did almost a full run-through and it felt great. I just need to chill the next couple of hours."

"You have to beat that little Russian girl," Sam said. "She was way too perky for me, and her costume was ridiculous."

"Was that the one who looked like a circus exploded all over her?" Phil asked.

"That's definitely Katia," I said.

"These two had a running commentary going about the costumes and the music while we were watching," Braden said.

"We had to do something to loosen you up," Phil said and looked at me. "He was chewing all his fingernails off before you skated."

"Really?" I smiled.

Braden's cheeks turned a light shade of pink. "I had full confidence in you. The competition atmosphere was just very intense."

"You should see my mom when I skate. The TV cameras catch her all the time, and she's hunched over in her seat, hands on both sides of her face, ready to cover her eyes at any moment. She's a mess."

"I don't know how she's watched so many competitions over the years," Braden said. "It's damn nerve-wracking."

"Just wait until nationals. It's the intensity of this event multiplied by a hundred," I said and glanced at the digital clock on the nightstand. "I'd better get to my room so I can try to take a nap."

"I'll walk you out," Braden said.

"Good luck," Phil said while Sam echoed him in a quieter voice.

Braden and I stepped into the hallway, and he gave my neck a light massage as he walked behind me. "We have to get on the road right after the event so I might not get a chance to say goodbye later. Sam has a ten a.m. class tomorrow that she can't skip."

Why had she come if she had to hurry back for a class? *Duh. You know why.* I did feel slightly relieved that Braden was missing the exhibition that night because I wasn't quite ready for him to see my emotional "Beneath Your Beautiful" show program.

"Thank you again for coming," I said. "It means so much to me that you're here."

I hugged him and fought the sadness weighing on my chest, trying to instead take in all the good sensations from being in his arms. Our goodbye hugs killed me every time.

"Can I ask one favor?" I said. "It's silly, but can you not yell my name before I skate? I don't like to think about who's there watching me."

He smiled and cocked his head to the side. "It makes you nervous that I'm watching you?"

I dipped my head and fiddled with the zipper on my jacket. "A little."

He didn't say anything, and when I looked up his face had grown pensive. "Would it be better if I left now? As much as I want to see you skate, I don't want to do anything to mess you up."

"No, I want you there," I said quickly and held my head high. "I want you to see me kick ass today."

"SKATERS, THERE IS ONE minute remaining in your warm-up."

I took note of the warning and slowed my pace around the rink. Unlike yesterday when I'd been the final skater in the group, today I was the first since the skate order went according to reverse standing. I needed to conserve energy for the four-minute program that lay ahead.

Weaving through the other girls, I came to a stop at Dad and Kathy, and I plucked a tissue from the box on the boards. The arena felt colder than yesterday, making my usual runny nose worse.

"Turn around for a second," Dad said.

I complied, and he straightened one of the criss-cross straps on the back of my slate blue dress. I felt ballerina-like in the gauzy material, my hair pinned into a perfect round bun. It was exactly the feeling I needed to get into character for the lyrical program.

When I faced Dad again, he squeezed my bare shoulders and gave me a big smile.

"You own this program," he said.

I nodded and took a long inhale and exhale. The other skaters had left the ice, and the crowd's cheers had reached a higher volume, anticipating my introduction. I turned toward the center of the rink, and the announcer called my name, setting off thunderous applause.

Standing in front of the judges seated rinkside, I made eye contact with all nine of them as I waited for the music to begin. The opening flute notes played, setting the delicate tone, and then I began to move, gliding toward the judges in attitude position.

I gained power with just a few pushes of my blades, and I curved around the corner to set up for the triple Lutz-triple toe combination. I was not going to miss it today. I vowed *never* to miss it again.

On a strong back outside edge, I vaulted myself into the air and contracted my body into making three turns. As I landed smoothly on one foot, I reached back and picked in with my opposite foot, sending myself upward again. Three more rotations later, I opened up for another clean landing, holding it an extra few seconds to earn more points. The audience went from hushed silence to exploding with cheers.

Sixth place is NOT where I belong.

I made my next two jumps also look textbook, and then I enjoyed my short "breathing" section, where I focused only on the choreography. I extended my short limbs as far as physically possible, stretching down to the tips of my fingers and toes. The music was so beautiful and dreamy that I was able to float along to it, but yet I still felt totally in control.

Passing the halfway mark of the program, I dug in and

prepared for the difficult elements ahead. With a quick snap forward, I jumped up into the double Axel and completed a double toe loop on the back end for my second combination. I followed that with a big triple flip. A rise in the music made me speed up my strokes, and I flew toward Dad and Kathy's end of the rink for my third combination. Blanking my mind, I let muscle memory take over, and it propelled me through the triple flip-half loop-triple Salchow. A huge roar from the crowd momentarily drowned out the music, and I let out a breath of relief, knowing I had only one jump remaining.

My thighs started to burn from working nonstop for three minutes, but I just pushed harder. I bent my upper body forward until my head almost touched my knee, and my legs went into a vertical split. As the crowd oohed and aahed, I came out of the split and immediately jabbed the ice with my toe pick. Three turns, spotless landing. Triple Lutz from a crazy-hard entrance DONE. More bonus points!

I twirled around and around in my closing layback spin, and I could see people in the audience rising to their feet already, their applause drowning out the music again. I ended the program in a deep lunge and watched the full standing ovation unfold all around me.

This is exactly what I need to do one hundred and twenty-two days from now.

As I bowed to the kiss and cry end of the rink, I saw Braden in the same corner section as yesterday. He was standing on the aisle steps with something in his hands, and he cocked back and pitched it onto the ice. Before the sweeper girls could converge on it, I sprinted over and picked it up. It was another stuffed dog, this one a miniature version of Papi. I looked up at Braden with a smile, and despite the distance between us, I could see him beaming back at me.

Dad greeted me with a big hug, and I gave Kathy a courtesy one as we walked to the kiss and cry. While we waited for the score I peeked inside the paper tag attached to the dog's collar.

In case Peter needs a furry friend.

My heart swooned, and I rubbed the dog's black fur before turning him to face the camera with me. We popped up on the Jumbotron, so I lifted mini Papi's paw to wave at the cheering fans. Wrapping my arms around him, I held on tight as the minutes ticked by, making me more anxious to hear my score.

The announcer read the high number, and impressed cheers erupted throughout the building. The score was in the neighborhood of what I'd wanted, so now I just had to wait and see if it was good enough to keep me in first place.

I did my press duty backstage while keeping an eye on the scores, and names kept falling under mine in the standings. With only Katia left to skate, I joined Dad and Kathy to watch her on the monitor. She proved that she deserved to be Russia's newest star with an impressive display of jumps, but mine had been bigger and more powerful. I'd also shown more maturity in my choreography.

Her free skate score came up on the screen, and it was lower than mine. I held my breath and tried to quickly do the math, but the announcer beat me to it. Katia's combined total put her ahead of me overall by two tenths of a point. Two freaking tenths. I squashed my frustration, and I put on a stoic face and clapped since there were media, officials, and other skaters milling around.

"You fought back hard today, and that's what matters," Dad said, hugging me to his side.

Kathy's scowl showed different feelings on the subject, but thankfully I got pulled away to get ready for the medal ceremony. Court and Josh were also backstage for the pairs ceremony, and the three of us embraced and talked about our silver-medal-winning performances. Hearing that I'd fulfilled Josh's vision for my program took away some of the sting of not winning. He was so excited about how I'd drawn the audience into the performance and had them captivated for the full four minutes.

The lights had been dimmed in the arena for the ceremony, and a spotlight lit up the podium on the ice. I congratulated Katia as I took my place on the second tier, but I didn't feel comfortable there. I had no doubt that I would be back on the top step at my next competition. Silver was *not* my color.

After the Russian anthem played and we posed for the necessary podium photographs, we took a victory lap around the ice and gathered for a few more official pictures. Braden, Sam, and Phil had worked their way down to the first row, and Braden had his phone aimed at me, either videotaping or photographing the pageantry. I skated over to him, and he engulfed me in his arms. His soft sweatshirt warmed my cold skin.

"You stayed for the ceremony," I said.

"No way was I missing this."

"You should've won," Phil said. "That was bullshit."

I gave him a smile of thanks. "It's my fault for messing up yesterday."

"What's up with these medals?" Sam took hold of the clear disc hanging from my neck. "They're like plastic."

"They're always like this at Skate America. The Olympic ones are made of the real stuff."

"I need a medalist selfie," Braden said.

I stood up against the boards to pose with him, and he leaned into me, his face close to mine. When he finished snapping, he turned slightly to look at me, and his warm cocoa eyes melted me like a marshmallow.

"You are incredible," he said.

There were no more cameras pointed at me, but I was still smiling so big. I was so happy now that Braden had shown up in Detroit, sneak attack and all. Having my worlds collide didn't have to be a bad thing. I loved feeling his excitement over being there. I hadn't realized how special it would be to experience all this with him. I hadn't realized how much I was missing by not having him in this part of my life.

ON THE DARK BUS I rested my head against the seat and closed my eyes, thoroughly exhausted from the day. The medal ceremony had been followed by the press conference, then a quick exhibition practice, and then the exhibition. I'd been so fresh with Braden feels that I'd had to fight back tears during my performance. Some of the lyrics hit so amazingly close to home.

It had only been a few hours since I'd last talked to him, but I had a deep need to connect with him, even if just via text. I took out my phone, and the screen illuminated the darkness.

Me: **Hope you're having a good trip home!**

Braden: **Sam passed out already and Phil and I are playing 20 Questions. I stumped him with Yoda.**

Me: **Is it weird that I wish I was with you guys instead of taking a quick two hour flight home tomorrow?**

Braden: **I wish you were here too.**

I smiled and stared at his text until the screen went dark. No sooner had it gone black did it light up again.

Braden: **There's something I need to tell you that I didn't want to tell you before you competed.**

I sat up straighter, watching anxiously as he typed his next message.

Braden: **My dad got the information on the accident.**

My eyes opened wide, now fully awake. I'd wanted to know what happened for so long, but I suddenly felt scared to have that knowledge.

Me: **He got everything?**

Braden: **The police report and the court files on the guy**

Me: **OMG**

Braden: **He looked through everything and he thinks it would be best to give it to you in person since it's such personal information.**

Now my pulse was really galloping. I could always change my mind…

Braden: **I can meet you at my parents' house whenever you're ready. Just tell me when and I'm there.**

You need to do this. You need to get the answers to the questions you've had for eleven years.

I looked at my calendar on the phone, and I saw the perfect opportunity to get it done. I just wished it was sooner because thinking about it for a week was going to be hell.

Me: **I'm driving to New York next weekend and can stop at your parents' house since it's on the way.**

Me: **If that works for your dad.**

Braden: **I'll ask him. Saturdays are usually good for him.**

I let out a puff of air.

Me: **Wow, this is really happening.**

Braden: **Sorry I hit you with it in a text. I thought you'd want to know as soon as possible.**

Me: **I'm glad you told me! Thank you again for helping me with this.**

Braden: **I hope you finally get all your questions answered.**

I knew the information that Braden's dad had found would probably answer my *Who?* and *How?* questions, but there was one question that could never be answered, and that was *Why?*

CHAPTER FIFTEEN

"CAN I GET YOU A CUP of coffee, Liza?" Mr. Patrick asked.

"No, thank you."

"Juice? Water?" Braden asked.

"I'm good, thanks."

The aroma of syrup and bacon lingered in the Patricks' kitchen, but my stomach was so jumpy that it didn't appeal to me at all. I'd arrived at the house shortly after breakfast and had been greeted by Mrs. Patrick as she hurried out the door for Tanner's soccer practice. Braden and Papi hadn't been far behind, and Papi jumped up on me, demanding my attention first. We'd all gone into the sunny kitchen where Braden's dad sat at the big oval table, surrounded by stacks of files.

"Is all this about the accident?" I asked quietly while Mr. Patrick stepped into the living room.

"No, that's some other stuff he's working on. He always has papers everywhere in here."

Mr. Patrick came in holding a thin manila folder, but just as he began to speak his cell phone rang. He took it from the holder on his belt.

"Detective Patrick," he said as he went back to the living

213

room.

"Are you sure this is a good time?" I asked while petting Papi's neck.

"Yeah, he shouldn't be long." Braden pulled out two chairs for us. "He just gets a lot of calls, even on his days off."

"It must be exhausting never getting a break, especially considering the awful things he probably has to deal with."

"That's why I never wanted to be a cop. Even though I admire the hell outta him, I couldn't do it. I wouldn't want to spend my life dealing with the awfulness that he does on a daily basis."

"Have you ever seen it take its toll on him?"

Papi stuck his nose between our two chairs, and Braden scratched behind his ears. "There've been some brutal cases where he was really beat down. He'd try to put up a good front for us, but I'd see him come home from the station and just sit in his car for like thirty minutes, staring out the window."

He kept his focus on petting the dog, and I touched the little silver nametag hanging from Papi's collar.

"Your mom is the perfect partner for him," I said. "She's such a warm and upbeat person. I bet she helps him put work behind him for the day."

A tiny smile twitched on his lips. "She's pretty awesome." He paused but still didn't meet my eyes. "I just know that whatever job I end up getting, I want to be able to come home and be with my family without needing a grace period first."

I put my hand on Papi's back, brushing his dark fur. "General Manager of the Sox can be a pretty rough job. One bad trade and all of Red Sox Nation will be calling for your head."

He finally looked up, his mouth curling into a full smile. Mr. Patrick returned, and I tensed up again as my eyes went to the folder in his hands. It was such an ordinary item to be holding the vital details I was seeking.

"I apologize," he said as he sat with us.

"It's okay," I said. "I appreciate you making time for me."

Braden started to push his chair back. "Liza, I can hang out upstairs if you'd rather–"

"You can stay," I said quickly. "I want you to stay."

He nodded, and I waited for Mr. Patrick to open the folder, but he just rested his hands on it.

"I hope I can fill in the blanks as much as possible. I was able to get the accident report, and it gave a clear picture of what happened."

The image of my parents' gray sedan flipping over and glass shattering everywhere flashed through my mind. It was how I'd pictured the accident since I'd first learned of it. The scene had jolted me awake many a night.

"Your parents were driving on a two-lane road, about–"

"Which road?" I asked.

"No one told you where it happened?"

"No one's told me anything."

His gray eyes gave me a sympathetic look. "It was Purchase Street near Barnes Lane."

I let out a tiny gasp and touched my mouth. "They were almost home."

Braden reached out and rubbed my back, and Mr. Patrick waited a moment before continuing, "They were driving south, and a young man driving north came into their lane. Your dad swerved to avoid him, but when the car went off the road it hit the retaining wall and flipped over."

A cold chill made all the hairs on the back of my neck stand up. The vision I'd had all these years was true. I shut my eyes as the image came to me again, now even clearer with all the details of the road I knew so well.

"Did they–" I opened my eyes but kept them on the table. "Were they killed instantly?"

"The report said they were deceased when the police arrived."

I could only nod a little as my throat constricted. The possibility that they'd been aware of what was happening, that they knew they were dying and we'd never see each other again had haunted me more than any other aspect of the accident. I'd had nightmares for years where I heard them crying for help. My eyes watered, and I quickly dabbed at them, not wanting to break down until I was alone.

"Who was driving the other car?" I squeaked out.

Mr. Patrick opened the folder and slid a piece of paper in front of me. It had a black and white mugshot of what looked like a teenage boy. Under the photo was the name Dominic DiManno.

"He's a kid," I said, blinking away my tears.

"He was eighteen at the time of the accident," Mr. Patrick said.

"I always... I always pictured someone older. Someone who looked dangerous." I stared at the pale, curly-haired boy in the photo. "Was he drunk or high? Why did he go into the other lane?"

"He was clean. He said the reason he lost control was... he dropped his phone and bent down to pick it up."

My head snapped up. "He *dropped his phone?*"

Mr. Patrick sighed. "I wish I had a better explanation to give you."

Braden cupped my shoulder, and I closed my eyes again as I tried to process the fact that such a trivial thing had been the reason my parents died. I'd been prepared for a number of causes but none of them as senseless as this.

"My mom said he went to jail," I said. "Is he still there?"

"He was released last September. Served ten years."

"So, I could've seen him around town and not even known it."

"I didn't get any information on whether he's still in the area."

I pressed my fingertips to my temple as I looked down at

the photo again. Dominic DiManno. I'd wanted to know the name of the person responsible for the accident for so long, but it wasn't giving me any sense of comfort. It just gave me more questions like why had he thought it was okay to take his eyes off the road to pick up his stupid phone?

"Braden, can you get Liza a glass of water?" Mr. Patrick said.

"I'm okay," I said. "I was just… thinking."

"It's a lot to digest," Mr. Patrick said. "That was everything I got from the department down there, but if you need anything else don't hesitate to ask."

"Thank you." I picked up the picture. "Can I keep this?"

"Of course."

He gave me the folder, and I slipped it inside. The grandfather clock in the living room chimed, reminding me where I was supposed to be. I swiped at my eyes one last time to make sure they were clear.

"I should get going to my mom's. Thank you again for everything, Mr. Patrick."

Braden walked me out to the wraparound porch, leaving Papi behind the closed door, and he motioned to the big swing in front of the living room window. "Why don't we sit for a few minutes? I'm not sure you should be driving just yet."

I wasn't visibly shaking, but somehow he'd seen the unsteadiness inside me. We slowly rocked back and forth on the swing, neither of us saying anything. Kids rode their bikes past the house, their laughter breaking through the crisp fall morning, and somewhere on the block a lawn mower roared to life, but my visual focus was entirely on the folder in my lap.

"I can't believe he's out of jail already. I assumed he'd be there for a really long time," I said.

"You know how the legal system is."

"Is he just going about his life now? Like he didn't kill two people?"

"I don't think it could be that easy. Any normal person would be scarred by that for the rest of their life."

"I want to know where he is and what he's doing." I took my phone from my purse. "Anyone can be found on the internet, right?"

"Are you sure that's a good idea?"

"I need to see if he looks–" *What? Remorseful?* "I just need to see what's become of him."

I clicked on Facebook, where almost anyone in the world could be found, and one hit came up when I searched Dominic's name. The residence was Scarsdale, New York.

"This is him," I said.

His profile picture showed him standing next to a shiny black pickup truck. His curly hair had been shaved to a dark, close cut, and his smile was a far cry from the shell-shocked look he had in the mugshot.

"He lives one town over from me," I read from his profile.

I scrolled through the few other photos, and they were all Dominic smiling with friends at parties or at the bar. No sign of remorse.

"He's only been out a year and he already has a normal life," I said.

Braden leaned closer to look at the phone. "It's hard to tell from pictures."

"He looks happy, doesn't he?" I enlarged one of the photos of Dominic grinning ear to ear, a beer in his hand. "Does he think about what he did? I'd love to know if he realizes how much damage he did. If I could talk to him, I'd tell him–"

"You're not going to try to contact him?"

"I didn't have the chance to be there when he was sentenced, and I never got to speak my piece. Why shouldn't I be able to now?"

"Maybe we should go back in and talk to my dad about

this."

"He'll just tell me to leave it alone."

Braden's eyes crinkled with concern. "I think I'd agree with him. I don't like the idea of you reaching out to an ex-con."

The phone rang, and I jumped at the noise. Mom's number appeared on the screen.

"She thinks I'm driving, so I'd better not answer. I should go before she calls back."

"Promise me you won't do anything crazy like message that guy online."

"I won't," I said. *Right now.*

I got in my SUV and hid the folder in my tote bag, but it taunted me from the back seat as I drove. I'd expected to be upset over finding out the details of the accident, but I had more anger than anything twisting my insides. How could my parents have died because someone dropped a phone? I would've preferred he'd been wasted or strung out because I could blame the alcohol or the drugs. This was just stupidity. Two seconds of stupidity had taken my parents away from me.

"A freaking dropped phone!" I yelled out to the universe.

Screaming out my frustration brought on tears, and I didn't try to hold them back. I had a three-hour drive to get out all my emotion, and then I had to act normal around Mom. How I was going to do that with this infuriating information crowding my mind remained to be seen.

⚬⚬⚬

"GIVE ME MORE EMOTION!" Kathy shouted as I began my step sequence. "I'm not getting ANY emotion!"

I was in the middle of my second short program run-through of the day, and I'd gotten so accustomed to masking my feelings the past few days that I'd become a robot on the ice.

I put my all into each step and dramatic reach, so much that I tripped on the final turn. After my closing spin, maybe four hands clapped together. The training atmosphere there didn't have the supportive family quality of my rink on the Cape.

Taking my time cooling down, I enjoyed the feel of my blades cutting smoothly into the ice. The cold air blew into my face and helped dry the sweat coating my skin. The exhaustion I felt from the workout and pushing my body to new limits satisfied me in a way that few things could. Being exhausted made me more energized to work harder, strange as it sounded.

The end of the session neared, and I dreaded getting off the ice because it meant talking to Kathy. We'd already argued that morning when she ranted over the jump layout in my short (the same argument we'd been having for months). I'd insisted it wasn't a problem, and she decided to remind me of my mistake at Skate America. "You can't make stupid mistakes like that at the Olympics. I haven't put in all these years of work for you to choke at the biggest moment."

My shoulders relaxed when I saw she had disappeared from the boards. I went over to the bleachers, changed out of my skates, and took my phone from my bag. I'd been obsessively checking Dominic's Facebook to see if he posted anything new.

Nothing had changed on his profile, but I clicked on his photo again, examining all the details. I stretched it larger and noticed for the first time the logo on his polo shirt. It was the name of a tire store nearby. *Is that where he works?* I used to drive by it every day on my way to school.

My heart started to pump harder as I thought about walking in there and seeing Dominic face to face. It would take nothing more than a ten-minute drive for me to meet the person who had taken my parents from me.

I twisted the colorful bracelet on my wrist and knew I had to talk this out before I went any further with the idea. There was only one person who I could talk to, who was aware of the emotions I was hiding.

Me: **How was your Psych test this morning?**

Braden: **Aced it! Who says you can't study and watch the World Series at the same time?**

I looked up and saw Kathy emerge on the other side of the rink, heading in my direction. Now seemed like a great time to run to the office to check on my mail.

Me: **I'll be back. Avoiding Kathy.**

I scurried to the front of the building and ducked into the office. The administrative assistant Tiffany gave me a smile from behind her desk.

"Picking up mail?" she asked.

"Yep, I forgot to stop by yesterday. Did it pile up while I was gone?"

"There's a good bit."

She reached under the desk and handed me a clear bag full of envelopes and packages. I got lots of letters from fans, mostly younger ones, sometimes including drawings of me or pictures of themselves on the ice. I also received a ton of autograph requests. Either Mom or Em screened my mail before I read it in case there was anything alarming. I saw enough creepiness on social media.

"Thanks, Tiff. See you tomorrow!"

I crept into the hallway in case Kathy lurked nearby. I just needed to evade her a few more minutes until it was time for my gym session. I slowly approached the open door of the coaches' room but stopped when I heard Kathy say my name. Not to me but to someone inside the room with her. I stood against the wall to listen.

"Did you see this?" a voice asked. It sounded like Russ, another coach and Kathy's good buddy.

"Oh, yeah. Funny how *I've* never been asked to pose for a

cover," Kathy said.

What is she—

Ohh, the federation's magazine.

Dad and I were on the cover of the latest issue. There was a feature on how we balanced our professional and father-daughter relationships.

"Did you read the article?" Kathy asked. "Four pages and I got one mention. One. But it goes on and on about her tragic past like every other article does."

"America loves when their athletes have a sad story," Russ said.

My face filled with heat as their snarky tones carried clearly into the hallway.

"Sad story," Kathy huffed. "She lives in a mansion, drives a Lexus. It's all turned out pretty well for her."

I winced as her words hit me like bullets. It was one thing to criticize my skating, but I never thought she would get so personal. And so cruel.

"I guess I shouldn't complain, though," Kathy said. "The more attention her crazy childhood gets, the more endorsements she gets."

And she receives a percentage of those earnings according to her contract. I became even sicker to my stomach.

"I've heard her say she hates talking about it in interviews," Russ said.

"Well, she better get over it. She might not care about the money, but if all goes well I can retire early."

I clenched my hands into fists. *Enough!* Before this conversation I was already *so* over all her screaming and her negativity and her entitlement. But now I was definitely *done.*

I marched into the room to the startled faces of Kathy and Russ. Skaters weren't allowed in the coaches' room, but I didn't give a crap about the rules at the moment.

"Liza," Kathy sputtered. "You're not supposed to be in here."

"Where should I be? Driving my Lexus to my mansion?"

She started to say something but it got clogged in her throat, so I kept going.

"I didn't mean to interrupt your fascinating conversation. Just wanted to let you know that I'm leaving and not coming back. Ever."

"Excuse me?"

"You are no longer part of my team. My agent will be in touch about terminating your contract." I started to leave, but Kathy caught me by the elbow. I yanked it loose.

"I'm not going to let you cut me out just like that," she said. "You're acting like a child."

"No, I'm finally acting like the adult that I am and taking control of my life. And I don't want you in it."

I grabbed my things, forgoing my gym session, and took off for home, my hands strangling the steering wheel. Mom and Dad were going to flip, but I'd lost the last shred of respect I had for Kathy. I couldn't stand to be in the same room with her much less work with her. It didn't matter how many years she'd been my coach. There was no trust between us anymore. None.

Mom was also going to flip over me living with Dad full-time, but that couldn't be helped. She'd have to understand that I was making the best move toward my bid for gold.

A Whitney Houston ballad was playing over the house sound system when I entered the kitchen from the garage. I stomped over to the refrigerator and chugged a glass of water. As I poured another, I heard Mom's footsteps on the back stairs.

"Did you skip the gym? Are you okay?" she asked.

I set my glass down on the island. There was no way to delicately break the news, so I just had to own it.

"I fired Kathy."

Mom's dark eyes widened and refused to blink. "You did what?"

"I tried to suck it up to not make waves, but she got personal and the things she said–"

Mom's phone rang on the island, and she looked at the caller. "It's Kathy."

"She's going to try to get you to change my mind, and I'm not doing it."

Mom answered and pressed the Speaker option. Kathy's grating voice came over the line. "Elena, how are you?"

Sure, pretend to be nice now.

"I'm concerned about what just happened at the rink," Mom said.

"Yes, Liza and I had a little misunderstanding, and we both said some things in the heat of the moment."

I hadn't said anything that I regretted.

"I'd like for us all to meet so we can put this behind us," Kathy said.

I shook my head at Mom and stepped closer to her. "I'm not changing my mind," I said forcefully into the phone.

"Liza, this isn't a move you want to make four months from the Olympics," Kathy said.

"Oh, it's the exact move–"

"I need to talk to Liza first," Mom interrupted me. "I apologize for how this was handled. We'll speak with you soon, Kathy."

Mom hung up, and I shook my head with more insistence. "She doesn't deserve an apology, and I'm not meeting with her. I've been telling you for months that it was a bad situation, so this shouldn't be a surprise."

"I knew things were strained, but I didn't think you'd do this without talking to your father and me first. What did she say to you today?"

My face flushed with anger again as I recalled Kathy mocking the tragedy I'd experienced as a child.

"She didn't say anything to me. I overheard her with Russ, and she was talking about how rich we are and how I get more endorsements because of what happened when I was a kid."

Mom shook her head and pinched the bridge of nose, and I continued, "And she basically said that she hopes the media keeps exploiting my past because it will mean more money for her."

I'd left out the part where she'd said what happened to me was no big deal since I had a lot of money now. It was so disgusting that I couldn't even repeat it.

"She's let a few comments slip to me before about our wealth, but I ignored her," Mom said. "I don't like that she spoke that way about you to someone else. It makes me wonder what she could be saying to other people."

"What's disturbing is not that she said it out loud. It's that she even thought it to begin with. As my coach she's supposed to look out for my best interests, not take advantage of me."

Mom quietly studied me as she tapped her dark red nails on the granite. "I think you should use the night to cool off, and tomorrow the three of us can discuss how to move forward. I'm not okay with her behavior, but we can't have people thinking that there are problems with your training."

"There *is* a problem. Its name is Kathy. I'm glad I stood up to her, and there's nothing more to discuss." I picked up my glass and put it in the dishwasher. "I'm driving to Dad's tonight so I can skate in the morning. I'm not going to let this mess up my schedule."

"So you're moving out? Just like that?"

"This is what's best for my skating."

Mom's expression wavered somewhere between sad and panicked, so I put my arms around her.

"I'll come back on weekends when I can, and I'll see you in Paris and hopefully Japan." If I did well at my Grand Prix event in Paris, I'd qualify for the Final in Fukuoka in December. "And you can drive up to the Cape any time."

"I know. It's just so sudden. When you go to your father's

for the summer I have time to get used to the idea of you being gone."

"You can go to Manhattan during the week and spend more time with George. Take advantage of the empty nest."

She tried to smile, but her mouth wouldn't fully comply. I gave her another squeeze.

"The weeks are going to fly by. We'll have the competitions and the holidays, and you'll barely notice I'm not here," I said.

I let her hold onto me a while longer, and then I went upstairs and checked my phone as I reached my room. I had a text from Braden sent shortly after our earlier exchange.

Braden: **Is Kathy harassing you today?**

Me: **She's harassed me for the last time. I fired her.**

I started tossing clothes into the suitcase that was still open on the carpet. My phone dinged, and I snatched it from the bed.

Braden: **GO LIZA!!!!**

I smiled, and my body relaxed for the first time that day, finally enjoying the relief of no more Kathy in my life.

Me: **Thanks for celebrating with me. It's not a popular decision with anyone else.**

Braden: **I'm proud of you! You don't need someone like that in your life.**

I dropped onto the loveseat in my sitting area and curled my legs under me.

Me: **I have other news.**

Me: **I found out something about Dominic from one of his pictures. I think he works at a tire place near here.**

Braden: **You're not thinking of going there?**

Me: **The thought crossed my mind.**

Braden: **What would you say to him?**

Me: **I don't know. I keep thinking of all these things I could say, but if I actually saw him I don't know if I could go through with it.**

Braden: **Then maybe it's better to leave it be. Talking to him might not make you feel better. Could make you feel worse.**

I looked up and my eyes fell on the photo of my adoptive parents on the nightstand. Dominic had never been forced to face me, and he needed to hear how his careless actions had affected me. Even though he'd served time, I wanted to be sure he really understood the consequences of what he'd done.

Me: **It just feels like something I have to do.**

Braden: **You shouldn't go alone to see him.**

Me: **I'm getting ready to drive back to the Cape so I'm not going right now, but I appreciate you looking out for me.**

Braden: **Well if or when you decide to do it, I'd be happy to go with you.**

He made me smile again, and I wondered for the hundredth time how I'd gotten so lucky to find a friend like him.

Me: **You're a saint for dealing with all my drama.**

Braden: **No need to canonize me. I kinda like talking to you and hanging out with you, if you hadn't realized it yet. Drama or no drama.**

Me: **That's good to know** ☺ **Because between now and Sochi, I can almost guarantee there will be lots more.**

CHAPTER SIXTEEN

I'D PICKED THE PERFECT TIME TO move back to the Cape. Two nights after I left New York, Dad and Em's house was rocking with a World Series viewing party. All the skaters they trained had been invited. If the Sox beat the Cardinals they'd be world champs, and Dad said we could push back the start of our training day a few hours in the morning.

"Liza, look!" Quinn said.

I turned toward the kitchen island. Quinn had two carrot sticks shoved under her top lip like walrus tusks. I grabbed two celery sticks from the veggie tray and tried to do the same, but they both fell to the floor. Quinn giggled and rambled away to show Alex, who looked like a walking advertisement for the Red Sox merchandise store. They'd both been so happy when I told them I'd be living there full-time. I'd been sure to make that announcement as soon as I arrived in case Dad had any objection. He wouldn't want to disappoint the twins after I'd made them jump around the living room with excitement.

Holly came in carrying a square container, and I tried to see through the side. "What you got there?"

"I made you 'Welcome Home' brownies." She put the

container among the array of snacks on the island. "I cut them small, so don't panic over the sugar content."

I hugged her. "You're the best."

"I'm so excited you're back for good. We're due for some Holliza time."

I was looking forward to that, too. I'd never talked much about my adoptive parents with her (I hadn't talked much about them with anyone until Braden), but I wanted to tell her about my investigation and how sweet Braden was being.

"I wish I'd left Kathy right after I graduated. It would've been a lot less messy." I opened the container and selected a corner brownie. "I have to pay her a settlement like we're getting a divorce. It pains me to give her another cent, but I'll do whatever it takes to make her go away."

"You know, there's another benefit to you being here all the time. You're closer to Braden." Holly's eyebrows danced.

Dad had popped up behind Holly, and the worried look on his face made me think he'd heard her. I took a bite of my brownie and offered him the container, hoping to distract him by appealing to his sweet tooth.

"Want one?"

Holly mouthed, "Sorry" to me and slinked off to chat with Court and Josh. Dad took a brownie and devoured it in one bite.

"Was there another motive behind firing Kathy that I should know about?" he asked.

"That was Holly talking, not me. I swear the only reason I left Kathy is because she wasn't contributing anything positive to my training."

He gave me a long look and then picked out another brownie. "Let's go in the library so we can talk."

"Dad, I promise you I'm not here so I can see Braden more or–"

"I believe you. Just take a walk with me." He touched my elbow. "And bring the brownies."

We maneuvered through the crowd surrounding the food and went down the short hallway that led to the library, the half bath, and the master bedroom. Dad took the container from me and put it on his lap as he sat on the leather couch.

"I'm stress eating and the game hasn't even started yet," he said.

"It's so cute how Em turned you into this huge baseball fan when you didn't know first base from third base when you moved here from Russia."

"I don't think she would've let me get my citizenship if I didn't know how to score a game." He chuckled.

I sat beside him and hugged one of the red throw pillows. "So, what are we talking about?"

He finished chewing his latest brownie before he answered, "The press release about Kathy comes out tomorrow. I don't want you going anywhere near the message boards or social media. If people make comments or ask what really happened, do not reply to them. All that needed to be said was done in the release."

"Don't worry, I won't say anything. I think the reason I gave that I want to train in one place until the Olympics was totally believable. Of course, that won't stop people from speculating that Mom and I had a fight or something, and that's why I moved out."

"There will be rumors on top of rumors, which is what I wanted to avoid." He hit me with a pointed look. "We just have to ignore them all and stick to the story you put out."

"I'm sorry I wasn't able to give you any notice that I was firing Kathy and moving here. I just came barreling in yesterday, declaring I was back for good."

"Sweetheart, don't ever apologize for being here. I wasn't happy with how things with Kathy were handled, but I'm thrilled you're here." He hooked his arm around my shoulders. "You know this is your home. Even though you've spent more time with your mom over the years, this is just as much your home."

A swell of emotion rose in my chest. "I know it is," I squeaked.

Alex careened into the doorway and screeched to a halt. "They're getting ready to sing the national anthem."

"Be there in a minute, bud," Dad said.

"They'd better win or he's going to be crushed," I said.

"Good thing his big sister is here for him just in case." Dad smiled and held out his hand for me as he stood. When I took it he wrapped me in a bear hug. "Nothing makes me happier than having us all together. We miss you so much when you're away."

There he went, making me teary again. "I miss you guys, too. Even Quinn's second grade playground stories."

He laughed and ruffled my hair. "Let's go get prime seats on the sofa."

The game started slowly, but the packed living room came alive in the third inning when the Sox put three runs on the board. I texted Braden a message with lots of exclamation points, and he sent back a video of Ross and him chest bumping in front of the TV. The Sox extended their lead in the next inning, and the atmosphere in the room went from tense to relaxed and jubilant. Braden and I continued to text back and forth, counting down the outs until only one stood between our team and the championship.

My phone rang with a FaceTime request, and I answered Braden's call as we all stood in anticipation of the final out.

"We have to celebrate this moment together since we started the playoff magic together," he said.

I grinned. "Absolutely."

Holly leaned over my shoulder and waved at the phone. "Hi, Braden!"

He got distracted by the action on the TV, and I looked up at our own gigantic screen. We were one strike away, so everyone began to clap in unison. Alex was standing two feet from the TV, clutching the pennant Dad had bought him at the first game of the Series. Even Quinn was bouncing up and down, and she couldn't care less about baseball. I held my breath as the Red Sox pitcher unwound and released the ball.

Swing and a miss!

Braden and I both yelled into the phone, but we were soon drowned out by the celebration at each of our respective parties. An arm choked Braden's neck, and Ross stuck his head into the video frame.

"World champs!" he shouted and then disappeared into the chaos behind Braden.

"Tell Holly to give you a hug for me," Braden said as he got sprayed with what looked like beer.

I smiled. "I will."

Dad had put Alex on his shoulders, and he was parading him around as Alex held the pennant aloft. I turned the phone so Braden could see them.

"I bet no one at your party is that adorable," I said.

"Warms my heart to see kids being raised right!" he said.

"I'll let you go celebrate. Don't burn anything down!"

Our guests slowly trickled out after the trophy presentation, and Court and I offered to help Dad and Em clean up, but they shooed us upstairs to get rested for practice. The later start in the morning was a big help, but we were already approaching the witching hour.

I snuggled under my down comforter and closed my eyes, but I was still too wired from the party to sleep. I started to think about everything that had gone down the past few days, and that kept me tossing and turning. I'd put aside thoughts of Dominic that night during the game, but now he crept back to the forefront again. Did he have trouble sleeping at night? Was he haunted by what he'd done?

I pictured myself confronting him, asking those questions. After standing up to Kathy, I felt empowered, more confident that I could face Dominic and speak my mind. And I needed to do it sooner rather than later so I could stop thinking about it and have my mind clear for my upcoming competitions.

The digital clock on the nightstand showed almost three a.m. I picked up my phone and squinted as the bright screen blinded me.

Me: **Are you still up?**

Braden: **Just got into bed. Don't tell me you're still partying?**

Our video chat earlier had spoiled me, so I didn't want to settle for texting. I clicked on the lamp and dialed up Braden on FaceTime, and he answered with a smile while smoothing his adorably rumpled hair. He was lounging against his pillow, shirtless and wearing his glasses. I was going to have some mighty sweet dreams whenever I got to sleep.

"The party ended a while ago. I couldn't sleep," I said.

"The one upstairs is still going strong. I have to give a presentation in class tomorrow, so I figured I should be coherent."

"Oh, I shouldn't keep you up then. We can talk–"

"No, don't go. I'm still winding down from the excitement. I won't be able to sleep just yet."

The fact that he was so eager to talk to me at three in the morning filled me with sparkly rainbow and unicorn feels. I could just stare at his hotness for the next hour, but I had to get to the reason for my call.

"I wanted to ask if you're up for a road trip to New York this Saturday."

"To see Dominic?"

"I have to get some more clothes and stuff from my house, so I thought I could stop by the tire shop."

He combed his fingers through his thick hair, messing it further. "You're positive you want to talk to him?"

"I don't think I can have peace until I do."

"I want you to have peace. We just don't know what this

guy's going to say, and I don't want you getting hurt."

My hand went to my heart, and I moved the phone higher so he wouldn't see the gesture. "I'll go in with low expectations and with my guard up."

"What happens if he's not there?"

I didn't want to consider the possibility of psyching myself up to meet him only to be disappointed. But even if we ran into a roadblock, at least I'd get to spend an entire day with Braden.

"Then I guess we'll just be taking a ride to New York for the day," I said.

He smiled and pushed up his glasses. "Sounds like a pretty good Saturday to me."

WHEN I'D DREAMT ABOUT my first road trip with Braden, I'd imagined us jamming to the radio, joking around, stealing flirty glances. Just being relaxed and carefree. I hadn't pictured us traveling to meet a man who'd committed homicide.

I'd woken up with a knot the size of a grapefruit in my stomach, and it hadn't gone away even after picking up Braden at his parents' house. His usual sunny energy had been dampened by anxiousness, too. Neither of us knew what we were getting ourselves into.

"Did you go bowling last night?" I asked. I didn't want to talk about the purpose of our trip. I needed as much distraction as possible.

"Yep, me, Phil, and Sam destroyed Jason, Britt, and Ross."

"Are Jason and Britt a thing? I kinda got the vibe they were into each other at the party."

"I think so. Ever since then they've been together whenever I see them."

"All your other friends are still single?"

"Yeah, Ross has never stayed with a girl more than two weeks, so I don't expect him to settle down any time soon. And anyone interested in Phil has to meet his girlfriend criteria which are stricter than admission criteria for Harvard."

I laughed and turned down the radio volume. It might be the perfect time to ask Braden something I'd been wondering forever but didn't know quite how to approach. It would be good practice for being bold with Dominic later.

"How come you didn't have a girlfriend when I met you? I see the way girls look at you," I said with a teasing smile.

His mouth opened slightly, and I could tell he was surprised by my question.

"I see how guys look at *you*," he said.

"Yeah, but my issues with dating are well-known. What's your excuse?"

He laughed loudly but also a touch nervously. "I've had girlfriends. I was just enjoying the single life when I met you."

"How many have you had?"

"Umm... two. Well... three if you count Jade from seventh grade. We would pass notes in history class, and I'd carry her books to homeroom."

"That's very cute. I can picture you as a little junior high Romeo."

"My game was strong. For Valentine's I gave her one of those supersized Hershey Kisses. I had all the girls swooning."

I laughed. "How did it end? Did Romeo break her heart?"

"She said some mean stuff about Sam, so I was like, 'Peace out.' She moved on to the eighth grade Casanova pretty quickly, so I don't think her heart was too broken."

Wow, so I wasn't the first person to be jealous of Sam. It had been happening since they were tweens. Had his other relationships also ended because of her?

"What happened with your other girlfriends? Breakup-wise?"

He peeked over at me. "I feel like I'm being interviewed."

"I have a lot of experience in the hot seat. It's my turn to ask the questions." I grinned. "And I'd tell you my dating history if it wasn't nonexistent."

"How convenient."

"We have a hundred and forty more miles to fill, so you need to entertain me."

"Okay, National Enquirer." He poked my arm. "My last girlfriend was fall semester last year. We went out a couple months, and then it just fizzled out. We were better as friends."

My mind immediately went to an unappealing place. If they'd dated a few months, they probably did certain things together. Not that I'd assumed Braden hadn't done *it* yet, but having a college girlfriend made it more likely. Why had I started asking these questions again?

"The other girlfriend I had was in high school. We were together two years," he said.

I mentally closed the door on his last relationship and focused on his high school one, where I could convince myself that nothing R-rated had occurred.

"Two years is a long time," I said.

"It was one of those situations where we stayed together because we were comfortable with each other. We got along really well, and we always knew we had dates for dances and stuff."

"So that one fizzled out, too?"

"Well..." He rubbed at a spot on his jeans. "After Scotty died... I was kind of a mess. I got real... I think 'clingy' was the word used. She said she felt smothered and wanted to do her own thing."

"She didn't understand that you'd just been through a trauma?"

"She knew Scotty well, too, because of me, but she reacted a lot differently than I did. She didn't want to talk about it at all, while I was consumed by it all the time. So, the two of us weren't a good combination."

I lowered the radio a few more notches. The peppy pop tune didn't exactly match the mood of the conversation.

"Were you able to talk about it with your other friends?" I asked.

"Most people shut down when the subject came up. Even Ross, who usually has something to say about everything." He tugged on his seatbelt and shifted in the leather seat. "My parents had me talk to the school counselor a few times."

"Did that help?"

He shrugged. "Everything she said made sense. That we never really know what's truly going on inside someone else's head, no matter how close to them we are. But..."

"You still feel like you could've done something to prevent it from happening."

"I've replayed so many of our conversations, trying to think if Scotty said anything that should've warned me."

"If he had said something, you would've picked up on it for sure. You knew him so well."

He looked out his window at the colorful foliage along the interstate. "It's just hard to make any sense of it. I don't know if I'll ever understand how it could've happened."

I chewed on my lip. "I wish I could tell you that time makes it easier to accept, but considering where we're going and what I'm about to do, I don't think I'm the best person to give advice on acceptance."

He turned so he was angled toward me. "I hope seeing Dominic can help you get there. I've been worried about you meeting him, but I understand wanting to know everything you possibly can about what happened. If there was some way I could get answers about Scotty's death, I'd do it in a heartbeat."

I took my eyes off the road for just a moment to meet Braden's, and I saw the pain that I knew all too well. The pain of grief that lived just under the surface, that never went away.

It waxed and waned, but it never disappeared.

After a few miles of silence, I suggested we listen to a new urban fantasy audiobook I had on my phone. I tried to focus only on the narrator, but my heart beat faster with every mile we traveled. As we entered Westchester County, I cracked open my window, seeking fresh air to breathe. My hands bounced from the wheel to my hair to my necklace and back again.

"Do you want to go to your house first?" Braden asked.

Mom was in Manhattan with George for the weekend, so I didn't have to explain to her why Braden had come with me to pack my stuff. She wouldn't even know I'd been there.

"Let's go to the tire shop. If I wait I'm just going to get more freaked out."

The commercial area of town around us was very familiar, but all the streets suddenly felt foreboding... as if they were leading me to a horrific end. I turned slowly into the parking lot of the store and pulled into a spot next to the beige-colored brick building. A nervous tremble had now taken over my whole body.

I can do this. I can do this.

Braden unsnapped his seatbelt and put his hand over mine, which was still gripping the steering wheel. "We can sit here as long as you need. There's no rush."

His touch took me to a much happier place, but I couldn't stall or I might lose my nerve.

"I'm ready," I said.

We walked toward the glass door, and I mentally rehearsed my plan for the hundredth time. I would ask the clerk if Dominic was working, and if he was, I'd say I needed to talk to him about my car. Once he stood in front of me, then I could tell him the real reason I was there.

I tugged on the door, but I stopped short in the doorway, my heart pounding in my ears. Dominic was behind the counter, going over some papers with a customer. He was less than twenty feet from me.

I spun around and pushed Braden back outside. "Oh my God, oh my God. He's right there."

Braden took hold of my shoulders, steadying me. "You don't have to do this. We can come back another time or never again. Whatever you want to do."

I shook my head. "I'm here. I have to do this. I just need a minute."

He held onto me as I slowly breathed in and out. *Be brave. Be strong.*

When I felt like I wasn't hyperventilating anymore, I returned to the door and opened it again. Striding forward with purpose, I passed the small waiting area and approached the counter. The customer ahead of me turned to leave, and Dominic looked up at me for the first time. His eyes went wide, the same expression he'd had in the mugshot after the accident. My stomach plummeted to the floor.

"What are you doing here?"

CHAPTER SEVENTEEN

"YOU KNOW WHO I AM?" I croaked, my mouth as dry as sandpaper.

Dominic's jaw tightened, and he glanced around the room at the two customers in the waiting area. "Come with me."

He marched out the door, letting it slam shut, and Braden and I followed. Dominic stood on the sidewalk with one hand on his hip, the other running over his cropped hair. His eyes darted everywhere but on me.

"I know you were the... the kid," he stammered, finally looking at me. There was fire in his light eyes. "Look, I did my time and I just wanna be left alone."

I struggled to find my voice. "I know you did, but–"

"You found your real parents, right?"

"Ye... yes–"

"There's no reason for you to be here. I did my time," he repeated. "I have to get back to work."

He hurried into the building, leaving me stunned and speechless. I'd gone over many potential scenarios all week, but Dominic recognizing me and running away hadn't been one of them.

"Are you okay?" Braden's hands cupped my shoulders again.

I was still at a loss for words. I just stared at the name of the shop painted on the glass door. How did Dominic know my face? I'd changed my last name to Dad's after we found each other, so I didn't have any public connection to my adoptive parents. And the likelihood of Dominic reading an article about a figure skater's tragic past and putting the pieces together was slim.

"He can't just blow you off." Braden started toward the door, but I grabbed his arm.

"Don't. He's not going to talk to me."

"Who is he to refuse to talk to you? He's the one who was at fault, not you. You deserve to be able to say what you came to say."

I did have so much emotion, so many things weighing on my chest that I wanted to let out, but I'd lost all my bravery, all my strength in the two minutes I'd spent with Dominic. I felt like he had the upper hand on me now.

"I can't... I can't go back in there."

I rushed over to my SUV and climbed inside, quickly turning the ignition and blasting the A/C. Braden wasn't far behind.

"I'm sorry, I didn't mean to push," he said. "I just know how much you wanted this."

"I didn't think... I didn't think he'd know who I am... that he'd know about my life." I gazed at the building and shivered. It was unsettling to think of Dominic knowing details about me, possibly keeping tabs on me all these years. As strongly as I'd wanted to confront him before, now I had just as strong a desire to leave.

I drove us to my house in silence and led Braden into the kitchen, where I dropped my keys on the island. I rested my elbows on the granite, holding my head in my hands.

"He didn't even apologize," I said. "What kind of person meets the child of the people he killed and doesn't say, 'I'm sorry'?"

"Not a good one," Braden said.

"I wasn't expecting him to be angry. I was supposed to be the angry one and he was supposed to be... I don't know... apologetic?"

"I get that he was surprised to see you, but he should've manned up and heard you out."

I lifted my head and pulled my hair away from my face. I couldn't stop thinking about what Dominic had said about me finding my real parents. It was the part of our brief conversation that bothered me the most.

"Do you think you'll want to go back there?" Braden asked quietly.

"Right now that's the last thing I want to do," I said, my voice hardening. The anger I hadn't had a chance to express to Dominic needed to be released. "He didn't seem sorry at all. I mean, was I supposed to be like, 'Okay, you served your time, so you don't owe me anything?' Even if I went back there, he'd probably refuse to listen to me and walk away again."

"Probably," Braden said, sounding just as irritated. "What a coward."

Just like I'd wanted to get far away from the tire shop, I suddenly wanted to get out of New York period. If Dominic didn't have the decency to speak to me, then I shouldn't waste any more energy thinking about him. He wasn't worth the time or the emotion. I hadn't even known his name a week ago, so I just had to go back to thinking of him as the anonymous person who'd caused the accident. He didn't deserve to have an identity.

"I'm ready to go home." I headed for the stairs. "Keep me company while I pack?"

Braden hesitated, looking at me with concern, but he didn't push me to talk any more about what I'd just experienced. We went up the narrow staircase, and when I turned on the overhead light in my bedroom, he said, "Wow."

"It's kinda big."

"*Kinda* big? You have your own living room." He pointed to the sitting area with the large TV. "Add a refrigerator and this is my dream bedroom."

"I'm pretty lucky I guess," I said, and *You found your real parents, right?* popped into my head. I shook it off and opened my dresser to pull out a stack of T-shirts.

Braden inspected the built-in stereo on the wall and pushed a couple of buttons. "Cannonball" by Damien Rice came through the speakers in the ceiling.

"Phil has satellite radio in his car. I discovered this coffee house channel when we drove to Detroit," he said.

"I listen to this a lot," I said. "Relaxing music is exactly what I need right now, so good choice."

While I transferred clothes from the walk-in closet to the large suitcase I'd left behind, Braden examined my collage of photos above the dresser and then moved on to the bookshelf full of my skating medals.

"You could open your own hall of fame with all these!" he said.

Watching him roam around my room, just existing in my personal space, was helping to lift my spirits. If only I could completely forget Dominic's heated words. They kept running through my head every time my mind wandered for just a second.

Braden sat on the bed and fell back onto the ivory comforter. "Damn, this mattress feels like a heavenly cloud."

"The benefit of my mom buying only the finest things."

"You must've felt like you were sleeping on the street when you slept in my bed."

I laughed. "I wasn't uncomfortable at all." Being in his bed had been quite heavenly. For reasons other than the comfort level of the mattress.

I took one last look in the closet and zipped up the suitcase. "I think I have everything I need."

Braden patted the comforter. "Come enjoy this cloud before we leave. It's the ultimate in relaxation."

I wasn't sure how much I could relax while lying beside him on my bed, but it was an invitation I couldn't pass up. I stretched out next to him, my feet dangling over the side. An acoustic version of Maroon 5's "She Will Be Loved" filled the room, and I closed my eyes to try to put myself at ease. It was futile with Braden so close to me. Our hands rested between us on the comforter, and even though a few inches separated us, I could sense the nearness of his fingertips, his pulse beating in them. Could he feel the pulse in mine?

I opened my eyes, and Braden's head was turned in my direction, his warm gaze watching me. He didn't look away, and my heart thudded louder.

"Liza?" Mom called out.

Braden and I both shot up just as Mom stepped into the doorway. Her eyes went from me to him and back to me with disbelief. The two of us hopped to our feet.

"What is this?" she snapped and turned off the radio.

"I thought you were with George," I said.

"He wasn't feeling well, and he didn't want me to get sick, too." She shook her head. "I can't believe I come home to *this*. All along you've told me you're just friends, and here you are sneaking off together. To another state!"

"We *are* just friends and we're not sneaking. I mean, no, I didn't tell you we'd be here, but we didn't come for the reason you think."

"I know all the tricks of hiding a relationship. I also know what guilt looks like, and you couldn't look guiltier."

"We're surprised, not guilty. We weren't expecting–"

"I knew from the beginning that a college boy would want certain things." Mom glared at Braden.

His eyes doubled in size. "Ma'am, we haven't done

anything–"

"But I expected more from you," Mom cut off Braden and turned her glare to me. "I never thought you'd do something like this after knowing all I went through with your father. I thought I taught you to make better choices, and here you are doing the same thing–"

"Mom, I'm not you! I'm not sneaking around, and I'm not going to end up pregnant!"

My outburst seemed to reverberate in the quiet room, and I regretted raising my voice. Braden stood motionless, probably wishing he could disappear. I wished he could, too, so he wouldn't be witness to the ugly scene.

"I'm sorry," I said. "I didn't mean to yell at you."

Mom breathed in through her nose as her bright red lips were clamped shut. "Braden, can you give us some time alone?"

He glanced at me, and I gave him a quick nod. Mom closed the door behind him and looked at me with a pained glare.

"I'm sorry," I said again. "I lost it because you weren't giving me a chance to explain."

"Okay, then, explain to me why you and your *friend* were alone in your bedroom, on your bed."

"I came to pack up more clothes." I pointed to the suitcase. "We were just resting before we drove home."

"Why didn't you tell me you were coming so I could see you? And why is Braden with you?"

I chewed on my lip. It was time I came clean and spilled everything about my investigation. Mom was already mad, so I may as well put it all out there.

"He's here as moral support because I went to see someone earlier. Dominic DiManno."

Mom's mouth opened, but it took her a moment to speak. "How do you know that name?"

"Braden's dad got all the information on the accident for

me. I looked up Dominic and found out where he works."

"And you spoke to him?"

"Just for a minute. He recognized me and couldn't get away fast enough."

She put her hand to her forehead. "Good. I don't want you to ever go near him again. Why would you bring up all this pain for yourself after all this time? How could Braden's father just hand over that information without speaking to me first?"

"Because I'm an adult, and I had a right to know what happened. I've always wanted to know, and you and Dad wouldn't tell me anything."

"We were trying to protect you. You didn't need to know those details. They were only going to make you hurt again. Leave the past in the past."

I had the feeling she meant more than leave the accident in the past. She meant leave all memories of my adoptive parents there, too. Even though they were her cousins, she hardly ever spoke of them, which was why I rarely talked about them around her. It might have been too painful for her to think about the years she'd lost with me, but I had a life during those years. One I didn't want to pretend didn't exist or feel guilty about remembering.

"It was a long time ago, but it was important to me to know," I said.

"I just don't understand why now." Mom studied me. "Or maybe I do. Since you met Braden, you've done some things that aren't like you."

"Like what? Being more assertive? Making decisions for myself? Those are good things."

"Lying to your parents? I'm sure you didn't tell your father you were seeing Dominic today."

"I had to do this on my own."

"With Braden," she said.

"He's been an amazing, supportive friend through all

this."

Mom folded her arms and stared at me for a long, agonizing minute. "I'm going to drive Braden to the train station and buy him a ticket back to Boston. I want you to stay here this weekend."

Is she serious?

"You're not going to ship him off on a train. I'm driving him home."

"You and I need to spend some time talking about the choices you've made lately."

"The choices I've made have all been good for me. I'm so happy training full-time with Dad. Being away from Kathy has reduced my stress level by a thousand percent. And even though Dominic wouldn't talk to me, I'm glad I found out everything I could about the accident. You don't know what it was like to have all those unanswered questions for so many years."

Her posture relaxed somewhat, but her face was still pinched with worry. "I just don't like all the lying. You've never kept things from me before. Even when you went on your first date, you didn't tell me until after it happened."

"Because I knew you'd freak out like you did just now."

"My reaction was justified."

I was emotionally drained from the roller coaster day and didn't have the energy to argue with her anymore. I could see her making us go round and round for who knew how long. All while Braden waited downstairs. I pulled on the handle of my suitcase and rolled it to the door.

"Can we talk when I get home? It's been an exhausting day."

"If you're trying to run away to your father's, I'm going to call him to let him know what you've been up to."

I kept moving, my suitcase behind me. "I was planning to tell him."

"That's fine, but I want to give him my perspective."

I stayed quiet and dragged my bag down the stairs. Braden was pacing around the island in the kitchen, and he jumped to help me with the suitcase. I gave Mom a swift hug, and she pulled me in for a longer one.

"Call me after you talk to your father."

"Okay."

"I'm sorry for any confusion," Braden said.

Mom just pursed her lips, so I turned to him and said, "I explained everything."

He exhaled, and we headed for the garage. My foot couldn't hit the gas pedal quickly enough. I couldn't wait to get out of that place, where both Dominic's and Mom's anger resonated inside me.

THE STREETLIGHTS GLOWED SOFTLY in the dusk as I turned onto Braden's street in Fall River. I'd told him about my conversation with Mom, and then we'd resumed listening to the audiobook. It distracted me for a little while from the thought of facing Dad's questions at home.

"I should've taken a few wrong turns. Circled Rhode Island a few times," I said as I parked in the driveway. "I'm not ready for part two of the 'we wanted to protect you' speech."

Braden opened his door. "Come on, I have the perfect hideout."

We went inside the house, and every room was dark except the kitchen. Braden called out, "Anybody home?" and no one answered. There was no sign of Papi either.

"Are you hungry?" he asked.

I hadn't eaten since we'd had sandwiches on the drive to White Plains, but I wasn't in the mood for a meal. I *was* in the mood for my favorite comfort food, though.

"I could go for some chocolate if you have any."

"You're in luck because my mom's a chocoholic."

He opened a few cabinets and presented me with a number of options – from chocolate chip cookies to mini candy bars to chocolate-covered fruit snacks. I selected the bag of dark chocolate-covered blueberries, and Braden led the way to the backyard.

"This is the best hideout," he said, letting me climb the treehouse ladder first.

I used my phone as a flashlight when I reached the top, and I switched on the lantern in the corner. Tanner's décor hadn't changed since I'd been up there during Braden's birthday party, but the temperature had dropped a lot since that day. I rubbed the goosebumps that sprang up on my arms.

Braden climbed inside behind me and opened the skylight. "After Scotty died I hid in here for a week. I couldn't face the reality of what was happening out there."

I crawled across the sleeping bag and sat against the pillows on the back wall, and Braden lowered his tall frame beside me. We each took a handful of blueberries.

"What did you do up here all that time?" I asked.

"I slept a lot. Or tried to sleep. Spent a lot of time staring up at that skylight." He glanced up at the cloudy evening. "Being here just felt safe."

I looked around at the dark knotted wood, how it seemed to form a cocoon around us. "It does feel safe. I would've escaped here too if I'd had a place like this."

"It had to be rough not having anything familiar around you after your parents died. Not just being taken away from your home but being taken to another country."

"I cried night after night after night. I didn't want to sleep because I hated waking up and realizing nothing had changed and the whole thing hadn't been an awful dream. My mom stayed with me every night and tried to comfort me, but nothing was helping." I toyed with the two blueberries remaining on my palm. "One night she came in with a book, *The Secret Garden*, and started to read to me, and listening to the story gave me something else to focus on. Her English wasn't the best back then, so I'd help her with some of the words. We'd read a chapter every night, and when it was time to go to sleep, I'd imagine I was part of the book. I'd make up my own chapters to the story so I wouldn't think about reality and get overwhelmed again."

"The book was your escape," Braden said.

I nodded and chewed slowly on my candy. "We didn't have a yard since we lived in an apartment, but my mom took me to this park one day, and she set up our own little secret garden. It was so pretty and just how I pictured it in the story."

"Sounds like she learned how to be a great mom right away."

"She really did. I'm so lucky that I had her to take care of me and that I met my dad just a year later. They drive me crazy sometimes, but they love me so much and have given me so much." I brought my knees to my chest and wrapped my arms around them. "Sometimes... sometimes I feel guilty for thinking about the accident and missing my adoptive parents."

"Why do you feel guilty?" Braden asked softly.

Dominic's question hit home again – *You found your real parents, right?* I knew exactly why he'd said that and why it had struck such a sensitive nerve.

"I have an amazing family with my mom, dad, Em, the twins... so I feel like maybe I shouldn't think about the past. I don't want anyone to think I'm ungrateful for what I have now."

"Your adoptive parents were your family, too. They were your whole world for almost eight years, the most important years of a kid's life. There's nothing wrong with missing them and mourning them."

My throat tightened, and I blinked swiftly as tears blurred my eyes. "I don't think Dominic would agree with you."

"Don't let anything that jerk said get to you. All he wanted to do was ease his conscience." Braden set aside the bag of chocolate. "Having your mom and dad in your life now doesn't mean you have to forget your adoptive parents or the pain of losing them. It's real. *They* were real, and you shouldn't feel guilty for how you feel about them."

I nodded a little, too choked up to speak, and he put his arm around me. Tears slipped down my cheeks, and I bent my head as I swept them away. It felt good to say those things out loud, something I hadn't been able to do with my family. Braden was such a good listener, and he had a way of connecting with my emotions that no one else did.

"Thank you," I sniffled. "For being with me through all this and being so supportive. I've never been comfortable talking about it with anyone else, but you really understand."

"You know that you can trust me. You can talk to me about anything."

He massaged my neck, and I leaned into the crook of his arm, laying my head on his shoulder. He gave me so much comfort, so much warmth. I loved how he looked out for me and always tried to understand my feelings. How he could lift me up with just a smile and make me swoon with just a look. I loved his gentleness and his genuineness and his fierce loyalty.

I'm in love with him.

My eyes pooled with more tears as I accepted my confession. I'd known for a while that I was in pretty deep emotionally, but I hadn't realized until now just how deep. I'd never been in love before, but I couldn't imagine feeling anything stronger than this.

He began to caress my hair, his fingers making silky strokes through the long strands, and I closed my eyes, fighting to contain my emotions. I was so confused, so conflicted. Not about how I felt, but about what I was supposed to do with those feelings.

Braden's lips pressed against my hair, and my eyes opened. All my instincts told me to lift my chin and look at him. To follow my heart. To not let another moment like this pass.

Our eyes met, and he held my gaze, soft but strong, not letting go as we drifted closer together. My heart, my breath, my everything sped up.

And then his lips were on mine.

I'd written many fictional kisses, imagining the sensations, the emotions of the moment, but none of it came close to what I was feeling. The softness, the sweetness of Braden's kiss filled me with heat, and following his lead felt so natural. He tasted like chocolate and all the wonderfulness that the world could offer. I thought I'd get some relief from finally being that close to him, but I only had more hunger, more longing. He made me want and need things I couldn't put into words.

We broke apart, but we lingered within a breath of each other, the anticipation of another kiss sparking the air between us. Braden lifted his eyes, searching my face, and I waited for him to make the next move.

"I'm sorry," he said.

That wasn't the move I expected. Or wanted.

His arm dropped from my shoulders, putting distance between us. "You're upset and vulnerable, and I don't want to be that guy taking advantage. Please tell me you don't hate me."

"I don't... I could never hate you."

He let out a breath of relief. "I don't want to mess up our friendship. I promised–" He stopped and looked down before meeting my eyes again. "You've become one of the best friends I've ever had."

Friend. Friendship. That's all he wanted. He'd kissed me

because he felt bad for me and had some momentary physical urge. His feelings for me were nowhere near mine for him. I took a hard swallow as a fresh set of tears threatened to emerge.

You can't be upset about this.

I'd set the boundaries. I'd told him I couldn't get involved with anyone. He'd played by my rules, and as a result, any romantic interest he'd once had in me had disappeared. That was my fault, not his.

"It's okay," I said, though my heart was crumbling. "It's been… it's been a crazy day."

"Yeah, it has." He slowly bobbed his head. "You've been through a lot. And I didn't mean to add any more complications. That's the last thing you need."

I didn't want to think of our kiss as a complication. It was one of the most exhilarating moments I'd ever experienced. My dream first kiss.

But I needed to put it behind me if I wanted to keep this awesome person in my life. He may not have been in love with me, but he cared about me, and I would be an idiot to throw away our friendship. If he was able to lose interest in me, then maybe eventually I would just think of him platonically, too. It could happen, right?

"We're good," I said. "I promise."

"You're sure?"

"Positive."

An awkward silence followed, an unusual occurrence for us, and Braden cleared his throat. Both of us were avoiding looking at each other. He finally made a movement and reached for the bag of candy. "More chocolate?"

I had every intention of staying friends with him, but I needed to remove myself from the current situation. He and I were too close together in the tiny, dimly-lit space, and my body was still humming from his kiss.

I picked up my phone and was glad to see a text from

Dad, giving me an out. "I should probably get home. My dad's texting me."

Braden observed me with doubt, and I wondered if he knew I was jetting for another reason.

"You want the chocolate for the road?" He asked, breaking into a little smile.

I did my best to smile back. "I'm good. Tell your mom thanks for letting me raid her stash."

When we got to my SUV, another round of awkwardness set in. Braden never hesitated to go all in for a big hug during our goodbyes, but now he stayed back. I didn't know how long it would be until I saw him again, so hell if I was going to let him rob me of what had become one of my favorite things on the planet.

"Thank you again for everything," I said and circled my arms around him.

He stiffened at first but then softened into me, strengthening the embrace. I clung to him, forgetting all the weirdness and enjoying the solidness of him pressed against me. We pulled back at the same time, but Braden's hands stayed cinched around my waist. I looked up at him, and his gaze flickered to my mouth, sending my heart into a tailspin again.

Just as quickly he let me go, and I peered into the darkness to read his eyes. He stepped aside to open my door for me, not letting me see what he was thinking. I thought I'd felt something more than friendship in that moment, but what did I know about boys and their feelings. I'd apparently misread many moments the past few months.

"Text me when you get home," he said.

"I will."

I watched him in the rearview mirror as I drove away, and he didn't move from the driveway. *Just when I'd thought the day couldn't get any more emotionally draining.* I would've never guessed when the day began that it would end with my first kiss. That had been the furthest thing from my mind when we'd started on our journey to see Dominic.

I was so unsettled and had so many jumbled thoughts. I knew I couldn't survive an hour drive, trying to make sense of them on my own. I had to talk to Holly. She'd made me promise to tell her right away if anything monumental ever happened between Braden and me.

The car took care of dialing her number, and when she answered she immediately asked, "How did it go?"

She knew all about the reason for the trip, so I filled her in on what happened with Dominic and then my mom. "I thought those would be the most newsworthy items I'd have to share, but... something else happened." I had to pause as the sensation of Braden's lips on mine came rushing back, making my breath catch. "Braden and I kissed."

"Oh my God! When? Where? How?"

"A few minutes ago in his treehouse when he was comforting me."

"Aahh! Your first kiss! How did it feel?"

"It was–"

I realized I could never adequately describe all the feelings Braden had given me in that moment. There was only one way to best summarize it.

"Perfect."

She squealed. "I'm so happy for you. Does this mean you're taking him out of the friend zone?"

I came back down from my high of remembering the kiss to recalling Braden's hasty apology.

"I wasn't really sure what I should do, but then he basically said that *he* doesn't want to take *me* out of the friend zone."

"What?"

"He apologized for taking advantage when I was upset and said he didn't want to mess up our friendship. That I'm one of the best friends he's ever had."

Holly was quiet for a minute. "I could've sworn that he was still into you."

"Well, it's been a while since you saw us together."

"Yeah, but he's always texting you and calling you, and he went all the way to Detroit to see you."

"He'd do that for any of his good friends, though. Look how close he is with Sam. I'm probably just another Sam."

"But he wanted to date you when you first met. He never wanted to date her."

"We don't know that for sure. He could be going out with all kinds of girls at school. I don't know where he is every night, and it's not my business because I told him I couldn't date him right now."

"But you really want to."

I let my head fall back against the seat. "I thought there was a good chance we could be more than friends later. Better than a good chance. But he's not interested anymore."

"I'm so sorry, girl," she said. "What did you say when he apologized?"

"I told him we were good. As much as it hurts to know he doesn't feel the way I do, I don't want to mess up our friendship either."

"It's not going to be easy now that you know, though. Unrequited feelings suck."

She was right, but I couldn't stomach the thought of not talking to Braden anymore. That would hurt way worse. Maybe the answer was somewhere in between. I could pull back a little – not rush to answer every text and call... stop myself from reaching out to him so often. We could still be friends, but he didn't have to be such a big part of my life. Then he might not be on my mind as much, and I could get over him.

Yes, that sounded like a good plan.

Winter

CHAPTER EIGHTEEN

MY SHORT PROGRAM WAS CURSED.

I had no other explanation for making mistakes in the short at every single Grand Prix event that season. At Skate America I'd popped the combination, in Paris I'd stumbled on the step sequence, and now I'd fallen on the double Axel at the Grand Prix Final. The double Axel! I'd been doing that jump since I was nine years old. I was convinced my blade hit a stone that had fallen off one of my competitors' costumes. World silver medalist Julia Lobacheva had skated right before me, and I'd picked up a number of silver stones from her dress while I'd waited to be introduced. She'd shed her sparkles all over the ice.

"I think George would love this," Mom said, holding up an alarm clock that looked like it belonged on a spaceship.

We were Christmas shopping at one of the gigantic malls in Fukuoka, Japan since I had a day off before the free skate, but my mind was still stuck on the event yesterday. I sat in third place because of the fall, almost seven points out of first. The roster was made up of only the top six skaters from the Grand Prix Series, so the event was like a mini world championship. With Sochi just two months away, everyone wanted to leave the best lasting impression on the judges and have good momentum going into the Olympics. I'd started the competition by putting doubt into the judges' minds.

I moved away from Mom and down the aisle of tech toys, and my eyes fell on a smart watch. My first thought was that it would be a great present for Braden. He could track the miles he ran every morning and check game scores right on his wrist.

I hadn't seen him in the month since we'd kissed, but I hoped to meet up with him sometime before Christmas. I'd stuck to my plan of distancing myself from him, though it hadn't been easy. Every time my phone dinged with a message from him, my heart twitched and I had to restrain myself from jumping all over it. I'd used lots of excuses of being busy (which I was) for my slower response time, but I worried he might've figured me out since his texts had become less frequent in recent days.

"Are you thinking of getting that for someone?" Mom asked.

I looked up with my hand still on the watch. "Maybe Braden."

"That's an expensive gift."

I gave her some subtle side-eye. In all the years I'd known her, she'd never deemed anything expensive. The word didn't exist in her vocabulary.

"He can use it every day," I said.

That was how I'd justify it to Braden when he'd protest the price of the gift. I'd held back on his birthday present, but I loved splurging on my friends. Holly and Court had accepted my extravagance a long time ago.

I contemplated the purchase a few more minutes and then brought it to the register. Mom wanted to look at ties for George, so I found a seat on a bench outside the store. Throngs of people streamed past me, their hands full with shopping bags. With my phone as my only entertainment, I went against Dad's "no social media" advice and pulled up Facebook. I'd still been occasionally creeping on Dominic's page. I knew I shouldn't care, but I couldn't stop myself from being curious.

He hadn't added any new updates or pictures, so I switched over to Twitter. One of the first Tweets on my feed was posted by Sam. A photo of a neon green snowboard accompanied it.

Finals looming but I'm dreaming about this. #WinterBreak #OfftheGrid

A coil twisted in my stomach. The snowboarding trip over New Year's to Phil's family cabin included all the roommates plus Britt and Jason. Braden had said they'd be in New Hampshire for five days, and they'd all agreed to turn off their phones. Thus, the "off the grid" hashtag. Braden and I hadn't gone five days without speaking since we'd met, but a forced separation might be beneficial with nationals starting shortly after that. He was good for my headspace in the fact that he still made me laugh and gave me a mental break from skating stress. But he was also bad for me because any contact with him stirred up all my emotions and got me questioning if I'd made the right decision keeping him in my life.

I sensed that I was about to revisit the night in the treehouse for the thousandth time, so I returned to scrolling through Twitter. My name caught my eye, and I clicked on the article link. A columnist who covered figure skating regularly had written an opinion piece on the short program. My performance, specifically. I started reading, blocking out all the noise from the shoppers around me.

Having lost only one competition in the past two years, Petrov was the clear favorite for Olympic gold coming into this season. But looking at the fall performances of Petrov, Lobacheva, and the rising star Katia Safina, the race has tightened considerably. Lobacheva and Safina have both skated flawlessly, and don't forget that they will be competing on home soil in Sochi. Petrov may have a Russian name, but the partisan crowd will not be swayed by her heritage.

The judges will also not be swayed if Petrov continues to lose critical points in the short program. She has always been a strong short program skater, so I have to wonder if the pressure of the Olympic season and being the favorite has become too much of a burden. With the dismissal of her long-time coach Kathy Field, there was also obviously some problem in her camp (I don't believe the move was done strictly to reduce Petrov's amount of travel). She once seemed invincible, but with the barrage of mistakes and the off-ice turmoil, her image of perfection has begun to crumble.

I scrolled below the article and scanned the reader comments. Many agreed with the writer, saying I was no longer a "sure thing." The consensus was that I was slowly coming apart, and by the time I got to Sochi, I'd completely cave from the expectations.

I closed the article and shoved the phone into my purse. I was *not* going to let the peanut gallery's psychoanalysis get to me. Yes, I had to deal with heavy expectations every day. I was reminded every time I saw myself on a Sochi promo commercial or an ad for one of the products I endorsed. Whose face was going to be on the cover of all the magazines' Olympic previews? Mine. Team USA was counting on me to not only represent but to *win*. To justify the pimping I'd received and be the golden girl in the marquee sport of the Games.

Those expectations were piling up higher by the day, but they were all out of my control, and I could not let any of them affect my skating. I had to stay focused on what I did on the ice. Nothing else. The "barrage of mistakes" I'd made had been flukes. They weren't a result of me crumbling under pressure. I'd set myself apart over the course of my career by standing strong as the spotlight grew bigger and brighter. Others had wilted, but I'd thrived. All I needed to do to shut up the critics was nail my free skate tomorrow and show that I was still the same fierce competitor I'd always been. They wanted perfection? I'd give them perfection.

STANDING ALONE AT CENTER ice, I raised my chin, presenting a confident stance in my opening pose. Every seat in the large arena was filled, but the crowd sat in total silence. The only sound came from the rapid clicking of the photographers' cameras, capturing the start of my free skate.

"Prelude to the Afternoon of a Faun" began quietly, and I exhaled slowly to calm the adrenaline pumping through me. I made gentle movements to match the music, corralling my energy for the jumps ahead. The first combination was approaching in a matter of seconds, so I increased my speed, taking charge of the ice. I switched to a back outside edge and propelled myself into the air, making three quick turns. Once I landed, I picked in again and turned three more times. I let out a breath as my blade cut a smooth arc into the ice. A clean landing was one of the best feelings in the world.

I flew through the triple loop and the double Axel (no stones tripping me up that time!) and relaxed more into the beautiful music. It was so calming, and even though I'd heard it a bazillion times the past seven months, I hadn't grown tired of it. The dreamy quality inspired me more with each performance.

With three jumping passes straight ahead, I came out of my sit spin with fervor and picked up my pace to set up for the first takeoff. I had to not only execute these jumps but execute them with a flourish to earn extra points. It was the only way I'd have a chance to climb to the top of the podium.

I jumped up into the double Axel with a world of aggression, and after two quick revolutions I landed on one foot with a firm thud. My blade worked hard against the ice, sending up a shower of snow, but I still had to pull off the second half of the combination. I reached back and muscled myself into the air for the double toe loop without any momentum helping me. Panic squeezed my chest as I sensed the lack of height on the jump. I came down way too soon and landed with a wide-swinging free leg, certain that the judges would ding me for the ugliness of it all.

I can't afford to lose any more points.

I knocked out the solo triple flip and then resumed my speedy flow across the rink, setting my eyes on the spot for my next combination. *This has to be perfect. BETTER than perfect.* Picking into the ice, I went airborne for my second triple flip, and something didn't feel right. I'd used too much force on the takeoff, and now I was off-axis and headed for disaster. My right foot connected with the ice, but I was so far back on my heel that I couldn't hold myself up. I crashed onto my butt, shooting a cold sting into my tailbone.

Bouncing up quickly, I reconnected with the music and did my signature Charlotte spiral into the triple Lutz, completing it by the grace of God. I ended the program with a dizzying layback spin and already saw the headlines that would appear in the papers.

Petrov Takes Another Tumble
Petrov Giving Away the Gold
What's Wrong With Petrov?

I had to ask myself the same question. *What IS my problem?* Was the peanut gallery right? Had I let the pressure get to me without even realizing it? Maybe all my mistakes really hadn't been flukes.

I left the ice with defeat sagging my shoulders, and I half-heartedly accepted Dad's hug at the boards. He didn't say anything, knowing all too well that nothing would be helpful at the moment. We sat in the ice blue colored kiss and cry, and Dad intently studied the replays on the monitor. I wanted to tell him not to bother because my issues weren't technical. Something was misfiring between my brain and the rest of my body.

My score appeared on the monitor, and my shoulders sank lower. I was in first place above the three girls who'd already skated, but my number would only hold up if Julia and Katia made major mistakes.

Dad and I stayed silent as we went backstage and watched Katia and then Julia skate. They showed no vulnerability, and they looked like the invincible ones. My name dropped to the third slot, and I stared down the standings as if they were my worst enemy. Placing third at the last big international event before Sochi was a sizable blow to my reputation. I'd managed to erase all the confidence the judges had in me as a consistent performer.

"Let's talk a minute," Dad said, ushering me away from the ever present cameras.

"Keep your head up at the press conference. The media are going to blow this up and make up their own reasons for your mistakes. Stay confident, stay positive. Don't let them lead you to a negative place."

I nodded and he continued, "The goal is to peak in Sochi, not here. You got ahead of yourself on the Axel and the flip, but everything was crisper than it's been all season. We know what we have to work on before nationals."

I kept nodding, but doubts still nagged at me. Doubts over whether I could mentally handle the final push to the Olympics. Dad hugged me, and that time I squeezed my arms around him, getting all the comfort I could before I faced the press.

In my harried state, I'd forgotten I had to go to the medal presentation first. I fake-smiled my way through the formalities and was ready to rid my neck of the bronze medal as soon as I left the ice, but I had to wear it to the media room for more photos. Julia entered the room to a huge round of applause, and she milked it as much as possible, taking her time in joining Katia and me on the stage. She was statuesque for a skater and had long blond hair and striking green eyes.

Every camera's dream.

The three of us each had to give an opening statement, so I stole verbiage from Dad's speech to me, emphasizing my goal to peak in February. Julia received the first question, and I did my best to mentally translate her answer ahead of the interpreter. I knew enough Russian to not feel lost when I attended competitions or visited my grandparents. From what I understood, Julia said the win gave her a new level of confidence for the Games, and the interpreter confirmed it. She'd never beaten me before, so I couldn't blame her for feeling more confident than ever. But the truth remained that she would not have been victorious if I hadn't messed up.

A reporter from IceNet stood and took the press microphone. "This question is for Liza."

I sat up straighter and took a sip from the bottle of water in front of me.

"You've made some uncharacteristic errors at each of your competitions this fall, and now you've finished third for the first time since 2011."

Thanks for the reminder.

"Are you concerned that your season hasn't been building toward the Olympics as it should?"

Of course I'm concerned, but there's no way in hell I'll admit that to the world. Dad's "stay positive" message echoed in my head.

"I'm disappointed that I haven't put out the performances I'm capable of, but I feel great about where I am with my programs right now. The month break until nationals will give me time to polish them even more and focus on executing every single element."

I leaned back from the microphone, and another reporter stood. "My question is also for Liza. You've always been at your best in high-pressure situations, but this season you haven't delivered in the big moments. Do you think the pressures and distractions of being a contender for gold in

Sochi have contributed to your troubles?"

I took another drink of water and cleared my throat. I couldn't share that I was still trying to figure out my psychological issues. If my "image of perfection" had already begun to crumble, admitting any mental weakness would totally implode it.

"Obviously, there have been more obligations, more distractions this season, but I've maintained my primary focus on training and improving every day. The mistakes I've made have been small technical errors that are easily correctable, and with time before nationals to nail run-through after run-through, I don't anticipate making those mistakes again."

I sat back, pleased with my answer, but the press wouldn't let the issue go. Question after question came to me as the reporters all but ignored Julia and Katia, and all the questions contained the words "expectations" and "pressure." They dug out every angle possible, including how daunting it must be for me to think about competing for gold in Russia, my parents' home country, and accomplishing something they weren't able to do. Fulfilling the destiny that they'd started so many years ago. By the end of the press conference my neck had gotten so tense that I had a pounding headache.

Returning to the hotel, I bypassed the post-competition merriment in the lobby and went directly to the room Court and I were sharing. She stood in front of the mirror, brushing her curly blond hair. She was wearing a cute jumper with heels, so it looked like she was on her way out.

"Point me to the aspirin," I said.

She put down her brush and hugged me. "I'm sorry you had such a rough week."

"I tried to blame it all on evil skate gods, but I think I was fooling myself. No one to blame but this supposed superstar."

"When I saw you going so hard into the Axel, I grabbed Josh's arm because I was already panicking for you. Same thing on the flip. It was just so unlike you to be so off on those jumps."

I went over to the nightstand and opened the bottle of aspirin. "I was thinking too much, trying to do too much."

There was a soft knock on the door, and Court gave me a sympathetic look before answering it. Josh came in and hugged me as I swallowed the medicine.

"Come downstairs with us and hang out," he said. "We're going to plan a birthday surprise for your dad tomorrow."

"That's so awesome of you guys. I need to lie down and try to get rid of this headache, though. Maybe I can help you plan over breakfast."

"Sure thing."

They left a few minutes later, and I put on my pajamas and reclined on the bed, phone in hand. I hadn't looked at it in hours, and I expected a text from Mom. Hers was at the top of the list followed by numerous ones from Braden. Resisting my initial urge, I clicked on Mom's first.

Mom: **Are you at the hotel yet?**

Me: **Just got back. Bad headache so going to sleep.**

Mom: **OK. Feel better sweetie. Just wanted to tell you I love you and I'm proud of you.**

Me: **Love you too.**

I scooted lower on the pillows and curled into fetal position to read Braden's messages.

Braden: **I'm not going to give you a rah rah speech because I know you're pissed at yourself and need time to work through it. I learned a lot in Detroit ;)**

Braden: **I've also learned a lot about skating from watching all these competitions, and I have to say (from a completely unbiased perspective) that you were still the best today. When you skate, you skate inside the music as if you're part of it. It's really amazing to watch.**

My eyes misted with tears, and I willed myself not to cry because it would make my head hurt worse. Common sense told me to stop reading, but the need to feel connected to Braden was too powerful.

Braden: **The Russian girls skate on top of the music like it's background noise. They're not even close to doing what you're doing. When you dominate all your jumps in Sochi (I have ZERO doubt that you will), the judges are going to give you all the points. Olympic record. World record. Drop the mic.**

I smiled and laughed softly into the pillow.

Braden: **Ok so I guess that was kind of a rah rah speech but that's what friends are for** ☺

My smile faded. Which word did I hate more at the moment – friend or bronze?

Braden: **I'm going for an early morning run now since I got up at the crack of dawn to watch you. Again, true friendship** ☺ **I woke up Ross with a pretty loud curse word when you fell. He still loves you, though.**

In my dream world, his next message would read – *And so do I.* But this was reality, where no such feelings were to be found.

Braden: **Have fun your last day in Japan. You deserve it!**

The time stamp on the texts showed he'd sent them right after the event ended, so he would be done with his run now. My fingers itched to dial his number, but I thought better of it. If he said the word "friend" again, I'd probably have an uncontrollable emotional outburst. Best to maintain a safe distance and not expose myself to more heartache. A simple reply would be the courteous and *friendly* thing to do.

Me: **Thank you** ☺

CHAPTER NINETEEN

MY ROOM LOOKED LIKE THE AFTERMATH of a Black Friday sale. Clothes and accessories were strewn all over the bed and the plush chair, and shoes littered the carpet. Holly occupied a small clear area on the bed, while Quinn sat on the floor of the walk-in closet, trying on my hats and scarves.

"I swear, packing for nationals is as stressful as the competition," I said, holding a red sweater and a black sweater in front of me.

"The black one," Holly said.

I tossed the loser into the closet and dropped the winner onto the pile forming inside suitcase #2. Suitcase #1 had no vacancy. Since I was going to be in Boston for six days and had a variety of activities on my agenda (practicing, competing, meeting with sponsors, doing autograph signings, watching my friends compete), I had to pack accordingly, which meant multiple outfit choices for each activity.

"We have to win Best Dressed Besties this year," Holly said. "We were robbed last year."

The fashions at nationals had become a huge sideshow over the years, and making IceNet's annual Best Dressed List had turned into an event just as competitive as the skating.

"Is there a Best Dressed Kid category?" Quinn asked.

I took a fedora from the top shelf and plopped it onto her head. "If you bring your A-game they might make it into a new one just for you."

"I know how we can win for sure!" Holly sprang upright. "We'll coordinate the colors of our outfits with the colors of each other's costumes on the days we compete. It will be the coolest show of support and a fabulous fashion story."

"I love it! So, I need to find something seafoam green for your short program and burgundy for the long." I scanned the racks of shirts, hunting for a green blouse I had in mind.

"Why didn't you give Braden his Christmas present?" Quinn asked from the other side of the closet.

I turned and saw she had the wrapped box in her hands, its tag clearly visible.

"We umm… we haven't had a chance to get together."

I also hadn't gone out of my way to make time for him. We'd both had a crazy few weeks – him with finals, holiday family time, and his snowboarding trip, and me with skating, pre-nationals media obligations, and Mom in town for a week over the holidays. Braden had offered to come to the Cape, but I'd gotten so spooked in Japan about my mental game and potential distractions that I'd decided I wasn't allowed to see him. We'd still been texting, but I'd avoided most of his calls.

"Isn't he coming back from New Hampshire today?" Holly asked.

"Yeah, I've been checking Twitter to see what Sam posts about the trip. I know she'll Tweet something as soon as she turns on her phone."

"I don't know how they survived without their phones for five days. I would've thrown myself off the mountain."

I laughed. "I should Tweet this disaster I've made of my room. Quinn, you want to pose with the mess?"

She bundled a purple plaid scarf around her neck and

pushed up the brim of the fedora. I snapped a photo of her in a sassy pose between the suitcases.

"Little sis helping me get ready for Boston," I read aloud as I typed the caption. "She wears the hat better than I do."

Holly went over to the electric blue cocktail dress hanging on the closet door and brushed her hand gently over the silky material. It was my outfit for the Olympic team reception at the end of the week.

"You're going to look so hot in this. Is there a way you can get Braden to see you in it? I think he'd reconsider this friends business."

"A dress won't change his feelings."

"He might really be missing you after a week of no contact. He had a lot of time to think about you in the mountains with no phone."

"I'm sure he was busy having fun snowboarding and playing games with his friends."

Holly held one of my discarded sweaters to her body and stepped in front of the full-length mirror. "Is he going to be at your practices this week?"

"I don't think so. His grandma has an all-event ticket so she'll probably be there, but he just has tickets for the short, the long, and the exhibition."

"You can give him his present," Quinn said.

"I don't know how much I'll see him," I mumbled.

I yearned to see him *so* badly, but I had enough distractions on my itinerary. Everyone was banking on me to win my fourth national title since the competition in Boston wouldn't be as strong as it was on the international level. But after the season I'd had so far, I wasn't taking anything for granted.

Quinn wandered out of the room, probably to go bug Alex, and I paused my search for the green blouse so I could check Twitter again. I was curious how long Braden would take to text me once he had use of his phone. I thumbed through the feed, almost scrolling past Sam's new Tweets.

I'm back! And EVERYTHING has changed. If I could've tweeted on New Year's Eve I would've posted this...

When your NYE midnight kiss is the kiss you've been wanting for so long. #BestTripEver #Happy2014

My heart stopped, and I read the Tweets over and over. There was only one person on that trip she'd wanted to kiss for so long. I'd seen the way she looked at Braden every single time I'd been around them. It had to be him.

EVERYTHING has changed.

That could only mean one thing. Braden and Sam had kissed, and they were together now.

"Oh my God," I whispered.

"What's wrong?" Holly asked.

When I didn't answer (because I felt like I was being strangled), she came and read over my shoulder.

"No way," she said quietly.

I walked on jelly legs over to the bed and sat on a pile of clothes. Scrolling through Twitter again, I looked to see if I'd missed any other posts by Sam or anyone else from the group. A new Tweet from her popped up just as I returned to the top. It was a string of ten heart emojis with no text. My lunch came up in my throat.

"He fell for her," I said. "It's exactly what I was afraid would happen."

"Maybe she's not talking about him."

"Of course it's him. It was so obvious how she felt about him and that she's been waiting to kiss him forever." I bent forward and bowed my head in my hands. "Oh my God, all his roommates have tickets for next weekend. The two of them are going to be there as a couple."

Holly sat next to me and put her arm around me. "You probably won't even see them. There'll be so many people there."

I kneaded my forehead as visions of Braden and Sam

kissing at the stroke of midnight assaulted me. Simply imagining them together physically hurt, so what would actually seeing them together do to me?

Holly's phone jangled with the ringtone she'd reserved for her mom, and she answered and said, "I'm coming in a few minutes."

"Time to go?" I asked as she ended the call. They were driving to Boston that night since Holly's practices started a day earlier than mine.

"Mom wants to get there before dinner. So annoying." She hugged me with all the strength in her petite body. "Call me if you want to talk. Just remember that you're way cooler than Sam, so it's Braden's loss."

I wished I had that perspective, but I felt like the loser in this situation. I'd still been holding onto hope that Braden would think of me as more than a friend again someday. That hope had just been destroyed.

I pulled my legs up on the bed and leaned back against the mound of black and white pillows. I'd lost interest in picking out cute outfits. I took my writing journal from the nightstand and flipped to the last page I'd written. I'd left off in the middle of a story about two pair skaters falling in love. They were currently flirting their way through a sushi dinner in Japan. Some of the banter had been inspired by conversations I'd had with Braden.

I slammed the journal shut and threw it aside. *Perhaps I should start a new story about a girl picking up the shards of her heart.*

Quinn returned sans the fedora and climbed beside me, flattening a few sweaters along the way. "Why aren't you packing?"

I snuggled her against me. "I needed a break."

"You look sad."

My phone lit up with a FaceTime request from Braden, and a sick feeling came over me, something I never thought I'd experience when I saw his face. The phone kept ringing, and I just kept staring at it.

"You're not going to answer it?" Quinn asked.

"I'm not okay to talk to him right now."

"Is he the reason you're sad?"

The ringing finally stopped, and I pressed my cheek to Quinn's soft curls. "I like him, but he likes someone else."

She raised her big blue eyes to mine. "He's stupid."

I laughed through the pain and hugged both my arms around her. The phone buzzed with a text, and I gave it a sidelong glance. Was he going to tell me about Sam?

"Let's read it," Quinn said.

I hesitated and then clicked on the message, holding my breath in advance of the additional pain it would bring.

Braden: **Happy New Year! Hope your 2014 is off to a great start** ☺ **The trip was a blast. Some crazy things happened that I have to tell you about. Give me a shout when you can.**

If the crazy things included Sam and him hooking up, he could keep that information to himself.

"Why is he texting you if he likes someone else?" Quinn asked.

"Because he thinks of me as his buddy."

"You should text him back and tell him to get lost."

I had to admit I was a little tempted to do that and just be done with this drama, but there was probably a more mature response I could use. I set the phone aside. "Help me finish packing and I'll deal with that later."

Alex popped in while Quinn helped me straighten the chaos in suitcase #2, and he quickly ran when he saw the mess. It took over an hour for me to finish selecting clothes for each day and then fit them into the luggage, but it was good busy work to keep me from breaking down. I could feel the tightness building in my chest. Once I'd packed everything, I asked Quinn to give me some space to compose my reply to

Braden.

Alone and gripping the phone, I mentally wrote and rewrote various replies, all delivering the same message – I wouldn't have time for texts or calls or socializing of any sort in Boston, so I was essentially disappearing for the week. My eyes welled up at the thought of no sweet, encouraging messages coming my way, but this was the best thing for my sanity. It didn't matter how nice he was or how good his intentions were. I couldn't think of him now without thinking of him with Sam, and that was too much for me to handle.

Me: **Happy New Year! I've been super busy as usual. Getting ready for Boston. I have so much on my plate that I won't be able to talk until after the event. It's my turn to go off the grid. Hope you understand!**

Mature and to the point. I watched the screen for his response and chewed on my lip as the little dots indicated he was typing.

Braden: **Of course. Do whatever you need to do to be at your best!**

He was so understanding that I felt bad for shutting him out. *Remember WHY this is necessary. He's with someone now. He should be focusing on HER.*

Me: **I have to go get dinner ready. Dad and Em are already in Boston with their novice teams, so Court and I are in charge around here. Hope you enjoy the competition!**

Braden: **I know I will! Enjoy competing** ☺ **You got this!**

I gazed at his text until the screen went black, my chin trembling as I held in the tears. *Let it out. Let it all out now and close the door on this.*

The first tears escaped, and I took Peter into my arms, muffling my sobs in his fur. Every memory from the past six months flooded over me – all the long talks, all the laughs, all the hugs, and of course the sweet, sweet kiss. I cried until my eyes burned and my throat was raw. I wanted to regret meeting Braden and putting myself through the emotional wringer, but the memories were too good, too precious. They didn't deserve to be lost. Just put away until they didn't hurt me so much.

I slowly lifted my head and dried my face with my sleeve. From now on I had to channel all my emotions into skating. It was the love that had been in my life through every good and bad day. The one constant I'd held onto through the tragedies and the turmoil. I'd relied on skating so many times to pick me up and give me happiness, and now it was relying on me to give it my greatest effort. I couldn't let it down.

WHIZZING PAST THE FIVE other girls on the practice ice, I looked over my shoulder at the boards. Still no Dad. He'd had to be at TD Garden for Court and Josh's short program, but he was supposed to hurry over here to the convention center for my short program warm-up as soon as they finished. Our team leader Marni stood at the boards so I wouldn't be alone, but I missed Dad. I wasn't competing for another five hours, and my knees were already wobbly and my palms sweaty. All eyes were on me to see which version of Liza would show up – the one who'd been unbeatable for two years or the one who skated like a head case.

I fiddled with my leotard and made long strides across the ice to loosen my legs. I had twenty minutes to practice the elements in my program. None of the skaters' music would be played as it was at our forty-minute sessions. The warm-up was strictly for focusing on the elements.

Without Dad to offer an alternative plan, I decided to run through all my jumps first. I wove through my competitors and found a lane for my triple Lutz-triple toe combination. Picking into the ice, I went up into three revolutions and came down on a shaky leg. I picked in for the triple toe, but my unsteadiness sent me off balance, and I had to step out of the landing. The crowd packed into the temporary seats applauded anyway, showing how much incredible support I had. It only made me more nervous, not wanting to disappoint the thousands of fans who'd be at the arena and the many more watching around the world.

Marni continued to stand alone at the boards, and I glanced at the clock overhead. *Where is he?* The Garden and the convention center were only a few minutes apart by shuttle. I was in dire need of one of Dad's pep talks.

I couldn't wait for him to arrive to do my next jump, so I pumped my legs and sped to the opposite end of the rink for the triple flip. I pulled in tight for the three rotations but again had a wild landing. I took a few deep breaths and dragged my palms down the sides of my black pants. *Calm yourself. Be the unbeatable Liza.*

A commotion behind the boards made me look up, and I spotted Dad sprinting toward the ice and flashing his credential at the volunteers. I raced over to him as he relieved Marni and stripped off his long coat.

"I'm so glad you're here!" I said, throwing my arms around him.

"I'm so sorry. The bus got off schedule and was late."

Perspiration beaded his forehead, and his face and neck were the same color as his red tie. I offered him my water, but he pulled a mini bottle from his coat.

"How did Court and Josh do?" I asked.

He took a long gulp and loosened his tie. "Court missed the Sal."

"Oh no."

Court and I had been dreaming for years of being roomies in the Olympic Village and competing together in the new team event (we'd even made a pinky promise called the Sochi Pact). Only the top two pairs would earn the trip to Russia, making the competition brutal. This was Court and Josh's last shot to go to the Olympics since they were retiring at the end of the season, so the pressure on them was just as monumental as it was on me.

"Let's talk about you," Dad said. "Have you done your jumps?"

"The combo and the flip. The landings were sketchy."

"Then let's do them again."

I nodded and rejoined the action on the ice. I completed the combination with yet another messy landing, so tight that I scraped the ice with the toe pick of my free leg. Dad waved me over, and he leaned his elbows on the boards so that we were at eye level. He gave me a little smile.

"Do you remember the first time you landed the Lutz-toe?"

I smiled back. "The summer I was thirteen. It was the day after Quinn took her first steps."

"You reeled off six clean ones in a row, each one higher than the one before it. Never saw anything like it."

"Everyone else stopped practicing and cheered me on."

He set his eyes on mine, holding my attention with his confident gaze. "That combo was made for you. You do it better than anyone ever has. Don't fight what's so natural to you."

I nodded slowly, thinking of all the years I'd done those jumps as if they were the most basic of moves. I'd taken so much pride in my success rate with them. I had to relax my body and let my training override my nerves.

"Do I have time to do it again?" I asked.

"One more. Then flip and Axel."

I slapped the boards with resolve and didn't waste any precious seconds getting into my jump setup, breathing evenly through each stroke. I visualized the technique step by step and then went into the air, enjoying the perfect spring from my toe pick. Every motion happened just as I'd pictured it, and I rolled right into the second jump with ease. A loud ovation punctuated the landing.

I stayed zoned in to the ice and executed the next two jumps with precision. Dad clapped as I skated past him and said, "Spins."

I knocked out all three, hitting the necessary positions and rotations, and I noticed only a few minutes remained in the session. Dad called me over and motioned to start my cooldown, so I worked my blades over the ice in methodic fashion, focusing on the familiar feel of the smooth motion. *Just another cooldown. Just another short program.*

The other girls went one by one to the center of the rink to bow before leaving the ice, and I waited until they'd all gone to make my exit. I bowed to the officials' side first and then turned to the face the audience. They roared to life, some even standing. My pulse ramped up again, and I dreaded waiting hours to compete. I had entirely too much time for thoughts of my past mistakes to resurface.

Dad and I hugged for a long minute after I put on my blade guards, and then he left me with this – "You're one hundred percent ready. All you need to do now is rest."

A small group of kids had gathered behind the barrier separating the credentialed area from the spectators, so I walked over in my skates and watched their faces light up with excitement. I went down the line signing programs and skates and cell phone cases, and I posed for every giggly selfie request. Their enthusiasm filled me with an abundance of positive energy. As I asked them how they'd enjoyed the practice, a much older fan joined the group – Braden's grandma.

"Hi, Liza!"

She squeezed between two tween girls and reached over the barrier to hug me. Her honeysuckle perfume wafted over me, reminding me of when I'd met her at Braden's party.

Braden's party. The treehouse. The kiss.

I jerked backward out of her grasp. "I... I don't want to get you all sweaty. How are you doing?"

"I'm having so much fun! I'm in skating heaven. I've been to all the events, even the ones with the teeny little kids. They were so cute!"

"I'm glad you're having such an awesome time."

"B told me not to bother you, but I just wanted to give you a good luck hug and tell you how much I've enjoyed watching your practices. You make it look so easy and so beautiful."

I smiled. "Thank you. I really appreciate that."

"I'll let you get back to your adoring fans." She patted my arm. "I'll be cheering for you tonight!"

"Have fun!"

The scent of her perfume remained in the air, and I quickly turned to the new crop of kids who'd raced down from the seats. Now was not the time to let my mind wander to memories of Braden. There was no room for sadness in my heart today. Only confidence and determination.

CHAPTER TWENTY

Her technique has abandoned her.

She's showing more nerves than she ever has.

I'd read all those things on the internet in the days leading up to nationals. Everyone was doubting me, questioning my resolve and my readiness for the most important six weeks of my skating career.

I stood at the door to the ice, about to skate my short program, and I had only one plan in mind. Not to prove to everyone that I was still the best in the world, but to have faith in the hours upon hours I'd spent training. I'd done everything humanly possible to prepare for this moment.

The girl who'd just completed her program finished her bows and headed for the kiss and cry, and the volunteer manning the door cracked it open for me. I ripped off my guards and burst onto the ice, and the building exploded with cheers. I focused downward and didn't allow myself to look up. I'd have time to take in the atmosphere after I skated. All I needed to do in these final minutes was become one with the ice.

After I circled the rink twice, I stopped in front of Dad at the boards. He'd changed his tie to a fuchsia one that matched my dress. I tightened my long ponytail and patted my head for any stray wisps, and then Dad took my hands in his. The huge crowd was still making a ton of noise, so he leaned in close to me.

"Skate with freedom and with joy. Let your natural power and your love for skating come through."

My face relaxed into a smile, and I exhaled a long breath to make my body do the same. Leaving Dad behind, I stood alone at the end of the rink, surrounded by applause and screams and people shouting my name. The announcer introduced me with enthusiasm, and the noise became overwhelming. My arms and legs trembled, and I shook them out as I found the spot on the ice for my opening pose.

The audience finally quieted, and the opening piano notes of "Nostalgia" broke the silence. My knees wavered as I made my first strokes across the ice, so I dug in harder, taking command of my movements. I entered the combination spin with all kinds of speed, and it kept me whirling swiftly through each position change. I followed that up with an equally fast sit spin, making sure to point my toes as I crouched low to the ice.

Shooting out of the spin, I worked up speed for my first jump, the double Axel. The disaster at the Grand Prix Final flashed through my head, but I quickly refocused on the technique. With a crisp forward snap into the air, I rotated and landed solidly on my right blade. Just like I'd been doing the past ten years.

The music tempo shifted from slow to upbeat, and I moved across the ice with the natural power that Dad had reminded me to use. I had so much speed that I eased up a bit as I approached the triple flip. *Stay in control.*

I sprang upward, and a rush of cold air whooshed over me and curled around me while I spun. I opened up for the landing, and I came down again on a neat, clean edge. The ovation that went up was the loudest yet, and it lit me up with even more energy.

Stay calm.

Keeping my breathing steady, I deepened my crossovers and sailed around the rink, heading for the biggest element, the triple Lutz-triple toe. As I switched to a back outside edge, my heart rate went into the stratosphere, and I yelled at myself, *Calm down! Your body knows exactly what to do!*

With a firm stab, I flew into the Lutz, snapping off three quick rotations. My right foot hit the ice, and my knee wobbled, but I would *not* give in to nerves. I punched the ice with my left toe pick and spun three more times, completing the jump with the strongest of landings. The crowd responded with a roar, and I held my pristine position a few extra seconds, hammering my point home.

I am still a champion.

I danced into the step sequence and concentrated on curving my blades at all the right angles to maximize my points. All the while I kept my head up, making eye contact with the audience and bringing them into the program with me. Their applause began again as I neared the end of the footwork, and I used their energy to zoom toward my final element.

I twirled into the layback spin and arched my back until I faced the ceiling. Reaching behind me, I grabbed my blade and pulled my leg up above my head. The faster I spun, the rowdier the crowd became, and on the song's final frantic notes I ended the spin with a dramatic stop. Not a single person was still in their seat.

Relief washed over me, and I stood frozen in my ending pose, my arms outstretched. Slowly I relaxed and turned in a circle, taking in the mayhem around me. The screams were so loud, the signs bearing my name so plentiful. Flowers and stuffed toys came flying from all directions. I clenched my fist, and I pumped it quietly at my side. That was the short program I'd been looking for all season.

I bowed and waved to every side of the arena, and I set off for the boards where Dad waited with a huge grin. A stuffed animal flew into my path, and even though it was face down I could see it was a light brown dog. My heart winced, and I hesitated a moment, but then I skated past it, letting the sweepers pick it up.

Dad embraced me and hugged me to his side as we stepped up into the kiss and cry. "You were in total control. The spins were some of the best you've ever done."

"They felt so fast," I said, slipping on my fleece jacket.

The technical panel didn't take long to finalize my score, and I pumped my fist again as the announcer read the enormous number. I looked up at the video board, and I was in first place by ten points. There were only a few skaters remaining, and I felt confident that none of them would approach my score. Dad kissed my cheek, and I stood to wave to the crowd, thanking them for their continued enthusiastic applause.

With the press conference and then the draw for the free skate, I didn't get back to my hotel room until almost midnight. Since roommates weren't required at nationals like they were at international events, Court and Josh were able to share a room, leaving me solo. I missed Court's company, but I couldn't blame her for wanting to sleep in Josh's arms. I'd never gotten to cuddle with Braden, but the warm, safe feeling I got from his hugs gave me an idea of how wonderful it would've been.

Thinking of Braden made me look to the bag of stuffies I'd carried from the arena. Somewhere in it was the puppy that I suspected had come from him. Why was he still giving me gifts that had special meaning? I stared at the plastic bag that was about to burst with toys. Had he attached a note to the dog like he'd done previously? I started to get my pajamas and my shower stuff together, but I couldn't fight the curiosity. I opened the bag and dug out the big-eyed puppy.

There was no note.

It made sense since he shouldn't be writing cute messages to someone who wasn't his girlfriend or whatever Sam was to him now. Maybe the dog hadn't even come from him. I had to stop thinking about him other than as the buddy he wanted me to be. I tossed the dog onto the carpet and stalked to the bathroom to get ready for bed.

Me: **On my way back from the arena. Want to hang out for a bit?**

Holly: **At dinner with the fam. Gonna be a while. Dad is telling stories of big games he lost when he played football in college to try to make me feel better.**

Me: **Text me if you need me to rescue you.**

Holly: **I got this. Get yourself to sleep so you can kick ass tomorrow.**

Me: **Love you!!!! ☺**

Holly: **Back at ya**

I PEERED OUT THE bus window at the Seaport neighborhood lit up by glowing streetlights. Slushy snow lined the curbs where it had been pushed aside after the last storm. I'd hoped for a dusting of snow tonight to cleanse the air of this not-so-fabulous day. The gloominess had begun that afternoon when Holly and Danny aborted a lift in their free skate, costing them the gold medal. I'd sat with Holly in her room afterward as she cried and cursed and beat herself up. She'd let me try to comfort her, but I knew from experience that nothing I said would make her less sad or frustrated. It would just take time for the sting to go away.

After leaving Holly, I'd met with Kristin about some pre-Olympics TV appearances she'd scheduled later in the month.

Being booked on talk shows before I'd even won the title was a reminder of what was expected of me. I'd started thinking about the monster scores the Russian girls had put up at their national championships and how I needed to top those numbers tomorrow to make a statement. As a result, I'd been tight on my jumps at my evening practice and not in tune with the music during my run-through. The other girls on the ice were also stumbling and missing jumps, and it seemed as if a bad aura hung over the practice session.

I'd thought the organized autograph signing on the concourse with the top four girls would get me out of my funk, but some fans got mad over the limited time of our appearance. In order to avoid chaos, the federation personnel working the table wouldn't let us sign anything after the line was cut off, but craziness ensued anyway with crying kids and angry adults. I'd offered apology after apology to the fans as we were ushered to the secure exit.

The bus came to a slow stop in the circle driveway of the Westin, and I hauled my rolling bag down the steps, careful not to trip in my heeled boots. Inside the lobby, the Friday night crowd had already started to gather around the bar. I noted the many familiar faces of coaches and former skaters and quickly looked away so no one would try to rope me into a conversation. I had a date with my PJs and the winter premiere of *Pretty Little Liars*.

I gasped and stopped in my tracks.

What the–

Braden was at the front desk, talking to the clerk and holding a shiny gold gift bag. My stomach flipped at seeing him for the first time in months, and then it sank.

Why is he here? I told him I couldn't talk to him this week. And he's bringing me a gift? This needs to stop.

I marched over to the desk, and he turned and saw me, surprise in his eyes.

"Hey, I didn't think I'd see you." He started to lean

toward me but stopped. "I was just leaving this for you."

"What is it?"

"It's your Christmas present." He handed the bag to me. "I thought part of it might be useful this weekend."

I gaped at him, searching for a calm response when all I wanted to do was scream. I'd been a fool to think that I could be friends with him. He was going to tear my heart out with every kind gesture, and it would be totally decimated because he was all about the kind gestures. I couldn't do it. I had to end this in quick fashion. Like ripping off a bandage.

"Thank you for the gift, but you shouldn't have come here. I umm... I don't think you should come to the Garden this weekend either. I'll reimburse you for the tickets for you and your friends."

"What–" he sputtered. "I don't understand. Is this because I brought the present? I really didn't plan to bother you. I just wanted–"

"This isn't going to work. I'm sorry, but I don't have time to be a good friend, so you should just forget about me. Forget about all of this."

He stared at me a long minute, disappointment on his face, and he stepped closer to me. "I think I know what this is really about." He lowered his voice. "It's about the kiss."

Heat filled my cheeks, and I lowered my eyes to the floor. Was he talking about our kiss or his and Sam's? Either way, it wasn't a topic to discuss in the lobby. The looky-loos hanging near the bar had started checking us out.

"Let's go talk in my room," I said.

I walked ahead of him, avoiding eye contact, and I stared straight ahead at the doors in the elevator. During the seemingly hour-long ride up to the fifteenth floor, I decided I had to be honest about my feelings. It was the only way Braden would get the message and leave me alone.

My room was so dark that I had to fumble along the wall for the light switch. I turned on the bedside lamp, too, and draped my coat over the desk chair. Braden took off his jacket, and he was wearing the gray UMass hoodie I'd worn when I slept at his house. *How did we get from the euphoria of that weekend to this?*

Braden gave the stuffed dog on the carpet a long look, and I thought he was going to say something, but he walked past it. I tugged on the ends of my sleeves, digging my nails into the wool sweater. Now that I had Braden up there, I couldn't lose my nerve. I had to attack my confession like I did the Lutz-toe combination. No doubts, no hesitation.

"You were phenomenal last night, by the way," he said, shoving his hands in his jeans pockets.

"Oh... thanks."

Awkward tension filled the small room, and I hated that his simple compliment could make me feel all gooey inside. I couldn't let him distract me from my mission.

"You were right," I blurted out. I kept my head down, focusing on my sleeves. "I know we're just friends, but when I saw Sam's Tweet about kissing you on New Year's, I was... I was jealous."

Silence came, and I held my breath.

"Wait, you thought that was about me?" he said.

My head snapped up. "It wasn't?"

"No. Sam hooked up with Phil on New Year's. Why would you think it was me?"

"She hooked up with Phil? I would've sworn on my life that she liked *you*."

He held up his hands. "All I know is apparently they were into each other for months. They didn't want to act on it because they thought it might be awkward being roommates."

I stood with my mouth open, processing the bizarre information I'd just gotten. "Sam and Phil?" I said in disbelief.

"That's the reaction we all had, too."

I slowly shook my head, realizing the situation was much different from what I'd believed it to be. Braden wasn't into

Sam. But that didn't mean he was into me. He'd still backed off that night in the treehouse.

"Now that we cleared that up, can we go back to the part where you said you were jealous?" Braden asked, one eyebrow raised.

"Oh... yeah." I averted my eyes again and took a long swallow, summoning the courage to spill my feelings. "I umm... I thought I wanted to just be friends. I thought that was what was best for me, but... when you kissed me... I... I didn't want you to stop."

He didn't respond, and I didn't dare look at him. He was probably trying to figure out how to nicely reiterate his lack of interest in me.

"Do you know how hard it was for me to stop?" he said quietly.

I froze and tentatively lifted my eyes to his. They were locked on me, full of emotion, and I was more confused than ever.

"Why did you?" I asked.

"Because I promised you I wouldn't cross that line. You said we could only be friends, and if I screwed that up, I was afraid you'd push me away and I'd never see you again."

"So, when you said you didn't want to lose one of your best friends..."

"I meant that. You are one of the best friends I've ever had." He took two small steps toward me. "But you're also so much more."

My flip-flopping stomach did an exuberant somersault, and my heart was totally overtaken by the gooeyness. Braden was saying everything I'd longed to hear, and it was time I said everything I'd longed to tell him.

"You're so much more to me, too." I took bigger steps toward him. "You didn't mess up anything when you kissed me. It was the best first kiss I could ever imagine. Because it was with you."

His eyes filled with bright light, and his lips curled into a smile. He finished closing the gap between us, touching his hand to my cheek. He traced my hairline with his fingertips, gently brushing the long strands from my face, and I shivered deep in my core.

"How do you feel about a second kiss?" he asked softly.

I slid my hands up to his chest and tipped my chin up to him, and he curved one hand behind my neck and the other around my hip. He bent toward me, and I met him halfway, sealing our lips in sweet bliss. I looped my arms around him and buried my fingers in his thick hair, and his breath came hot against my mouth as his tongue skimmed the seam of my lips. I parted them and breathed him in. He stroked the small of my back, pressing our bodies together, and I melted into his warmth.

He pulled back just enough for our eyes to meet, and I lost myself completely in the affection in his gaze. He kissed the tip of my nose and then my cheek and then my earlobe, and I went weak in the knees. I knotted his wavy locks between my fingers, holding him tight against me.

"How did you not know how I feel about you?" His lips tickled my ear, and he brought his head back to face me. "As hard as I tried to hide it, I thought for sure it was so obvious. Phil said I had little hearts popping out of my eyes whenever I saw you."

I laughed. "There were times I thought you were still interested in me, but I'm so clueless about guys that I wasn't sure if I was misreading everything."

"You didn't misread anything. I never stopped wanting to be with you. I prayed every day that you'd give me another chance, and I was going to wait as long as I had to."

I cupped my hands under his strong jaw. "I felt the same way, but I was so scared that another girl would steal you away before I could be with you."

"No one could ever steal me from you. This is all yours."

He patted his heart.

I smiled and leaned into him, but my phone trilled in my purse. My body was pulled toward Braden's like a magnet, but knowing the call could be competition-related, I reluctantly left his embrace to answer it. Mom's name was on the screen.

"Hey, Mom."

"Hi, sweetheart, I just wanted to check in before bed. Do you want to have breakfast in the morning?" Her voice was loud enough where Braden could probably hear her.

"Umm…" I glanced at him, unsure how he might fit into my plans. "I'll probably just get something small since I'll have an early lunch before the warm-up."

"Okay. Just call if you want to meet. Hope you get a good night's rest."

"I'll try."

"Love you."

"Love you too."

Braden circled his arms around my waist and pressed his lips to my forehead. "Do you have to go to sleep soon?"

I tightened my grip on him and rested my head on his chest. "I don't want you to go."

"Believe me, the last thing I want to do is leave you, but I don't want to throw off your schedule."

I burrowed my face into his soft sweatshirt. I couldn't bring myself to let him go. Not after going months without seeing him. Not after finally admitting our feelings to each other.

"What if you stay and we cuddle and fall asleep together?" I said.

He combed his fingers through my hair. "That's a very attractive offer, but are you sure I won't be in your way?"

"You're exactly where I want you to be."

His mouth spread into a smile, and I felt it still on his lips as he kissed me. And kissed me again. And then again until we broke apart, both of us breathless. If I'd known how freaking incredible kissing him like this felt, I would've thrown myself at him a long time ago.

"We need to get you to sleep," he said, touching his forehead to mine.

I sighed. "Yes. Sleep."

I went over to my suitcase and searched for the perfect pajama combination, finally settling on a Red Sox tank and a pair of little gray shorts. Braden said he was going to text Ross his whereabouts while I changed, and as soon as I closed the bathroom door I did a dance of glee.

He wants to be with me.

He said I have his heart.

I can kiss him whenever I want.

I fanned my hands in front of me and took a few deep breaths before changing my clothes, brushing my teeth, and washing my face. Looking in the mirror, I smoothed down my shirt and chewed on my lip. *Is this cuddling going to get frisky? How frisky do I want it to get?* The thought of Braden's hands on my skin made me tremble with anticipation. I trusted him wholeheartedly and knew he'd never push me to do anything I wasn't ready to do.

I went back into the room, and Braden was holding the stuffed dog. He raised his head, and his eyes traveled over me, shining with appreciation.

"How come you didn't wear that when you stayed at my place?"

I smiled. "I had on my friendship pajamas then."

He grinned and held up the stuffie. "What happened to my note?"

"There was a note?"

"Yeah, it was hooked to the collar."

"It must've fallen off. What did it say?"

He sat the puppy on the edge of the bed. "It said, 'Missing you but so proud of you.'"

I touched my heart and gave him a long hug. "It's probably better that I didn't see it last night because I would've sobbed and thrown it in the trash."

He laughed. "The treatment a guy gets for being nice."

I looked over his shoulder and noticed the gift bag on the desk. "I need to open my present! Yours is still at my house."

"Yeah, probably in the garbage," he teased.

I tapped his arm with a little punch and reached inside the bag, and my hand touched two books. The first was a paperback – a collection of *The Far Side* cartoons.

"I thought you could read it tomorrow while you're waiting all day to compete. I guarantee it will make you laugh," he said.

"This is awesome. I'm always looking for something to keep me entertained on a long competition day."

I took out the other book and discovered a journal with a pretty pink floral pattern on the cover.

"For all that smut you write," he said. "Which you definitely need to let me read now. Boyfriend privileges."

My eyebrows shot up, and he stammered, "Sorry, that was... that was presumptuous–"

"It's okay." I smiled so big my cheeks hurt. "It's more than okay."

He smiled just as big, and he took me into his arms, wrapping me in one of his fantastic hugs that I'd missed so much. In less than an hour, the day had gone from being a total downer to one of the most amazing days of my life. And I was about to end it by cuddling with Braden. *Winning!*

I set my phone alarm, and I also rang the front desk to arrange for a wake-up call. As I peeled back the blanket and the cover sheet, Braden went around to the other side of the bed and kicked off his sneakers. Grabbing my lotion from the nightstand, I massaged the jasmine-scented liquid into my arms and hands.

"Oh, wow, that smell," Braden said.

"Is it bad?"

"No, it's good. Very good. It was all over my sheets after you slept there, so it was like you were still there after you left. I didn't want to get out of bed."

I smiled at the fact that we'd had similar experiences that weekend. "The bed smelled like you when I got there, and I wondered if you'd notice if I stole your pillowcase." I laughed.

I crawled under the sheet, and Braden tugged his hoodie over his head, lifting up his T-shirt with it (*sigh*). He pulled it down and then slid between the sheet and the blanket so we weren't completely under the covers together.

"You can umm… you can take off your T-shirt too, if you want," I said, not succeeding in hiding my grin.

"Are you trying to take advantage of me?"

I hid my face halfway in the pillow. "I just want to touch your abs."

His eyes widened and he laughed. With a quick tug, his shirt came off and landed on the floor. Settling back beside me, he took my hand in his, bringing it to his lips. He kissed the tips of my fingers and then guided them down to his stomach, his eyes staying fixed on mine. He pressed my palm against his warm skin, and a surge of heat went through me. I took over control and splayed my fingers over his tight muscles. His soft gaze sharpened with desire, and he covered my mouth with his, kissing me long and deep and… *oh my God, this is so good.*

Somewhere between Braden biting my neck and me exploring every inch of his chest, I realized the longer our make-out session lasted, the more I wouldn't want to stop, and time was not my friend.

I groaned. "It's getting late."

He placed a soft kiss on my collarbone and looked at me with hooded eyes. "To be continued."

"Definitely."

I reached over to turn off the lamp and then snuggled

into Braden's arms, my back to his chest. He pecked my shoulder and said, "Goodnight, my superstar."

I turned my head to him and wrapped my hand around his bicep. "You're *my* superstar. First date, first kiss, first boyfriend..."

He went totally still, and then his lips found mine in the darkness. He retreated with a tingling, feathery kiss.

"I want to be your first everything."

CHAPTER TWENTY-ONE

I COULDN'T HEAR MY MUSIC WITH the noise of over ten thousand people screaming and clapping, but I'd practiced the program so many times that I could hear the Debussy piece in my head. I leapt into the air in a split flying leaf and took a few steps before twirling into the layback spin. With the crowd feeding me enough energy to skate a hundred more minutes, I completed the closing spin at a frenetic pace.

The cheers reached a deafening level as I lunged into my ending pose, and I couldn't remember experiencing a louder crowd in all my years of competing. I came up from the ice and looked around me, peering all the way up to the nosebleed seats. I'd just had one of the best skates of my life, so if this was my last nationals, I couldn't have asked for a better goodbye.

I took my time bowing to all four sides of the building, wanting to hold onto the incredible love from the audience. My career was a question mark after the Olympics, so I didn't know if I'd ever get to feel the special vibe of nationals again. Tears misted my eyes, and the faces in the crowd blurred together.

Except one that managed to stand out.

The one standing at the foot of the corner aisle, holding an enormous stuffed dog. I burst into laughter and skated over to Braden and his canine companion.

"He's bigger than Papi!" I said.

"I trained him to give great hugs," Braden said, holding out the dog's plushy black arms.

I wrapped mine around its body and tipped my head up close to Braden's. Everyone was watching, including my parents (who didn't know yet that Braden and I were dating), but I didn't want to hide how I felt about him. I was so excited and proud to be with such an amazing guy.

I planted a quick kiss on Braden's lips, and his surprised look melted into a smile. I backed away from the boards and hustled over to the kiss and cry, where Dad was now the one with wide eyes. He hugged me and said, "Beautiful skate."

The three of us sat on the small bench, me between Dad and the dog, and I hooked my arms around both of them. I couldn't stop smiling, and Dad eyed me with curiosity.

"Is there a new development I'm not aware of?" he asked.

"I'll tell you all about it later."

His scrutiny ended when my score was announced, and the crowd went bonkers again. My jaw dropped, and I started laughing at the number, which was higher than I'd ever received. I'd wanted to top the Russians' scores, and this took care of that worry. *God bless nationals inflation!*

As I stood atop the podium a few minutes later, I searched the stands for Braden and my family. The lights had been dimmed, and I was under a big spotlight, making it hard to see anyone, much less my favorite people. Finally, I spotted Quinn and Alex leaning precariously over the boards from the front row. Mom, George, and Em were to their right, while Court and Josh were to their left. They'd punched their ticket to Sochi that afternoon, and I couldn't wait to celebrate with them.

Braden stood beside Josh, and when he saw me looking his way, he tapped his grandma's shoulder. She began waving wildly at me, and I did my best to reciprocate, but I had my hands full with flowers and the champion's pin and trophy.

After the photographers dismissed us, I went straight to Mom and gave her my bouquet of red roses. She held me in a teary embrace and said over and over, "My gorgeous girl." I didn't think she was going to let me go, but the twins started clamoring for my attention. I shared squealing hugs with them and also Court and Josh, and then I met the beaming smile of Braden. He swallowed me in his arms, and I pressed up against the boards to get closer to him.

"Watching you was like watching the Super Bowl, the World Series, and the Stanley Cup all rolled into one," he said.

"That's high praise from a sports superfan."

We grinned at each other, nose to nose, and I felt my family and friends watching us intently. Holly was the only person who knew about the change in our relationship. Braden had left early that morning to let me start my competition day routine, and I'd met Holly at the coffee shop in the lobby. She'd let out such a high-pitched screech over my news that everyone sitting around us had turned to stare.

Braden's grandma took my hand and squeezed it. "Can I get a picture with you and your medal?"

"Of course!"

Braden snapped the photo with his phone, and Grandma Joann leaned in close to me. "I'm so thrilled that you and B are together now. You make the sweetest couple."

I hugged and thanked her, grinning at Braden over her shoulder. Sounded like he'd been busy spreading the good news.

"We made it down from the rafters!" a familiar voice said.

Braden's mom came down the aisle steps with his dad and his sisters behind her.

"You didn't tell me your whole family was coming," I

said.

"Well, Tanner's not here. I'll spare you his thoughts on watching four hours of skating," Braden said. "They've had tickets for a while. I didn't want to tell you since I knew you were already nervous about having so many familiar faces here."

I scooted over slightly so I could see all of them. "Thank you so much for coming. It really means a lot to me."

"You were amazing!" Tarah said. "And the crowd was so wild. I had no idea a figure skating crowd could get that loud."

"It was louder than the last Bruins game we saw here," Mr. Patrick said.

"Liza, they're motioning for you guys to go," Court said.

The other medalists were gliding toward the exit and the press conference that awaited us, so I waved and blew kisses to my cheering section and gave Braden one last hug.

"Meet me at the hotel?" I said.

"I'll be there."

MY PHONE RANG AS the bus made its final turn to the Westin, and I switched from texting Holly to answer Mom's call.

"Are you on your way, sweetheart?"

"Almost there."

"George and I are in the small bar, so we'll come out to meet you. Your father's in the restaurant, but he said they're closing soon, so he'll be out in a few minutes."

"Sounds good."

Braden was already in the lobby, so this was going to be an interesting gathering. I hoped my parents would accept him as my boyfriend and realize how much I needed him for the Sochi home stretch. He wasn't a distraction. He was a lifeline.

I rolled my bag and carried my gigantic puppy through the glass doors of the lobby (Dad had taken my other gifts for me), and I headed for Braden and Ross lounging on the sofa.

"Hey, you." Braden jumped up and put his arms around me. "Ross came to keep me company so I didn't look like a creeper."

"Thank you, Ross."

"I've been watching the skater traffic going by," Ross said. "Man, there are some smokin' hot girls in this sport. You need to hook me up."

I laughed. "You realize a lot of those girls are probably underage? The makeup can be deceiving."

"Creeping on jailbait." Braden slapped his shoulder. "Classic."

"I'm getting out of here. Going to Britt's party where I don't have to check IDs." Ross hugged me. "Liza, you're a rockstar. I don't know what you're doing with this chump, but I guess you could do worse."

"Thanks, dude," Braden said, and they shared a bro hug.

Quinn and Alex came running across the lobby, Dad and Em behind them, and Quinn inserted herself between Braden and me. She folded her arms and tilted her head way back to look up at him.

"Do you like Liza now?" she asked.

He grinned and crouched to her level. "I've always liked her very much."

"You promise you won't make her sad again?"

He glanced up at me, his eyes warm with affection. "I will never, ever make her sad."

She gave him her best intimidating glare, and I bent to her ear. "It wasn't his fault I was sad. I misunderstood a lot of things. He's a really, really good guy."

Dad and Em were watching Quinn's cross-examination with amusement. She stared at Braden a few seconds longer and then stuck her hand out to him.

"Then I'll let you be her boyfriend."

We all laughed, and Braden shook her hand. I squeezed her and kissed her cheek. "I'm so lucky to have a little sister who's got my back."

"Quinn, you did my job for me," Dad said, his hands on his hips.

"Yes, the interrogation portion of the evening is over," I said as Mom and George folded into the group.

"I just have one question for Braden," Dad said.

I groaned inside, and Braden stood tall to face him.

"Would you like to join us at the Olympic team reception tomorrow night?"

"Really?" I squeaked.

"I'm sure the fed can accommodate one more guest."

"After all the things I've done for them, they'd better," I said.

"Thank you, sir. I'd love to go." Braden reached out to shake his hand. "Thank you."

I hugged Dad, and he cupped his hand around my bun as he kissed the top of my head. "Since Braden can't go to Russia, I thought this would be the next best thing," he said.

"Thank you so much," I said. "You're the best."

Mom wasn't sharing in all our smiles. She looked like she was trying, but her lips were pressed too tightly together to move. Hoping to ward off any comments she might make, I asked, "Where's Court and Josh?"

"They ran upstairs after we finished dinner," Em said. "I think they were ready to start their own party."

I knew the feeling. As soon as I saw Braden after I skated, I'd begun thinking about his "to be continued" from last night. I was ready for the continuation the moment I could get him up to my room.

"So, when did you two decide to start dating?" Mom asked.

Something tells me her interrogation will be a lot harsher than

Quinn's.

"Yesterday. Last night," I said.

"It's an odd time to start something, don't you think? You're going to be in Russia for the whole month of February."

"We can text and FaceTime while I'm there. We're pros at staying in touch when we're apart." I smiled at Braden, and he laced his fingers through mine.

"Your schedule is going to be crazy after the Olympics, too, if you… if things go well," she said.

"I have no doubt Liza will be very busy," Braden said. "I'll be here watching every TV show and reading every article until she comes back."

Mom studied me, her mouth pinched again. "I just want to make sure you're not distracted by things at home."

Ha! I knew the word "distraction" would be used by at least one of my parents.

"Of course I'm going to miss him, but I am one thousand percent focused on my goal, and Braden supports my skating one thousand percent. He's known me long enough now that he understands the craziness of my life."

"Speaking of craziness, tomorrow is going to be insane, so we should get these two to bed." Em gathered up the twins. "We'll have much more time to celebrate tomorrow night."

I could always count on Em for a convenient subject change.

"Yeah, I have to get up early for exhibition practice." I looked at Braden and patted the stuffie. "Help me carry him to my room?"

"George and I can help you," Mom said.

"Why don't we go have one more drink?" George said, taking Mom's hand. "Wind down a little bit."

She didn't budge, but Braden had already picked up the dog. I gave Mom and George quick goodbye hugs, and we walked with Dad, Em and the twins to the elevator. Dad had his concerned Papa Bear look in his eyes. I could only imagine his thoughts on Braden coming up to my room.

"You have a long day tomorrow," he said.

Ah, the subtle approach.

"Yep," I said.

"Braden, let me know where your family is sitting for the exhibition," Em said. "We didn't get to talk long at the medal ceremony."

Thank you, Em, for saving me once again.

"For sure," Braden said. "My grandma was beyond starstruck when she met you tonight. She'll probably ask for a picture with you tomorrow."

"She's the cutest," I said.

The elevator opened on my floor, and Braden and I bid everyone goodnight. Dad was still staring us down as the doors shut. I unlocked my room, and I took the stuffie from Braden as I turned on the light.

"I won't be needing you tonight," I said to him as I hugged the puppy. "I have a new friend to cuddle with."

"Oh, really?" Braden smiled and moved behind me, snaking his hands around my waist. "Can your new friend do this?"

His lips grazed my neck, and I closed my eyes and leaned back into him. "What else you got?"

He nipped softly on my earlobe, turning me into a puddle of mush, and I loosened my grip on the stuffed animal.

"I'm almost convinced," I said.

He spun me around, and the dog fell from my grasp. My feet came off the carpet, and I laughed and wound my arms around Braden's neck. He brushed my lips with a tease of a kiss and then captured my mouth with an intense caress. When I finally caught my breath I whispered, "You're in."

BRADEN PARKED HIS JEEP in the long driveway next to his apartment, and he quickly came around to help me climb out. The heels and the short dress made it difficult. We'd driven over from the hotel after the reception, which had been an emotional celebration. With all the emotions, eating dinner hadn't been a priority, so Braden had offered to make us a couple of his famous omelets.

We walked into the living room, and Sam and Phil were snuggled together under a blanket, watching TV. The sight of them as a couple was so bizarre that I found myself staring longer than necessary.

"What are you doing slumming down here when you have a fancy hotel room?" Phil asked.

"I was promised an omelet," I said. "Fancy party food doesn't hit the spot."

"How was it? The party?" Sam asked.

"Liza was named captain of the figure skating team," Braden boasted as he took off his dark suit jacket.

"Very cool," Phil said.

I hung my coat over one of the kitchen barstools, and the chilliness of the room hit my bare arms and shoulders. I rubbed them to erase the goosebumps. "I see Ross has taken control of the thermostat again."

"We've been battling him all night. He's sleeping, but he senses when the temperature goes up two degrees," Sam said. "I can loan you some clothes if you want."

"You sure?"

"You could borrow one of my T-shirts," Braden said with a sly grin.

"How selfless of you." I tugged on his red tie. "I think I'll stick with Sam's wardrobe."

I followed her to her room, and she opened the closet. Not another item could fit on the rod or on the shelves.

"T-shirt and yoga pants okay?" she asked.

"That's perfect."

She pried a couple of racks apart, and I shook my head at how quickly things had changed. A few days ago, I would've never been able to picture myself in Sam's room, borrowing her clothes. I hadn't had time to get the details from Braden, and I was curious to hear the story of what happened on the snowboarding trip.

"So, you and Phil," I said. "I was so surprised when Braden told me."

She turned to me with a white T-shirt and black pants. "Because you knew I had feelings for Braden."

Awkward.

"I umm... I had a strong suspicion."

She handed me the clothes and shut the closet door. "I had a major crush on him for a long time, and I thought he'd see me differently once we started rooming together. But then he met you, and..."

SUPER awkward. What was I supposed to say? Should I apologize? I should've just taken the clothes and skipped the conversation.

"I thought when you came to visit for the weekend that you'd realize you really were better off as friends, but it was pretty obvious you still liked each other a lot," she said.

That explained why she'd wanted me to visit that weekend and her confusing behavior once I'd arrived.

"Was that when Phil came into the picture?" I asked.

She smiled a little, and I breathed easier.

"No, it wasn't until Detroit. That was my last gasp effort to get closer to Braden. Phil saw what was going on, and he had a 'come to Jesus' talk with me, basically telling me that I should let go of any hope with Braden because I was just going to keep getting hurt."

I knew from my months of misinterpreting Braden's feelings how awful it felt to have unrequited ones. It had to be especially excruciating for Sam living with him and seeing him every day.

"I'm really sorry," I said.

"It wasn't your fault. Even if Braden hadn't met you, he'd probably still think of me as a little sister. That's just the way he's always seen me since we were kids. I was finally able to accept that when I realized there was this other great guy in my life who'd been going through something similar." She eased into a smile. "Phil had been secretly crushing on me since we'd moved in."

"We all thought he was picky about girls when really he just didn't want to date anyone who wasn't you," I said.

"We started talking a lot after Detroit, but it was always when no one else was around. It was like our little secret friendship. Until New Year's when we kissed in front of everyone."

"That must've been awesome. I wish I could've seen all their faces."

"Ross said, 'Are we getting *Punk'd?*'"

Phil stuck his head into the room. "I'm going to put the movie on in my room."

"You guys don't have to move because of us," I said.

"It's cool. My room is warmer." He grinned at Sam, and her cheeks turned pink.

"You can change in here," she said to me as she went toward the door.

"Thanks. I'm really glad we talked."

"Me, too. Oh, and I don't think Braden knows about my crush on him or any of that, and I'd like to keep it that way."

"Of course. I totally understand."

She and Phil left, and I changed into the comfy clothes. They were just a tiny bit larger than my size. Since I was still chilly, I went into Braden's room and stole one of his hoodies to complete my new outfit.

I returned to the living room, and Braden looked up from chopping veggies in the kitchen. He'd taken off his tie and rolled up the sleeves of his white button-down.

"Don't you look cozy?" He smiled.

I sat on one of the stools so I could watch him cook over the bar. "Sometimes I wish I could compete in yoga pants."

"Noooo, you can't lose the costumes."

"Are you a fan of the sparkles?"

"I'm a fan of *you* in the sparkles." He peeked up at me. "You are sexy as hell in those little dresses."

My face grew hot, and I laughed as I dipped my head. "I've never thought of myself that way."

"You should because you are. And it's not just because of how you look. It's because of how powerful you are when you skate." He stopped dicing, and he fixed his eyes on mine. "First time I saw you I thought, 'She is the most gorgeous girl I've ever seen.' Then I watched your videos, and I thought, 'Wow, she's beautiful *and* she's a mega talented athlete. *Please* let her come to another game and buy another Slush Puppie.'"

I grinned. "The first thing that I noticed about you was your laugh. And then your smile. They were both so full of life and genuine... and hot."

"I totally caught you checking me out."

"And I totally panicked when you caught me." I laughed.

Braden whipped up the omelets and plated them on the bar, and we sat on the stools with our knees touching as we ate. I hummed with appreciation as I took a bite filled with avocado and peppers.

"Tell me about your trip," I said. "Sam filled me in on her and Phil. Anything else crazy happen?"

"Jason wiped out doing a stunt, and we thought we were going to have to medevac him off the mountain."

"Oh no."

"He was okay. Just sprained his knee. He loved having Nurse Britt taking care of him the rest of the trip."

I laughed. "You and Ross ended up being there with two couples."

"Yeah, they were cozied up by the fire, and we were like,

'When did this turn into a romantic getaway?'" He took a drink of his orange juice. "Since we didn't have our phones, Ross and I were pretty much stuck hanging out together to entertain ourselves. It turned out to be a good thing because we ended up talking about Scotty."

"Really?"

"I was thinking about him a lot, just how he would've been there with us, doing all the crazy stunts better than everyone else. Ross said he was thinking about him, too, and we talked about feeling guilty over what happened and stuff. He'd been blaming himself, too."

"All this time you've been going through the same thing."

"It was a really good talk. We realized that maybe we shouldn't feel so responsible. That it was Scotty's choice. He had other options, and he made that decision."

I touched Braden's knee. "I'm so glad you're finally able to make some peace with it."

"I guess Ross and I should've talked a long time ago."

"It might've been too soon then. It's probably better that it happened now."

He set down his glass and covered my hand with his, giving me a long concerned look. "I wish you could find the same kind of peace. Have you thought anymore about trying to talk to Dominic again?"

I looked down at my empty plate. "I've still been checking his Facebook page. I don't know why."

"Because you still have things you need to say to him."

"I really want to ask him how he knew about my life."

Braden rubbed his chin. "Maybe you could write him a letter and send it to him at work. He might answer your questions if he doesn't have to face you."

I nodded slowly. "It might be easier for me to say what I'm feeling on paper, too."

My phone buzzed, and I figured I should check it since

the hour was so late. I quickly read the message.

"It's from Kristin, reminding me of my schedule tomorrow." I would be making the rounds on the local TV stations, discussing my big win and looking ahead to the Olympics. "I have to be ready to go at six a.m. for the first morning show."

"Does this mean I need to get you back to the hotel soon?"

I locked the phone and hopped onto Braden's lap. "Nope. All I need in the morning is a strong cup of coffee and I'll be good to go. No one is cutting into my time with you."

He smiled and kissed me, and I wrapped my arms around him in a fierce hug. I'd spoken confidently about handling our impending separation when Mom had brought it up, but now that I had time to really think about it, my throat tightened. We'd been apart for two months, but I hadn't known then what it felt like to spend the night lying next to him. To hear the sound of him sighing in his sleep. To feel his soft arm hair tickling my skin. To watch his heart pound under my fingers as I pressed my hand to his chest. Would it have been better if I didn't know what I was missing?

He kissed me again and cradled my face in his hands, gazing at me adoringly and leaving me with no doubt. *This* was definitely better.

CHAPTER TWENTY-TWO

I FLEXED MY WRIST AND MASSAGED my fingers. Signing my name on five hundred magazine covers had pretty much crippled my hand, and I had no idea what Kristin planned to do with the autographed items. I'd had so many things shoved in front of me to sign since nationals. I stared at the final copy from the pile on the coffee table, the image of me in my slate blue costume dominating the cover. I'd posed for the action photo at the Media Summit, so my hair was down and curled into long waves unlike my usual competition bun. The headline sprawled under my leaping figure was *Golden Destiny*.

In nine days I would be leaving for Sochi to fulfill my "destiny," and it couldn't arrive fast enough. I wasn't looking forward to saying goodbye to Braden, but I was more than happy to say goodbye to the media and the hype machine smothering me. I'd had to spend the last few days in New York, wasting time in front of TV cameras when I should've been on the ice or in the gym. But what the network wanted, the network got. They needed me and my backstory to get people excited for their million hours of Olympic coverage.

"You finished all those already?" Mom asked as she came in from the kitchen.

"The faster I went, the less time there was for my hand to cramp."

"I was hoping you wouldn't finish so quickly so you'd be here longer." She sat on the sofa behind me and put her arm around my shoulders. "Why don't you stay one more night? We can go shopping in the city."

I smiled and capped the black marker. Bribing me with a trip to Fifth Avenue may have worked once upon a time, but not when I had the sweetest, hottest guy on the planet waiting for me in Boston.

"I promised Braden we'd spend the weekend together. You'll get to spend time with me in Russia, so he has dibs."

"He should've come down here for the weekend. It would be more comfortable for you than staying the night at his apartment. With all his roommates I'm sure it's noisy and messy."

"His roommate Phil is a neat freak, so the place is spotless."

Mom reached out and straightened the nearest pile of magazines. "Still... with all those people around there are so many germs. You don't need to catch anything the week before you leave for the Olympics."

"I've been around people at the TV studios, and I'll be around a lot more on the flights to Russia."

"But that's unavoidable."

I got up from the plush carpet and stretched my legs. "Mom, I really don't want to argue about this."

"I don't want to argue either. I just want to make sure you know what you're getting into. You've only been dating Braden for a couple of weeks, and you've never spent the night at a boy's house before."

I wanted to tell her I had, but it would only lead to a new argument about me lying to her. I could offer up another bit of information, though. One that might help her see that I was mature enough to handle the situation.

"Braden spent the night in my hotel room at nationals. A couple of nights."

She popped up from the sofa. "What?"

"We didn't do anything. We just cuddled."

She put her hand to her forehead and let out an audible exhale. "Well, I hope that's all you'll be doing tonight, too."

I'd be lying if I said I hadn't thought about going further, but the idea of it was a lot different from actually doing it. Considering I'd just had my first kiss a few months ago, I wasn't really emotionally or physically prepared for any big moves.

"Don't worry. As you said, we've only been dating for two weeks. I'm not rushing into anything."

I went up to my room to grab my luggage and returned to Mom standing at the foot of the stairs. She pulled me into her arms and hugged me as if she was the one who wouldn't see me for a month.

"You know I only worry because you are the most precious thing in the world to me. I want nothing but the best of everything for you."

"Braden is the best person I could ever be with. I can't wait for you to get to know him better."

"I'm looking forward to that, too. Any time you want to bring him here, he's welcome." She finally loosened her hold on me. "You know, like tonight."

I laughed. "Nice try."

"I am serious about the invitation. I was impressed with how Braden handled himself at the Olympic team reception, and his family was very nice when I spoke to them at the exhibition. I do think you've made a good choice."

Now I was the one who went in for a big hug.

She helped me carry my bags to my SUV, and as I climbed inside she blew me a kiss. "See you in Sochi, sweetheart!"

I waved to her as I backed out of the garage, and I turned up the stereo for the long drive to Boston. Sunshine peeked through the gray clouds, giving some much needed light to the early afternoon. I was so looking forward to the weather in the seaside town of Sochi, which would feel like summer after the winter we'd had in the Northeast.

I pulled up to the stoplight across from the tire shop, and my knuckles went white around the steering wheel. Dominic was standing in front of the building, smoking a cigarette. I watched him take a puff and then tip his chin up to blow the smoke skyward. His free hand was shoved in the pocket of his dark jacket.

If I turned into the parking lot, I wouldn't have to wait and write a letter to Dominic. I could make him talk to me right now. Refuse to leave until he agreed to hear me out.

The light switched to green, and a jolt of adrenaline overtook me, leading my hands to steer the vehicle into the lot. I parked away from the building and jumped out before I could have any second thoughts. Dominic saw me emerge from behind the row of cars, and he paused while lifting the cigarette to his mouth. I could see the protest forming in his mind, but I wasn't going to give him the chance to speak first this time.

"I'm not here to harass you," I said. "I just want to talk to you about what happened. I think I deserve at least a few minutes of your time."

He took a long draw on the cigarette and then doused it in the ashtray atop the garbage can. "I'm working."

"Do you get another smoke break?"

He didn't respond as he fiddled with a pack of gum from his pocket, and I was about to press him again when he said, "The shop closes in an hour."

"I can wait until then," I said, heading for the door. He'd have to physically remove me from the building to get rid of me.

He slowly followed me inside, and I sat in one of the plastic chairs lining the wall. Only one lady was waiting for her car to be serviced. I took out my phone and debated texting Braden my whereabouts. He was working at the UMass basketball game, and he'd only get distracted and would worry if I told him. I closed the text box and opened a book on my ereader instead.

I found my mind wandering, skipping over whole sentences as I went over the things I wanted to say to Dominic. I needed something to pass the time that required less concentration. I switched to the internet and searched for inspirational quotes. As captain of the figure skating squad, I'd been texting my teammates motivational quotes and videos every day. The daily search had also provided me with great material for my own personal pep talks.

While I surfed the web, I listened to Dominic speak on the phone to customers. He was well-spoken and professional – not the image I'd had of him. I'd convinced myself that he was a rude jerk to everyone.

The hour dragged, and I watched the hands on the clock move in slow motion for the final ten minutes. My knees bounced up and down just like they did right before I competed. When the clock struck two, Dominic went through a door behind the desk, and I held my breath. If he snuck out the back, I'd chase him down in the parking lot. He was *not* ditching me this time.

He returned a few minutes later, and I sprang to my feet while putting on my coat.

"We can go to the coffee shop down the block," I said.

"I'd prefer to do this here. We can go outside."

"It's freezing out there. Let's meet at the coffee shop."

Once again I didn't give him the opportunity to object. I marched out the glass door and straight to my SUV, waiting to turn the ignition until Dominic started his truck. He drove toward the exit, and I trailed him just feet behind. When we reached the coffee shop, I ordered a cup of green tea while Dominic got coffee with no sugar or cream. We found a table far from the bustling counter, and a couple of teenage girls looked over at us. I hoped they didn't recognize me. Now was not the time for photos or autographs.

Dominic kept his jacket on as he sat across from me, and he kept his eyes on his small coffee. "Why do you want to talk to me?"

He didn't sound angry. His question was quiet and tentative. I'd been rehearsing my opening while I waited for him, but I wasn't sure I needed so many words.

"I didn't have the chance when the accident happened, and I just recently learned all the details."

"So, you know why it happened."

The image that had haunted me so many years returned again. The car swerving, the car flipping, the car smashing beyond recognition. All because of Dominic's stupid decision.

"You dropped your phone," I said.

He looked across the room, his eyes fixated on anything but me. "I was talking to my girlfriend. The phone slipped out of my hand."

"Why didn't you pull over before picking it up?"

"I bent down for just a second–"

"Didn't you see a car in the other lane? Why would you take your eyes off the road with another car coming in your direction?"

My blood pressure had skyrocketed, and my face felt as hot as my smoking cup of tea. I'd thought I could stay calm during the conversation since I'd had so much time to think about it, but my emotions wouldn't be denied. They had waited too long to be unleashed.

Dominic wrapped his hands around his cup but didn't drink. He just continued to stare at it.

"I don't have any good answers for you. I was eighteen

and planning my Saturday night and not thinking about anything else. I don't know what I can say except I'm sorry."

He still wouldn't look at me, and I couldn't tell if his apology was really sincere.

"If you're sorry, why did you bring up my birth parents when I first saw you? Were you saying that I shouldn't care about the accident because I have them in my life? How do you know about them?"

He finally lifted his eyes and made contact with mine. "I *am* sorry."

Part of the mask he'd been wearing fell away, and I saw his true remorse. It cooled some of my anger but created a huge lump in my throat. I took a sip of tea to chase it away, but I could hardly swallow.

"After I was arrested, I was told that the people who died had a kid." Dominic looked down at the table again. "I asked my lawyer to find out what was going to happen to you, and he said that you were being taken to Russia by your birth mom."

"How did he know she was my birth mom? No one knew that."

"It was in some court documents." He raised his coffee but then set it down. "When you came back here and started skating again and winning competitions, someone recognized your name and told my mom."

I nodded a little. "I still had my old last name for a while after I moved back."

"I asked her to keep me updated on what you were doing, and she showed me all your competition results and the articles about you and your real parents."

I pictured him in his prison cell reading about me. It gave me a queasy feeling. "Why did you want to know all that?"

"I needed to know what happened to you. If I'd completely screwed up your life. Every time I read something new and saw how successful you were... it gave me some relief."

The queasiness turned into sadness, adding more confusion to my mess of emotions. He'd honestly been concerned for my well-being. The smile he wore in his photos may have been another mask. It sounded like he'd been haunted by his actions just as much as I'd been.

"Do you still think about the accident?" I asked.

He rubbed his hand over the slight stubble on his jaw. "Always. Even more lately since you've been on TV a lot."

My first instinct was to apologize, but then I realized I hadn't done anything wrong.

"I don't like to talk about it. I'm trying to start my life over, so that's why I didn't want to see you. I haven't talked about it in a long, long time." His eyes lowered, and I watched him drift far off in thought. "I actually thought you were in the car that day. With your parents. I saw the pink bike fly off, and I thought there was a kid in the car."

"Pink bike?"

"Yeah, there was one hooked onto the car."

I shook my head. "I didn't have–"

A pink bike.

My birthday.

The present I wanted.

My body went cold as the realization hit me like an icy wave.

My parents had gone out that afternoon to buy my birthday present. That was why they were on the road. That was why they died.

Because of me.

"Was it someone else's?" Dominic asked.

His voice sounded far away, and all the coffee shop noises – the cappuccino machine, the cash register, the customers typing on laptops – they all faded to a quiet hum. I could only hear my heartbeat throbbing in my ears.

"It was... it was for me. My birthday was the next week."

I swallowed hard. "I asked for a pink bike."

"I'm sorry. I shouldn't have mentioned it."

"They said they had to run errands." I leaned forward and put my head in my hands. "I was the reason for their errand."

"If you're saying that you–" Dominic started and paused. "The reason doesn't matter. It's not why the accident happened."

Yes, it does matter. They wouldn't have been in the car if it hadn't been for me.

My blood pressure spiked again, and my hands began to tremble. I wanted to get out of there. I *needed* to get out of there.

I pushed back my chair and grabbed my coat. "I have to go."

"Wait." He stood along with me. "Forget what I said about the bike. I never should've–"

"Thank you for talking to me. I won't come around again."

I hurried to the door while shoving my arms into my coat, and I quickly jumped into my SUV, started the engine and zoomed toward the highway. Memories that I didn't know I still had pushed their way to the front of my mind. Me seeing my friend Hope's new pink bike and asking my parents for one just like it. Mom telling me that my small white one was in good shape and I didn't need a new one. Me pleading for it, saying that was the only present they needed to buy for my birthday.

Tears flooded my eyes, and I choked on a sob. Why couldn't I have been satisfied with what I had? I should have known they would get the bike for me. They loved surprising me and making me happy. Mom used to say my smile was her favorite thing to see every day. It was her personal sunshine.

The highway became blurrier, and I dragged the back of my hand across my eyes. They lost their lives because they loved me so much. How did I deserve to have not one but two amazing sets of parents? Why had I been given so many blessings?

Boston seemed so far away, and I just wanted to curl up in Braden's arms and hold on tight to him. I wanted to bury myself in his comfort, his safety. Knowing that I would soon be on display before the whole world turned my stomach. Me and my tragic backstory. No one knew that I was the reason for the tragedy.

When I reached Braden's apartment a few hours later, my tears had dried, but the heavy pressure on my chest remained. It weighed me down as I walked up to the house. I rang the bell and took a long breath, but all the suffocating emotion threatened to burst out again. Braden opened the door, and the brilliant happiness in his eyes when he saw me was exactly what I'd longed to see for two hundred miles. I crumbled into tears and reached for him, dropping my bag in the doorway.

"What's wrong?" he asked as he sheltered me in his arms.

I heard footsteps in the hall and then Ross' voice. "Hey, Liza's here."

I lifted my head to wipe my eyes, and Ross said, "Oh, I didn't–"

"Let's go to my room," Braden said, picking up my tote and walking us to the hall, his arm never leaving my shoulders.

He closed the door, and we sat on the unmade bed. I sank into his embrace, and he rubbed my back and kissed the top of my head.

"Talk to me," he said quietly.

I sniffled against his T-shirt and started to speak, but I couldn't bring myself to say it. He caressed my hair away from my face and gave me another kiss.

"Baby, what is it?"

I squeezed my eyes shut as more tears burned and blinded me.

"They died because of me," I whispered.

He pulled back a little, and I opened my eyes, finding confusion in his. "Who? Your parents?"

I nodded.

"Why would you think that?"

"Because it's true."

His jaw tightened. "Did you talk to Dominic? What did he say to you?"

"He didn't realize what he said was important, but it was. He said my parents had a pink bike on their car. That was going to be my surprise birthday present. They went out that day to buy my present. *I'm* the reason they were in the accident."

Braden's expression softened, and he cupped his hands around my face and locked his eyes on mine. "You are not the reason they were in the accident. Dominic is. He is the only one to blame."

"But they wouldn't have been in the car if I hadn't begged for that stupid bike."

He shook his head. "You don't know that. They probably went a million other places. They were running errands on a Saturday afternoon."

"That's what they said, but what if they just went to get my present?"

"Even if they did, that doesn't mean it was your fault. There is nothing about this that makes it your fault."

I wanted to believe him, but I couldn't shake the heavy weight, the feeling of guilt that I'd had a major part in the awful chain of events. I bent my head, but Braden gently nudged my chin upward.

"Liza," he said softly, almost a whisper.

There was sadness but also steadiness in his gaze. "You told me so many times that I shouldn't feel responsible for Scotty's death, and I know now that you were right. Just like I didn't put the pills in his mouth, you weren't driving

Dominic's car. *He* took his eyes off the road. *He* caused the accident. Nothing you did played any role in it."

I stared into his eyes and felt his belief. If only I could live there inside his certainty and make it my own. I returned my head to his shoulder, and he eased us back against the pillows. We stretched out together, and I burrowed into the crook of his arm, repeating what he'd said over and over in my head. It made sense, but my heart had a mind of its own. Guilt had taken up residence there and wouldn't be easily removed. My haunting image now contained a pink bike lying in the middle of the road, and I couldn't unsee it. It would be there forever. A lasting reminder of my connection to that horrible moment.

CHAPTER TWENTY-THREE

I STOWED MY TOTE BAG ON top of the two extra-large suitcases in my SUV, and Braden shut the rear door. We stood at the end of his driveway, the light of dawn just beginning to brighten the sky.

"Are you sure you don't want me to come to the airport with you?" he asked.

"I'm sure. I don't want our goodbye to be in the middle of a crowd at the security line."

He circled his arms around my waist. "Are you afraid I'm going to give you a kiss that's not appropriate for public viewing?"

I brushed a tiny snowflake from his jacket. "I'm counting on it."

He smiled and kissed me sweetly as a warm-up. Pressing our bodies together, he deepened the next kiss, knotting his hands in my hair. The cold, damp morning hung over us, but the heat from Braden's mouth erased every bit of my chill.

We stayed clutching each other in silence, clinging to the final minutes we'd have together before our twenty-four day separation. I'd slept over again that weekend and had tried to put everything except Braden out of my mind, but what Dominic had told me continued to lurk between all my thoughts. Braden had reminded me again and again that I was an innocent party, a victim of Dominic's carelessness. I'd leaned on him so much the past week, spending every evening on the phone with him. He was the only one who knew what I was battling, and he understood exactly what I was feeling. But now we were about to be thousands of miles apart.

"It's not too late for you to come to Sochi," I said. "I can buy your plane ticket, and you can sleep on the floor of my mom's hotel room."

He laughed. "I'm sure she'd love that."

"It would be a great way for you guys to bond."

He hugged me tighter and touched his lips to my hair. "I wish more than anything that I could be there, but I'll be just a phone call away any time you need me. Midnight, three a.m., five a.m. I don't care what the time difference is."

I looked up at him and threaded my fingers through his hair, where more little snowflakes had fallen. "I can't touch you over the phone."

"But I'll be with you every night when you sleep. I saw you swiping my pillowcase." He tapped the tip of my nose.

"I left you something in return. Check under your pillow."

His mouth spread into a slow smile, and he lifted his hand to my cheek. His thumb stroked under my bottom lip and swept over my jaw, and I concentrated on committing to memory all the spine-tingling sensations of his touch.

"Next time I see you, the whole world will have fallen in love with you. Just remember who fell for you first. So hard." He bent his head toward me, his eyes capturing mine. "I love you, Liza."

He kissed me, and I felt as if I was floating like one of the snowflakes dancing in the air around us. Unlike the snow, I melted easily into Braden's embrace.

I held his face in my hands, his early morning stubble prickling my palms. "First date, first kiss, first boyfriend... first love."

He grinned and kissed me again, and I whispered against his lips, "I love you, too."

SHATTERED GLASS.

Mangled metal.

A pink bike sprawled on the cement.

I gasped and jumped, and my eyes flew open. They darted around the room, not recognizing my surroundings until I remembered I was in Sochi. Bright daylight streamed through the sliding glass door to the balcony, and I checked the time on my phone. I'd laid down for my post-practice nap almost an hour ago. I hadn't wanted to nap because every time I slept I had the same nightmare, but between the jet lag and the restless nights, I had to squeeze in as much rest as possible.

I got up and straightened the blanket, and I moved my Olympic swag from the floor to one of my overflowing suitcases. Mom was coming to visit in a few minutes, so I needed to make the place a little more presentable. I hung up some of my clothes and then organized Court's mess of shirts and jackets on her twin bed. We'd only been in the Village a couple of days, but it looked like we'd been living there for a month.

Mom messaged me that she was outside, so I went down to the security checkpoint to meet her. There was advance paperwork and an involved process to grant access to visitors, but I'd made sure to get it all timely done. Mom hadn't gotten the chance to compete at the Olympics, so I knew how important it was for her to experience all of it with me. She'd loved every minute of Vancouver in 2010, but I had a feeling this time would be even more special since we were in her home country.

I took her on a tour through the dining hall and the game room, and then we walked under the palm trees to the Team USA dorms. She looked around my large room and went to the glass door, sliding it open and letting in the cool sea breeze.

"You have a beautiful view," she said as she gazed out at the calm water of the Black Sea.

"It's very serene. I should do yoga out there."

She sat next to me on the bed and started to open her small purse but stopped. She turned to me, examining me with her worried look that I knew so well.

"You looked a little tired at practice."

"I'm still recovering from all the traveling. I just need to get comfortable here."

"Maybe you shouldn't go to the Opening Ceremony tomorrow night. You could use the extra rest before you skate on Saturday."

My individual competition wouldn't start for another two weeks, but I had to skate in the team event as soon as the Games started.

"I don't want to miss the Opening Ceremony. It was one of my favorite parts of Vancouver. If I skip it, I know I'll regret it later."

She didn't protest, and she stayed silent, unlike the usual pattern of our disagreements.

"Is there another reason you haven't been sleeping well?" she asked.

She was still staring at me, and I wasn't sure what she was thinking. Was this about Braden? Did she think I was losing sleep because I was missing him?

"I know you talked to Dominic," she said.

My mouth dropped open. "H–how?"

"He came to the rink last week looking for me before my class. He told me about your conversation, and he asked me to give you this."

She unzipped her purse and took out a plain letter-sized envelope. She held it in her lap, not yet handing it over.

"It's a letter he wrote to you. I read it because I had to be sure he was being sincere before I gave it to you. I didn't know if I should wait until we get home, but when he told me how upset you were..." She pressed the envelope tightly between her fingers. "He said you might be blaming yourself for the accident."

I bowed my head as tears snuck up on me. "Did you know? About the bike?"

She was quiet for a long minute. "Yes," she finally said, her voice as shaky as mine.

"I know I shouldn't blame myself, but I can't stop thinking about it. That they wouldn't have been there if–" I couldn't catch my breath enough to finish.

She grasped my hand and squeezed it hard, and I looked up at her. Her eyes were wet.

"I spoke with Peter that day. I called to tell him your grandfather was in the hospital because of his heart condition, and he and Carrie were at the grocery store. They'd just finished shopping for your present."

"They were at the grocery store?" I croaked.

"They were doing a lot of shopping that afternoon. Not just for you."

I bit my lip to steady my quivering chin. "You talked to them right before they..."

She gave me a tight nod. "Yes. So maybe they would have been on the road sooner if I hadn't called. You could blame me just as easily as you're blaming yourself, but you have to see that neither of us is to blame."

Her fingers pressed against mine, emphasizing the importance of what she'd said. The new information swirled around in my head, trying to find its place in the picture I'd created of that day.

"I think this might help you see it more clearly, too," she said.

She held out the letter, and I hesitated before accepting it. I took it from the envelope and unfolded the sheet of paper. It was filled with lines of neat print, penned in black ink.

Liza,

I've written you many letters over the years, but I didn't send any of them. I wanted to apologize for my actions and for causing you such a huge, terrible loss, but I decided it would be better not to bother you when you had obviously worked very hard to overcome your loss. This time I need to speak up, though.

I can't allow you to blame yourself for the accident. There were many inconsequential things that led your parents to be on that road at that moment – how fast the clerk checked them out at the store, the traffic they encountered going to and from their destination, how quickly the stoplights changed from red to green. The list goes on and on. But none of those things can be blamed for the accident. Your parents' deaths were undeniably my fault and my fault only. It's taken me many years to accept that I made a careless decision that killed two people. I struggle with that knowledge every day. But that is for my conscience to bear. Not yours.

I hope I've been able to give you some clarity, and I need to tell you again how sorry I am. Please know that I will regret that day for the rest of my life.

Dominic

I read the letter once more and then carefully folded it and slipped it inside the envelope. Hearing Dominic take full responsibility was something I'd needed since the moment I'd first heard his name. Even before I knew he existed. What he said about all the little things that happened the day of the accident resonated with me. I wasn't blaming Mom or the clerk at the store, so why was I blaming myself?

Mom put her arm around my shoulders. "Everything he said in that letter is true."

I slowly bobbed my head. "Braden's been telling me all

week that I should focus on Dominic's carelessness... that it was the only thing that mattered. But I couldn't get the image of the bike out of my head. It made me feel like I was there. Like I was part of what happened."

"I wish I could erase that image. I never wanted you to know all these details. I kept them from you because I was trying to protect you from any more pain. You suffered so much already."

"Is that why you never talk about them? Peter and Carrie?"

She sniffed back her tears, her own pain apparent in her dark eyes. "I watched you suffer every day, so heartbroken, so lost. I worried that you would never be happy again. But then you started to smile a little and come alive again, and I didn't want you to go back into that darkness. I thought the best thing for you was for us to move forward and not look back. I thought any reminder of them would just hurt you all over again."

"I'm always reminded of them. You know I take this everywhere." I touched the bear next to my pillow.

"I thought that was for comfort, something familiar to always have with you."

"It is, but it's mostly so they're still with me in some way. It doesn't hurt to think about them. It hurt more thinking that you didn't want me to talk about them with you. It felt like you wanted to pretend I'd never been with them."

"No, no, sweetheart. I am so grateful that you had them in your life. I don't know what I would've done if I'd had to give you to strangers. I would've died not knowing if you were okay." She smoothed her hand over my hair. "They loved you so much, and I owe them everything for taking such good care of you."

My chin trembled uncontrollably, and I blinked rapidly to see through my tears. "You've taken really good care of me, too. I don't thank you enough for that."

She wrapped her arms around me, and we cried together quietly, letting out years of emotion that we'd kept from each other. As I laid my head on her shoulder, I was brought back to the nights when we'd snuggle in my bed and read together. Those were the moments that had helped me smile again, and Mom was the one responsible.

"I love you, Mom."

"I love you, too, sweetheart. So very much."

We slowly broke apart and dried our tears, and I stared down at the envelope in my lap. It couldn't have been easy for Dominic to write those words, to lay his guilt out on paper.

"I wish I'd told you about Dominic years ago so you didn't have to go look for answers," Mom said.

"If you'd told me, I still would've been curious about him. I'm glad I got to talk to him. Seeing his remorse was really... it was important to me. I needed that just as much as I needed to know the how and why."

She took my hand between both of hers. "I hope you see now that you were not part of the why."

I looked up at her and nodded, my throat tightening again. "It was just such a shock when Dominic told me about the bike. I hadn't thought about it in so long."

"Any time you want to talk about Peter and Carrie, I'm here to listen. I don't want you to hold back anything anymore."

I nodded again and hugged her. "As long as you promise to do the same."

CHAPTER TWENTY-FOUR

How much more waiting could I take?

I'd waited two weeks to get to my short program day, and now I was on hour twelve of waiting to compete. I'd practiced so early that morning that it felt like a year ago. I was last in the start order of thirty ladies, which was good for scoring purposes but not for my nerves.

I adjusted my earbuds and turned up the volume on my phone, blaring the classical piece "Meditation." Circling around Dad, I took a seat along the mirrored wall of the empty warm-up room. My knees jiggled, and I bent forward, resting my elbows on my thighs, but the shaking persisted. I'd thought skating in the team event would make me more comfortable for my individual competition, but I was antsier than ever. We'd won the silver medal, and I'd been so proud to share the moment with my teammates, but I'd made a couple of errors that had me spooked. I couldn't go back to my pattern of stupid mistakes again.

Dad touched my shoulder, and I removed one earbud.

"It's time," he said.

I bid goodbye to my calming music (not that it was doing

its job) and gave Dad my phone for safekeeping. The two TV cameramen stationed in the doorway moved aside, and they followed us down the corridor to the ice. The closer we got, the louder Katia's music became. I stopped just inside the backstage entrance and tried to shut my ears to the tinkly instrumental version of "Send In the Clowns." I imagined my own program music and me flying through jump after perfect jump.

You did it at nationals. You can do it again.

Katia struck her closing pose, and I moved toward the ice, ready to finally end the hours and days and years of waiting. The cameramen moved with me, and photographers lined almost every inch of the blue-papered boards. Boards covered with the Olympic rings.

This isn't nationals.

The crowd roared around me, and Katia was all smiles as she skated toward the kiss and cry. I took off my guards and handed them to Dad, and as soon as my blades hit the ice, chants of "Rus-si-a! Rus-si-a!" began, reminding me that I was not on friendly turf. I pushed off and sped around the ice, the crowd's nationalism fueling my adrenaline.

As I lapped the rink, I couldn't help but hear Katia's huge score and the announcement that she was in second place. That meant someone, probably Julia, had scored even higher. I quickened my strokes to work out my shakiness, but my knees continued to wobble.

Just skate. Forget the score.

I glided over to Dad and took a sip of water, gripping the bottle hard between my trembling fingers. He watched me with an easy smile, and he gently captured my hands, warming and steadying them.

"Take a breath," he said.

I slowly inhaled and exhaled, focusing on him and nothing else. He was calmness personified.

"You've put in the time and the work, and you have the

determination," he said. "This program is in your blood. Let yourself be in the moment and enjoy every step."

I nodded and closed my eyes for a few seconds, absorbing his speech, and then I opened them and kept my gaze on Dad as I backed away from the boards. When I finally turned to face the long sheet of ice, my eyes fell on the colorful rings painted in the center.

Vancouver had been my coming-out party, my chance to show everyone my potential. I'd skated over the rings then with confidence and exuberance. I had to find that looseness again. Forget all the current pressures and channel that bright-eyed fifteen-year-old with nothing to lose.

"Our next skater represents the United States of America." The announcer paused for the Russian translation. "Liza Petrov!"

Polite applause met me as I skated past the judges and curved around the icy rings. A few American flags waved in the audience, and a couple of people started up with the "Rus-si-a!" chant again. They were soon drowned out by shouts of "USA! USA!" and I was sure I recognized the voices of Court and Josh. I stared at one of the big flags and saw myself draped in it, gold medal in hand.

Slow down. Take this one moment at a time, just like Dad said.

I froze in my opening pose, looking right at the judges, and I waited yet again, that time for my music to begin. My heart thumped more powerfully as the seconds of silence stretched on and on. I was about to burst with contained adrenaline when the first note sounded in the big arena.

My body moved on instinct with the music, and I wheeled into the combination spin. I reached back to grab my blade for the donut position, and my index finger hit the sharp edge, the sudden burn startling me. I fumbled to take hold of the blade but managed to catch it, bringing it close to my head as I spun.

I opened up and drove into the next spin, crouching low

to the ice, and I felt stickiness on my hand. Blood. I couldn't tell how much as I spun around and around, but as long as my finger was still intact, I had to keep moving.

I came out of the spin, and a spot of red flew onto the ice. Blood trickled down my index finger, and selecting fuchsia instead of white for my dress suddenly became one of my best decisions. I couldn't worry about the mess on my hand. I had a double Axel to do in a couple of seconds.

The music neared its tempo transition, and I slowed a beat to get my timing in sync. I whipped into the air and turned swiftly, keeping my balance in check throughout the jump. I unfurled for the landing, and I connected with the ice on a solid edge, earning a round of applause from the crowd.

With the added excitement in the music, I upped the amplitude of my movements as I stroked toward the triple flip. Picking into the ice, I went high into the air and tightened my body into three rotations. I came down for the landing, and I held my head up and my shoulders back in textbook posture. My pulse jumped with exhilaration knowing that I was halfway home.

I sped around the corner of the rink, digging deep into the ice, and my stomach tightened over the magnitude of the upcoming combination, the triple Lutz-triple toe. Miss it and my golden dream would be in major jeopardy. My pace slowed, and I took quick breaths as I reversed direction into the takeoff.

Attack! Don't be afraid!

I stabbed the ice and pulled in my arms, spinning through the Lutz. My blade skidded on the landing, but I gritted my teeth and willed myself up into the triple toe. I landed on a sticky curve, but I rode it out, making it look as pretty as I could.

All jumps DONE!

I raced into the step sequence, and I leaned so far on an inside edge that I had to quickly adjust or I'd fall on my face. I settled into the footwork, finding my zone, and I maintained my speed as I sailed into the final element, the layback spin. I had to grab my blade again, but I didn't feel any pain as I wrapped my fingers around the cool steel. I only felt giddiness.

I just did a clean short program at the Olympics!

The song hit its big final note, and I jabbed my toe pick into the ice to hit my ending pose. I didn't get the ovation that Katia had received, but my scattered fans in the audience jumped to their feet and made their presence known. I looked up into the stands, and I spotted Quinn first. She was hard to miss with the huge red and blue pompoms she was shaking. Mom had her hands on her chest, and I prayed she would survive the long program if her heart was already in distress.

I headed for the boards, and Dad waited with a huge grin and his arms spread open. I leapt into them, releasing all my leftover energy.

"That was beautiful," he said.

He set me down so I could put on my guards, and as I held onto his arm I remembered my sliced finger.

"I'm getting blood all over your suit," I said.

"Your blade got you?" he asked as he inspected the cut.

"On the first spin."

He took a pack of tissues from his jacket and wrapped my finger while we sat in the kiss and cry. The camera in front of us lit up, and I waved with my non-bloody hand.

"Hey, everyone back home! Holly, everyone at the rink, I miss you. My Boston crew – Ross, Sam, Phil – see you soon! Braden, I love you!"

I blew a kiss to the camera and touched my heart, and Dad hugged me to his side. We watched the video board for the score, and again the wait dragged on forever. A long delay usually meant the technical panel was reviewing one of the elements.

"What could they be looking at?" I muttered.

"Everything looked clean to me," Dad said.

The pop music playing over the sound system quieted, and I sat up straighter, eyes glued to the screen. Dad tightened his arm around me.

"The short program score for Liza Petrov of the United States of America."

Another pause. Another wait. *GAH!*

"Seventy-five point four eight. She is currently in first place."

"Yes!" I pumped my fist.

Dad embraced me, and I stood to wave to the audience as was expected of the leader. I looked up at the video board, and I studied the numbers on the screen. I had less than a point lead over Julia and just a little more than a point over Katia. Zero breathing room.

Dad patted my shoulder. "You're in a great spot."

I nodded, but I knew the spot that was most important – the one I would draw in the start order for the free skate. If Julia or Katia skated last and skated clean, the last impression in the judges' minds would be the partisan crowd's deafening applause for them. That kind of noise was impossible to ignore.

I could already hear Dad in my ear – *You can't control the draw or the judges. You can only control how you skate.* I was going to have to repeat that again and again the next twenty-four hours. And what a long twenty-four hours it was going to be.

I FLIPPED OVER ONTO my side and buried my face in Braden's pillowcase. Clamping my eyes shut, I waited for sleep to overtake me. And waited. And waited.

Still wide awake.

I turned onto my back and looked over at Court. She was

curled into a ball, blanket up to her chin, lost in the deep sleep that I sought so desperately. My stubborn brain just wouldn't cooperate. It had me thinking about all my years of competing, how I'd set and achieved so many goals. I'd enjoyed the daily work and the challenges. I'd felt satisfaction with every new skill I learned and every victory I notched. But I knew I would feel incomplete if I didn't accomplish this one final goal. It was the ultimate validation of my career.

Ugh, stop thinking!

I reached over to the nightstand, and I picked up my phone to see the time.

Fifteen hours until the free skate.

When Josh and I had started working on my long program last spring, this day had seemed ten lifetimes away. Now it was here, and I would be a zombie for the biggest competition of my life because I couldn't get five minutes of sleep.

I put the phone on the bed, and my bandaged finger hovered over the Twitter app, which I had avoided the entire time I'd been in Sochi. Resisting my curiosity, I clicked on my photo albums instead. I scrolled down, and I stopped on the one with the pictures of my adoptive parents. As I swiped through them, I smiled at the memories each one of them brought up, especially those from the photo of us with my first gold medal. My dad had videotaped my program, and he showed it to everyone he knew, treating it as if it was an Olympic champion's performance. I wished I could see his reaction to that tape being played in one of my commercials on national TV.

I believed that he could see me now, that he and Mom were watching every second of my journey and cheering me on, but it wasn't the same as being here for it. Being able to hug me and celebrate with me and cry with me. My eyes filled with tears, and I took Peter from the nightstand, caging him inside my arms.

"I wish you could be here," I whispered.

I kept scrolling through the photos, looking at their faces and imagining their excitement and what they'd say to me if I'd win gold. I could hear my dad's booming voice and my mom's squeaky one mixing with each other, not making any sense because they'd be so emotional. But the pride on their faces would say it all.

My phone lit up with a text, and I dabbed at my eyes to read it clearly.

Braden: **You probably won't read this until morning, but Ross is posting your shout-out to him all over social media. He thinks he's famous now.**

I muffled my laughter in Peter's fur. Braden and I had talked earlier, and his roommates had all yelled their thanks in the background for their shout-out. I'd wanted to chat longer, but I'd had to get to bed. I didn't know it would be a fruitless effort.

Me: **It's technically morning here. Four in the morning. I can't sleep. HELP.**

Braden: **I'm sorry you can't sleep, but I'm excited I get to talk to you** ☺

Me: **Get ready to be even more excited. I'm going outside to call you** ☺

I dragged the blanket off the bed and swaddled myself in it, and I tiptoed to the door. Court didn't stir an inch, and I stepped out into the hall.

I sat along the wall and dialed Braden on FaceTime. His bright smile illuminated the dim hallway.

"Hey, you," he said. He was sitting with his back against the headboard of his bed. I longed to be there, nestled into the crook of his arm. Maybe then I could get some rest.

"What are you up to?" I asked.

"Just reading some notes my friend Tom took in stats class."

"What would've happened if you'd had a test while I was

skating and couldn't skip class?"

"Oh, I would've had a talk with my professor. Girlfriend in the Olympics trumps everything else."

I smiled and stifled a yawn.

"Am I making you sleepy already?" he asked. "I should be offended, but I'm happy I could help."

"My body is tired, but my brain isn't. That's the problem."

"Too many thoughts about tomorrow?"

I rubbed my forehead. "*So* many thoughts."

"Maybe it'll help if you talk about them."

I pulled my hair away from my face and rested my head against the wall. "I just can't believe that this day is finally here. I've been dreaming about it and planning for it almost my entire life. Literally. When I was three years old and watched Michelle Kwan in the 1998 Olympics, I pointed at the TV and said, 'I'm going to do that,' and I've worked my butt off day after day to put myself in position to do it, and now it all comes down to four minutes on the ice. Four minutes that can change the course of my life forever. If I win the gold medal, there's no limit to the things I can do. If I want to write a book, people will line up to help me. If I want to start a charity, my name will bring in support from everywhere. I can do so many amazing things just because I have the title Olympic gold medalist. And it all depends on what I do in those four minutes. Actually, it doesn't all depend on that. I'm not skating last, so even if I have the best performance ever, I have to hope that my score stands up after Katia and Julia skate." I finally took a breath. "Those are some of the thoughts that are terrifying me."

Braden wore a sympathetic smile. "I'm giving you a big virtual hug right now."

"You don't know how much I need it."

He shifted positions and propped his arm behind his head. "Can I ask you something? When you were three and you pointed at the TV, what made you want to skate at the Olympics?"

"It looked so fun and exciting, and I wanted to win and be considered the best skater in the world."

"Do *you* believe you're the best skater in the world?"

"I know I am."

He grinned. "I love how confident you are in your ability."

"I've always been confident in my ability. Whether I use it to its full potential in the biggest moment of my career is what's panicking me."

"You're going to do it. No doubt in my mind. And I'm not saying that because I'm crazy in love with you and I think you're freaking amazing. I'm saying it because I know you. I know the fight in you. The competitiveness. The love you have for skating. You're going to use all those things when you get out there on the ice for those four minutes."

My eyes misted again, and I wiped them with the edge of the blanket. "Have you ever thought about going into coaching instead of the front office? You're a natural at these pep talks and rah rah speeches."

One corner of his mouth curved up. "You give me a lot of inspiration."

"I could really go for another one of those virtual hugs right about now."

"Grab onto my pillowcase, and I'll take a whiff of this." He reached off camera and showed me the bottle of my lotion that I'd left under his pillow. "It'll be just like we're together."

I smiled and gazed into his warm, chocolate eyes. "You know what you are? You're my personal sunshine."

I didn't think my mom would mind me using her term of endearment for me on Braden. I knew she would adore him and agree that the description fit him perfectly.

"Personal sunshine?" he said. "I like that."

"You always make everything brighter."

"But have I made you sleepier? That's my main job right now."

I laughed. "You let me get out my stressful thoughts, and you've made me smile and laugh and feel relaxed enough where sleep is more a possibility now. I'd say you were very successful."

"Then I'll let you get to bed while you're still under my relaxation spell." He smiled and sat up. "I'll talk to you tomorrow to give you one last reminder of how much you're going to kick ass."

"I'm looking forward to it."

We exchanged *I love you's* and virtual kisses, and I crept back into the room. Court was still in the same position. Hugging my pillow, I gave it a tight squeeze and directed my thoughts away from skating and toward images of Braden. I saw our goodbye in his driveway, and I bit my lip as I remembered our last incredible kiss. Flashing forward, I saw us at our reunion next week, me jumping into his arms and giving him an even more passionate kiss. And what was that hanging around my neck? Oh, yeah, the gold medal.

So much for not thinking about skating.

CHAPTER TWENTY-FIVE

I stood on the ice in front of the judges, moments from my free skate, and my entire career was flashing before my eyes. My first competition in a bright pink dress. My first lesson with Dad, just days after meeting him. Falling three times at the Junior Grand Prix Final. Earning the highest score ever at Junior Worlds. Dominating nationals at every level from juvenile through senior.

Winning the short program at the Olympics.

The last was the freshest memory but the one I had to forget. I couldn't rely on the miniscule lead I had after the short. Attacking the long program was my only option.

If I didn't hurl all over the ice first.

I swallowed the anxiousness rising in my throat and posed as still as I could with every part of my body quivering. What if I blanked and forgot all the choreography? What if I had a real panic attack in the middle of the program? My heart was pounding so fast that my chest hurt. I glanced over at Dad, and he watched me with nothing but confidence in his eyes. He was so sure that I could do this.

You CAN do this.

You've faced much more frightening circumstances in your life, and you made it through. You are strong enough to rise above your fear and skate this program with all your heart. Be the champion that you know you are!

The music began, but my choreography didn't start until a few seconds into the piece, so I took the time to let out a measured breath. On my cue, I pushed forward in attitude position and opened my arms, inviting everyone into the program with me. I concentrated on the soft, peaceful flute, and my body slowly relaxed into the familiar steps. The ones I'd done every day, multiple times a day for the past nine months.

I made easy, sweeping strokes across the ice, building up speed for the triple Lutz-triple toe, and I visualized it in perfect slow motion. I'd owned that combination since I was thirteen. I could *not* be afraid of it.

With a quick jab into the ice, I flew upward and relied on my muscle memory to take over through the first jump. I landed on a clean edge and let my years of training do their job again as I vaulted into three more swift rotations. Another smooth landing followed, and I extended my arms down to my fingertips, putting a confident flourish on it.

No fear. All strength.

I settled into the music and twirled into the combination spin, making a clean catch of my blade – no blood shed that time. When I finished the required revolutions, I stroked toward my next jump. I'd fallen on the triple loop during the team event, so I cleared my mind of everything but the technique. I saw it like a movie in front of me, and then I pushed off from my back outside edge, mimicking the movie in exact form. Three turns, spotless landing, more applause.

The double Axel came easy after the opening triples, and I floated into the step sequence, one of my favorite sections of the program. I loved the rise and fall of my knees with the music, how Josh had designed each step to flow effortlessly with the ethereal piece. I found myself feeling calmer and steadier with every breath. I took that serene energy and let it guide me into the next section, the most difficult of the four minutes.

I sprang forward into my second double Axel, getting more air under me than I had on the first, and I used the boost to propel myself into the double toe, completing the combination. After a few transitions, I conquered the triple flip and gained even more momentum.

Keeping the powerful mood going, I stroked around the edge of the rink, making full use of the space. I went from one end to the other and picked into my second triple flip with no hesitation. A windy blur of rotations later, I did a quick half loop and then went up into the triple Salchow. I landed with my head up looking straight at Dad, and he slapped his hands together and pumped his arms in the air. I gave him a huge smile and turned back toward center ice.

I am so close. I am SO close.

My heart began to race with anticipation, and I felt my movements getting ahead of the music. I slowly exhaled and deepened my edges, forcing myself to stay with the melody. I had one jump left. One jump between me and the Olympic skate of my dreams.

I glided backward, lifting my right leg high behind me until I was in a full vertical split. The crowd cheered and then grew louder as I took off for the triple Lutz. I coiled into the turns and exhaled as I opened up for the landing, expertly finding the ice with my blade. It made a long, easy cut into the ice, and a rush of emotion rose up inside me. I wanted to cry out with joy, but I had to maintain the quiet tone of the program.

I spun into the layback, and I saw the American flags already going up in the stands. I steered my attention back to the spin and counted the revolutions, not wanting to give away a single point. *Focus to the end!*

Debussy's final notes softly faded away, and I bent into a lunge to close the program. I stayed frozen in that position, letting the reality of the moment set in.

I did it.

I skated the best that I possibly could.

I have a very good chance to be Olympic champion.

The audience gave me a more enthusiastic response than they had after the short, but I couldn't find the strength to rise and thank them. The emotion I'd been holding in crashed forth and sank me to my knees. I gasped for breath as the onslaught of tears came, rivers of relief streaming down my cheeks.

I pushed myself up from the ice and took my bows, and I turned toward Dad. His fist was against his mouth, his eyes about to overflow. I was halfway to him when a stuffie flew in my direction. I looked up into the seats, and Court was jumping up and down in the aisle.

I picked up the white stuffie, and laughter and sobs got all caught up together in my throat. The dog was a stuffed version of the Slush Puppie mascot, complete with the blue T-shirt and beanie. I hugged him against my body and sprinted over to Dad.

He swallowed me in an embrace and tried to speak, but he choked on his words. He kissed the top of my head, and we walked with our arms around each other to the kiss and cry.

"I'm so proud of you," he croaked.

"I never could have done it without you," I said.

He gave me a tissue, and I patted my eyes and my face dry. I sat the puppy in my lap and opened the little tag pinned to his shirt, and I soon needed a new tissue. This was Braden's shortest but most meaningful note yet.

I LOVE YOU.

I faced the camera and waved, and I gave the puppy a kiss on his little black nose. The announcer came over the loud speaker, and I clung to Dad and let out a puff of air. I'd done everything I could, but would the judges do the same?

The score popped up on the screen, and I bounced in my seat. "A personal best!"

Dad hugged me, and we quickly went backstage as Katia got ready for her introduction. My score had been massive, but there was nothing stopping the judges from eclipsing it if Katia or Julia delivered. The scores were always ridiculously high at the Olympics. I started to feel shaky again as I prepared for yet another waiting period. Everything was now out of my hands, and that made it all the more worse.

I went through the line of media, trying to focus on the questions, but I was straining to hear what was happening on the ice. Dad was positioned in front of the monitor backstage, but I couldn't see him. After I talked to the last reporter, I hurried to join him, and my heart jumped at the sight of a smile on his face.

"Katia's in second," he said. "She skated great. Just not as great as you."

I nodded and gulped.

Just one more skater.

Dad put his arm around me, and we watched Julia strike her opening pose. The dramatic bells of *Carmen* rang out in the arena, and I hugged my stuffed puppy and bowed my head. Mom and Dad had planned to skate to *Carmen* in the Olympic season before they found out Mom was pregnant. No way could I lose to someone using that music.

I couldn't bear to look at the screen, but the loud cheers told the story. Dad's grip on my shoulder grew tighter with every jump Julia landed, and I started to pray.

Please, please don't let her score be higher than mine.

Multiple TV cameras were aimed at us, waiting for either my tears of joy or tears of disappointment. I couldn't believe it had all come down to this. The judges had to ask themselves just one question – had Julia performed better than I had?

Her standing ovation went on for minutes, and I pressed

my nose to the dog's fuzzy cap. A crowd had formed around us – media, our team leaders, other skaters and coaches. If I didn't win, I wouldn't be able to make a quick exit. I took deep breaths, preparing myself to not have a breakdown in front of millions watching around the world.

"The free skating score for Julia Lobacheva of Russia," the announcer said.

I stopped breathing. Dad had done the math, so if I heard anything less than 154.12, I'd win the gold medal.

Please, please.

"One hundred fifty-one point two three–"

"Oh my God!" I screamed.

Dad picked me up and swung me around, and I held onto him as my head spun with dizzying thoughts and emotions. I started laughing and crying again, but soon there were only tears. I pressed my face to Dad's collar and sobbed, relieving myself of all the tension, all the worry, all the angst.

I AM THE OLYMPIC CHAMPION!!!!

"I did it, Dad," I choked out.

"Yes, you did, sweetheart," he said, his voice strangled. "Yes, you did."

Everyone around us had stepped back to give us our moment, and they were applauding and scurrying with their cameras to get the best shot. When Dad reluctantly let me go, the crowd swooped in with congratulations and hugs. I was still clutching my stuffie, and I wrapped my arms around it, the closest I could get to hugging Braden. I felt like I was in a daze, but there was no time to reflect on what had just happened. The media awaited for another round of interviews.

From the press area I was ushered back to the ice for the flower ceremony with Julia and Katia. We wouldn't receive our medals until the next day in the Olympic Park, so we stood on the podium with just bouquets of flowers. As we took our victory lap, I searched the crowd for my family and found them above the vacated judges' table. With the stands elevated from the ice, I couldn't get close enough to touch them or even talk to them. All I could do was take in the emotion on their faces. Mom and Em were weepy messes, my grandparents were beaming with pride, Court and Josh were shaking pompoms and videotaping me, and the twins were jumping up and down and yelling my name. I waved at all of them and shouted, "I love you!" hoping they could hear me.

I returned backstage and was bombarded with more congratulations and then given directions on where I needed to be next. I only had a few minutes to change out of my costume and get over to the Main Press Center for more media obligations.

I went to the locker room, and the space was empty and quiet, giving me my first chance to breathe in an hour. I sat next to my bag and scrolled through the dozens of texts on my phone. So many of my skater friends from around the world had reached out to me. Holly's had me laughing out loud as they were line after line of happy and excited emojis with no words. My fingers flew over the rest, reading as many as I could, and then they landed on Braden's messages. I teared up yet again.

YESSSSSSS!!!!!!

You are brilliant!

The best ever!

GOLD MEDALIST!!!!!!

I fully admit that I cried. Multiple times.

God, I just want to hold you and kiss you and see your beautiful, ecstatic smile up close.

I wiped my eyes and dialed him on FaceTime, and his phone rang and rang. I began untying my skates, and Braden finally popped up on the screen.

"Hey, I didn't think you'd have time to call! I was just getting a beer to toast to you!"

Ross' head appeared next to Braden's, and he lifted his

bottle. "To Liza. You rule the world!"

I laughed, and Braden clinked his beer against Ross'.

"The gang's all here," Braden said as Ross departed. "We were all going nuts. You're the freaking Olympic champion!"

I shook my head. "It doesn't seem real!"

"Just wait until you get the gold medal and you hear the national anthem."

"I'm going to be crying so hard I won't be able to see the flag."

"I just looked up the time of the ceremony, and I'll be skipping class again. I've become a delinquent like Ross, but it's so worth it." He grinned. "Do you realize how good you were today?"

"It felt really, really good. Like a dream."

"I knew all along this was your time. I've known it since the day I first watched you practice."

I bit my lip as my tear ducts continued to get a workout. "I can't wait to celebrate with you."

He smiled and angled closer to the screen. "Get ready for the celebration to end all celebrations."

"GOOD MORNING!" DAD SAID.

"Best morning ever!" I said.

We walked down to the dorm exit and out into the brilliant sunshine. A car was scheduled for us at the entrance to the Village, ready to take us to our first stop of the day – finally meeting up with the family at their hotel. I'd been at the network studio until the wee hours of the morning giving interviews, and I'd gotten only two hours of sleep, but I was bright-eyed and ready to go. Knowing I'd achieved my lifelong dream made it easy to jump out of bed.

"So, do you feel any different today, champ?" Dad asked. "Is it all starting to sink in?"

"I feel so much lighter. Like the relief I get after Worlds times a thousand."

He rubbed my shoulder. "You deserve to be stress-free for a very, very long time."

"I know I'm going to have a lot of demands on my time, and there will be a lot of decisions to make, but I just want to enjoy all of it. I don't want to let any of it stress me out."

"You have a great team around you, and your mom, Em, and I will be watching out for you, too. Em can give you her perspective on how she's handled all the demands."

"I should ask how *you* feel now." I bumped his arm with my elbow. "Being the coach of both a gold medal-winning pair *and* a gold medalist in singles. That's a pretty rare and awesome accomplishment."

"I'm just lucky to have had such phenomenal talent come into my life. You, Em, and Chris are three of the best skaters in the history of the sport."

"We might have the talent, but we wouldn't have made it to the top without you. You taught me so much, and you gave me all the support I could ever need. I never felt alone on the ice because I had you right there at the boards. That meant everything to me."

He put his arm around me and kissed the top of my head. "I've loved every minute of being at the boards for you. The only thing I've loved more is being your dad."

I hugged him and swiped at my damp eyes. "My first and definitely not my last tears of the day."

We met our driver and arrived at the hotel after a quick ride, and a few people stopped me for photos as we headed to the restaurant. Mom saw us outside the door and came rushing over, unable to contain her excitement. We blubbered together as we embraced, and then the festival of waterworks continued with Em and my grandparents.

"Welcome to the club," Em said as she hugged me.

"I won't have to stare longingly at your medal on the wall

anymore." I laughed.

My grandmother kissed both my cheeks and squeezed my face between her hands. "Liza, you make us so proud. We are so happy you do this in Russia."

"I'm so happy you could be here," I said.

Quinn and Alex latched onto me, and I hooked my arms around them. "My loudest cheerleaders," I said.

"Mom said she got to go to Disney World after she won the Olympics," Alex said.

"Can we go with you?" Quinn asked.

"If I go to Disney World, you'll be on the top of my guest list."

"Yeah!" they shouted in their perfect twin harmony.

"We have toast," my grandfather said.

I looked at the table, confused when I didn't see any bread. He lifted his glass, and I laughed to myself. *Oh, THAT kind of toast.*

Everyone gathered around the table, and I picked up one of the glasses of juice. My grandfather was a quiet man and not too comfortable with English, so I was surprised he wanted to make a speech.

"Liza, we do not have chance to see you often, but we watch you grow through skating," he said. "You work very hard, and you bring us all very much joy. Congratulations to our beautiful champion."

I touched my heart, and we all brought our glasses together. I went around the table and hugged my grandfather.

"Spasibo, dedushka," I said.

He kissed my cheeks and said, "My sweet" in Russian, his favorite name for me. I returned to my seat between Mom and Dad and looked over the menu. For the first time in forever, I could eat whatever I wanted and feel zero guilt. Pancakes, French toast, potatoes...

"What looks good?" Mom asked.

I inhaled the smell of bacon in the air, and my stomach

rumbled. "All of it."

THE NIGHT COULD NOT be any clearer or more gorgeous. Across from the Medals Plaza, the Olympic torch blazed, its fiery orange flames bright against the dark sky. The podium stood one step away from me on the huge stage, and beyond it was a sea of people stretching far and wide. They exploded with cheers as Julia stepped onto the podium to receive the silver medal, and I bounced on the heels of my sneakers. My time was coming in just a few moments.

"Gold medalist and Olympic champion, representing United States of America – Liza Petrov!"

I took the top step of the podium and raised my arms in the air, waving at the thousands who'd waited in the cold to watch the ceremony. They treated me to a long ovation, and I squinted under the bright lights to see faces in the crowd. My family had been promised a spot up front, but all I could see were throngs of coats and hats and fan-made signs.

The official giving out the medals stepped in front of me, and I bent forward so he could loop the blue ribbon around my neck. The medal was so heavy! I kissed the smooth, gold surface and looked skyward, something I'd never done after any performance or any medal ceremony. But I wanted to acknowledge the two people who had first believed in me. Who'd believed the little girl who said she was going to win the Olympics someday. Who'd started me on the journey to making all my dreams come true.

"Ladies and gentlemen, the anthem of the United States of America."

I placed my hand over my heart and watched the Stars and Stripes rise between the two Russian flags. I'd fully expected to cry, but I couldn't stop smiling and I had an overwhelming sense of peace. The weight of the medal hanging from my neck felt like it was part of me. As if it was always meant to be there. I glanced down at it and then back up at the flag, bursting with pride. My "golden destiny" had finally been fulfilled.

I LIFTED THE PLANE'S window shade and smiled at the sight of the blue Boston harbor below us.

Home.

The wheels of the plane hit the runway with a thud, and I reached into my tote for my two medals.

"Why are you putting those on?" my seatmate Quinn asked.

"There will be TV cameras waiting for me at baggage claim."

"We're going to be on TV? I'm not wearing my cutest outfit."

I smoothed her curly ponytail. "You look adorably chic as always."

"I thought you brushed your teeth and your hair because you're going to see Braden."

"I did. I can't have twenty-hour airplane breath when I see him."

"Because you're going to–" She puckered her lips and made loud kissing noises.

I laughed. "Yes. Yes, we are."

Just like I hadn't wanted our goodbye to be at the airport, I didn't want our reunion to be all over the news, so I was meeting Braden at his apartment. I shot him a quick text that I'd landed, and I got back one word.

YESSSSS!!!!!

Court and Josh walked beside me wearing their Olympic bling too, and travelers all along the concourse applauded as we made our way to baggage claim. The moment we stepped through the security exit, a loud roar went up, and my eyes widened at all the fans who'd come just to welcome us home.

Dad and Em took care of getting our luggage while we talked to the TV crews and signed autographs. I had my phone in my pocket, and I felt it buzz while I was between fan selfies.

Braden: **ETA?**

Me: **It's crazy here. Coming soon I promise!**

The reporters kept multiplying until finally there were no more microphones in my face. I stored the medals in my tote, gathered the rest of my bags, and texted Braden from the parking garage.

Almost there!!!!

I lifted my head and stopped short, and Court rolled her suitcase into me from behind. Braden was standing next to my SUV, holding a bouquet of pink roses.

I squealed and ran to him, leaping into his arms and hooking my legs around his waist. I buried my face in his jacket and breathed in the scent of his cologne. This was *so* much better than hugging a pillowcase.

We looked at each other, and I basked in the glow from his smile. The brightness in his eyes could light up the whole world.

"Hi," I whispered.

He smiled even bigger. "Hi."

His lips found mine, and the butterflies in my stomach were stronger than they'd ever been. I strengthened my hold on him, afraid I might fly away with happiness.

"How did you know where I parked?" I asked.

"I texted Court. I wanted to surprise you away from the cameras."

"You definitely surprised me."

He handed me the roses, and I brought them to my nose to smell their sweetness. Dad and Em held us up, chatting a few minutes with Braden, but soon he and I were off to his place in our two-car caravan.

Braden unlocked the front door, and I grinned at the big "Congratulations" banner hanging above the kitchen bar. Gold balloons floated all around the empty living room.

"This is for your party later. My family's coming, the roomies of course, the upstairs crew… but for now it's just you and me," he said, drawing me into his arms.

I smiled and curled my fingers into his hair. "I very much appreciate you skipping class again for me."

"I might flunk out, but at least I have a kick-ass girlfriend."

"I can get you a job. You can be general manager of Team Liza."

"Am I allowed to make out with the star of the team?"

"That's one of the main job duties."

His eyes dropped to my lips, and he slipped his hands under my jaw, gently guiding my head toward his. He brushed my mouth with a soft kiss and then came in hotter, hungrier. I gave his bottom lip a tender bite, and he pulled me closer, melting us together.

We dropped onto the couch, and we kissed until my lips were swollen and my skin was on fire from his touch. I took a breath and rested my head on his shoulder, my hand over his racing heart.

"Do you want to see my gold medal?" I asked.

"Is that even a question?"

I jumped up and got it from my bag, and I displayed it proudly on my palm.

"Can I touch it?" he asked.

"No."

His face dropped, and I laughed. "Of course you can."

His grin reappeared, and he cradled the medal in his hands. "You were right. It's really heavy." He read the inscription on it and laced the ribbon between his fingers. "I want to see it on you again."

He put it around my neck and then sat back. His intense

gaze on me sent my butterflies fluttering again.

"That's hot," he said.

I smiled and leaned forward, kissing him hard.

"That's one of the things I love most about you," I said, still breathless.

"The fact that I'm turned on by you wearing a gold medal?"

He kissed my neck just above the ribbon, and I filled with nothing but swoon. I had to take a moment to regain my thoughts.

"The fact that you appreciate everything it took for me to win this. You got on board as soon as we met, and you supported me even when I tried to pull away. You embraced my dream with your whole heart."

"I'm just glad you let me come along for the ride. I told you that you were way out of my league."

I studied him and tapped my chin. "Maybe you're right. What am I doing with such a sweet, smart, caring guy who also happens to be extremely easy on the eyes?"

"You forgot amazing kisser."

"Are you? I don't remem–"

His lips captured mine, and I framed his face with my hands. If there was a Boyfriend Olympics, Braden would win all the gold medals. No contest.

Spring

EPILOGUE

I DIDN'T THINK I WOULD EVER be so nervous again, but throwing a baseball in front of a rowdy, sold-out Fenway Park had my heart pounding and my palms sweating. I was about to deliver the ceremonial first pitch to David Ortiz aka Big Papi, and all eyes were on me as I stepped onto the mound. Braden had given me pitching lessons, but my fingers were having trouble getting a good grip on the ball. The competitor in me wanted my throw to make it the full sixty feet and six inches to home plate.

I planted my back foot on the mound and cocked my arm back, humming the ball toward the plate. It flew high and wide, and Big Papi had to pop up to catch it, but I'd covered the distance! The crowd gave me a loud cheer, and the Red Sox slugger hugged me as he gave me the souvenir ball. I walked toward the dugout, grinning at Braden, who was in absolute heaven. I'd gotten field passes for both my family and his, and they'd all watched batting practice and met the Sox players. Braden had stayed on the field for the first pitch while everyone else was upstairs in a luxury suite.

He threaded his fingers through mine, and we followed

the Sox PR people through the hidden corridors of the ballpark. Braden's eyes were going everywhere, taking in every sign, every piece of equipment. I was giddy watching his excitement.

"One day you'll be walking these halls, making all the big decisions," I said.

He grinned. "I can't even imagine what that would be like."

We walked into the suite, and everyone applauded my pitching effort. "Wild thing!" Ross called out. I gave him an exaggerated bow and high-fived Holly as I headed for the buffet.

"Hey, your mom just told me you turned down *Dancing with the Stars*," Tarah said over the platter of chicken tenders. "How could you pass that up?"

"I might do the fall season. They said they'll still have a spot for me. I just have so many other things going on right now that I couldn't commit two months to it. I'm doing the *Stars on Ice* tour, making a bunch of appearances, shooting commercials... and I might be guest starring on one of my favorite TV shows." I crossed my fingers.

"You're living the life!" Tarah said.

"She deserves it," Braden said, smiling at me with pride.

He and I grabbed plates of food, and we stood at the bar overlooking the field. Alex and Tanner sat below us, comparing the autographs they'd gotten on their baseballs, and Quinn sat in front of them, staring at Tanner. She'd been all googly-eyed since she met him down on the field.

"I think Miss Quinn has her first crush," I said.

"The irresistible charm of the Patrick men strikes again," Braden said.

I laughed. "As does their incredible modesty."

Braden's mom came up and hugged one arm around me. "Liza, thank you again for including us. I still can't believe I shook Big Papi's hand! I don't think Tanner's going to stop talking about this for the rest of his life."

"I figured it was a great way for me to score points with him," I said. "He wasn't too happy with me being in his treehouse."

"Oh, he's definitely forgotten about that now," Mrs. Patrick said. "And he's got a new buddy in Alex."

"And a new admirer." I pointed at Quinn. "I'm pretty sure Tanner thinks she has cooties, but that's not stopping her from following him around."

Mrs. Patrick gasped. "How perfect would it be if they got together one day? Our families already know each other, and they would have the best meet-cute story."

Braden and I both laughed. "Mom, they're seven and nine," he said.

"I'm saying *in the future*. It could happen!"

She left us, but we still couldn't stop laughing. I watched her go over to where Braden's grandma had Dad and Em cornered.

"She'll probably try to arrange Quinn and Tanner's marriage with them. Dad might go for it if it means Quinn doesn't get to date. He already knows she's not going to be afraid of boys like I was."

"You weren't afraid of *me*." Braden smiled.

"No one could ever be afraid of this face." I pinched his cheek. "Actually, I lie. I was a tiny bit terrified of you the first two times you talked to me."

"But then you fell under the spell of my charm, and the rest is history."

"An incredible history." I stood on my tiptoes and gave him a kiss. "And an even better future to come."

OTHER BOOKS BY JENNIFER COMEAUX

Edge Series
Life on the Edge (Edge #1)
Edge of the Past (Edge #2)
Fighting for the Edge (Edge #3)

Ice Series
Crossing the Ice (Ice #1)
Losing the Ice (Ice #2)
Taking the Ice (Ice #3)

Gold Rush

To stay up to date on Jennifer's new releases, join her mailing
list:
http://eepurl.com/UZjMP

Jennifer loves to hear from readers! Visit her online at:
jennifercomeaux.blogspot.com
www.twitter.com/LadyWave4
www.facebook.com/jennifercomeauxauthor
www.instagram.com/jcomeaux4
jcomeaux4@gmail.com

Please consider taking a moment to leave a review at the
applicable retailer. It is much appreciated!

EXCERPT FROM LIFE ON THE EDGE

Go back to the beginning with the Edge Series and discover how Emily and Sergei fell in love and Liza came into their lives. Enjoy this excerpt from *Life on the Edge (Edge #1)*:

BAM!

MY ELBOW WHACKED CHRIS'S FOREHEAD FOR the fourth time during practice. He grunted and caught me before I hit the ice. Though I'd skated over half of my nineteen years, I'd never had so many collisions. Of course, until a year ago, I'd never skated with a partner.

I cringed and touched Chris's sweaty brow. "I'm so sorry."

"It's okay." He raked his hand through his thick dark hair. "A little head trauma never hurt anyone."

I laughed wearily and arched my neck, stretching the sore muscles. The cold air wasn't helping loosen them. Looking up, my eyes honed in on the red, white, and blue banner above the rink:

Emily Butler and Christopher Grayden–2000 National Silver Medalists

Only four months had passed since Chris and I placed second at our first national championship, but it seemed like a lifetime. The triple twist, the high-flying element we needed to learn before next season, continued to elude me. *If we don't master this move, we'll never compete with the top teams in the world.*

I grasped Chris's hand. "Let's try it again."

We took matching determined strokes across the ice, and the burst of wind cooled my face and loosened damp tendrils from my long ponytail. With a quick motion, Chris squeezed my hips and launched me into the air. I wound myself tight and spun but fell into Chris's waiting arms before finishing three revolutions. A sigh heaved my shoulders.

Sergei glided toward us around the other practicing skaters. Our coach was often mistaken for one of us because of his youth. He nodded and regarded us with his deep blue eyes. "The rotation is getting faster. Focus on what you did right today. I see a lot of improvement."

I relaxed into a smile. Before I'd started working with Sergei, I'd heard many horror stories about Russian coaches. Sergei demanded discipline and maximum effort, but his energy stayed positive, and he provided constant encouragement.

Chris and I left the ice and sat on the short set of wooden bleachers. My ankles thanked me as I untied my skate laces and gave them space to breathe.

"I guess it's an improvement I didn't give you another black eye," I said.

Chris poked his swollen freckled cheek. "I kinda like my shiner. Makes me look tough." He grinned, displaying his dimples.

"You're going to need more than that to make you look tough," I teased as I walked away.

Inside the locker room, the musty scent of sweat and metal contrasted with the cool freshness of the ice. After stowing my skates in my locker and slipping on a pair of sneakers, I pulled a fitted T-shirt over my leotard and winced as I bumped the fresh bruises on my arms. If people only knew how much pain went into chasing the Olympic dream.

I needed to talk to Sergei before his next lesson, and I found him in the rink's upstairs lounge, which overlooked the ice. He was holding a cup of coffee and talking to a couple of the skating moms. As usual, they sat captivated, totally engrossed in his words, and I couldn't blame them. When I'd met Sergei, I stammered through our introduction, spellbound by his captivating eyes and gleaming smile. His personable manner had quickly put me at ease, though, and I'd gotten past staring at his good looks. Important, obviously, if I wanted to get any work done on the ice.

As Sergei spoke to the moms, I remembered I had to phone my own mother. She expected a daily call once I'd moved from Boston to Cape Cod a year ago. I lingered near the water cooler and read the announcements stapled to the bulletin board until Sergei finished his conversation and moved toward the stairs.

"Sergei, do you have a minute?"

"Sure." He glanced at his sport watch. "I have about ten. What's up?"

"I was thinking of doing some coaching in the afternoons like I used to in Boston. Just a few kids, but I wanted to see what you thought." I toyed with my silver cross and chain. "If it might be too much to take on right now."

He took a long sip of coffee and gave me a pensive look. "I might have a better idea. Walk with me."

I followed him down the narrow steps to the rink, and he set his paper cup on the boards. Skaters swooshed past us, creating a chilly breeze.

"Would you be interested in helping me with one of my

novice teams?" Sergei asked. "Teaching them the pair elements would reinforce everything you've learned."

I bobbed my head with vigor at his show of confidence. "That sounds like a great idea."

He spread his hands apart. "Don't I always have all the answers?"

"Yes, Oh Great and All-Knowing Coach." I performed a playful bow.

"I've never had an assistant before. Maybe you should call me Mister Petrov when we work together." He lifted his cup to his mouth, a hint of a smile on his lips.

"You're joking, right?"

His eyes widened with innocence. "Why would I be joking?"

"You're only six years older than me." I laughed and started for the weight room, and Sergei chuckled behind me. "I'm not calling you Mister."

WITHIN A WEEK, I began assisting Sergei with his newest and youngest team of twelve-year-old Courtney and fourteen-year-old Mark. They were struggling with their double loop throw jump, so I acted as Sergei's partner to demonstrate the technique. The kids stood next to the boards while Sergei's strong hands grasped my hips and vaulted me across the ice. A double felt light and easy compared to the triples I normally did.

Courtney and Mark studied us attentively and tried the throw on their own. Attempt after attempt, Courtney failed to land on a clean edge. Her pink cheeks deepened to crimson as she huffed with frustration.

"It's alright." Sergei patted her shoulder. "Mark, she needs a little more height. Make sure you've got your weight balanced on the takeoff."

"Courtney, also try pulling in tighter and quicker." I brought my arms sharply against my chest.

Our students worked on the element each afternoon, some days having more success than others, but Sergei never lost patience. Watching him handle Courtney and Mark's roller coaster of emotions with gentle authority gave me a new level of respect for him. He knew just how to reassure the kids and light up their eyes with understanding.

After Courtney and Mark's sessions, I often stopped at the Starbucks near the rink on my way home. I learned Sergei was a frequent patron, too, and every time we ran into each other, our conversations grew longer.

One afternoon, we finally gravitated to one of the tiny tables and had been sitting there over half an hour. Sergei had gone to the counter for a refill, and when he rejoined me, he caught me softly singing Sting's "Fields of Gold" along with the piped-in radio.

"Are you a Sting fan?" he asked, stirring a packet of sugar into his black coffee.

"Huge." I sipped my latte. "Are you?"

"I have all his CDs. 'Fields of Gold' is one of my favorite songs."

I leaned forward and rested my elbows on the small table. "Did you know he's having a concert up in Mansfield next weekend? None of my friends want to go. They said his music is for old people." I frowned.

Sergei laughed. "Yeah, I don't know anyone interested in going either."

"I wonder if there are tickets left. Maybe we could go together."

He stared at me over his cup, and I shifted backward in my seat. I hoped he didn't think I was suggesting anything like a date. The U.S. Figure Skating Federation wouldn't approve of a coach and student dating.

I hastily added, "You know, since no one else wants to

go… and we don't know when he'll have another show here."

Sergei nodded and his mouth gradually opened into a smile. "Yeah, we should go. The last concert I went to was about five years ago, right after I moved to Virginia from Moscow. It was Dave Matthews Band. I hadn't heard of them, but some people at the rink invited me."

"Ahh, I love them. I've never seen them live."

"They were great. Turned me into a big fan." He tapped his fingers on his cup. "But what I remember most about that night was the taxi ride home. I didn't have a car, and I lived *way* outside the city. The taxi driver didn't speak good English and neither did I at the time. I fell asleep, and when he woke me up, I had no idea where we were. He'd misunderstood me and taken me to a town twenty miles from where I lived."

I burst into laughter. "Oh, no!"

"When he finally got me home, I didn't have enough cash to pay the ridiculous fare, and we got in an argument about whose fault it was he took me to the wrong place." He chuckled and shook his head. "I gave him all the money I had and left him outside my apartment, cursing me out."

Giggles echoed in my throat. "That's crazy. Well, the good news is we can drive ourselves to Mansfield. Speaking of which, I should get home and check on the tickets." I snagged my car keys from my purse. "If I find some, I'll go ahead and order them."

"Let me know later how much I owe you."

"Don't worry, I won't curse you out if you don't pay me right away." I smiled, and Sergei laughed.

With my keys in one hand and my coffee in the other, I stood and aimed for the door. "I'll call you when I get them!"

Typical summertime traffic slowed my drive home. I loved the beauty of the Cape during summer with the hydrangeas in bloom and the deep orange sunsets, but I missed the peacefulness of winter on the island. After crawling bumper to bumper on Route Six from South Dennis to

Hyannis, I finally arrived at my parents' vacation townhouse, which had become my year-round home.

In the sun-splashed living room, my roommate, Aubrey, was hunched over one of her ice dance costumes, needle and thread in hand.

"What happened to your dress?" I dropped down beside her on the beige chenille couch.

She pushed a few stray blond hairs out of her eyes and squinted at the pink fabric. "Some stones fell off last time I wore it."

I picked up my laptop from the coffee table and drummed my fingers while it booted up. With a few clicks, I landed on Ticketmaster.com.

Aubrey glanced at the screen. "What are you buying tickets for?"

"Sting's concert in Mansfield. Turns out Sergei is as big a fan as I am."

Her perfectly-shaped eyebrows curved upward. "You're going on a road trip with Sergei?"

"Mansfield is an hour away. I don't call that a road trip."

She straightened the short skirt of the costume and examined the shimmering silver stones around the hem. "You two seem pretty chummy these days," she said with a sidelong glance.

I shrugged. "We like to talk when we get coffee. No big deal."

"It's a big deal when you start going out at night together. Coaches aren't supposed to be that friendly with their students. Especially not young, hot coaches."

My face warmed, and I focused on the computer screen. "We work together and have a few common interests. It's nothing more."

"I'm just trying to look out for you, Em. You need to be careful."

My fingers paused on the keyboard. Aubrey was the

same age as me, but her dating history could fill a book three times the size of mine. She'd been breaking hearts since I'd met her at thirteen. Our gap in boyfriend experience sometimes led her to treat me like a little sister.

"Sergei and I have a professional relationship. You don't need to worry."

She didn't look convinced, but she didn't press the issue. I turned back to the computer and concentrated on selecting two seats for the concert, ignoring the tiny voice in my head that echoed Aubrey's warning.

A RUMBLE OF THUNDER rolled in the distance, and both Sergei and I looked skyward. Fast moving clouds hid the moon. A roof covered half the amphitheater but not our seats in the farthest reaches of the venue. Sting had finished his first set, and I was regretting not bringing my rain slicker.

Sergei rose from the long bench. "Do you want a soda or anything?"

"I'll take a bottle of water." I reached into my jeans pocket for the cash I'd stashed.

He waved away the money. "I've got it."

I smiled as I watched his long legs take him down the packed aisle. I hadn't been on a date in so long that I'd forgotten how nice it was having a guy do the little things like fight the crowd for concessions and... *Wait a second.* I shook my head. *This isn't a date, remember?* Just because Sergei opened his car door for me and wiped the dirt off my seat at the amphitheater didn't mean our outing was anything more than friendly. *He was being polite.*

The smell of popcorn wafted past me as people returned from the concession stand and climbed into our row. Sergei came back with two bottles of water and handed me one.

"This is definitely the best concert I've been to," he said.

"I saw U2 a few years ago in Boston, and they blew me away." I paused, and Sergei raised an eyebrow. "But so far, this is even better."

A lone raindrop plopped on my nose, and my eyes drifted to the sky again. "I think we're about to get drenched."

A few more drops fell, and Sergei said, "If it gets too bad, we can leave if you want."

"No way. I don't wanna miss any of the show. Unless you're afraid you're going to melt?" I bit my bottom lip to stifle a smile.

He laughed. "No, I can handle it."

The drops soon increased to a steady drizzle and pelted us on and off through the rest of the show. I sang along to every song while the rain coated my lips. Next to me, Sergei patted his leg in time to the beat of each tune, and every now and then, his arm bumped mine. His skin felt warm despite being wet, and with each touch my arm tingled.

By the time Sting finished his second encore, my navy T-shirt clung to me and my hair was soaked, but I was too awed by the music to care. I peeked at Sergei, and his short golden brown hair had darkened from the rain, making his blue eyes stand out even more. We moved with the thick crowd to the parking lot and had just hopped into Sergei's SUV when the drizzle became a downpour.

"We got out of there right in time," I said.

"You mean you wouldn't want to sit outside in this? What, afraid you would melt, Emily?"

I laughed. "Oh, I could've handled it."

The windshield wipers slapped back and forth, drowning out the classic rock on the radio. Sergei turned on the heater and drove slowly until we reached the interstate and pointed south to the Cape.

"I'm so glad we came," he said. "He sounded amazing live."

I combed my fingers through my hair, unknotting the

long, damp waves. "I know. I'd see him again in a heartbeat."

"Next time he comes, we'll have to get tickets early so we can be closer to the stage." He shot me a smile. "And out of the rain."

"Definitely." I returned his smile.

A shiver sped down my spine at the thought of spending another evening with Sergei. I didn't know if I was still on a high from the concert, but being in the dark car with him was heightening all my senses. I'd always thought he was attractive, but only now did I notice how his smile softened the sharp angles of his face, how sexy my name sounded in his Russian accent, how his T-shirt hugged his lean yet muscular chest.

I gulped and set my eyes on the highway in front of us. *You need to put those thoughts out of your mind right now.*

ACKNOWLEDGMENTS

THIS IS THE LONGEST book I've written, and I wouldn't have been able to survive the long road of writing it without my faithful beta readers Melissa, Debbie, Sylvianne, and Teresa. A big thank you also to Alokya, Mara and Ashley for critiquing the early chapters when I was struggling with direction.

I can't thank my friends Christy and Darlene enough for beta reading and working through all my plot conundrums with me. There were many! I also have to thank Marni, Alex, and Jimmy for taking time out of their schedules to do multiple photo shoots for the cover. Your generosity is so very much appreciated!

Finally, a big thanks to all the skaters who inspire me and motivate me to keep writing about this beautiful sport. Special thanks to skaters Marissa Castelli and Tarah Kayne and skating moms Ann Bowes-Shaughnessy and Jacqui White for answering all my research questions!

ABOUT THE AUTHOR

JENNIFER COMEAUX is a tax accountant by day, writer by night. There aren't any ice rinks near her home in south Louisiana, but she's a diehard figure skating fan and loves to write stories of romance set in the world of competitive skating. One of her favorite pastimes is traveling to competitions, where she can experience all the glitz and drama that inspire her writing. When she's not writing, traveling, or calculating taxes, you can find her feeding her television addiction.